Eden approached her tentatively. She almost looked desperate for approval.

A rake in her hand, Sheila just stared at her. Dylan's daughter had been hiding a lovely face behind that awful Goth makeup.

But as far as Sheila was concerned, she was still a monster.

"I thought I'd start cooking my dinner—if that's okay with you," Eden murmured.

"Fine."

"Listen, I'm really sorry about what happened to your garden," she said, her voice quivering a little. "I know you don't believe me, but I had nothing to do with it. Anyway, I'd like to help tomorrow, getting it back to the way it was."

"It'll be a long, long time and a lot of work before it's back to the way it was," Sheila said coolly.

"I'd like to help out just the same."

Sheila figured this was her cue to toss aside the rake and hug her. But she couldn't. She kept thinking of Eden and that ███████ ████ stalking her, the texts, and today, the gar█████ ███████

"Go make █████ ███████ ██████ ██████ening her grip on the r████ ██████ ██ ████████ ████ething in mind . . ."

"What?" Eden ███.

"If one of my kids gets sick or hurt, ██ some sort of freak accident happens to any of them, I'm holding you accountable. I promise, I'll make you pay . . ."

Books by Kevin O'Brien

ONLY SON

THE NEXT TO DIE

MAKE THEM CRY

WATCH THEM DIE

LEFT FOR DEAD

THE LAST VICTIM

KILLING SPREE

ONE LAST SCREAM

FINAL BREATH

VICIOUS

DISTURBED

TERRIFIED

UNSPEAKABLE

TELL ME YOU'RE
SORRY

NO ONE NEEDS
TO KNOW

YOU'LL MISS ME
WHEN I'M GONE

HIDE YOUR FEAR

THEY WON'T BE
HURT

Published by Kensington Publishing Corporation

KEVIN O'BRIEN

THE BETRAYED WIFE

PINNACLE BOOKS
Kensington Publishing Corp.
www.kensingtonbooks.com

PINNACLE BOOKS are published by

Kensington Publishing Corp.
119 West 40th Street
New York, NY 10018

All Kensington titles, imprints, and distributed lines are available at special quantity discounts for bulk purchases for sales promotions, premiums, fund-raising, educational, or institutional use.

Special book excerpts or customized printings can also be created to fit specific needs. For details, write or phone the office of the Kensington sales manager: Kensington Publishing Corp., 119 West 40th Street, New York, NY 10018, attn: Sales Department; phone 1-800-221-2647.

First Pinnacle printing: August 2019

10 9 8 7 6 5 4 3 2 1

ISBN-13: 978-0-7860-4507-5
ISBN-10: 0-7860-4507-8

Printed in the United States of America

Electronic edition: August 2019

ISBN-13: 978-0-7860-4510-5 (e-book)
ISBN-10: 0-7860-4510-8 (e-book)

This book is for my friends, the Kelly Family: Ed, Sue, Ryan and Eric.

ACKNOWLEDGMENTS

Many thanks to my Kensington family for all their hard work to help make this book happen. I'm so lucky to have been with them for the past twenty-two years. Here's to twenty-two more! A special thank-you goes to my brilliant editor, John Scognamiglio, for his guidance, his patience, and his friendship. John's creative contribution is here on every page.

My gratitude also goes to the lovely and talented Meg Ruley, the talented and lovely Christina Hogrebe, and the marvelous team at Jane Rotrosen Agency for helping make my dreams come true.

Another big thank-you to my writers' group pals, David Massengill, Garth Stein, and Colin McArthur, for making it through the first rough one hundred pages of this book and helping me see where it needed to be polished up or completely gutted.

I want to give a special thank-you to my friends with Seattle 7 Writers, especially Dave Boling, Erica Bauermeister, Carol Cassella, Laurie Frankel, Suzanne Selfors, Jennie Shortridge, and Garth Stein. You guys are the best!

Another thank-you goes to the amazing Dante and Pattie Bellini.

Thanks also to the following individuals and groups for their support and encouragement, and for putting up with me: Dan Annear and Chuck Rank, Jeff Ayers, Ben Bauermeister, Pam Binder, A Book for All Seasons, The Book Stall, Marlys Bourm, Amanda Brooks, Terry and

Judine Brooks, Lynn Brunelle, George Camper and Shane White, Barbara and John Cegielski, Barbara and Jim Church, Anna Cottle and Mary Alice Kier, Paul Dwoskin, Elliott Bay Book Company, John Flick and Dan Reich, Bridget Foley and Stephen Susco, Matt Gani, Cate Goethals and Tom Goodwin, Bob and Dana Gold, Cathy Johnson, Elizabeth Kinsella, David Korabik, Hallie Kuperman, Stafford Lombard, Paul Mariz, Roberta Miner, Dan Monda, Jim Munchel, Bob and Gerry O'Brien, Meghan O'Neill, the wonderful folks at ReaderLink Distribution Services, my faithful friends from Sacred Heart School, Eva Marie Saint, John Saul and Mike Sack, John Simmons, Roseann Stella, Dan Stutesman, George and Sheila Stydahar, and Marc Von Borstel.

Finally, thanks so much to my family. You guys are the greatest!

CHAPTER ONE

9/5 Wed—12:30 A.M.

"I have only a few sunny days left."

That's what Antonia announced in a Facebook post several days ago. Like we're all supposed to give a shit.

Antonia and her tan. Okay, I admit: At forty-four, she looks pretty good—what with all her exercising and all that sun. But the way she talks about her tanning sessions and how important they are, you'd think she was doing work for the United Nations: "Oh, no, I can't be there for that . . . I'll be tanning!" Every damn summer, it's the same thing. As soon as she gets off work at the Hilton, Antonia hurries home, makes herself a Cosmopolitan (still thinking she's Carrie Bradshaw in Sex and the City), changes into her bikini, and heads up to the roof of her apartment building with her Coppertone, her blanket, and the Cosmopolitan in a thermos. All her friends and former boyfriends know about her sacred routine.

The roof has no protective railing, and it's seven stories high. No one's supposed to be up there. If Antonia stumbled and plunged to *her death from that roof, would anyone be all that surprised?*

Would anyone really care?

She's a terrible mother. I'll certainly vouch for that. I guess a couple of her work friends at the hotel might miss her, but hell, they don't really know her—not like I do. She's currently single (it's been an off-month for her), so she won't leave behind a devastated boyfriend to shed any tears for her. And I sincerely doubt her two loser ex-husbands or any of her loser ex-boyfriends will show up at the memorial service.

I can imagine the preacher giving the eulogy, struggling to come up with something nice to say about her: "Okay, so she was a self-centered, uncaring bitch, but Antonia had a killer body and a terrific tan. And, by all accounts, she was great in the sack. She lived fast and died young . . ."

Too bad she won't leave a good-looking corpse, not the way she's going to die.

And she isn't exactly young . . .

I admit, I'm being hard on Antonia here. I read a while ago—I don't remember where—that some people, when they know they're going to die, they push their loved ones away. It's supposed to make the separation easier for the survivor. Maybe I've been doing something like that in reverse—to make it easier for me to pull this off. But I really don't think I'll miss her when she's gone.

I know she has her good side. She can be a hell of a lot of fun at times, and she has a great laugh.

But really, right now she's just in the way.

If everything is going to happen as I want it to, Antonia can't be around. I've known that for weeks now. And I've prepared myself for it.

According to the weather report, Portland is supposed to be warm and sunny tomorrow, so it's a sure bet that Antonia will be soaking up some rays on the roof.

But she won't be completely alone.

Antonia was right. She's used up the last of her sunny days.

Thursday, September 6—4:12 P.M.
Portland, Oregon

Antonia Newcomb—"Toni" to most of her friends—had a conflict of major proportions. It was a perfect afternoon for a rooftop tanning session. But she'd come home from work five minutes ago to find a second notice stuck to her mailbox in the lobby of her apartment building: The post office was holding a package for her. She'd ordered an item online from Barneys a couple of weeks ago. It was supposed to be like Botox in a bottle, and cost a small fortune: $180. The trouble was that her neighbors in the building had recently complained that someone was stealing their packages. So, for the time being, no parcels were left in the lobby.

Antonia had to work late tomorrow. If she didn't pick up the package now, she'd have to wait until Monday afternoon—and hope it was still there at the post office.

Meanwhile, it was gorgeous out, and the Weather Channel predicted rain for next week. It was probably the last decent afternoon before autumn rolled in. The days were already getting shorter.

For a few minutes, Antonia stood, staring through the window of her messy sixth-floor apartment. The appeal of "Botox in a bottle" was strong, but the appeal of her rooftop tanning time was even stronger. She'd been looking forward to it all day. And with every minute of indecision, she was losing precious sun time.

"Screw it," she said, heading into the kitchen to make her usual rooftop cocktail. She'd take her chances at the post office on Monday.

Ten minutes later, Antonia stepped out of her apartment and locked her door. She wore sandals and had a Chris Isaak T-shirt over her bikini. In her backpack, she carried a beach towel, her smartphone, sunglasses, Coppertone, and the thermos with her chilled Cosmopolitan.

In the dim hallway, she turned toward the back stairwell and spotted old Mrs. Pollakoff stepping off the elevator with two bulging grocery bags. Mrs. Pollakoff lived next door and was a nice old biddy. But she liked to talk, slowly, and usually about something excruciatingly boring. All it took was one "Hey, Mrs. Pollakoff" to get her started, and then Antonia would have to stop everything and listen to the old woman drone on and on: "Well . . . I . . . heard . . . from . . . my . . . niece . . . today. And . . . her . . . son . . . has . . . this . . . particularly . . . terrible . . . ear . . . infection . . ."

A coworker at the Hilton once told Antonia that you can always tell if someone is engaged with you and really listening by looking at their toes. If their toes pointed toward you, they were engaged. If their toes pointed in another direction, they wanted you to shut up so they could move on. That was how it was with old Mrs. Pollakoff. Antonia's toes always pointed in another direction whenever Mrs. Pollakoff stopped to talk to her.

Antonia thought about ducking back inside her apartment, but it was too late. The old woman had already spotted her. "Well . . . where . . . are . . . you . . . off . . . to?" she asked, between gasps for air as she lugged her grocery bags toward her unit.

"A friend's pool," Antonia lied. Her toes were already

pointing away from Mrs. Pollakoff, who looked like she was about to have a heart attack from the load she carried. The roof access was one flight up the back stairwell, and the last thing Antonia wanted to do right now was stop and help Mrs. Pollakoff with her groceries.

"Would . . . you . . . mind . . . giving . . . me . . . a . . . hand . . . here?"

Antonia tried not to wince. She quickly nodded and grabbed one of the bags. "I'm just going to take this to your door, Mrs. P," she said, walking ahead. "Hope you don't mind, but I'm running kind of late . . ."

"Have . . . you . . . noticed . . . lately . . . at . . . the . . . Safeway . . . that . . . more . . . and . . . more . . . people . . . are . . . bringing . . . their . . . dogs . . . into . . . the . . . supermarket . . . even . . . though . . . it's . . . supposed . . . to . . . be . . . against . . . the . . . law?"

Antonia ended up carrying the bag into Mrs. Pollakoff's kitchen, which was about ninety-five degrees and smelled like sour milk. She also listened to the old woman go on and on about how no one paid attention to the "No Pets Allowed" signs anymore.

The good-deed side trip took only three or four extra minutes, but it felt like an eternity before Antonia got out of there. She hurried down the hallway to the back stairwell. Up on the top floor, there was a metal spiral staircase blocked by a chain. A faded sign hung from the sagging chain: DO NOT ENTER.

Antonia swung her leg over the chain and started up the slightly wobbly stairway to a little room, no bigger than a closet. The caretaker kept a broom, a dustpan, and a bucket in there for the rare occasions when he swept the roof. The beige paint on the walls was peeling, and cobwebs swathed all four corners of the high ceiling. A door—with a fogged, mesh, safety-glass window—led outside to the roof. It had one of those push bars that activates the fire alarm when the door was opened. But the janitor had the key to a lock just below the bar, and that bypassed the alarm trigger.

Antonia had "borrowed" the key from the previous janitor years ago. She kept it on a rubber bracelet specifically for these sessions. No one else in the building had access to the roof. She wasn't supposed to be up there, either, but so far, she'd never been caught. She slipped her key into the door.

It wasn't locked.

"Oh, crap," she muttered.

Was someone out there now? She hoped not. It would ruin her whole afternoon.

With a bit of trepidation, Antonia opened the door and stepped outside. She didn't see anybody, and nothing looked different. A couple of puddles had formed from the rain two nights before, but that was all.

Antonia figured maybe she'd forgotten to lock up when she'd been up here on Monday afternoon.

Ducking back inside, she grabbed the broom, stepped out again, and wedged the broomstick in the doorway. She was always slightly paranoid about the door slamming shut and getting stuck, leaving her stranded up there.

Outside at last, Antonia felt the sun's delicious warmth. Heat seemed to waft up from the faded black tar covering the rooftop. She took her sunglasses out of her backpack, put them on, and ambled over toward her usual spot.

Ten chimney-like air ducts were staggered across the flat roof. The ledge around it was only about two feet high. Beyond the ledge, she had a beautiful view of Portland's Northwest neighborhood. There weren't any other tall buildings within two or three blocks, so Antonia had some privacy.

That was why, once she laid out her blanket, she

usually sunned topless. This afternoon would be no different. Antonia sat down on her beach towel, pulled the T-shirt over her head, and removed her top. As she rubbed Coppertone on herself, she breathed in the lotion's scent. It always reminded her of orange blossoms, trips to the beach, and sex. She often imagined some slick, handsome, executive vice president in a high-rise office building a few blocks away, looking at her through high-powered binoculars. Maybe he knew about her tanning sessions and looked forward to them as much as she did. Maybe he got off on seeing her sunbathing semi-nude. It was a nice fantasy. In reality, no one had ever bothered her while she was up on the roof—except two summers ago, when a low-flying helicopter had visited her on a few occasions. She'd figured it carried a rush-hour traffic reporter for one of the radio stations. The first time the chopper hovered over her, Antonia had automatically covered herself up. But during the return visits on other afternoons, she'd decided to give them a peek—more than a peek, a good long look. She was proud of her body, and she liked showing it off.

She set her thermos and the backpack on top of her T-shirt and top so they wouldn't blow away. Then she poured some of her Cosmopolitan into the thermos cup and sipped it. Popping in her earbuds, she listened to Sheryl Crow on Pandora, blocking out the noise from the street seven stories below. Antonia sipped her drink once more.

She reclined on the blanket and felt the warming rays on her smooth, lubricated skin.

Antonia was about to close her eyes when she heard something slam. Was it the door to the little shed? She sat up and squinted at her only entry back into the building. The broomstick was still lodged in the door.

She figured the noise had probably been from a

dumpster lid shutting in the alley below. All Antonia had to do to check was walk a few feet and peer over the ledge. But she didn't want to put her top back on.

She glanced once more at the rooftop shed. Was someone hiding behind there—or maybe crouched behind one of the air ducts?

Despite her bravado about being nearly nude outdoors, Antonia couldn't help feeling a bit skittish this afternoon. Off and on, for a couple of weeks now, she'd had the feeling someone was following her, watching her.

On several occasions, she had spotted her daughter Eden's creepy new boyfriend hanging around the apartment building—even when her daughter wasn't there. Was he the one stalking her? Antonia thought she'd seen him in the Hilton lobby earlier this week, too. His name was Brodie, and at nineteen, he was three years older than Eden. Antonia wouldn't have been a bit surprised if he was into drugs or some other kind of criminal activity. In fact, when her neighbors in the building started to complain about their missing parcels, Antonia immediately figured Brodie was stealing them. She didn't understand what Eden saw in him. He was all skin and bones—with a mop of dirty, blond hair. She often wanted to remind the scrawny SOB that every time he touched her underage daughter, he was setting himself up for a statutory rape charge. But Antonia decided any efforts to interfere in her daughter's love life would only push Eden closer to the worthless creep.

But why the hell would Brodie be hiding on the roof right now? Had Eden told him that her mother liked to sunbathe topless up here?

Well, if he'd come up for a peek, and she caught him spying on her, then maybe she could convince Eden to dump his sorry, skinny ass. Of course, knowing her daughter, if anything like that actually happened, Eden would merely blame her.

Antonia finished off what remained in her thermos cup and refilled it. Removing her sunglasses, she lay back on her blanket and listened to her music. After a few minutes, her mind started to drift. She might have even fallen asleep for a spell. But then, past the music, she thought she heard footsteps.

With a start, Antonia sat up again. She automatically crossed one arm over her bare breasts. She plucked out her earbuds. "Who's there?" she called. "Is anyone there?"

She glanced toward the janitor's shack. She didn't see anyone. The shack's door was still propped open with the broomstick.

Yet Antonia called out once more: "Is anyone there?"

No one answered. She could hear cars down on the street below—and someone tinkering on a piano in a neighboring building.

A cloud passed over the sun. Shuddering, Antonia grabbed her T-shirt and clutched it to her chest. She didn't know why she was so spooked. But she no longer felt safe muting the outside noise with her music, so she switched off her phone and stashed it in her backpack— along with the earbuds. "Shit," she muttered. She liked listening to her tunes while she tanned. Maybe this rooftop sun session was a bust after all. Maybe she'd be better off going back to her apartment and finishing what was left in her thermos down there.

Frowning, she glanced up at the sky. There was just the one little cloud. Was she going to let that ruin her afternoon?

She wouldn't let her silly paranoia spoil things, either. This could be her last tanning session of the year, the last of her sunny days.

Antonia took another gulp of her Cosmopolitan.

The sun came out from behind the cloud, and she basked in its reassuring warmth once more. She reclined on the towel. Antonia was just starting to relax again when she heard something squeak, followed by a little tap. *It's not the shed door, stupid*, she told herself, keeping her eyes closed. *You're all alone up here, and that sun feels delicious*. She wasn't going to sit up again. There was a creaking sound, which might have been footsteps—or just about anything else. *Ignore it*, she told herself. It was probably just a neighbor moving around directly below in one of the top-floor apartments—or maybe someone down in the alley, taking out their garbage.

She felt the kiss of a slight breeze against her naked skin. It gave her goose bumps.

A part of her wanted so much to sit up and check one more time to make sure no one was creeping toward her, but she didn't move. It was like a contest now. How long could she lay here with her eyes closed? Besides, even if someone else was up here, why should she care? What did she think would happen? So they'd see her boobs. Big deal. And if it was the janitor, ready to chew her out for sneaking up here, she'd simply tell him this was her first time on the roof, and the door had been unlocked. Wasn't it his responsibility—to keep the roof door locked? And how long had he been staring at her practically naked before he'd made his presence known?

Antonia giggled at the thought of turning the tables on Sid, the building janitor, who had never seemed to like her much.

Something blocked out the sun once again. Probably another cloud.

Without opening her eyes, Antonia blindly felt around for her thermos cup. Her fingers brushed against something: a foot. She felt the laces of a sneaker.

Antonia opened her eyes and gasped. She couldn't see who was standing over her—just the shadowy silhouette between the sun and her. Sitting up, she quickly grabbed her T-shirt to cover herself.

Past all the sounds she'd been ignoring, Antonia could hear her visitor's voice, though it was merely a whisper.

"Why did you have to be in my way?"

The custodian, sixty-two-year-old Sid Parsons, lived in the basement of Antonia's apartment building. He was proud of the job he did keeping the building clean, safe, and secure. That was why it irked him to find that some jerk had left a near-empty, sixteen-ounce cup from McDonald's on the newel post at the first-floor stairway landing. The same jerk must have tossed the used McDonald's bag onto the lobby floor. Now the entryway smelled like old cheeseburgers. Outside, crows were fighting over scraps of greasy paper and French fries on the small front lawn. The birds scattered the fast food trash over the walkway and trimmed grass.

Sid had a pretty good idea who the guilty party was. It was probably that seedy creep who hung around with the daughter of Newcomb in 6-B. The scumbag and the daughter seemed high half the time. Talk about a couple of lowlifes. Since the guy had first started coming around a few weeks ago, several residents' packages had been stolen. Also, someone had broken into the storage room and made off with all sorts of things, leaving behind a hell of a mess. And Sid kept finding trash in and around the building. He often noticed the guy's cigarette butts out by the front door, too.

Sid had already said something about it to Newcomb the Nympho. That was what he called her, though he kept the nickname to himself. She was always buzzing in some new guy. She didn't seem to have any problem getting boyfriends, but she sure couldn't keep them. Each one would move in and make himself very much at home there. But by the time Sid learned the guy's name he'd be gone, and there would be another to take his place. The woman's taste in guys wasn't all that much better than her daughter's.

As he gathered up the sorry son of a bitch's trash, Sid figured he'd send an email to the condo board about it. Maybe one of them would give Newcomb the Nympho a talking-to.

Opening the dumpster lid, Sid tossed the garbage inside.

Suddenly, he heard a scream directly above. He thought it was a seagull. But when he looked up, he saw a nude woman plummeting down from the roof. Arms and legs flailing, she hurtled right toward him—and the open dumpster.

Horrified, Sid reeled back.

Her body hit the edge of the bin with a loud, terrible, ripping thump.

But Sid didn't see what happened to her.

He couldn't see, because of the blood that had splattered into his eyes.

CHAPTER TWO

Trying to keep out of the rain, Sheila O'Rourke vied for a spot in the bus stop's small shelter. Four other people were waiting for the number 49 at her stop in the North Broadway neighborhood. Sheila had already made up her mind that the filthy looking, twentyish, blond-haired guy among them was a board-certified jerk. Here they were, huddled under the crowded shelter roof to-gether, and the guy lit up a cigarette. Yes, they were all outside, but he was blowing smoke in the faces of four other people. An elderly lady with an empty shopping tote on wheels coughed repeatedly and waved her hand in front of her face, but the guy didn't notice.

Something about him was familiar. He wore a baggy army camouflage jacket, along with a backpack. He seemed totally oblivious whenever the backpack banged into someone. He didn't seem to notice Sheila frowning at him, either. His smoking didn't bother her that much, but it clearly bugged the old lady—and that bothered her.

The bus pulled up to the curb, making a hissing sound as it stopped. The old lady needed the special ramp lowered—with a *beep, beep, beep*—so she could get on the bus with her shopping tote. Sheila boarded after her, took a vacant window seat near the front, and set her purse on her lap.

Tossing away his cigarette, the blond guy stepped on after her. "Hey, man," she heard him tell the driver. "I don't have any money, and I really need to get downtown. And it's raining. Could you cut me a break?"

The driver grumbled something back to him. Sheila wondered how often the poor bus drivers in this city had to listen to sob stories like that. But the driver must have said yes, because the homeless-looking guy shook off the rain and plopped onto one of the seats usually reserved for elderly and disabled riders. He immediately took off the backpack and set it on the seat next to his so he was occupying two spots. From the bag, he took out a bag of Fritos, wolfed some down, and spilled a few more onto the bus floor.

The old lady who had been so annoyed with him at the bus stop gave him a dirty look—probably because he sat right beneath a sign that said NO DRINKING OR EATING on the bus.

Sheila was fascinated with the whole scene unfolding in front of her. She wondered if the old lady would say something to the guy—because, if she did, he'd probably tell her to fuck off, or something sweet like that.

He stashed the chips in his backpack, spilling more on the floor. Then he pulled out an iPad, checked it, and tucked it inside the bag again. As the bus came to a stop, he took a smartphone from the pocket of his camouflage jacket and started working it with his dirty thumbs.

Sheila stared at him, half amused, half disgusted. *Unbelievable.* And here she'd thought he was homeless. The creep had an iPad and a smartphone, and he could afford cigarettes at $9 a pack, but he couldn't cough up $2.50 for public transportation.

She didn't realize she was scowling at him until he turned and scowled back at her.

Flustered, she looked out the rain-beaded window.

What was her problem? If some guy was shameless enough to beg for a free ride on the bus, what business of that was hers? Why should she care?

Here she'd thought there would be some sort of confrontation between him and the cranky old lady. But *she* was the cranky old lady—or at least, she felt that way today: a cranky old lady at forty-three. It was probably because she hadn't slept well last night. Plus, it was raining, the bus stank, and her stupid car was still in the shop.

According to the auto mechanic, somebody was trying to kill her.

On Monday morning, she'd backed her Toyota Highlander out of the garage and gotten to the end of the driveway when she realized the dashboard warning light for the brakes was flashing. The parking brake wasn't set, and the regular brakes seemed to be working. Sheila glanced toward the garage and noticed the sporadic trail of oily-looking fluid on the driveway. "Oh, crap," she muttered. She decided not to take any chances and inched the car back into the garage. She found an empty plastic pan and shoved it under the car to catch the leak.

"Somebody must be out to get you," said the slim, slightly cross-eyed mechanic from Hilltop Auto that afternoon. He'd shown up, looked under the car and then at the pan full of oily fluid. He and Sheila were standing in her garage with the big door open.

Sheila didn't understand his comment—or the lopsided little smile on his face.

"I'm sorry?" she asked.

"It's the brake fluid," he said, wiping his hands on his coveralls. "In the movies, when somebody's out to kill somebody else and wants to make it look like a car accident, they usually drain the brake fluid . . ."

Dumbstruck, Sheila stared at him. "Are you saying someone tampered with my car?"

He quickly shook his head, "Oh, no. I . . . I mean, yeah, your brakes aren't working. But it's anybody's guess why. I didn't mean to scare you, Mrs. O'Rourke. Though I guess it's pretty scary when you stop to think about it, because—well, if you'd kept driving the car while it was leaking brake fluid like that, you'd have had a serious accident, no doubt about it. Good thing you noticed it in the driveway and not on the highway . . ."

With a hand over her heart, Sheila looked at the car and then at him again. The Toyota was their family vehicle. She imagined driving on the interstate with one or all three of her kids in the car when the brakes gave out.

"Y'know, I was joking earlier about someone trying to kill you," the mechanic muttered. Obviously, he could see how upset she was. "It's just that, in the movies, there's usually a winding, mountain road, and the brakes are gone and—and, well, I'll shut up now." He cleared his throat. "Um, about the car, Mrs. O'Rourke. I'll call a tow truck. We should have the problem fixed by tomorrow afternoon . . ."

While getting dinner ready that night, Sheila had told her husband what the mechanic had said.

"Well, that's a stupid remark," Dylan said as he poured them each a glass of wine. " *'Somebody's out to get you.'* How insensitive can you get? I should give that garage a call, I really should . . ."

"Oh, honey, no," she sighed. "I don't want to get him into trouble. His eyes were kind of crossed, and . . . well, I felt sorry for him. I really wasn't upset about what he said. It's the idea that we could have had a major accident. He was just joking. It's not worth making a federal case."

That had been on Monday, the night before last. The shop had called yesterday afternoon to say the car wouldn't be ready until the end of the week. Sheila could tell she was talking to the same mechanic from before. She asked if he'd figured out what had caused the brake fluid leak. This time, there were no jokes: "The brake line was all chewed up. We can't be sure exactly what caused that, Mrs. O'Rourke. Anyway, we want to run a few more tests to make sure the problem's nipped in the bud."

So Sheila was without a car for another couple of days. It was a pain, but not the end of the world—and not worth haggling with the insurance company for a loaner. She was always chauffeuring around her three kids and their friends. So she sort of welcomed the break. As far as work was concerned, she often took the bus anyway because parking was a total nightmare in the trendy, congested Pike/Pine corridor of Capitol Hill, where Sheila taught dance lessons at the Century Ballroom three afternoons a week. The number 49 dropped her off just a block away. It was practically door to door.

Sheila told herself if having to take the bus was the worst thing that could happen, then she had it pretty easy. To appreciate how easy she had it, all she had to do was look back at her life seventeen or eighteen years ago, when she and Dylan had been living in Portland. She'd been working as an accountant at Neff Intermodal Limited, taking care of her dying mother, and going slightly crazy in the early stages of her first pregnancy. That was just the beginning of a horrible period for her—with one devastating thing after another.

Including three deaths.

"I know you must feel God is testing you right now, Sheila," she remembered an old, booze-breathed priest friend of her mother's saying. "You're just going through a rough patch."

The priest had convinced Sheila that if she could make herself forget about these terrible occurrences, it would be like they never happened. In other words, he'd advocated total denial. Maybe not the healthiest coping method, but it sort of worked. At least, that was how she managed to carry on at the time.

After her mother died, Sheila decided that too many people in Portland knew about her personal tragedies. Too many familiar locales brought back too many painful memories. In Seattle, she and Dylan made a fresh start, and once there, she almost managed to convince herself that the "rough patch" had never happened.

About five years ago, on a lark, she'd signed on for dance lessons at the Century Ballroom: waltz, fox-trot, and swing. She discovered she had a knack for it—and was so enthusiastic that the teacher often asked her to assist or fill in. Eventually, Sheila began instructing—individual, couple, and group classes. She didn't make nearly as much money as she had as an accountant, but it was a hell of a lot more fun. And dance proved to be the best therapy in the world for her problems. It was hard to stay glum when she was moving around on the dance floor.

As she stared out the window of the bus, Sheila told herself that she'd perk up once she started teaching her East Coast Swing group this afternoon.

She checked her watch—and then glanced over at the blond guy once more.

He was still staring at her. He clearly mouthed the word "bitch."

Flustered, Sheila quickly looked away again. Maybe somebody should have explained to this jerk that if he blew smoke in people's faces, weaseled his way onto the bus without paying, took up two seats in the disabled/elderly section, and made a mess on the bus floor, he shouldn't be so damn sensitive when he got a dirty look or two.

Ignore him, she told herself. *You should have ignored him in the first place.*

Her face flushed, she stared at the seatback in front of her. Sheila suddenly realized where she'd seen the guy before. It had been about ten days ago—at the supermarket. He'd been with a Goth-looking, blond-haired girl. Sheila had spotted him slipping a bottle of wine inside the same baggy camouflage jacket he wore now. He'd smirked when he caught her looking. Sheila remembered scowling back at him. She'd said something to one of the checkout clerks about the two street kids who were shoplifting, but had no idea if the clerk had followed up on it.

She wondered if he actually recognized her from over a week ago. It didn't seem likely—unless of course, he'd been busted for shoplifting that particular day and he somehow figured she was the one who had reported him. Still, would he really remember her?

Sheila never considered herself all that memorable in the looks department. "Cute" was the word people used to describe her, and she was content with that. Tall and thin, she had blue eyes, a pale complexion and wavy, shoulder-length, auburn hair—or more precisely, *light mocha brown*, according to the description on the Nice'n Easy box. It had been her color for about eight years. But it wasn't like the street punk would have remembered the lady with the light mocha brown hair. She remembered being dressed differently the last time they'd seen each other: She hadn't been wearing this purple coat at the supermarket ten days ago. So she couldn't imagine how this kid could remember her. Was it possible he'd been following her around for a while now?

He couldn't have been stalking her—not for the last ten days, not without her noticing. Sheila dared to look at him again. Yes, it was the same guy from the supermarket.

And yes, damn it, he was still staring at her.

Swallowing hard, she looked away again.

The bus ground to a stop. A few people had gotten up and moved to the door. Hers was the stop after this one— in three blocks.

Sheila loathed the idea of him following her off the bus—if he was indeed following her.

The young man stopped staring at her to look at his phone.

Sheila glanced back and saw the last person heading out the bus's middle door.

Springing to her feet, she ran to the door and hurried off the bus. She was in such a rush that she almost tripped stepping down to the curb.

With a whoosh, the doors closed after her. Then the bus pulled away—with the blond creep still on it.

Catching her breath, Sheila stood there on the sidewalk, in the rain. She waited until the bus was a little farther down the street, then she ducked under the awning of a Panera Bread. She wasn't sure what to do. It wasn't like she could call the police. The guy really hadn't done anything except scare her a little.

She stepped into Panera and was overwhelmed by the smell of fresh-baked bread. If she weren't so unnerved, the aroma might have made her hungry, but right now, her mouth was dry and she just wanted a bottle of water. Someone was in front of her, so it took a couple of minutes.

When she stepped outside again with her water, Sheila thought she saw the creepy blond guy across the street—in front of the community college. She stopped in her tracks.

A semi-truck rumbled by her. When it had passed, the guy was gone.

Sheila anxiously gazed across the street to see if he was hiding behind a lamppost, a telephone pole, or a car. She knew she hadn't imagined him. He'd been there just a minute ago, watching her. He must have gotten off the bus at the next stop and then backtracked.

She remembered the son of a bitch telling the driver he was going downtown.

Sheila couldn't see him, but she knew he was there somewhere across the street. She could feel his eyes on her.

Her phone rang, startling her. With a shaky hand, she pulled it out of her raincoat pocket. It was a text, sender UNKNOWN. *Was it him?*

Standing under the awning, she bit her lip and opened the text:

Maybe u should ask ur husband about this.

There was a link.

Sheila knew she shouldn't open a link from some stranger. She checked the time. She had only a few minutes to get to the Century Ballroom to teach her dance lesson. She told herself to delete the damn thing and get on her way.

But she wondered what Dylan had to do with this cryptic link.

She couldn't help thinking the blond-haired creep was behind this. It seemed like too much of a coincidence that a stranger was following her—at practically the exact same time she received this strange text. There had to be a connection.

She clicked on the link.

An article from *The Oregonian* popped up—with the headline:

Portland Woman Falls to Her Death From Apartment Building Roof

Sheila immediately checked the date. It was from almost two weeks ago.

As the rain tapped on the awning overhead, Sheila read the article about a forty-four-year-old divorcée, Antonia Newcomb. Sheila didn't know her. She'd never heard of her. The woman was survived by a sixteen-year-old daughter. The victim appeared to have been sunbathing on her apartment building roof before she fell. The article didn't say if her death had been an accident or suicide, or if foul play was involved. Apparently, the police hadn't determined that at the time the article was written.

Sheila felt sick to her stomach.

She had no idea who this woman was. But the way she'd died was too horrible—and too familiar. And it had happened in Portland, of all places.

She wondered why Dylan was supposed to know about this.

Clutching the phone in her hand, Sheila gazed across the street again—for the seedy-looking blond guy.

But there was no sign of him.

CHAPTER THREE

Wednesday—5:11 P.M.

Dylan O'Rourke's phone rang as he walked down the corridor toward the men's locker room at the Pro Club. There were signs posted in the locker room prohibiting cell phone use, and Dylan refused to be one of those d-bags who thought their particular call or text was the exception to that rule. So he stopped, stepped aside, and pulled the phone out of his pocket. It was another text from Sheila:

> When will u b home from the gym?

Dylan sighed. She was driving him crazy. She'd left him a voicemail earlier while he'd been in a lunch meeting. She'd sounded upset, and asked him to call her. He'd called back and left a message, asking what was the matter. She'd replied with a text, saying it could wait until tonight. But then, after an hour, she'd left another voicemail—to see if they could talk before her next dance class. She wouldn't tell him in any of her messages what the hell was wrong, not even a clue. But they were supposed to talk when he got home from the gym tonight.

Sheila had pulled this same routine on him about two weeks ago: all these messages back and forth because she needed to discuss something with him. Dylan had figured one of the kids had had an accident and she'd been afraid to tell him in a message. But Sheila had insisted it could wait until he got home. It had turned out she'd just wanted to know if he was okay with going to a neighbor's dinner party that weekend.

So Dylan convinced himself that whatever this current "crisis" was, it could wait until he was home tonight. He texted her back:

B home usual time . . . 6:45 XXX

He shoved the phone back into his pocket, and then headed into the locker room.

Dylan had a rigid routine he followed at the gym, right down to using the same machine for each exercise—if it was available. On the second level, the club had a dozen elliptical machines lined up in front of the floor-to-ceiling windows, and the machine he liked was at the end—near the TV that was always tuned to CNN. But his machine wasn't working today. Someone had unplugged it. His workout was already getting off to a bumpy start.

Dylan tried the apparatus beside it, and that put him next to someone else—a thirtysomething blonde with her hair in a ponytail. She wore gray sweatpants, a white T-shirt, and glasses. She had a book on the holder of the machine's dashboard, and she barely looked at him when he stepped onto the neighboring apparatus.

That kind of bothered him—which was funny because Dylan usually tried to isolate himself at the gym. It was his time to tune everything else out. His job was in public relations for Starbucks, and he spent nearly all his work day dealing with people, doing his best to be diplomatic or charming. At the gym, he really didn't want to talk to anyone. And yet, people were always striking up conversations with him. "Well, *duh*," Sheila had told him when he'd mentioned it. "That's because you're not exactly hard on the eyes, hon. And please, don't act like you don't enjoy it, because I know you lap up the attention."

She was right, of course—about liking the attention and connecting with people. And yeah, he knew he was good-looking. He worked hard to keep in shape. And he was lucky because he had thick, wavy, dark brown hair and green eyes—almost the color of a 7UP bottle. He was forty-four, but looked several years younger. He liked hearing that he was handsome. But at the gym, he just wanted to get in and out of there. Plus, nearly half the people who approached him there were guys who ended up asking him out. And then he was never sure if he was getting a friendly invitation or hit on. He always told them thanks anyway, but his wife was waiting for him at home.

The blond woman ignoring him was pretty—with a turned-up nose and full lips. Something about her was familiar. As he started his warm-up, Dylan tried to figure out where he'd seen her before. It wasn't here.

She glanced at him for a second, but as soon as their eyes met, she went back to her book.

But Dylan was thunderstruck. His first assessment of her was wrong. She wasn't just pretty. She was beautiful. He didn't want to stop looking at her.

She kept her strides at a leisurely pace. Dylan guessed she was just getting started on the machine or she was cooling down. He didn't want to be caught staring, so he gazed forward—out the rain-beaded window at the buildings and construction cranes around South Lake Union. But it was dark enough out that he could shift his focus to their reflections in the glass. He kept looking at her, all the while wondering where he'd seen her before. She turned and glanced at him.

Dylan smiled at her. "Hi, I know I've met you before . . ."

She politely smiled back, but shook her head. "I don't think so." She wiped the perspiration off her forehead and went back to her book.

Now that he'd heard her voice, Dylan remembered how they'd met. It had been about three weeks ago. He was in one of the busiest areas of Broadway, on his way to the supermarket for Sheila and waiting for the light to change. The WALK sign went on. He was about to step off the curb when someone grabbed his arm. Before he realized what was happening, a car tore around the corner, its tires screeching. The damn thing just missed him.

His Good Samaritan was an attractive blonde. She wasn't wearing her glasses then. As they crossed the street together, Dylan thanked her for saving his life. Just as they reached the curb on the other side of the street, her grocery bag tore. Dylan gave her the canvas grocery bag he'd had with him. It was from work: a high-quality Starbucks tote bag with Edward Hopper's *Nighthawks* on it. Dylan remembered she didn't want to walk off with his fancy tote. He assured her that he had a ton more like it at work and at home. On the sidewalk, he helped her transfer her groceries into the bag. After they said goodbye and parted company, Dylan recalled turning to look at her—and he caught her looking back at him, too. She gave a shy wave, and then moved on. It was strange, but in their brief exchange, Dylan felt a real connection to her.

Now here she was, at his gym.

"We met on Broadway," Dylan said. "You stopped me from getting mowed down at the crosswalk by some nut."

The blonde warily glanced up from her book, and then at him. She started to shake her head again. "I'm sorry . . ."

"I gave you my shopping bag," he said.

She paused on the machine. "Of course!" she exclaimed, breaking into a smile. She was slightly out of breath. "I still have it. The Edward Hopper tote, it's a new favorite. I use it every time I go shopping. I hate to tell you, but you're never getting it back."

"It's all yours," Dylan said, increasing his pace on the machine. "It was a thank-you for rescuing me, remember?"

"Well, it was my pleasure." She started walking in place again. "I'm sorry I didn't recognize you earlier."

"That's okay," Dylan replied. The machine's dashboard showed his heart rate was increasing. "This is the first time I've seen you here. Are you a new member?"

"No, my husband and I joined about a year ago." She smoothed back a strand of damp hair from her forehead. "I used to work out in the mornings, but I have a part-time job and the hours changed last week. So now I'm trying to adjust to coming here in the early evenings."

Dylan noticed she'd gotten that *my husband* reference into the conversation mighty early. Did she think he was trying to hit on her? He glanced over toward the free weights area, and then at her. "So—is your husband here with you tonight?"

"No, he hasn't been—well, no, he—he's home tonight." She faced forward again, and Dylan was pretty sure she was checking his reflection in the window—the same way he'd been looking at her before.

"So you have a part-time job?" he asked.

"I work at Children's Hospital, patient and family services. It's mostly customer service or public relations—sort of what I gather you do for Starbucks."

Dylan's face lit up. "So you do remember me. I'm flattered."

"Well, actually, it's the Starbucks bag I've been lugging around for the past three weeks." She gave him a tiny, contrite smile. "I seem to recall you saying you had a bunch of them from work . . ."

He was a little disappointed. Apparently, the Starbucks shopping bag had made more of an impression on her than he had—and usually, he was so good with people.

She nodded at his left hand. "I see you're married, too. Is your wife here?"

"No, she's not a member. She gets plenty of exercise with her job. She teaches swing dancing and the waltz."

"That must be a fun job. I'm envious." She gave him a sidelong glance. "On top of everything else, I'll bet you're a wonderful dancer."

"Actually, I'm her worst student," Dylan admitted. "I can do the twist and move around the dance floor okay, but when it comes to remembering the steps, I'm utterly hopeless."

She was still gazing at him. Dylan was getting such mixed signals. From her dreamy smile, he now thought maybe she liked him. Even if he hadn't made much of an impression on her the first time they met, perhaps he was making one now.

She seemed to realize she was staring and quickly looked down at her book again. Her pace on the machine quickened.

Dylan was going to ask about the book she was reading, but instead, he heard himself say something else. "Would you like to get together for lunch sometime this week?"

She glanced up from her book and sighed. "I don't think that's such a good idea."

"Why not? It would just be lunch—that's all. Besides, I'd like to repay you . . ."

"You already did that—with the tote bag."

He chuckled. "Well, I hope my life's worth more than a tote bag. Seriously, I'd like to thank you."

Slowing down her stride, she set her bookmark on the page and closed her book. Then she switched off the machine and gave him a tight smile. "That's all right. You've thanked me enough."

She stepped off the elliptical, grabbed the spray bottle and rag from the holder on the side of the dashboard, and sprayed down the grip bars.

"Hey, listen," Dylan said, slowing down on the machine. "It was just a friendly offer. I think you're very nice. I hope I didn't offend you. It's not like I was . . ." He trailed off.

Without looking at him, she wiped down the dashboard. "It's okay, I was wrapping up here anyway."

"Well, it was really nice to run into you again," Dylan said.

She returned the bottle and rag to the holder, then grabbed her book. "You, too," she said, turning away. She hurried toward the stairs to the first level.

Working the grip bars, Dylan started to increase his speed on the machine again. "God," he muttered to himself. "I'm such an asshole."

Once he'd finished his workout, showered, and dressed, Dylan headed out of the locker room and checked his phone. There hadn't been any more messages or texts from Sheila in the past ninety minutes. That was a good sign. Or was it? For all he knew, while he'd haplessly flirted with that blonde, his wife's problem—whatever it was—could have blown up into a major catastrophe.

Why hadn't Sheila just told him what was so damn important? He didn't know whether to be worried or annoyed.

As he headed downstairs to the gym's lobby, he kept telling himself that if it were a real emergency, Sheila would have urged him to come home.

He approached the glass doors to the street, then stopped.

The blonde was standing just outside the doorway, trying to avoid the downpour.

Dylan took a deep breath and pushed the door open. He worked up a smile for her. "Hi, again," he said. "Listen, I'm sorry about earlier. I'm happily married. I don't want you thinking I'm one of those guys who go to the gym to hit on women."

"I didn't think you were," she replied with a wistful smile. "And I really was finished with my routine. Anyway, no need to apologize." She held her gym bag in one hand and her phone in the other. She wore a lightweight olive jacket with the collar up. The jacket's shoulders were water-stained and her hair was wet. It looked like she'd started out in the storm but turned back.

"Do you need a ride?" he asked.

She squinted up at the rain. "Oh, I think it'll let up soon."

"Well, I live in Roanoke Park. If you're headed up to Capitol Hill, I'm going in that direction anyway." He nodded at the black BMW parked by the curb in front of the building. "My car's right there. I've got rockstar parking."

She checked her phone. "Typical. It's pouring out, so naturally, my Uber app has gone haywire on me." She looked at him and smiled. "A ride would be great, thanks."

They ran through the downpour to his car, and Dylan opened the passenger door for her. Then he hurried around to the driver's side and jumped in behind the wheel. He listened to the rain pelting the car roof.

"I really appreciate this," she said, a little out of breath. She set her gym bag in front of her on the floor. "By the way, my name is Brooke . . . Brooke Crowley."

Dylan shook her hand. "I'm Dylan O'Rourke. Where are we headed?"

She lived on Belmont Avenue, which wasn't far away, but involved crossing a high overpass to Interstate 5 with nothing to shield her from the wind and rain. The rest of the walk was up a steep hill.

Even in the downpour, they had a sweeping view of the city and Lake Union from the overpass. For a few moments, there was an awkward silence. The only sounds were the windshield wipers squeaking, the rain, and the traffic noise on the interstate below. Then Brooke asked if he and his wife had any kids.

She'd asked in a very friendly way. At the same time, Dylan wondered if she was trying to make a point about him being married.

"We have three kids," Dylan said, eyes on the road ahead.

"So tell me about them. I'm interested."

"Well, there's Hannah, who's sixteen, going on twenty-seven. She's very popular and just starting to date, which scares the hell out of me. Steve is fifteen, and he's into trains . . ."

"Is he like you?" she asked.

"No, he's smarter than me. He takes after his mom. He's very sensitive, too. He recently had his hair all shaved off to help raise money for children with cancer. It's just starting to grow back, thank God. Strangers look at us with such pity when we're out together. I want to tell them, 'He's okay, don't worry . . .'" Dylan laughed and glanced at her.

They were at the stop sign at the end of the overpass. A streetlight was shining from above. Shadows of raindrops on the windshield dappled her face, and for a moment he thought she was crying.

"You all right?" he asked.

She nodded, and then cleared her throat. "You said you had three kids. What about the third one?"

Dylan shifted gears to head up the steep hill. "Well, Gabe is ten and a total jock. Every Saturday, he has a game somewhere. So—Gabe's the King of Saturdays. Most of our weekends are scheduled around him."

She nodded. "Belmont is coming up," she said. "You'll take a right here."

Dylan followed her directions. "What about you and your husband?" he asked. "Do you have any kids?"

She hesitated, and then pointed to an apartment building on the right. It was one of three buildings in a row—each about ten stories high. "That's me, right there."

Dylan turned into the driveway. "Nice," he murmured. "Do you have a view?"

She nodded. "Yes, and it's pretty incredible, too. We're on the ninth floor. Everyone comes over on New Year's to see the Space Needle fireworks—whether we invite them or not."

Pulling in front of the lobby's glass double doors, Dylan let the car idle. "So—no kids?" As soon as he asked this, he regretted it. She'd skirted the question earlier, and obviously, there was a reason for that.

"Not anymore," she said quietly. "We had a son, Aaron, who died. It'll be two years in November. He had leukemia."

"I'm so sorry," Dylan murmured. He didn't know what else to say. He felt terrible, joking a minute before about Steve's shaved head.

"It's weird," she sighed. "When I meet someone who's married, I sort of automatically ask if they have any kids. I keep forgetting that they're bound to ask me the same question. I've had practically two years to figure out how to answer them, and I'm still not sure."

"I think you can just be honest," Dylan said, shrugging.

"Yeah, only they get uncomfortable when I tell them the truth. But whenever I say I don't have any children, it feels awful—like I'm pretending Aaron never existed. It seems so cold-blooded. I felt bad enough when we moved here . . ." She looked out the car window at her building. "We used to have a house in Queen Anne, and once Aaron died, Paul—that's my husband—he said we should move. I didn't want to, but I understood. Aaron had been sick for so long. He spent his last two months in the hospital. You'd think Paul would've gotten used to that empty bed-room. But after Aaron died, Paul couldn't take it."

"Of course not," Dylan whispered.

"Paul said that even if we gutted it and tried to change the bedroom into a study or something, it would've always been Aaron's room. Anyway, we moved here about a year and a half ago. And I'll bet right now you're very sorry you asked if I had any kids."

"No, I'm not," he said. "I'm glad you told me. Was he at Children's Hospital?"

"Yes, I started volunteering there after we moved here. You know, moving here didn't really change things too much, not for me. Maybe I didn't want things to change. I'm still constantly walking past or revisiting Aaron's room at the hospital. There've been scores of children in that room—in that same bed—since Aaron. But to me, it's still Aaron's room. It's one of the main reasons I work there. I want to be near his room. Isn't that crazy?" She reached into her coat pocket, pulled out a tissue, and wiped her nose. "I haven't admitted that to anyone, not even my close friends."

"Sometimes it's easier to talk to a stranger," Dylan offered.

She smiled at him. "You don't feel like a stranger."

Dylan was speechless. One minute she seemed wary of him, and the next, she'd say something like that. The signals she sent were so mixed, and somehow that intrigued him. In their silence, he listened to the rain on the car roof. He wanted to reach over and touch her tear-stained cheek, but he kept his hand on the wheel.

"I didn't mean to get so serious on you." She let out a sad little laugh. "Poor guy, you offer a girl a ride home, and she practically breaks down crying in your car. You're probably thinking this is the last time you ever ask anyone out at the gym."

"Actually, I was thinking that I'd really like to see you again," he said quietly.

She grabbed her gym bag and opened the passenger door. The interior light went on. "I should go before I say yes."

He didn't want her to leave. Still, he quickly jumped out of the driver's side to help her with the door. *Ding-ding-ding,* the alarm chimed. He'd left his key in the ignition. Ignoring it, Dylan ran around the front of the car and reached her door just as she was stepping out. He shut the car door for her.

"Do you usually walk to and from the gym?" he asked, a little out of breath. He felt like he was on the elliptical machine again.

She nodded.

The two of them stood in the rain for a moment.

"And this is the time you usually go there?" he asked.

She nodded again. "My new time, yes . . ."

"Will you be working out tomorrow?"

She shook her head. She didn't offer more.

He managed a smile. "Well, maybe I'll see you there again sometime."

"Thanks for the ride, Dylan," she said. Then she turned and started toward the building's glass double doors. She took her keys out of her pocket.

Dylan stood by the car, watching her. The driver door was still open, and the alarm was still *ding-ding-ding*ing.

She stopped and turned around. "I'll be working out on Friday," she called.

"Friday," he repeated, slightly breathless again.

She nodded. Then she hurried to the door and let herself in.

CHAPTER FOUR

"**A**re you sure you don't know who she is?" Sheila asked. "Or *was*?"

Dylan sat at their breakfast table, which was actually a booth, something out of a fifties diner with green vinyl seat cushions and a green "cracked ice" pattern tabletop trimmed in chrome. They'd bought the house nine years ago because Dylan had loved the kitschy midcentury modern kitchen—wood cabinets, green and brown boomerang-patterned countertops, and outdated, bronze-colored appliances. Sheila wanted to tear it all out and put in an island, granite countertops, and stainless-steel appliances. But Dylan wouldn't hear of it. As a compromise, he bought her the stainless-steel appliances, but wouldn't make any other changes. It was his favorite room in the house. Sheila tolerated it. The other anachronistic compromise to the midcentury look was a small flat-screen TV at one end of the diner-style table, by the window. At the moment, *The Big Bang Theory* was on mute. But Dylan paid no attention to it. He was looking at Sheila's phone, reading the *Oregonian* article someone had texted to her.

"Antonia Newcomb," he read the name aloud. Then

he shook his head. "Babe, it doesn't ring a bell, not even a distant one."

"Are you sure?" Sheila asked, glancing over her shoulder at him. She was at the stove, stirring a pot of sloppy joe. "I thought maybe she was someone you knew back in school—or when we lived in Portland . . ."

Dylan shook his head again. He had no idea who the woman was. He sipped his scotch and soda. He allowed himself one drink when he got home every night. Sheila, obviously shaken, had already knocked off her second glass of merlot.

The boys were watching TV down in the basement recreation room, and as usual, Hannah was barricaded in her bedroom, on Instagram or texting with one of her friends. The family always ate a bit late on the nights Dylan went to the gym. He'd arrived home even later than usual tonight. And he was glad Sheila hadn't asked why he'd been delayed. She'd been too preoccupied with the text and some creep she'd encountered on the bus.

Though Antonia Newcomb was a total stranger to both of them, the way she'd died was eerily familiar. Dylan was reluctant to say anything about it, and he knew Sheila was, too. In fact, he was surprised she'd even brought up Portland.

They didn't talk about their time there. Though he traveled to Portland for work occasionally, Dylan did his damnedest to avoid even mentioning the city in Sheila's presence.

"Are you sure this text wasn't meant for someone else?" he asked, setting Sheila's phone down on the tabletop. "It doesn't mention either one of us by name. You said you tried to reply to this thing, right?"

"Twice," Sheila answered, taking the salad out of the refrigerator. "And both times, my texts bounced back as undeliverable."

"That just proves what I'm saying. It wasn't meant for you, or it's from someone trying to screw with you."

Dylan didn't want to say anything beyond that. Sheila's name had been in the Portland newspapers seventeen years ago. Maybe someone remembered and sent the article out of spite. People could be pretty awful sometimes.

He now understood why she'd become unnerved and left him so many messages today. He sighed. "Honey, I don't think you should worry about this. Just delete it. And don't open any more strange texts with links. They could have a virus or spyware. You could have really screwed up your phone, or far worse. You could have—"

"I know, I know," Sheila huffed. She pulled the merlot out of the liquor cabinet and refilled her glass.

That's three, Dylan thought. She was really tipping back the wine tonight. Sheila drank a little bourbon sometimes when she couldn't fall asleep at night, but it was unlike her to get plastered before dinner.

"So—you're saying it's all just a coincidence? *Portland Woman Falls to Her Death* . . ." Sheila's voice cracked as she recited the headline. She took a gulp of the wine. "Some coincidence. I'm on the bus, and I see this shoplifting creep from ten days ago. He calls me a bitch. And after I slip out the back door without him noticing, he jumps off at the next stop, and in less than five minutes, he's across the street from where I am. He must have backtracked—running—four blocks. The guy was obviously following me. The text came, like, a minute later . . ."

Dylan slid out of the booth. He stood up. "You didn't tell me that he called you a bitch."

"He mouthed it at me," Sheila said.

"Is something burning?" he asked.

"Damn it, the buns!" Sheila grabbed a potholder,

yanked open the oven door, and pulled a cookie sheet of hamburger buns from the top rack. Some of the buns were black around the edges. She dropped the sheet onto the stovetop's vacant burners. Two of the bun tops fell onto the floor. "Goddamn it!" she hissed. "And we don't have any buns left . . ."

"Honey, chill," he whispered. "It's not the end of the world."

She frowned at him. "Y'know, one of the worst things you can say to someone who's having a meltdown is 'chill.'"

"Point taken, hon." He handed Sheila her wineglass, then steered her to the booth and sat her down.

Picking up the hamburger buns, Dylan got a knife out of the drawer, moved over to the sink, and started scraping the scorched edges off the buns. He watched a layer of black crumbs form around the drain. "Sheila, you should have told me about this creep on the bus when you left me your first voicemail. I would have come and picked you up at the ballroom. Please tell me, after all that, you didn't take the bus home from work."

With the glass in her hand, she shrugged. "Well, I made sure the guy wasn't anywhere around . . ."

Shaking his head, Dylan set out the dinner plates. "You know how much I hate the idea of you taking the bus to work. Every other week, you're telling me about some incident or crazy person you encounter on that stupid bus. If you don't want to take the car to work, call a cab or take Uber—"

"That's so expensive," she murmured.

He started to get exasperated. "I don't understand. If he was harassing you on the bus and chasing after you, why didn't you call the police?"

"Well, he—he wasn't exactly *harassing* me. He caught me scowling at him, and he scowled back. And I can't be a hundred percent sure he followed me. I only caught a glimpse of him across the street. Maybe I'm just blowing it all out of proportion."

Dylan took the tater tots out of the oven, set the baking pan on a trivet, and turned to stare at her. A minute ago she was telling him how the guy had jumped off the bus one stop after her so he could hunt her down. And now she wasn't even certain the guy had been following her. Apparently, all he'd done was give her a dirty look on the bus. Was the dirty look even meant for her?

This was so typical of Sheila. She'd get upset over something and tell him about it—until she worked him into a state. Then once he was good and mad, or worried sick, she'd suddenly play down the whole thing. It drove him nuts.

He took a deep breath. "Well, I don't want you taking that bus anymore. And if you see this creep again, just call the police—and then call me."

Sheila nodded. "What do you think I should do about this text?"

That was what really upset her, the text—and the story about the Portland woman falling to her death. He understood, and he felt terrible for her. No wonder she was numbing herself with wine. Dylan was convinced someone must have seen the article and sent it—just to be cruel. Maybe it was somebody one of them had known back in Portland, or maybe a stranger. How the culprit had gotten Sheila's contact information was a mystery.

Dylan moved over to the breakfast table, smoothed back Sheila's hair, and kissed her on the cheek. "Like I told you. Delete it, hon."

"Are you sure you don't know this Antonia person?"

Dylan sighed. "For God's sake, Sheila, who are you going to believe—me, or this jerk sending you some anonymous text? It probably wasn't even meant for you. Just delete it, okay?"

He stepped away and headed around the corner. Then he called down the basement stairs: "Hey, guys, dinner's ready!"

His fifteen-year-old son, Steve, came to the bottom of the stairs. With his recently shorn brown hair, he looked like a gangly, scared, underage marine recruit. He always had a slightly vulnerable, deer-in-the-headlights look to him, which made Dylan wonder if he was getting picked on at school. Despite his wide shoulders and long limbs, he wasn't much of an athlete, though he was trying to be. Unfortunately for him, sports were more of his kid brother's forte.

"*Anchorman* is on. Can we eat down here?"

Dylan frowned at him. "Isn't that rated R, or something? Gabe shouldn't be watching that."

"It's on TBS, and they're cutting out all the dirty stuff."

"Fine," Dylan said. He figured the kids didn't need to be around their mother after she'd had three glasses of wine. "Could you do me a favor? Could you go upstairs and tell your sister to get off Instagram because dinner is ready? And pass the word that we're all eating wherever we want tonight."

He headed back into the kitchen to serve up dinner.

Sheila was still sitting in the breakfast booth, staring at her phone. Her wineglass was empty.

CHAPTER FIVE

Thursday, September 20—1:43 A.M.

Antonia Newcomb's Facebook page displayed several posts from her friends: "We'll miss you, Toni!" and "I can't believe she's gone . . ." Antonia's photo gallery showed a flashy-looking, tanned woman with dark hair, a little too much mascara, and a nice figure. She looked like a real party girl, too. In most of the pictures, Antonia had a drink in her hand—or her arm around some guy. She'd posted plenty of selfies, too. The story from *The Oregonian* had mentioned a daughter, but the girl wasn't in any of Antonia's Facebook posts.

Sheila didn't have a Facebook page, but her daughter had one she hadn't posted on in ages because, apparently, it was no longer cool, or something. Sheila used Hannah's account password to check on people. "Facebook stalking" was the term for it, according to Hannah. If Sheila did have a Facebook page, one thing was certain: She'd be posting pictures of her kids and bragging about their accomplishments all the time. She wondered why Antonia had completely ignored her daughter on the site.

Sheila sat at her desktop computer in her little office nook, an alcove off the kitchen by the corridor that led to the garage. It was a little chilly tonight, so she'd put on a pair of socks and thrown an old cardigan over her pale blue, cotton pajamas. She sipped bourbon from a jelly glass. Two shots, she'd measured. On these nights when she couldn't sleep, she'd get out of bed and have a couple of shots to relax her. Of course, booze-induced slumber was the worst kind of sleep, but with five and a half hours before she had to be up, she couldn't be picky.

It was too late to take an Ambien. Besides, she didn't like mixing it with alcohol. She didn't drink at all in the evenings if she was taking Ambien. She worried about destroying her liver. She'd even talked to her doctor about it. He'd made her fill out a four-page behavioral health questionnaire. After looking it over, he said she wasn't an alcoholic, but could be on her way to becoming one. Apparently, her answers on the questionnaire indicated she had some issues with depression. The doctor recommended she see a therapist, and he gave her a list of behavioral health services they offered.

What with looking after the kids, the house, and her garden, teaching her dance classes, and volunteering at a retirement community (she taught a waltz class there every week and organized a monthly dance), she didn't have time to get psychoanalyzed.

No, self-medicating with booze and prescription drugs is so much smarter.

The truth was, she didn't want anyone trying to get inside her head. And she didn't want to be reminded about things she'd worked so hard to forget.

Her big mistake had been throwing back so much wine before dinner tonight. She'd barely eaten a thing. She'd conked out on the sofa in the den just minutes after dinner, leaving Dylan and Steve to wash the dishes.

Now she was wide awake, drinking again, and on Antonia Newcomb's Facebook page. She was looking for familiar names among the dead woman's friends and even scanning the party photos for a possible glimpse of Dylan. He traveled to Portland on occasion. Maybe he knew Antonia from one of his trips—or from several of them.

Why else would that texted news story be accompanied by a note suggesting she ask her husband about it?

She couldn't help thinking that Dylan had to know something. He had to be involved somehow.

But Sheila wasn't coming up with anything on Antonia's Facebook page. And she couldn't find a follow-up article in *The Oregonian* about the woman's death. Sheila still had no idea if it was an accident, or a suicide, or a murder.

She took another sip of bourbon and glanced out the window by the breakfast booth. All the lights were off in the Curtis house next door just on the other side of a low hedge. Last month, the Curtises had left for a yearlong stay in Europe. Their place was up for rent, and Sheila found it slightly unsettling to have this big empty house right next door.

In fact, about three weeks ago, when Dylan had been out of town, she'd been sitting in this very spot, reading online about where all the cast members from *Grease* were now (oh, the things she desperately needed to know at two in the morning). That was when she noticed a strange light in the window across the way. She knew the Curtises had set some light timers, but this wasn't a lamp or an overhead fixture. It wasn't a headlight reflecting on the window, either. It was someone with a flashlight, lurking around their darkened dining room. Sheila thought it looked like a man, but that was just a guess.

For several moments, she sat glued to her desk chair, afraid to move. If she could see him, he could see her.

The flashlight suddenly went off, and then, beyond the window, there was only darkness. Sheila had no idea where the intruder had gone. She thought of her children asleep upstairs—and imagined him on his way over to make sure he left no witnesses.

Sheila got to her feet and hurried across the kitchen to where she'd left her purse on the counter. Digging inside the bag, she ducked into the shadowy dining room and pulled out her cell phone. As she dialed 9-1-1, she kept looking out the dining room windows for a sign of him. She could almost feel him watching her. At any minute, she expected to hear him kicking down the kitchen door.

Whispering into the phone, she reported what she'd seen in the empty house next door. The 9-1-1 operator kept asking her to speak up, but Sheila was terrified that, somehow, the prowler could hear everything she was saying.

Two police squad cars pulled up in front of the house within ten minutes. By then, Sheila had awakened the children, and they were all huddled on the stairs, hastily dressed. Steve clutched a baseball bat that belonged to Gabe.

The police got the Curtises' real estate agent out of bed, and it took them over an hour to determine there were no signs of a break-in next door. All the while, Sheila did her best to come off as calm and controlled. She even offered the policemen Cokes and what was left of the Rice Krispies treats she'd made the night before. She wondered if they could smell the bourbon on her breath.

But she wasn't drunk. And despite the police not finding any evidence of a break-in next door, Sheila knew someone had been inside that house.

Now she wondered if the elusive intruder might have been the blond creep she'd seen on the bus the day before. According to the police, it didn't look like anything was missing at her neighbors' home. Had someone snuck into the house next door for the sole purpose of spying on her—or her family? Maybe when she'd spotted that creep in the supermarket two weeks ago, he'd already been following her for a while.

But why would he be tailing her all this time? It didn't make any sense.

Still, Sheila couldn't help wondering if he was over there now in the Curtises' dining room, sitting at their table in the dark, watching her.

She immediately got up from her desk and lowered the blinds to the window by the breakfast booth. Wandering back to her desk, she finished off the rest of her bourbon.

Another neighbor had told her that the Curtises had found a renter for the place, a divorcée without any kids. Sheila would be glad once the woman moved in. Maybe the house would be occupied before Dylan took his next business trip.

Then it hit her. Had Dylan been out of town two weeks ago when Antonia Newcomb had fallen to her death in Portland? Sheila wasn't sure. She checked the calendar on the wall by her computer. Steve had given her the calendar last Christmas: *Beautiful Gardens of the Northwest*. She still used an old-fashioned paper calendar to mark appointments and reminders. And there it was, under a photo of Seattle's Japanese Garden: The last week in August, Dylan had been in San Francisco. He was home again on Friday the thirty-first. She flipped the calendar back to September and hung it on the wall again.

Antonia Newcomb had died on Thursday the sixth. Dylan had been home that week. Sheila had hosted a dance that evening at Summit Park Retirement Home, and hadn't gotten home until after ten. She remembered now that the kids had to order pizza for dinner because

Dylan had to work late, too. He'd had to wine and dine the Midwest region manager. Or so he'd said.

Was it possible that he'd driven down to Portland that day—and then come back? A car trip to Portland was almost four hours each way—if traffic wasn't awful. And traffic on Interstate 5 was usually awful. Still, Dylan certainly could have made the trip down and back that day.

Sheila reached for her glass of bourbon again—and realized it was empty.

She had to be a little drunk if she was thinking Dylan could have had anything to do with that woman's death.

But obviously, someone else thought so.

Sheila kept telling herself that Dylan hadn't lied to her, not about this. But there was a way of double-checking— just to put her mind to rest. Whenever Dylan bought gas, he stashed the receipt in the glove compartment of his BMW. It was a routine. He logged the mileage when he drove the car for company use; he kept all his gas receipts—whether they were for a company trip or not— and then went over them at the end of the month.

If he'd driven down to Portland on September sixth, he'd have had to buy gas—if not on that day, then the day before or the day after.

Sheila knew it was crazy, but if she expected to fall asleep tonight, she needed to check the glove compartment of Dylan's car.

She stared at the door to the garage—just a few feet away from her desk. It was only going to take a minute. She'd leave the door open. She'd be okay.

She grabbed his car key from a bowl on the kitchen counter. Then she stepped over to the door to the garage and unlocked it. As Sheila opened the door, a chill passed through her, and she clutched the edges of her cardigan. She switched on the overhead light. With her car still at the shop, there was plenty of room, and Dylan had parked his BMW in the middle of the garage. Yard equipment, tools, folded-up lawn-chairs, sports paraphernalia, bags of fertilizer, and stacks of empty plastic plant pots were all shoved against the far wall. A crack ran through the glass of the window in the corner.

Pressing the button on the key fob, Sheila unlocked the BMW. In her stocking feet, she padded over to the car. The cement floor felt icy, and she shuddered. Opening the passenger door, she climbed inside and got a whiff of something flowery. It smelled more like Chanel No. 5 than air freshener.

A woman had been in Dylan's car recently. Antonia Newcomb? *Yeah, Sheila, smart. The woman's been dead for two weeks and Dylan's car still smells like her perfume.* No, a woman had been in the BMW within the last day or two.

Sheila opened the glove compartment and searched through the receipts. She found one for September second and another for the thirteenth, both from gas stations in Seattle. She didn't find anything from Portland around September sixth.

She stashed the receipts back into the glove compartment and shut it. She felt very silly.

But who the hell had been in her husband's car recently?

Climbing out of the BMW, Sheila quietly closed the passenger door. She headed toward the doorway to the house and switched off the overhead light. Then she pressed the button on the key fob to lock his car. She watched the emergency lights blink for a moment, then turn off completely. At that same moment, she heard something rustling outside the garage. In the sudden dark, she could see only the afterimage of the emergency lights and the faint outline of a tree through the garage's cracked window. The branches swayed slightly in the breeze.

Was that what she'd heard?

All at once, someone darted past the window.

Sheila gasped.

Something banged against the garbage cans at the side of the garage, creating a loud, tinny clatter.

Terrified, Sheila bolted back into the house, slamming the door behind her and locking it. She raced toward the front of the house—to the stairs. Halfway up, she saw a shadowy figure standing at the landing. From the dimly lit second-floor hallway, he seemed to loom over her.

She froze and tried to scream, but nothing came out.

Clutching the banister, Sheila suddenly realized she was looking up at Dylan.

He hurried down the steps to meet her. "Jesus, honey," he whispered. "Are you okay? What's going on?"

She collapsed into his arms. "Outside," she gasped. "Someone's right outside the house. I saw him . . . in the window, I saw him."

CHAPTER SIX

Thursday—2:20 A.M.

Steve was only half asleep when he heard a door slam somewhere down on the first floor. Then he heard the pounding of footsteps racing up the stairs—as if someone were being chased.

His heart beating furiously, Steve sat up in bed.

For a few seconds, he stayed still.

Down the hallway, footsteps came from his parents' bedroom. He figured his dad must have gotten out of bed to see what was wrong.

Steve started to reach for the baseball bat he'd kept at his bedside since his mom had spotted a prowler next door three weeks ago. He'd practically had a heart attack that night because it had happened while his dad was out of town. But his dad was home tonight, and Steve hesitated. His hand hovered by the bat. He wished he knew what was happening. He wasn't sure if he should go out to the hallway to see if his parents needed any help, or if he should just sit there in bed and wait it out. He could hear them whispering.

He figured if they were standing out there, having a conversation, it probably meant he shouldn't panic. Maybe the crisis was over. Steve had always thought he'd know what to do if someone broke into the house. By *someone*, he meant a homicidal maniac or a serial killer.

He'd recently developed a morbid fascination with true crime—serial killings in particular. It had started by accident, early in the summer. He'd gone online to look up a girl he had a crush on, a senior named Barbie Grimes, who was incredibly popular and had no idea he was alive. What Steve found instead were several articles about the Grimes sisters: Barbara and Patricia, two Chicago teenagers who, one night in December, 1956, went to the movies to see Elvis Presley in *Love Me Tender* for the eleventh time. They never returned. An intensive search for the missing girls went on for over a month—until a construction worker on his lunch break by a bridge on a deserted road noticed two "flesh-colored things" amid the patches of melting snow in the gully below. The girls' naked bodies had been frozen in the snow for weeks. Their murderer was never found. The article referred to other murders in Chicago in the nineteen-fifties and sixties, and, of course, Steve had to find out about those, too.

Over the summer, he read articles online about dozens of heinous murders and murderers over the last seventy years. Among them: Ed Gein, the Butcher of Plainfield, Wisconsin, upon whom the fictional killers in *Psycho*, *The Texas Chain Saw Massacre*, and *The Silence of the Lambs* were modeled; the Boston Strangler; the Candy Man in Houston, who tortured and murdered at least twenty-seven teenage boys; the Shoe Fetish Slayer; Son of Sam; Ted Bundy; the Interstate Killer; and John Wayne Gacy, the Killer Clown, who had the bodies of nearly thirty teenage boys buried in his basement.

Steve wasn't particularly interested in the killers, but he wanted to know about the victims and their families. In so many cases, no one had any idea what actually happened in the last minutes of the victims' lives—what they did or tried to do, what they were feeling. Steve was left to wonder. He read up on details of various crime scenes in an attempt to figure out what really occurred near the end. He remembered reading about the eight student nurses who were slain in Chicago in 1966. Someone described the kitchen of their townhouse dorm as "tidy— except for a box of Ritz crackers left on the counter." That stuck in Steve's head. He wondered if one of the girls was having a late-night snack just hours before being strangled or stabbed to death. Some evenings, before going to bed, he'd glance in the kitchen, and if anything was left out on the counter, he'd put it away. A box of crackers on the counter now seemed like bad luck to him.

Having all those details of all those murders rattling around in his brain, Steve was a nervous wreck most of the time. The nights when his dad was out of town were the worst. Sometimes, it would take forever for Steve to fall asleep—especially when he realized he was the only one in the house still awake, the only one to hear the sounds in the night. He hated taking any kind of satisfaction in his mom's troubles, but he always fell asleep easier those nights when she had insomnia and went downstairs to read because then *she* was the guardian of the night, the one hearing those unexplainable, creepy sounds.

In all his imagined scenarios of someone breaking into the house, Steve's father was out of town. Steve imagined everyone else asleep when he heard the intruder downstairs. He figured he'd call the police, grab his bat, wake up Gabe and Hannah, and then hustle them into the master bedroom—which had a lock on the door. They'd hole up in there, along with their mom. He'd blink the bedroom lights so the cops approaching the house would know where to find them.

In all his scenarios, he was so clearheaded. He assessed the danger and knew exactly what to do.

Now, Steve listened to his mother anxiously murmuring to his dad in the hallway. But he caught only fragments of the conversation, and he still couldn't be sure what was happening. It sounded like his mom had seen a man lurking outside their garage.

Grabbing the baseball bat, he crept out of bed and padded to the door to listen.

"What were you doing in the garage at this hour?" he heard his father ask. "Hon, have you been drinking?"

In reply, his mother murmured something that Steve couldn't quite hear, but she sounded scared. Her voice was all shaky.

Still clutching the bat, Steve opened the door and stepped out to the hallway. He saw his parents by the top of the stairs—his mother with a cardigan over her blue pajamas, his father in white boxer shorts. Steve slept in a T-shirt and long pajama bottoms, even when it was hot out. He was so pale and skinny, he felt uncomfortable sleeping shirtless. His father didn't have any such problem.

"Is everything okay?" Steve asked nervously.

"Oh, Jesus," his father muttered, looking exasperated. "It's nothing. Stevie, go back to bed. You'll wake Gabe and Hannah—"

"It's not nothing!" his mother whispered.

His dad patted her on the shoulder. "Okay, okay. I'll go down and check. Stay put. If I'm not back in five minutes . . ." He trailed off.

"If you're not back in five minutes, what?" she asked.

"Nothing, I'll be back in five minutes. God."

Steve joined them at the top of the stairs. "I'll go down with you," he offered.

His dad sleepily kissed him on the forehead. "Stay here with Mom, keep her company. And try to be quiet, okay? No use waking up the whole house—at least, not until we know what's what."

Steve offered him the bat. "Here, Dad, take this."

"You hang on to that. I'll be okay." With a sigh, his father started down the stairs.

Watching him, Steve put an arm around his mother. "Should I get my phone in case we need to call the police?" he whispered.

She nodded. "Good idea, honey."

Steve broke away and hurried back into his room, where he snatched his smartphone off the desk.

When he stepped back out to the hallway, he didn't see his mother—and his heart stopped for a moment. Then he noticed her halfway down the stairs, peering over the banister at his dad. Steve crept down the steps to join her. He clutched the phone in one hand and the bat in the other.

He watched his dad check the front door. His dad stepped into the living room and looked out of the windows. Then he headed into the dining room, out of sight.

Since reading up on so many serial killings, Steve had become squeamishly aware of just how easy it would be to break into their home. There were no fewer than four entrances. The front door was solid with some good locks on it. But the kitchen door and another door in the den, down the hall, had French-style windowpanes. All an intruder had to do was break one little pane of glass, reach inside, and unlock the door. There was a flimsy chain lock near the bottom of the door in the kitchen, but one good kick and that chain lock was history. Finally, there was a basement door off the laundry room—which,

out again, louder this time. His voice
e you okay?"
for leaves rustling.
he bat tighter. He felt his mother's
r.
igure in the shadows coming from
t took a moment for him to realize it
hing them.
e," he announced, rubbing his hands
ere dirty. "A raccoon must've tipped
arlier. Left a hell of a mess."
th, Steve lowered the bat. He stepped
e doorway for his dad.
on," his mother insisted. "I heard the
ust seconds after I saw someone in
"
ped his bare feet on the mat. Then he
he door. He bent down to fix the chair
n of the door. "Well, I looped around
no one's out there—at least, not any-
g up, he headed to the sink and started
"I think we're okay, hon. But I still
were doing in the garage."
heard something," she replied. "I
check, and that's when I saw him run
She rubbed her forehead. "I'm sorry,
safe. I think we should call the police.
be around."
off his hands with a paper towel.
kay? Please? Would you feel better if
e?"
iously. "The basement, too."
is dad as he stepped from the kitchen
dad switched on the overhead light.
nny tree gently swaying outside the

fortunately, seemed pretty sturdy. A concrete stairwell outside led down to it.

Their house was a Craftsman, surrounded by tall hedges. West of them, the Curtis house was only about thirty feet away. Steve used to reassure himself that, if one of them screamed in the middle of the night, Mr. or Mrs. Curtis would probably hear and call the cops.

But that house was empty and dark now.

Bordering them on the other side was an alley, and across from that, another neighbor's garage. Steve had a view of it from his bedroom window. In front of the house, across the street, was Roanoke Park—a square block of trees, shrubs, grass, and pathways. The small playground, made up of a swing set, jungle gym, and slide, was on the opposite end of the park, so Steve and his family were spared the sound of squealing, laughing children during the day. But the park could be pretty creepy after sunset. In one of the true-crime stories Steve had read, a family of four were robbed and killed in their Denver home. Their murderer had confessed that he used to watch them from the park across the street. He'd sit on a park bench, have his lunch or a book with him, and he'd think about how he was going to break into the house and kill them all.

Steve didn't like living in a house with a similar setup. He wondered if the man his mom had seen outside their garage had been scouting their place for a while. Was he just checking up on them tonight? Did he plan to come back some other night—when Steve's dad was out of town?

He listened to his dad's footsteps. It sounded like he'd moved from the dining room to the den. Both rooms had a lot of valuable stuff a prowler might want. They had a ton of silver in the dining room breakfront, and on his dad's desk in the den, there was a notebook computer.

They'd just bought a TV, which sat on the shelf beside an expensive music system. Steve wondered if his father double-checked the lock on the door in the den. He must not have discovered anything suspicious, because soon Steve heard him in the kitchen at the back door. At least, Steve hoped it was his father at the door. The chain lock rattled.

Biting his lip, he crept down to the bottom of the stairs and peeked into the kitchen. The backyard lights were on. His father had left the door open while he stepped out into the yard—barefoot, and in his underwear, no less. His dad obviously wasn't scared, or shy. He was about as self-conscious in his boxer shorts as a boxer would be.

"I wish he'd taken the bat," Steve's mother muttered, coming up behind him in the hallway. She rubbed his shoulder. "He doesn't believe me, but I saw someone."

Steve glanced back at her for a moment. "Well, he's outside checking right now," he whispered. But maybe his mom was right. His dad seemed to be making this house and perimeter check just to appease her. That was probably why he hadn't taken along the baseball bat. And why he'd gone out there in just his underwear. He must have been pretty damn sure he wouldn't run into anybody.

But Steve kept wondering, *What if someone is really out there?*

He handed the phone to his mom. "Could you hold on to this?" He wanted to have both hands free in case he needed to use the bat.

From where he stood in the front hall, Steve had a partial view out through the living room and dining room windows. If his dad was checking around the entire house, there was no sign of him yet.

Steve stepp
outside any o

He couldn
boomerang-p
crackers. It wa
right about h
drunk—just s

Steve look
why his fathe

It was deat
silence to be
curdling scre
The killer cou
slit his throat.
a waitress ha
killer, the onl

With trepi
"Honey, no
him into the k

He hesitate
backyard. So
his mother's
stones, plants
It was a whit
claimed look
never though
looked a littl
trees that bro
lights fixed
breeze, shad

"Dad?" St
He could
on his bare a
But then h
Frozen in

"Dad?" he ca
was shaky. "Dad
Silence—exc
Steve clutche
hand on his shou

He saw a dar
around the garag
was his dad appr

"Everything
together as if the
over the trash ca

Catching his b
back and cleared

"It wasn't a rac
trash can tip ove
the garage windo

Steve's father
closed and locked
lock near the bott
the entire house a
more." Straighten
to wash his hand
don't get what yo

"I—I thought
stepped out there
past the window.'
but I still don't fee
This guy could st

His father drie
"Honey, let's not,
I checked the gara

She nodded an
Steve followed
into the garage. H
Steve noticed a sl

cracked window where his mom said she'd seen the man. His dad stepped back into the kitchen. Steve followed him and watched him lock the garage access door. Stopping by the desk in the office nook, his father reached over and nudged the computer mouse. The screen lit up. It showed some woman's Facebook page. Steve didn't know her.

Frowning, his dad picked up the empty glass on the desk and carried it to the sink. Then he put the bottle of bourbon away in the cupboard.

With Steve's phone still clutched in her hand, his mom glanced at the floor.

"I'll go down to the basement with you, Dad," Steve piped up.

"Thanks," his father muttered.

He noticed his parents weren't looking at each other. He wasn't sure why his dad had checked what was on his mom's computer screen. But it was obvious he objected to the drinking. Steve wasn't dumb. He knew his mom drank sometimes late at night to help her fall asleep. But he didn't think that necessarily made her an alcoholic. Then again, maybe it did. He wasn't sure.

At the door to the basement, he switched on the light. With his dad right behind him, Steve felt safe enough to lead the way down the carpeted stairs. His mom remained in the doorway at the top of the steps. "Be careful!" she called in an amplified whisper.

Steve worried about her—working too hard, not sleeping enough. A while back, last year sometime, they'd all gone to a school play Hannah had appeared in. His parents had gotten dressed up for it like it was a very big deal. Steve recalled them all rushing around to get ready before they left for the high school. When the play was over and everyone piled into the car to go home, his mom caught a look at herself in the rearview mirror. She had on a little jacket that went with her dress, and she noticed a big rip in the shoulder. Some of the padding was even sticking out. His mom went nuts. "Am I invisible?" she asked everyone in the car. "Didn't anybody even notice this? I'm so busy rushing around at the last minute, fetching things for everyone else, that I leave the house looking like a complete idiot! All I'm good for is cooking, cleaning, and doing the laundry. Otherwise, I'm the invisible woman! I can't believe this."

At the time, no one had seemed to take her too seriously. It had just been their mom blowing off steam. Sitting next to Steve in the back seat, Hannah, still wearing her stage makeup, had barely glanced up from her phone. "Well, don't yell at me. I didn't rip it."

But maybe his dad had been paying attention that night. And maybe that explained what happened about a week later—at least, Steve remembered it being about a week later. His dad had had another business trip coming up, and he was supposed to be gone longer than usual. The night before he left, he stepped into Steve's bedroom and talked to him about how he'd be the man of the house for the next several days. Steve remembered him saying, "Your mom gets a little fragile sometimes— I mean, emotionally. So I'm counting on you to look out for her, Stevie, cheer her up if she's blue. Make her feel appreciated, you know?"

That week while his dad was out of town, Steve had accompanied his mom to one of her dances at the retirement home where she volunteered. She was so good with the old folks, so patient and friendly. She ran the whole show like a combination master of ceremonies and disc jockey. Everyone there—the staff, the old people, the visitors—they all adored her. Steve felt like the son of a superstar. He was proud of her.

A few nights later, he walked through the kitchen

while his mom washed the dinner dishes, and he realized she was crying. She saw him and tried to pretend like everything was fine. He pretended not to have noticed. But he was left to wonder what she was crying about. Was she lonely for his dad, or lonely in general? Was she really emotionally fragile, like his dad had said? Or maybe she just hated washing dishes.

After that night, Steve almost always washed the dinner dishes for her. He didn't mind, really. He figured it was the least he could do to help his mom feel appreciated. Plus, it gave him an excuse to procrastinate on his homework.

Now, as he walked through the basement with his father, Steve realized his dad was probably right, both tonight and that night months back. His mom was a bit fragile. And in all likelihood, she'd had too much to drink tonight and imagined she'd seen someone through the garage window.

But God bless his dad, still going through the motions and giving the place the once-over. He started in the family room, which was carpeted, and had a big-screen TV, a sectional sofa, and a foosball table. Framed vintage travel posters covered the walls.

Down a short corridor off the family room, his dad switched on the light and stuck his head inside the basement's guest room. The twin beds were stacked with junk: piles of stuff that was supposed to have gone to Goodwill weeks ago and rolls of wrapping paper. It was the most ignored room in the house. Steve's parents hadn't had an actual guest sleep in there since his dad's widowed mother stayed with them two years ago, and she was dead now.

It was also the most coveted room. Steve, Hannah, and Gabe sometimes used the room when a friend spent the night. Hannah had recently been campaigning to make it her bedroom, but she was too lazy to make the move, which would require first cleaning up her pigsty of a bedroom. Meanwhile, Steve had also put in a bid for the room. His current bedroom was tiny, and so close to the master bedroom and the siblings' bathroom that he felt like he didn't have any privacy at all. He was always worried someone would barge in while he was in the middle of whacking off. Plus, the basement bathroom was right across the hall, so it would practically be all his.

If his parents ever decided to let him have the room, he'd have to get accustomed to being alone down there at night—two floors away from where everyone else slept. Just down the hall from that coveted bedroom was the laundry room, which connected to a storage room, a furnace room, and his dad's workroom. If there was a creepy section of their house, those rooms were it. They were the bowels of the place, probably unchanged since the house was built in the 1930s: cement floor, exposed pipes, and plaster peeling off the dingy walls.

Now he and his dad checked those rooms, which, except for the laundry area, always seemed sort of dark and creepy—no matter what wattage light bulb they tried in the old ceiling fixtures.

Steve watched his dad jiggle the knob on the laundry room door to make sure it was locked. "Think we should check outside?" he asked his father. "I mean, if I was going to hide, that stairwell would be a pretty good place."

His dad's shoulders slumped, and he gave him a look that seemed to say, *Are you really going to make me do this?* With a sigh, he unlocked the door.

It suddenly occurred to Steve that, if they were in a movie right now, this was when the killer would pop out from the shadowy stairwell on the other side of the basement door, when everyone least expected it. Steve tightened his grip on the bat.

The door was stuck, and his dad had to tug it open.

For a horrible moment, Steve wondered if someone was holding onto the knob on the other side.

But his father finally yanked the door open, and there was no one out there. A couple of dead leaves blew in. The dirty cement floor felt cold under Steve's bare feet.

"You and your mom . . ." his dad mumbled as he closed and locked the door.

"Me and mom . . . what?"

His father hesitated, smiled and quickly shook his head. "Nothing. C'mon, let's go up and tell your mother the coast is clear." He put his hand on Steve's shoulder.

Steve was pretty sure his dad had been about to say something along the lines of *like mother, like son*. Then he must have thought better of it. But he would have been right if he'd said it. Just as Steve's mom couldn't have slept until his dad had checked every corner of the house, Steve wouldn't have been able to fall asleep, either. He wondered if his dad considered him "emotionally fragile," too.

His father switched off the lights in the basement family room, and they headed upstairs together.

Steve's mom was waiting in the kitchen, his phone still in her hand. "Well?"

"All clear," his dad said, turning off the basement light and closing the door behind him.

"I still think we should call the police," she muttered.

His father sighed. "Honey, in less than four hours, we all need to be up. I don't know about you, but I'm seriously beat." He took a deep breath and turned to Steve. "Why don't you hit the sheets, okay, Stevie? Thanks for helping out."

Steve glanced at his mom to make sure she was okay.

With a tight smile, she handed him back his phone and then kissed him on the cheek. "G'night, honey. Thanks."

His father rubbed Steve's stubbly scalp, where his hair used to be before he'd shaved it off for the cancer fund-raiser. He'd raised only $140—a hundred of which was from his parents. He could have raised a lot more if he'd had some uncles or aunts, or living grandparents.

With the baseball bat resting on his shoulder, Steve shuffled up the front stairs. But he paused when he heard his parents talking again. His mom had whispered something.

His dad responded, "Honey, we just had the police here on that false alarm when I was out of town—what, three weeks ago? Do you really want to call them again? Have them look around and find absolutely nothing *again*? I know you're upset after what happened on the bus yesterday, but I've checked the house inside and out. No one has tried to get in. We're safe. Let's just go to bed, please."

Steve heard his mom murmur something about not being able to sleep.

"Well, why don't you take half an Ambien?" his dad offered.

"Then I'll sleep until eleven! Besides, I can't take Ambien now, not after I've been drinking."

"Fine, have another shot of bourbon then, if it'll calm you down. But don't blame me if you have a hangover tomorrow."

After a few moments, Sam heard a glass clink.

"How long has Steve been sleeping with Gabe's base-ball bat?" his dad whispered.

"I think it started when you were out of town last month. He doesn't sleep with it. He just keeps it near his bed."

His dad muttered something. Steve leaned over the banister a bit, straining to hear.

"He gets nervous sometimes, that's all," his mom said. "Listen, before I forget. Earlier, when I was in the garage, I—I climbed into the front seat of your car for a second—"

"Why did you do that?"

"I was worried someone might have tried to break into it. So I wanted to make sure everything was okay inside the car. Anyway, while I was in there, I smelled perfume."

Steve listened to the silence.

"I thought maybe you took a woman client to lunch—or a coworker, or something," his mother explained.

"No, I gave a woman a lift from the gym to her place on Capitol Hill. It was raining, and she looked stranded, so that was my good deed for the night."

"You picked up some strange woman—or is this someone you know?"

"Barely. We talked for, like, two minutes on the elliptical machines. And then we happened to be leaving at the same time, so I offered her a ride."

"Why didn't you tell me about this?"

"Well, as you might recall, you kind of had other things you wanted to talk about earlier tonight. Plus, I just didn't think it was very important. Now, c'mon, honey, finish that up and let's go to bed."

Steve saw the light go out in the kitchen. He quickly crept up the rest of the stairs and tiptoed to his room. He closed the doorway behind him, careful not to make a sound. Setting the phone down on his desk, he held onto the bat as he wandered over to the window. He glanced down at the narrow alley that bordered their yard. He didn't see anyone lurking there.

What if his mom was right? What if someone had been watching her from the deserted house next door three weeks ago—and again tonight from the backyard, and by the garage?

He listened to his parents' footsteps on the stairs.

He didn't want to think it, but maybe his mom wouldn't be so "emotionally fragile" if his dad wasn't out of town so often—and if, when he was in town, he wasn't giving rides to women from his gym.

Steve carefully leaned the baseball bat between his headboard and the nightstand. Then he climbed into bed and tried to sleep.

CHAPTER SEVEN

9/20 Thurs—4:45 A.M.

Too wired to sleep.

Maybe I need two or three shots of bourbon to help me relax—just like that stupid bitch, Sheila. I'll bet she needed a whole pint to help her nod off tonight. Hell, she's probably still wide awake, tossing and turning in bed, driving him crazy.

I sat in the park and watched the last light go out in the house at around 3:20. I've been damn careful not to be noticed, but my days of hanging out in that park are behind me—now that I've been seen. But I figured I could stick around tonight. I knew, no matter what she told him she saw, he wouldn't call the cops—no, not after she had the police there three weeks ago for absolutely nothing. I still get a laugh when I think about the two nights before that one, wandering through the house next door with a flashlight, just waiting for Stupid Sheila to notice. All the while, there she was at her desk in that tacky retro kitchen of hers, too busy surfing the web and slowly getting sloshed to notice anything—not until my third visit. Third time's the charm.

Tonight, I got another chuckle, watching him stomp around outside the house in his underwear.

*I couldn't hear, but I could clearly see him
muttering to himself, so tired and disgruntled,
so fed up with his frumpy, stupid wife and her
neuroses.*

*"Study of a Family Ready to Fall Apart." That's
what I kept thinking as I sat and watched the
show from the park across the street.*

*The son could be a problem. Him and his
baseball bat. I can tell he'll get in my way. He's
awfully close to the mother, and he's on his guard
all the time—jumpy as hell, in fact. He's not as
self-involved as the other two. Anyway, Mama's
Boy may need to go. I'll think of something
creative. Maybe he and Mama can go together—
two birds, one stone.*

*He's always jumping into the car to
accompany her to the store or on errands. I can't
figure out if she's dragging him along by the
umbilical cord or if he's her surrogate husband,
or whatever. It's just too bad that business with
the brake fluid in her car couldn't have taken
them both out of the equation. I knew it was a
long shot. But it was worth a try.*

That would have been quick and easy.

*Then again, it wouldn't have been very
satisfying. All my plotting and planning would
have been in vain. Yes, the result would have been
the same, but where's the fun in that? I loved
listening to Antonia scream as she fell. It was
such a rush—like an orgasm. But really, thinking
about how I'd make it happen, the foreplay, all
the little rushes—that was the real thrill.*

*It's how I felt tonight—and how I'm going
to feel until I hear Stupid Sheila let out that
final scream.*

CHAPTER EIGHT

Friday, September 21—6:37 P.M.
Seattle

"**D**ante, you don't need to bring your hand up so high," Sheila called out. "If you raise your arm just a little—enough to clear Pattie's head—that'll make it easier for her to do the spin. Otherwise, you guys are great. Okay, everyone. Rock-step, side, side . . . Let's all try the pull around. Leads, get ready."

Several of Sheila's regular couples had shown up early for a practice session before the Century Ballroom's monthly East Coast Swing Dance. The dance was from seven until nine. From advance ticket sales, Sheila expected about a hundred people, with probably the usual mix of straight and gay/lesbian couples. She used to address the leads as "gentlemen" or "guys," but then one time she'd called it out while standing right next to a couple of women and realized how foolish that was.

For now, there were only eight couples on the floor, some of them dressed in their best retro swing attire. Sheila wore a vintage red-and-black cocktail dress she'd found in an upscale consignment shop. The disco ball above them spun, refracting light around the huge room. But the effect was slightly lacking because the overheads hadn't been dimmed yet and everyone was practicing without music.

The ballroom was in the turn-of-the-century Oddfellows Building on the second floor, just down the hall from a popular restaurant and a second, smaller ballroom/dance studio. Once the dance started, the doorway usually would become choked with people—including several spectators. The ballroom had a bar and a seating area with small tables, but most everyone came for the dancing.

For some of Sheila's students, this event would be sort of a test run. Dante and Pattie were learning East Coast Swing so they could dazzle the guests at their wedding reception in two weeks. This event would be their first time trying out in public what Sheila had taught them in a series of private lessons. They were a cute young couple, and Sheila could tell they were a bit nervous.

She was nervous, too, but for totally different reasons.

She hadn't received any more anonymous texts. And though she continued to search online, she hadn't found a follow-up story about the Portland woman's death. Nor had she had another encounter with that creep from the bus. Still, Sheila had been on her guard for the last two days. Yesterday around dusk, from her living room window, she'd spotted a sketchy-looking guy wearing an army jacket and a knit cap. His back to her, he'd been shuffling down the path in the park across the street— too far away for her to see if he was the blond guy from the bus. She'd waited until long after he wandered to the opposite side of the park and disappeared behind some shrubs. Only when she'd been pretty certain he wasn't coming back did she finally move away from the window.

Yesterday, Dylan had insisted she take an Uber to the ballroom to teach her classes. He didn't want her riding the bus for a while. He'd been particularly attentive and sweet since Wednesday night's "false alarm." That was what he had called it, a *false alarm*—like she'd been seeing things. All his special attention sort of made her feel like a recently released mental patient. Dylan claimed to believe her about the man lurking outside their house. But Sheila could tell he was trying to placate her. He seemed to think she'd have the whole situation nipped in the bud if she just avoided public transportation for a while.

On the subject of who believed whom about what, Sheila had snuck out to the garage last night and checked inside Dylan's car. The perfume smell had dissipated to nothing. She'd felt awful doing it, but couldn't help double-checking.

One good sign: Dylan hadn't suddenly bought one of those pine tree–shaped cardboard air fresheners for the car or tried to cover up the smell with something else. There was no covering up, nothing to hide.

This morning, she'd gotten her Toyota Highlander back from the repair shop—to the tune of $600. So Sheila had driven to the Oddfellows Building tonight. The building was across from a huge park and playfield that became a bit dicey late in the evening. Though busy and trendy, the area attracted a lot of panhandlers and street people and often reeked of marijuana. Dylan had been worried about how far she'd have to walk to her car after the dance finished at nine. This was nothing new. He always fretted about her walking around that area by herself late at night.

She'd parked about three blocks away on a shadowy, tree-lined street on the other side of the playfield. It was hardly ideal, but she couldn't find a space that was closer or more in the open. She'd made a mental note to ask Dante and Pattie to walk her to her car after the dance. Dante was a big guy. No one would mess with him.

Sheila told herself she'd be okay. Mostly, she was

worried about her kids. Hannah was spending the night at a friend's—and yes, the parents were home; Sheila had double-checked. The boys were staying in and planned to order pizza once Dylan came back from the gym. After what had happened the other night, she hated the idea of them being at home alone tonight—even for just an hour or two. She knew Steve was nervous about it, too, the poor kid. She'd texted him a few minutes ago, and he'd texted back that he was fine.

The other dance instructor—a thin, attractive, thirty-something blonde named Hallie—showed up along with the bartender and the two guys who would bus tables and work the door. Someone dimmed the lights. Hallie had the song list on her laptop. She gave Sheila a hard copy and her wireless headset. Sheila and Hallie would take turns announcing the songs and the dances, pushing drinks at the bar, and promoting upcoming events. Sheila donned her headset. As the ballroom started to fill up, she stashed her purse behind the bar and helped herself to a bottle of water.

Hallie got things started early with The Manhattan Transfer's "The Boy from New York City." People started dancing—including a "show-off" couple. Each dance had at least three or four couples who demanded attention and way too much space on the dance floor. Half the time, they were nowhere near as good as they thought they were. This couple, two thirtysomething lesbians in zoot suits, were pretty decent dancers though. They were regulars: Linda and Camille.

"Can I get a sound check on your mic, Sheila?" Hallie's amplified voice rang out over the music from her makeshift DJ booth—an already-cluttered table she'd set up on the small stage across the room.

"You certainly can, Hallie," Sheila chimed back,

emerging from behind the bar. She heard just enough feedback to confirm the mic was working. "It looks like the joint is already jumping—and the bar isn't even open yet. But it will be in just a few minutes!"

She noticed, over by the door, that the hallway had become congested with ticket-holders waiting to get their hands stamped and others, craning their necks to gape at the dancers.

As The Manhattan Transfer wound down, Sheila checked the playlist. "Now things are about to get a little crazy with Big Bad Voodoo Daddy and 'Go Daddy-O!'" she announced over the music and din.

The dance floor became more crowded, boxing Linda and Camille in slightly. Sheila carefully wove around the frenetic, whirling bodies, paying special attention to her newer students. She was pleased to see that they seemed to fit right in. Hallie cranked up the volume, and Sheila could feel the bass beat on the hardwood floor. The temperature in the ballroom had grown hotter in a matter of minutes. Sheila glanced over toward the door again. Among the couples streaming in, she recognized the regulars who didn't miss a dance. And in the packed corridor, amid the gawkers, she recognized the creep from the bus.

Sheila froze.

If the guy had hoped to be discreet about following her, he was doing a miserable job of it. He wore his baggy army jacket. Once again, his blond hair looked unwashed and unkempt. He'd come with his punk girlfriend, the pale blonde who had been shoplifting with him at the supermarket. She wore a red hoodie, along with dark, Goth eye makeup and lipstick that was practically black. He kept his arm slung over the girl's shoulder. She seemed to be picking her nose, but then Sheila realized she was fiddling with a stud in her nostril. Neither one of the pair seemed to have spotted her yet.

Sheila knew they were stalking her. It was no coincidence they were here. If only she could snap their picture, she'd show it to the police—and she'd show Dylan. Then he'd know she wasn't crazy.

She backed away, hoping they wouldn't see her amid the kinetic crowd on the dance floor. Threading through the dancers, she hurried toward the bar. She kept glancing over at the door to make sure the punk couple was still there. As she ducked behind the bar, she knocked over a drink. The glass smashed onto the floor. Booze splashed across the front of her dress and ran down her legs.

"I'm sorry, Jay!" Sheila whispered to the bartender. She heard a murmur of feedback over the music, a reminder that her headset mic was still on. But she was too frazzled to care about that now. She had to get to her phone.

Crouched behind the bar, the hem of her dress dragging in the broken glass and spilt liquor, Sheila frantically dug into her purse. She finally found her phone. With a shaky hand, she switched it on and pressed the camera icon. Clutching the phone to her chest, she came out from behind the bar and ventured across the teeming dance floor. Everyone seemed charged up by the loud music and the pulsating beat. One dancer slammed into her, and Sheila almost dropped her phone. Couples kept moving and twirling between her and the door. Past all of them, Sheila could see the blond creep and his girlfriend, still in the crowded corridor.

Making her way closer to the door, Sheila locked eyes with her stalker.

They both froze for an instant. He gave a tiny smirk of recognition.

Then he pulled his girlfriend's arm—as if about to retreat with her. Sheila had no idea why they were leaving. Maybe now that he'd seen her, he planned on coming back later, or they'd be waiting for her outside at the end of the dance.

But she couldn't let him get away.

"Wait!" she screamed. "I see you!"

The mic blasted her shrill voice over the swing music. Several couples stopped dancing.

Sheila rushed to the door, colliding with a woman who had just entered the ballroom. "I'm sorry!" Sheila said. And again, everyone on the dance floor heard it—along with a deafening boom as her headset mic was knocked askew. But Sheila kept moving toward the corridor.

"Stop, you two! I see you!" she yelled again at the couple. She raised the phone camera over her head and snapped several shots in a row. "Who are you? What do you want?"

The blond creep and his girlfriend stopped to stare at her.

The music was suddenly shut off.

"Sheila, are you okay?" Hallie asked over her mic. Her voice seemed so loud without the throbbing music. "Is there a problem?"

Sheila realized that everyone had stopped dancing. They stared at her.

Lowering the phone, she glanced over at her friend on the stage. She could hear the confused murmuring from the crowd—and then, one voice from the hallway, ringing out over all the others: "Crazy bitch."

Sheila swiveled around in time to see him ducking back into the crowd, pulling his girlfriend down the hall toward the stairs.

Sheila almost chased after them. But at the threshold of the jam-packed corridor, she came to a stop. It was hopeless. Even if she called the police right now, the two punks could easily give them the slip in this crazy, crowded neighborhood. The streets and sidewalks were always jammed on Friday nights.

"Sheila?" Hallie asked over the mic once more.

Shaking and out of breath, she turned toward the ballroom. It was dead quiet under the swirling disco light. Everyone looked at her with what seemed like concern or pity. At any other time, Sheila would have been utterly humiliated, but not now.

She glanced down at the phone in her trembling hand. She had a clear shot of her stalker and his girlfriend. With their mouths open, they looked slightly startled.

She had something she could show Dylan later tonight.

Sheila straightened her headset. "It's okay," she heard herself say. "We had a little problem. But I think it's going to be okay."

CHAPTER NINE

Friday—6:44 P.M.

The pretty young brunette at the Pro Club's front desk was folding white towels and neatly stacking them on the countertop. It was part of the towel service they provided for the members.

Dylan managed a smile for her. He'd already worked out, showered, and dressed. With his gym bag in tow, he headed toward the door. "Thank you," he said.

"Have a nice night!" the girl called in a perky voice.

He pushed the door open and headed down the stairs toward the building's lobby. His "nice night" would be pizza and Netflix at home with Steve and Gabe.

Dylan had secretly been planning for something quite different this evening. He'd hoped to bump into Brooke again. She'd said she would be working out tonight.

He wasn't sure where it would have gone from there. He'd thought maybe he could persuade her to wrap up early and go for a walk with him—or maybe grab a drink someplace. It wouldn't have mattered what they did. He'd wanted to see her, even if it meant just talking while on the elliptical machines again. Hell, he would have settled for that. He hadn't expected to get laid—not tonight, at least. She clearly wasn't the type. That was obvious from their last conversation. Telling him about her son dying of leukemia was hardly the kind of thing a woman talked about when she was ready to jump in the sack with a guy. What she seemed to feel for him was a lot more serious.

Or maybe he was projecting because he felt that way about her. It was strange that it could happen like that to him so fast. The last time around, he'd gotten such mixed signals from her. Dylan really needed to know where he stood with her. Did he even have a chance?

He certainly wasn't going to find out tonight. He'd spent most of the last ninety minutes wandering around the club's two floors of machines and weights, looking for Brooke. He had had one false alarm—a slender blonde with her hair in a ponytail who looked exactly like Brooke from behind. And every time he'd passed a mirror, he checked out his hair to make sure he looked his best for her. But it was all in vain.

Wasn't meant to be, he thought, heading outside. He really hated that expression.

Dylan could feel fall in the night air as he walked down the block to where he'd parked his car. He pulled out his phone to order the pizza for the boys and him. He was scrolling down the phone screen for the number when he heard someone say, "Well, hello."

Dylan glanced up to see her standing in front of him on the sidewalk. She carried a gym bag and wore a long black cardigan and jeans. Her blond hair was loose and wavy, framing her lovely face. She wasn't wearing her glasses. Maybe she had some makeup on, but he couldn't tell for sure. He just knew she looked even prettier than he remembered from Wednesday night.

"Hi," Dylan said, happily dazed.

"Looks like we're just missing each other," she said.

Dylan gave a hesitant smile. He wondered if he should lie and pretend he'd just arrived at the club. He could say he'd started back to check on something in his car. Then they could work out together. He didn't mind going back and working out again. But then, his gym clothes were already sweat-soaked and wrinkled.

"Are you okay?" she asked.

He laughed. "Yeah. I was kind of hoping I'd see you in there."

"Well, I'm usually here earlier in the evening. But my husband had a last-minute work dinner thing tonight, and I was late heading out. It's a long story." She smiled. "You know, I thought about you last night."

"Yeah?" He liked hearing that.

She nodded. "There was something about the railroads on the History Channel, and I remembered you said that your older son was into trains. Do you know the program I'm talking about? Did he see it?"

Dylan shook his head. "I don't think so. Maybe we'll catch it On Demand." When she said she'd thought about him last night, he'd been hoping for something else entirely.

"Well, anyway," she said. "It was nice running into you again, Dylan." She started to move past him.

"Hey, would you have dinner with me?" he heard himself ask.

She stopped, turned, and stared at him.

"Just dinner," he explained. "My wife is working at a dance tonight. So I'm supposed to have pizza with my two boys in front of the sequel to a sequel of some Marvel Comics superhero movie—and they couldn't care less if I'm there or not."

Dylan could see she was about to say no, so he kept talking: "You said your husband had a work thing. When's he getting back?"

She shrugged and let out a little laugh. "Eleven, but—"

"Well, then you'll be eating alone—alone and late, if you're working out first. What were you going to have anyway?"

"For dinner?" She rolled her eyes. "Weight Watchers' lasagna."

"You don't look like you need Weight Watchers."

"Good to know those meals are paying off," she said. "I'm not in the program. But I eat the microwave dinners sometimes."

"You sure I can't talk you into letting me take you out to dinner? I'd have you home by nine."

She sighed. "I'm afraid I better pass."

Dylan kept the pleasant look on his face. He'd already been a lot pushier with her than he wanted to be. He nodded politely. "I understand. Listen, have a good work-out. I hope we run into each other again."

Her smile waned. Dylan wondered if she was sorry he'd given up when he did. She stood there for another few moments.

"You know what?" she finally said. "I would love to go someplace for dinner with you. Can we?"

Dylan felt elated. "Well, yes, of course. Good." He moved toward his car—a few feet away. "I'm right here."

In his mind, he started checking off the precautions. He was getting ridiculously ahead of things, but after the restaurant, on his way back from dropping her off, he'd have to remember to drive home with all the windows down. He didn't want Sheila smelling her perfume in the car again.

He had to cover his tracks with the boys and come up with some excuse for why he wouldn't be back home for another hour or two. Then it occurred to him. What if something happened to them while he was off having dinner with this woman? What if Sheila was right about someone watching her and watching the house?

Dylan reminded himself that he'd walked all around the house in the wee hours of Thursday morning and hadn't found any evidence of an attempted break-in. Sheila had just been on edge that night . . . and a little hammered, too.

He'd be back before nine o'clock. The boys would be fine.

He opened the passenger door for Brooke. "Why don't you get in while I order the pizza for my kids?"

She climbed into the front seat, and Dylan shut the door. He phoned the pizza place and paid for it with his credit card, including a tip for the delivery person. Then he stepped farther away from the car as he called home.

He didn't want Brooke to hear him lying to his sons.

"I want to watch this one," Gabe announced, waving the DVD of *Y Tu Mamá También* at him. "It says on the back, it's 'unafraid of sexuality.' And on the front, it says, 'Wildly erotic.' What's erotic?"

"Erotic is another word for sexy," Steve answered, studying the back of a DVD of *Boogie Nights*.

They sat on the floor of their parents' bedroom, an open blue plastic storage bin about the size of a laundry basket between them. In the bin, beneath a pile of sweaters, their dad had stashed about thirty DVDs—all of the movies rated R or unrated, which usually meant super dirty. The bin was kept in the back of their parents' bedroom closet—until just a few minutes ago, when Steve and Gabe had dragged it out to the bedroom. They'd left the closet door open, and the light was on, spilling just enough light into the darkened bedroom for Steve and his ten-year-old brother to examine the adult DVDs their parents had tried to hide from them.

Gabe was a head shorter than Steve, with a solid,

athletic build, unruly golden-brown hair, and big green
eyes. "Oh, he's going to be a real heartbreaker when he
grows up," one of his mom's friends had said about Gabe
recently. Steve figured he'd lucked out as far as kid
brothers were concerned, because Gabe looked up to him
and was annoying and obnoxious only about fifteen percent of the time. Steve didn't really mind babysitting or
hanging out with him—except for that fifteen percent
of the time.

They had planned on watching a movie with their dad
tonight, but Steve had gotten a call from him about ten
minutes ago. His father had forgotten that he was supposed to meet with a trainer at the gym, so he wouldn't
be home until nine o'clock. He said he would grab something to eat on the way home. But he'd ordered a large
sausage pizza for them, and it was supposed to arrive
around seven-thirty. "Is everything there okay?" his dad
had asked.

After what had happened the other night, Steve didn't
want to be alone in the house with just Gabe while it was
dark. But he figured he should grow a pair and tough it
out until nine. He didn't say anything to his father except
that he and Gabe were probably going to watch *Black
Panther* again on Netflix. That was okay with his dad.
"Just nothing rated R," he said. Steve thought that was
kind of a silly thing to say, since every TV and computer
in the house had parental controls.

As soon as Steve hung up, he checked all the doors to
make sure they were locked. Then he explained the situation to his little brother. Gabe's eyes widened. "We're
here alone until nine? Can we watch a dirty movie?"

"Y'know, at your age," Steve replied, "watching a
movie with sex and nudity could warp your mind. So,
hell, yeah! But I'll kill you if you tell Mom and Dad."

Steve didn't know who his parents thought they were

fooling with the hidden treasure trove of forbidden movies. He and Hannah had known about it for about three years now. They'd seen about half the movies in that bin. He'd watched *Basic Instinct* at least five times—or parts of it. He hadn't been aware that Gabe knew about the dirty movie collection, but apparently Hannah had spilled the beans to him a while back.

"I want to watch this '*Yo-Yo Mama*' one," he said, handing the DVD case to Steve.

He glanced at the back of the case and returned it to him. "Subtitles. Do you want subtitles running across the naked bodies? I don't think so. And don't get these out of order. Dad might have them stacked in there a certain way. If he sees it's all screwed up, he'll know we were looking at them."

They finally decided on *Body Heat*, which delivered the goods right away with a glimpse of a naked woman getting out of bed with a guy right after the main titles. The boys watched it on the big-screen TV in the basement rec room. An awestruck Gabe made Steve replay the brief nude scene three times. Steve felt like he was corrupting him.

The next ten minutes of the movie featured just courtroom and lawyer's office stuff, and a long scene in a restaurant with people talking about how hot it was out. Steve decreed that if it didn't get better in five minutes, they'd fast-forward for nudity. Meanwhile, Gabe played a game on Steve's phone and Steve started browsing through his dad's high school yearbook, which had been gathering dust on the rec room bookshelf.

The yearbook was from his father's senior year. He had about a dozen page numbers after his name in the index. The yearbook editor must have been in love with him or something because, besides all his sports team and extracurricular activities photos, there were several candid shots of his dad—and not a gawky one in the lot. For Steve, it was hard to believe his dad was only two years older than him in these pictures. He seemed so mature, handsome, and confident. Plus, it looked like practically the whole damn school had signed his yearbook.

Steve wasn't very popular, but he'd never really cared about that until this year. Suddenly it mattered to him that he had nothing better to do on a Friday night than watch an R-rated movie with his kid brother.

Steve's best friend since fourth grade had been Adam Bartleson. He was a pint-sized, good-looking kid with an olive complexion. He was also funny as hell. He had lived only three blocks away, and he and Steve had been inseparable. Looking back, they had done the dorkiest things together, but they'd always had fun. Then Adam moved away in July: Carlisle, Pennsylvania. Steve was miserable most of the summer. Going to the beach or to Dick's Drive-In, exploring the city on his bike, and even playing video games just weren't the same without his friend. Apparently, Adam wasn't having the same problem. He'd already made a new best friend in Pennsylvania—Brad Something. After a few weeks, Steve's and Adam's texting and Skype sessions had fallen off drastically. In his last correspondence, Adam wrote that he and Brad had smoked some weed and gotten high. Steve was flabbergasted. His friend had had absolutely no interest in anything like that before he moved—and marijuana was legal in Washington State, although not for kids, of course. But Steve and Adam had been practically the only ones at school who hadn't messed around with it. It was like his friend had moved away and completely changed on him.

So Steve spent the summer hanging out with his parents, watching TV, and reading about serial killers. Lots of fun. Steve figured if he wanted to avoid going crazy from boredom and loneliness, he'd better sign up for a sport at school. He picked gymnastics because it meant no one would try to hit him or expect him to catch or throw a ball. The team coach said Steve was starting out pretty late in life, but with his long legs, he might do well on the pommel horse. Plus, no one else from the sophomore class specialized on the horse, so by the time Steve was a senior, he might just be good enough to represent the school in some gymnastics meets.

Right now, he sucked, but he'd been practicing for only three weeks. The coach called him "Keeps Getting Up," like some kind of honorary Native American name. It was a politically incorrect but painfully accurate moniker, because Steve was always falling and getting back up on the pommel horse. Still, he liked trying to master something. His hands were all blistered and calloused, which was actually kind of cool, even though they hurt. He hadn't made friends with anyone on the team yet, but everybody was nice enough—at the very least, they seemed to tolerate him.

He'd recently shown his sore, raw-looking hands to his dad. And when Steve mentioned that he'd probably be sitting on the bench for most of the year, his father got a concerned look. "Listen," he said. "If you don't want to be on the gymnastics team, that's okay. I mean, if you like it, great. But I hope you aren't doing it for me."

Puzzled, Steve shook his head. "No, actually, I'm kind of having fun."

To Steve, it came across like his dad was saying, "Don't bust your ass going out for a sport on my account, because it's not going to make me like you more."

Or maybe his dad was just trying to tell him that he loved him either way. And Steve knew that. But his father was so proud of Gabe, the jock of the family. And though she could be a total brat sometimes, Hannah had their dad wrapped around her little finger.

Steve knew his father tried hard to be his friend. But he didn't have to try at all with Hannah or Gabe. With them, the connection was effortless.

His dad was under the impression Steve was still crazy about railroads from a brief fascination he'd had with old passenger trains for a couple of months back in eighth grade. His dad was still giving him railroad crap—miniature engines and cabooses, commemorative railroad spikes, mugs with railroad logos, and all sorts of memorabilia. The walls to Steve's small bedroom were covered with old railroad posters. Steve didn't have the heart to tell his well-meaning dad that he'd lost interest in railroad junk at least two years ago.

Steve remembered the other night, when his dad almost said "like mother, like son." The truth was, he was a lot more like his mom than he was like the handsome jock in this old yearbook.

"This woman sounds just like Jessica Rabbit," Gabe commented, squinting at the screen. "Do you think she's going to take her clothes off?"

Steve set the yearbook aside. "Your guess is as good—"

A series of knocks upstairs silenced him.

"Pizza!" Gabe announced.

"They're early," Steve murmured, glancing at his watch. He paused the movie in the middle of a scene with Kathleen Turner showing William Hurt the wind chimes on her balcony. He hurried upstairs to answer the door, and his brother followed him. "Get the Cokes and napkins, will you?" Steve asked as he passed through the kitchen. He headed toward the front hallway and the door.

But only a few feet from the door, he hesitated. Something was weird.

There was a stained-glass window on the upper half of their front door. At night, whenever a car with its headlights on pulled into the driveway, the colors in the stained glass became vivid—far brighter than when just the front porch light was on. Right now, the colored glass was dull and muted.

He wondered why the pizza guy hadn't used the doorbell or knocked again. It had been at least a minute since the first series of knocks. Steve checked the peephole to the right of the window. He didn't see anyone out there.

He took a deep breath, then unlocked the door and opened it.

The front porch was empty. And so was the driveway.

The night air gave him a chill. He glanced across the street at the park. At the far end, near the playground, he spotted someone passing under a streetlight along the walking path. Then the shadowy figure disappeared into the darkness. Whoever it was, they were walking away from the house. They were way too far away to have knocked on the front door just a minute ago.

Steve heard something rustling in the bushes alongside the house.

The hair stood up on the back of his neck. He quickly ducked inside, shut the door, and locked it.

He told himself it was probably just the wind passing through the bushes.

"Gabe?" he called.

No answer.

He hurried toward the kitchen. "Hey, Gabe?"

The kitchen was empty. Steve suddenly couldn't get a breath. "Gabe!" he yelled.

He heard the toilet flush in the bathroom around the corner. "What?" his brother called back through the door.

Steve sighed. "Nothing," he said, his heart still racing. He felt pretty stupid. Yet he checked the door to the garage and the kitchen door. Both were still locked. Then he glanced out the window at the Curtis house, where his mom had seen the prowler a few weeks ago. The place was completely dark. He figured the light timers must not have gone on yet.

Gabe emerged from the bathroom. "Where's the pizza?"

Steve shook his head and shrugged. "It's not here yet."

"Well, who knocked?"

"I don't know." He glanced out the window again. "Must not have been the front door. Maybe it was just a noise outside."

Gabe wrapped his hand around the refrigerator handle and stared at him, wide-eyed. "Maybe it wasn't a noise outside. Maybe it was a noise *inside*. Maybe somebody's in the house with us."

Steve stared at his brother. He tried to laugh. "That's crazy. We—we would have heard the footsteps. And plus, all the doors are locked."

"Well, what if it was the pizza guy at the door, but before you got there, somebody killed him and dragged his body into the bushes and then he drove off with our pizza?"

Steve rolled his eyes. "Yeah, sure, that's probably what happened. I don't know why I didn't think of that."

But he could tell Gabe was scared. "Well, then who knocked? Somebody knocked."

"Like I say, it was probably just a noise from outside." Steve wanted to convince himself of that as much as he wanted to convince his kid brother.

Gabe glanced up at the ceiling. "What was that?"

"What was what? I didn't hear anything."

"I thought there was a noise."

"Listen, can it, okay?" Steve said. "There wasn't any noise. You're creeping yourself out. And you're creeping me out, too."

It was funny that Gabe was so fearless and tough on the football field, but just like him, his brother could be a total basket case about unexplained noises in the night and the thought of serial killers. And Steve hadn't even told him much of what he'd read online about famous murders, only a few details about a couple of the more grisly cases.

"I heard something upstairs," Gabe insisted. He moved over to the counter, where their mother had a crock full of kitchen utensils. He grabbed a steel meat-tenderizer mallet. "I swear, it sounded like someone's in Mom and Dad's bedroom."

Taking a step toward the hallway, Steve shushed him. "Well, shut up for a second and let me listen."

The house was quiet except for the hum of the refrigerator.

What if his brother was right? Steve remembered how they'd left their parents' bedroom—with all the lights off, except for the closet light. They'd left the closet door open and the bin full of DVDs on the floor, near the dresser. Was someone creeping around that room right now, looking for jewelry or money?

He still didn't hear anything. But he didn't want to discount Gabe the way their dad had discounted their mother about what she'd seen and heard the other night. Steve realized he had to be the brave one here. Yet it was hard, especially when he imagined their father coming home tonight to find him and Gabe dead, blood dripping from the kitchen walls. Or maybe his father would find nobody home and their bodies would be discovered days later in some woods, the victims of a psychotic pedophile.

He turned to his brother. "Listen, let's go down to the basement and get the movie. We need to put it back. We need to put everything back where it's supposed to go in Mom and Dad's closet. I—I'll show you there's nobody up there. We'll check every room, every closet. You can bring that hammer-thing if it'll make you feel better. It's going to be okay. If anybody's hiding up there, between the two of us, we can beat the crap out of him. Right?"

Gabe just stared back at him with uncertainty.

Steve wasn't sure he believed what he'd just said, either. He thought about John Wayne Gacy, who had killed dozens of boys in Chicago. He was a big man who liked to dress up as a clown for charity functions. Steve imagined someone like that waiting up there for them. Maybe he was even dressed like a clown.

He crept into the front hall, with Gabe right behind him. At the bottom of the stairs, Steve glanced up at the second floor. "The hall light's on up there," Gabe said under his breath. "We didn't leave the hall light on. It was dark in the hallway."

"No, it wasn't," Steve replied in a hushed voice. "You switched the light on earlier, I'm almost positive."

But the truth was, they'd both been so excited over the prospect of watching a dirty movie, they wouldn't have noticed if a hippopotamus had been in the upstairs hallway.

"I don't think we should go up there," Gabe whispered anxiously. "When's Dad supposed to come home?"

"Not until nine."

"I think we should call him, have him come home *now*."

"No way," Steve whispered. "I'd rather face a serial

killer than try to explain to Dad how we snuck into his dirty video collection."

It took a while, but Steve finally convinced his brother to go along with his plan. They retrieved *Body Heat* from the DVD player in the basement, returned it to its spot in the storage bin, and shoved the bin back into the master bedroom closet where it belonged. Then, switching on the lights along the way, they checked every room and every closet on the second floor. Steve got the baseball bat out of his bedroom while his brother held on to the meat-tenderizer mallet.

It was a miracle of restraint that neither of them freaked out and bashed in the brains of the pizza delivery guy after he rang the doorbell.

They didn't want to go back down to the basement, where they couldn't hear if someone was trying to break in. Gabe seemed convinced an intruder was still hiding inside the house—just one step ahead of them during their earlier room-to-room search. So with weapons nearby, they ate their pizza in the kitchen breakfast booth and watched a *3rd Rock from the Sun* rerun on the small TV.

Steve didn't have much of an appetite. He nervously counted the minutes until his dad was supposed to come home.

Dylan had consumed only half of his cheeseburger and a few fries. He was too nervous to eat. He noticed that Brooke hadn't eaten much, either. Maybe she was a little nervous, too.

They were at Harry's Fine Foods, a neighborhood restaurant that used to be a mom-and-pop grocery store. It still had the squeaky wood-plank floor, and behind the bar were a couple of the old, pull-handle, glass-door refrigerator cases. The restaurant was only two short blocks from Brooke's apartment building on Capitol Hill, but she assured Dylan that none of her neighbors knew her or her husband very well. So no one was about to recognize her there. "Besides, we have nothing to hide, right?" she'd added.

"At least, not yet," Dylan had said offhandedly.

She'd looked right into his eyes. "I was thinking the same thing—only I can't joke about it."

Talking with her was effortless. During the few, fleeting silent moments, they just smiled at each other, and she was so damn cute when she blushed. He brushed his ankle against hers under the table and she reciprocated.

But now, near the end of the meal, she said the very last thing he wanted to hear: "So—tell me about your wife."

"You want me to talk about Sheila?"

Leaning back in her chair, she nibbled on a French fry. "All I know about her is that she's the mother of your three children and she teaches ballroom dancing."

"What else do you want to know?"

"Well, for starters, where'd you two meet? How long have you been married? Were either of you married before?"

"Wow, when you start in with the questions . . ."

She shrugged. "I'm just curious. Aren't you curious about my husband?"

Dylan considered it, and then slowly shook his head. "Not really. I'm a lot more curious about you."

She glanced down at the table and pushed her plate away. "So—how did you meet your wife?"

"College," he answered. "University of Oregon in Eugene. Sheila worked part time in a coffee house. I used to go in there to flirt with her. She reminded me of a young Diane Keaton, back when she did *Annie Hall*. We started dating our senior year, but broke up a few months after graduation. It was a very amicable split. Then we ran into each other again in Portland three years later and that was it. We've been married for nineteen years. And I forgot your other question . . ."

"Any other marriages?"

"That's right," he murmured. Then he shook his head. "No other marriages."

Brooke's eyes wrestled with his. "Have you . . . ever been unfaithful to her?"

"Well, that's pretty direct," he muttered. He took a sip of his beer. "I've come close once or twice. We've had our share of tough times—like everyone, I guess. About two years after we got married, Sheila had sort of a nervous breakdown. It almost did us in. That was the worst. She was—well, she was close to suicidal. The thing that worries me is she never really got any help for it."

"You mean, she never saw a therapist?"

"I really wanted her to, but she refused. She talked to some old priest, and that's about it."

"Well, does she suffer from depression, or what?"

Dylan shrugged. "I'm really not certain. Like I say, she was never diagnosed or treated. Instead, we just left Portland, severed all ties to the past and moved to Seattle. Sheila felt if she could put it all behind her and forget about it, then it would be like she had never had any problems. I guess she's made that work for her. It's been seventeen years, and she's been fine. I mean, she's had her moments, but she's generally good. She's been a great partner, a great mom. But always, in the back of my mind, is the fear that she'll fall apart again."

Brooke shifted in her chair. "What made her fall apart the first time?"

Dylan sighed. "I don't think I can talk about that—at least, not yet. I'm sorry. Sheila and I don't even discuss it. I know it sounds weird, but telling you would be like a violation."

"I understand," Brooke said pensively. "I guess I'm curious, because Paul and I are going through a tough time right now. In fact, his work dinner tonight, I'm pretty sure it's something else. I have a feeling he's seeing someone. And there's a part of me that doesn't really care." She smiled at him. "By the way, that has nothing to do with me accepting your invitation to dinner tonight. It's not because I wanted to get even with Paul or anything. And it's not because I didn't want to be alone, either. I'm here because I like you."

Dylan felt a little jolt of pleasure just hearing her say that. "Well, I'm sure, by now, you've figured out how I feel about you."

Blushing again, she nodded. "To be honest, I've been . . . struggling with that ever since you first said hello to me the other night. Do you want to hear something kind of perverse?"

He laughed. "Yes, please."

"Well, if you think it's strange that I'm asking a lot of questions about your wife and kids, it's because one of the things I find so attractive about you is that you're a family man. I think it's sexy. What does that say about me? I mean, I don't want to break up anyone's marriage and family, most of all yours. And yet I have these feelings for you . . ."

Dylan's phone vibrated in his pocket. He wanted to ignore it, but knew he couldn't. He winced at her. "I'm sorry. Hold that thought, please."

He took his phone out and checked it. The call was from Sheila. He noticed the time: 8:21 P.M.

"I'm sorry," he said again, getting to his feet. "I really need to answer this."

"Go ahead," she murmured.

Hurrying to the door, Dylan stepped out of the restaurant and clicked on the phone just before it went to voicemail. "Hey, hon," he said, a little out of breath.

"*Where are you?*" she asked. Her voice was loud and a bit shrill to compete with the music booming in the background. "Didn't you get my text earlier?"

"No, I—I must have missed it," he answered, honestly. All he could think was that he'd been too distracted. "What's going on? Is everything okay?"

"Everything's *not* okay. I just talked to Steve. Why aren't you home?"

"Didn't Steve explain to you about the trainer at the gym?"

"Yes, he explained. But you could have rescheduled. After what happened the other night, I don't know how you could leave the boys alone in the house—"

"Honey, I tried to get out of it, but I couldn't—at least not gracefully." Through the restaurant window, he could see Brooke sitting alone at their table. She looked a little sad. "Anyway," Dylan said, "I figured the boys would be okay. It's not even nine o'clock yet."

"Well, I spoke to Gabe, and he said the two of them were scared out of their wits."

"Why? What happened?"

There was a pause, and all he could hear was the pulsating music.

"Sheila, what happened?" he asked again.

"What happened is that they were supposed to have pizza with their father tonight, and he blew it off. You should have been there."

"All right, I'm sorry. What happened to them?"

"They got spooked because someone knocked on the front door and then disappeared."

"When was this?"

"About an hour ago," she answered.

"An hour ago, and nothing since?"

"I guess the pizza arrived about fifteen minutes later," Sheila said, "but nothing else after that."

"Honey, I think they're going to be okay. It's not like—"

"Where are you?" she interrupted. The music was still playing in the background. "Are you still at the gym?"

"No, I'm done there. I just swung by a restaurant to pick up a cheeseburger to go. I'm practically on my way home now. I should be there in fifteen minutes."

"Good," she said. "By the way, the creep from the bus was here at the dance tonight—with his girlfriend. I took their picture, and we can show it to the police if we have to."

"Are they still there?"

"They're gone now. But for all we know, they could be outside the house right now. I can't believe you left the kids home alone."

"I'm sorry. I'm on my way right now."

"Text me when you get there," she said. Then she hung up.

Clicking off the phone, Dylan headed back inside Harry's Fine Foods. He waved at their waiter and made a check sign in the air. Then he sat down at the table with Brooke.

"Was that Sheila?" she asked.

Dylan pulled out his wallet. "Yes, I'm sorry. I have to head home."

"Is everything okay?"

"I think so." He pried his credit card out of his wallet.

"It sounds like there's a minor crisis with one of the boys—at least, I hope that's all it is. Like I say, I'm really sorry about this." He figured Sheila was being slightly alarmist about the boys' safety. The guy who was supposedly following her couldn't be at her dance and their home at practically the same time. Still, he knew he had to get home and make sure everything was all right.

The waiter came by with their check. Without even looking at it, Dylan handed the check back to him—along with the credit card. "Could you box these up, please?" he asked, pointing to the food on their plates.

"Not mine, thanks," Brooke said.

"You sure?" Dylan asked.

Brooke nodded. She waited until the waiter left with their plates and their check before speaking up again. "You know, ever since we walked in here, I've had the sensation that someone's been watching us. It's silly, because no one knows me very well around here. So I must be paranoid, or I'm feeling really guilty."

"What do you have to feel guilty about?" Dylan asked. "We've just had a nice dinner, that's all. It's perfectly innocent."

"I'm not telling my husband about this dinner, and I'm pretty certain you won't tell Sheila. So it's not perfectly innocent." With a forlorn look, she gazed down at the table. "In a way, I'm glad you got that phone call when you did. It gave me time to come to my senses. The good news is we haven't done anything we'll regret. Nothing has really happened."

I don't consider that good news, Dylan wanted to say. But he knew it was wrong, so he just kept his mouth shut and nodded.

"I'm pretty vulnerable right now," she admitted. "And

I—I'm very attracted to you, Dylan. As I started to say before that phone call, it's been a struggle for me."

"Me too," he whispered. He reached across the table and took her hand. "For the last two nights, you wouldn't believe how much I've been looking forward to going to the gym, just to see you again. I've never felt this way about anyone before. It crazy, I know, after only a couple of short meetings. But you're the most exciting thing that's happened to me in a long, long time."

With a sigh, she gently pulled her hand away. "You're not making this easy for me at all. I asked you earlier if you'd ever cheated on your wife. But you haven't asked if I've ever been unfaithful to my husband."

Dylan shrugged. "I figured you'd tell me eventually. But I'm guessing you've been faithful."

"You're right. I've never cheated on my husband. I think I'd be pretty terrible at it. I don't know Sheila. But I'm guessing she's a nice person. And despite the problems we've been having, my husband's a kind, decent guy. I think they both deserve better."

The waiter returned with the check, Dylan's credit card, and the boxed leftovers. "Thanks a lot. You folks be sure to come back soon."

Nodding, Dylan worked up a smile for him. Then he signed the dinner receipt and put his credit card away. He sat there for another few moments and gazed at her.

"You should go," she said.

"Can I at least drive you home?"

She shook her head. "I'm just two blocks away, and I want to walk. You go home to your family, Dylan. I'm going to sit here a little longer. I may even buy myself a drink."

He stood up. "So that's it?"

She looked up at him, smiled, and nodded.

He took a step back from the table.

"Don't . . ." she cleared her throat, "don't forget your leftovers."

Frowning, Dylan grabbed the box. "It was nice meeting you, Brooke," he murmured.

She nodded and looked down at the table.

Dylan hurried out of the restaurant and down the block to where he'd parked the car. Jumping into the front, he put the leftovers box on the passenger seat and slammed the door shut.

"Goddamn it!"

Saturday, September 22—1:10 A.M.

Usually, Dylan fell asleep just seconds after his head hit the pillow. Not tonight. Sheila, who usually had trouble with insomnia, was sound asleep beside him. She'd taken an Ambien around midnight, and that had immediately knocked her out. Dylan was left to toss and turn, mulling over his shitty evening.

Thwarted expectations were bad enough. But he couldn't even bellyache to anyone about how disappointed he was. On top of that, he felt like a total jerk for leaving the boys home alone earlier tonight. They were fine, of course—just a little shaken up. Still, Sheila was pretty damn unforgiving. And she was right, damn it.

Yet, given the choice, he'd do it all over again if it meant he'd have another chance to be with Brooke.

Dylan climbed out of bed, put on a pair of sweatpants and a T-shirt, and then crept downstairs. He was tempted to try Sheila's trick with a couple of shots of bourbon. But he hated bourbon. Besides, he didn't want to wake up in the morning feeling even lousier with a hangover. He needed to be *bright-eyed and bushy-tailed* tomorrow (his mother's favorite expression). Gabe had a football game in Auburn, and Dylan was one of the carpooling parents.

He checked the refrigerator for something to eat. He eyed his leftover burger and fries. He'd thought about finishing up the dinner earlier, after returning home. He'd ended up watching *Black Panther* with the boys—or some of it.

A little more than halfway through the film, Sheila had come home. Dylan had joined her in the kitchen while the boys remained down in the basement with the movie blaring. As she fixed a peanut butter and jelly sandwich for herself, Sheila lit into him again for leaving the boys alone at home.

Dylan just kept on apologizing.

She showed him the photo she'd taken of the guy from the bus—along with his girlfriend. Dylan felt awful for not taking her more seriously. It was now frighteningly obvious that this blond kid was indeed stalking Sheila, for one reason or another. Whatever—or whomever— she'd seen outside the house the other night could no longer be dismissed as the product of too much bourbon and an overactive imagination. And maybe she was right about this stalker sending her that strange text.

The guy in the photo was a sketchy-looking creep. Dylan wished he could call the police on him, but the son of a bitch hadn't really tried anything yet. He hadn't even gotten within twenty feet of Sheila. And they couldn't prove he'd been anywhere near the house. What could the police do?

Even Sheila agreed that, at this point, it seemed useless to get the police involved. "Maybe he'll back off now that I have his photo," she said. Still, she texted the photo to Dylan, Hannah, and Steve so they'd all be on the lookout for the guy and his girlfriend. Sheila talked about printing up the shot and taping it to the refrigerator door, just to keep the kids extra aware. Dylan wasn't sure that was such a terrific idea. It would be like the creep was already inside their home, scaring the kids.

Dylan had talked her out of it for now.

He heated the burger and fries in the microwave and opened a root beer. He sat in the dinette booth and ate. He'd left his phone recharging on the table earlier. Unplugging it, he once again looked at Sheila's photo of the lowlife guy and his girlfriend.

Scumbag, he thought. The girlfriend looked like a junkie. Dylan thought she might have actually been pretty without all the obnoxious Goth affectations. In the photo, she seemed startled and slightly out of it. She also had a strange, childlike innocence.

She actually had a very sweet face.

Though Dylan had never set eyes on the girl before, he somehow recognized that face.

CHAPTER TEN

Monday, September 24—1:24 P.M.

Sheila was in her element. Gardening was right up there with dancing as ideal therapy for whatever bothered her. She wore her comfy, ancient, University of Oregon sweatshirt, gardening gloves, and an old blue baseball cap, which Dylan claimed made her look like Donna Reed in *It's a Wonderful Life*, specifically the scene in which they're helping the Martini family move into their new home in Bailey Park. She couldn't help feeling a bit like Donna Reed whenever she wore it.

She was kneeling on a cushioned pad on the ground, planting perennials for fall: Coral Bells Cassis and Day-lily Daring Deception. She'd propped open the door to the den so she could listen to the eighties station on the radio. Right now, they were playing Journey's "Don't Stop Believin'," which they repeated about four times a day. But she didn't mind right now.

Lush with blooming plants, flowers, and two small Japanese maple trees, her three-tiered garden took up about a third of the backyard. Carefully arranged stones and boulders divided up the beds. Dylan said it was a work of art. The garden's birdbath centerpiece attracted an array of feathered friends, and bees buzzed around the flowers. Her garden was this living, breathing thing that she took care of. Sheila would start working on it and forget all about the time. In fact, she had her phone balanced on a nearby rock with an alarm set for two-thirty so she'd remember to stop, get cleaned up, run to the store, and be back before the kids came home from school.

She didn't want any of them to be alone in the house, not even for a few minutes. She hadn't seen the blond creep since snapping his picture at the dance on Friday night. But she wasn't taking any chances. That was another reason she had her phone close by, just in case something happened.

Now that Dylan had seen proof of her stalker, he seemed genuinely concerned about her and the kids. It made her feel as if they were protected—finally. Even with him at work right now, she felt more secure than she had last week. It was as if Dylan was now doing all the worrying for everyone.

On Saturday morning, he'd ordered two mini-canisters of pepper spray from Amazon, one canister for her and one for Hannah. They had arrived this morning in the kind of heavy-duty cardboard and thick-plastic packaging that could only be opened with garden shears or a buzz saw. Sheila hadn't taken them out of their packages yet.

She'd noticed two college-age guys unloading some boxes from a Starving Student Movers truck in the Curtises' driveway on Saturday. No one had seen the new neighbor yet, but it looked like she'd moved in. A car had been parked in the driveway for the past two nights. With the house next door once again occupied, Sheila knew she wouldn't feel quite so isolated. She wouldn't be spooked by the darkened windows across the way.

She made a mental note to take some garden flowers to the new neighbor—and maybe a bottle of wine.

She was spreading mulch around the new plants when her phone chimed.

Taking off her gloves, Sheila reached for the phone and squinted at the text notice. She didn't recognize the sender. Immediately, she thought of the last text she'd received from a stranger, and a little jolt of dread hit her in the stomach.

And up until just a few seconds ago, she'd been feeling so content.

Frowning, she clicked on the message. All it said was:

He knows.

The text came with an image attachment that had been blocked.

With the phone in her hand, Sheila got up and moved into the den so she could see the screen better. She noticed the standard warning about the blocked image. For a few moments, she wasn't sure what to do. The other night, Dylan had reminded her about all the potential hazards of opening a link from an anonymous sender. But Sheila kept staring at that message: *He knows*.

"Shit," she muttered, clicking on the attachment.

Someone had scanned a handout from a memorial service for *Antonia "Toni" Newcomb*. There it was: that name again, this time with a slightly out-of-focus photo of the pretty brunette beneath it. Smiling over her shoulder in the shot, she had her hair up and looked about ten years younger than she did in her Facebook photos. Under the photograph was a sort of stencil drawing of a rose above more text: *In Remembrance, 1974–2018*. At the very bottom of the page was the funeral parlor's name in small print—MARCH-MIDDLETON FUNERAL SERVICES, PORTLAND, OREGON.

It looked like the cover of a thin leaflet. Sheila

couldn't figure out why anyone would text this to her. *He knows.* What the hell did that mean? Had Dylan lied when he'd said he'd never met this woman? As much as she tried to suppress the thought, she wondered if Dylan was connected to her death in some way.

Sheila still couldn't get over the horrible way Antonia Newcomb had died.

She tried to reply to the text. But her hands shook so much that she kept making mistakes and having to back-track. She finally spelled out the short message:

Who are you?

She clicked on Send.

Within moments, the text bounced back as undeliverable.

"Damn it!" she hissed. She wanted to throw the phone across the room, but she stifled the impulse and set it down on Dylan's desk. Almost automatically, she reached for the handle to the top drawer and yanked it open. All she could think was that Dylan must be hiding something from her. She started riffling through the drawers, feverishly piling things on top of the desk: a box of staples, a packet of Sharpies, envelopes, notepads, receipts, papers. She had no idea what she was looking for—just some kind of proof that he knew Antonia Newcomb. Maybe her name was on a cocktail napkin, or perhaps he'd saved an old love letter or two. Sheila anxiously read over the receipts to see if any were from Portland or somehow connected to "Toni." When she didn't find anything, she tried the other drawers and found work papers, old contracts, warranties and pamphlets for their TV, the music system, and his computer. In the bottom drawer, she uncovered birthday cards he'd saved from her and the kids. They went back for years.

Sheila started crying. She was so frustrated—and so mad at herself for suspecting him. But she couldn't help it.

Heading across the hall to the bathroom, she plucked a couple of Kleenex from the pewter tissue box on top of the toilet tank. She wiped her eyes and blew her nose. After throwing out the tissues, Sheila reached over and switched on both the light and the vent fan. She was the only one at home, but out of habit, she shut the door before she sat down on the toilet. While she peed, she thought about the awful mess she'd made in the den. How was she going to explain to Dylan why everything from his desk was in the wrong drawers?

Past the churning of the vent fan, she could hear Michael Jackson's "Thriller" on the radio and a strange, shuffling noise, like something had fallen from the mountain of papers and junk she'd piled on top of Dylan's desk.

She realized she'd left the den door open when she came in from the garden.

Had someone snuck inside the house? Was that what she'd heard—or was it just a breeze rustling the papers on Dylan's desk? Sheila couldn't be sure, not with the radio on and the bathroom vent humming.

Now she heard footsteps.

She felt so helpless and stupid, sitting there. She quickly grabbed some toilet paper, wiped herself, and then pulled up her underwear and jeans. If someone was in the house, she didn't want them knowing where she was. She didn't flush the toilet, but quietly lowered the lid. Then she crept over to the door and listened.

Someone was whispering. And it wasn't the radio.

Sheila's hand hovered over the doorknob with the button lock in the center. She'd left her phone on Dylan's desk, and the pepper spray was on the kitchen counter, still in its packaging.

She couldn't breathe. What good would locking herself in the bathroom do? There was no window for her to escape. All they had to do was kick down the door. Still, she slowly pushed in the button until it clicked.

There was more whispering. It sounded like they were in the den or the dining room. She heard a man cackle— a horrible, smug laugh. Someone shushed him.

Sheila glanced around for something to defend herself. She wondered if she could extract the towel bar from its holders without making too much noise. Like that would be any defense against two intruders.

She'd left her purse with her wallet inside on the kitchen table. She wished they'd just take it and leave. But Sheila was convinced that the blond creep and his girlfriend were the ones who had invaded her home. And they weren't here just to steal money. No, they had some sort of other agenda.

Suddenly, they got quiet. Sheila couldn't hear anything beyond the vent fan. She waited a moment, then reached for the vent switch and turned it off.

The radio was still on. It was playing The Police's "Every Breath You Take." Past the music, Sheila could hear footsteps again. Then a door shut. She couldn't tell if the sound came from the den or if it was the door to the basement or the closet.

After that, there was just the music, no other sound.

Her heart racing, she listened to the song end. Then the disc jockey started talking.

Sheila remained paralyzed with fear for several minutes. She kept waiting for the next footstep or whisper or that awful cackle. She couldn't hear anything but the DJ on the radio. She finally reached for the doorknob and slowly turned it. The lock button popped out with a click. Wincing at the sound, she opened the door.

Across the hall, in the den, she saw her blond stalker glancing at some of the papers on Dylan's desk. He was wearing his army jacket. A few papers fell out of his hand and drifted to the floor as he glanced over at her. He grinned.

Frozen in the bathroom doorway, Sheila gasped.

"Hey." The voice came from the kitchen.

Sheila swiveled around to see the punk girl gazing back at her. The girl had a pink streak in her greasy-looking platinum blond hair. She wore a red hoodie, unzipped in the front to reveal a torn, black T-shirt. She carried a huge brown purse. The girl had a framed photo of Dylan in her hand, one that Sheila kept on her computer desk.

Sheila was speechless. The two intruders seemed so nonchalant about breaking into her home; they might as well have wandered into a furniture store and started browsing. It took a few moments for Sheila to get any words out. "What—what are you doing? You have no right to be in here."

The blond creep snickered.

"I mean it!" Sheila yelled, unhinged. "You need to leave—now!"

"God, chill," the girl said. "We knocked, and no one answered."

"The door was open, lady," the creep chimed in.

"It's not like we're stealing anything," the girl said. Approaching Sheila, she held out the framed picture. "This is your husband, right? This is Dylan O'Rourke."

Sheila glanced over at the blond creep who had wandered over to the bookcase. He took a CD off the shelf to glance at it.

She turned toward the girl. "Yes, that's my husband,"

she said, a tremor in her voice. "And he's upstairs right now. So you'd better leave."

The guy laughed. "Yeah, right," he said, inspecting another CD. "We saw him go off to work this morning."

"Who are you?" Sheila whispered. "What do you want?"

"Why don't you call your husband at work?" the girl said. "Tell him I want to see him."

"Just who are you?" Sheila asked again.

"I'm his daughter," the girl said. "Tell him that his daughter wants to see him."

Sheila stared at her.

"Call him," the girl whispered.

"I'll call him," the blond creep said, tossing aside the CD. "He's supposed to be upstairs, right?" He sang out: "Daddy! Hey, Daddy, your little girl's here!"

The girl turned to him. "Don't be an asshole, Brodie. Can't you see you're freaking her out? Go outside and have a smoke."

"Don't fucking boss me around," he muttered.

She sighed. "Okay, *please*, take your ass outside and smoke a goddamn cigarette. Just get out of here! God."

"Screw this," he grunted, pulling a pack of cigarettes out of his jacket. "I'm going to Jimmy's. I'm taking the car. You're on your own. You want to meet me there later, you can get a ride from Daddy—or maybe your new step-mom." He lit up his cigarette, headed out through the den door, and tossed the match away.

The girl handed Sheila the framed photograph of Dylan. "Call him."

Sheila finally stepped away from the bathroom door. She set the framed picture on the kitchen counter. Then she turned toward the girl again. She clutched the edge of the counter to steady herself. "I don't believe you're his daughter," she whispered. Yet, even as she said it,

Sheila thought of how much this girl—as she'd argued with her boyfriend—reminded her of Hannah whenever she pitched a fit. "Who are you?" she asked.

"My name's Eden," the girl said, reaching into her big purse. It took her a few moments to find what she was looking for. "Shit," she muttered in the middle of her search. She finally pulled out an old, stained legal-size envelope. She handed it to Susan. "My birth certificate's in there."

Her hands still shaking, Sheila took the document out of the worn envelope.

"'Baby girl born July first, two-thousand-two at eleven-something in the morning,'" the girl said, liberally quoting from the document. "'Mother: Antonia Spiro. Father: Dylan O'Rourke.'"

Sheila gazed at the parents' names. *Antonia* again.

"Is your mother the woman in Portland who killed herself a couple of weeks ago?"

The girl frowned. "She didn't kill herself."

"You and your—your friend," Sheila interrupted, waving the birth certificate in front of the girl. "You're the ones who have been sending me those texts—the article about your mother, the notice from the funeral home."

The girl snatched the document out of her hand. "I don't know what you're talking about. I haven't sent you anything!"

"Then your friend did. And the two of you have been following me."

"Okay, yes, we were following you. I was curious. Can you blame me? But I didn't send you any texts, and neither did Brodie."

"Well, somebody did. I think you and your friend—"

"You goddamn fucking bitch, would you just call your husband?" the girl screeched. Then she started crying.

She carelessly stashed the birth certificate and envelope back inside her purse, scrunching up the paper.

Sheila noticed the snot dripping from the girl's pierced nostril.

The girl took a few deep breaths. "Listen, lady . . . I know this isn't easy for you," she said quietly, the words a little broken. She wiped her nose with the back of her hand. Mascara ran down her cheeks. "But do you think it's easy for me? I'm sixteen years old. My mother's dead. And I don't have anyone else to go to . . ."

Dylan's daughter locked eyes with Sheila. "I need my father."

CHAPTER ELEVEN

Monday—3:17 P.M.

Now Dylan knew where he'd seen the punk girl's face before—in old photos of his mother as a teenager. Of course, his mom had never had platinum and pink hair or sported a stud in her nose. But there was certainly a resemblance.

The girl sat slumped in the chair across from him at the dining room table. Stone-faced, Sheila occupied Dylan's usual seat at the head of the table. He'd taken Gabe's seat. It was odd for him not to be in his regular spot. But then, the whole damn situation was surreal.

The family ate in the dining room only on formal occasions. This old mahogany table, with a Wedgwood soup tureen as a centerpiece and a crystal chandelier sparkling overhead, was where they usually sat down to have "serious discussions" with the kids—sometimes collectively, sometimes individually. At the moment, Dylan kept thinking how this seemed more like an office conference table. Sheila and the girl even had bottled waters—on coasters, no less—in front of them. It seemed like they should have had laptops, too. It felt so impersonal and official.

No one spoke.

Instead of a laptop, Dylan had the girl's birth certificate

in front of him. It was slightly soiled and wrinkled, the paper soft with age. But the words on it cut like a razor.

Sheila had called him at work and told him to come home immediately. The kids were fine, she'd said. No, she wasn't having another *scare*. There was no reason to call the police. She needed to see him and didn't want to discuss it over the phone. No, it couldn't wait.

He immediately thought of Brooke. Had Sheila somehow found out about the clandestine dinner on Friday night? Maybe a friend of hers had seen him with Brooke at the restaurant. But the place was so small that he'd certainly have noticed a familiar face among the diners. The only other way Sheila could have found out was if Brooke had told her. But she didn't seem like the type who would do that. Besides, it was all perfectly innocent. Nothing had happened—and nothing *would* happen. He and Brooke had ended it before anything got started. The thought of her still made his heart ache. He'd been miserable all weekend. Brooke had said she didn't want to ruin his marriage or hurt his wife. No, she wouldn't have told Sheila anything.

It had to be something else that was bothering Sheila. During his drive home, he felt slightly annoyed with her for not telling him what the problem was. She'd said she wasn't scared. In fact, she'd sounded a bit hostile.

When he pulled into the driveway, he noticed Sheila's Toyota parked in the little bay on one side of the garage. No other cars—so no surprise visitors. He still wasn't sure what to expect.

Dylan parked in the garage, and let himself in through the kitchen. He heard Sheila call to him from the dining room: "I'm in here!" From the edgy tone of her voice, he almost took it as a warning.

Dylan didn't even remove his suit coat. He passed through the kitchen, then past the basement stairs and bathroom. Glancing toward the den, he noticed his desk was in shambles. A mountain of papers was strewn across it and spilling onto the floor. It looked like someone had emptied out all the drawers and dumped everything on top of his desk. He wondered if they'd been burglarized. But Sheila had said on the phone there was no need to call the police.

He turned toward the dining room and balked. A strange girl was sitting at their table, in Steve's usual spot. It took Dylan a second to recognize the street girl from Sheila's photo.

He looked at Sheila and nodded toward the den. "Hon, what—what happened in there?"

Sheila kept her hands folded on the table. "That's not important right now." She motioned to the teenager on her left and then glared accusingly at him. "Do you know this girl?"

"Yes." He frowned at the sullen-looking kid. "Why have you been harassing my wife?"

"No, I mean, did you know her from *before*?" Sheila pressed.

The girl sighed. "Lady, I already told you. He doesn't know me."

"Tell him who you are," Sheila said.

The girl's heavily made-up eyes locked onto him. "My name is Eden O'Rourke. I'm your daughter."

Stunned, Dylan just stared at her. The words she uttered rang in his ears for a few moments.

Sheila had said something after that, but it was lost on him. Hell, he didn't even remember sitting down in this chair a few moments ago. He had no idea if it had been Sheila or the girl who had slid the birth certificate across the table at him.

But there it was—and there was the girl who looked so much like his mother, sitting at his dinner table.

Dylan looked at the parents' names on the document. "Antonia Spiro," he murmured.

"No one called her Antonia except me," the girl said. "For everyone else, it was always *Toni*."

Dylan just nodded. *Toni Spiro*. It was a lot different from that other name. He hadn't made the connection when Sheila had shown him the article about the Portland woman who had fallen to her death.

"Antonia Newcomb," Sheila said—as if reading his mind.

"She got married twice after you knew her," the girl explained, "back seventeen years ago."

Dylan felt sick to his stomach. He turned to Sheila. "Seventeen years ago, that was when—when things weren't going so well with us. I thought we were . . ." He shrugged. It was a time in their lives that they never talked about. And here he was, talking about it—in front of a stranger, no less, a stranger who claimed to be his daughter. Dylan rubbed his forehead. "If I hadn't been so lonely and half out of my mind at the time, nothing would have happened. Toni, she was—well, she was just there. I mean, she was a nice person. But believe me, it wasn't anything serious . . ." He looked at the girl. "I'm sorry. But I'm sure your mother would back me up on that."

She curled her lip at him. "My mother can't do anything. She's dead."

"I had no idea she got pregnant. She never told me about you." He turned to Sheila again. "I knew Toni for maybe a month. And when I realized . . ." he sighed. He had to remember to keep breathing. "Honey, when I realized you and I could work things out, I stopped seeing her. I ended it. It was a—a clean breakup, no hard feelings. I never heard from Toni again."

"He's telling the truth, lady," the girl said, giving Sheila a glib smile. "My mother used to say the likelihood of him knowing about me was right up there with the likelihood of you knowing about the two of them—not likely at all."

"But she gave you *our* last name," Sheila said.

The girl nodded. "Yeah, I guess she did."

Sheila looked at her watch—and then at him. "Gabe has football practice, and Steve has gymnastics," she announced in a cool, controlled tone. "They won't be home until five. Hannah, depending on her social schedule, might not be home until dinnertime—or she could come through the front door in fifteen minutes. Are you going to explain to her who our guest is? Or do you expect me to do it?"

Dylan was in agony. "Honey, I'm so sorry," he whispered.

Sheila stared at him. Then suddenly, she hauled back and slapped him hard across the face.

It hurt like hell and left him dazed. So much rage had gone into that slap. The side of his face throbbed and burned.

Dylan blinked a few times. He watched Sheila spring up from the chair and march toward the kitchen. She snatched her purse from the breakfast table. Then he lost sight of her as she headed toward the front hallway. Touching his mouth, Dylan felt blood. He listened to her footsteps. He heard the front door open, then slam shut.

He glanced over at the girl who claimed to be his daughter. He didn't want to believe it, despite all the evidence in her favor—including the family resemblance. He didn't want to believe it, because, right now, he hated her.

The little bitch smirked at him. She leaned back in the chair again. "Y'know, I didn't exactly expect a warm and fuzzy father-daughter reunion, but I didn't anticipate a shit-storm of this magnitude, either."

Dylan listened to the car pulling out of the driveway. Touching his mouth again, he frowned at the girl. "Why didn't you come to me first?"

She gave an offhand shrug.

"Maybe you and your friend thought it would be a lot more *fun* this way. Am I right?"

"Maybe," she muttered, glancing at the tabletop.

"Well, why didn't you pick on me?" Dylan said. "Why did you pick on my wife? Why put her through the wringer? What were you doing, following her around and sending her that text—"

"Hey, listen. I already explained to her, I didn't send her any text," the girl said, a bit peevishly.

"Then your lowlife friend must have. Maybe he tinkered with my wife's car, too—"

"What the hell are you talking about? Neither one of us touched your wife's car. And where do you get off calling my boyfriend a lowlife? You haven't even met him."

"I've seen the guy's picture. And I heard enough about him from my wife. The two of you were stalking her, harassing her. I notice you haven't denied that yet."

"I wanted to see what my stepmother was like," the girl said. "I was curious. Is there anything wrong with that? We were watching you, too."

Dylan tried to keep a poker face. But he couldn't help wondering if they'd seen him with Brooke outside the gym or at the restaurant. "Did this—*surveillance* include lurking outside our house at two in the morning on Thursday?"

She squinted at him. "Why the hell would we do that? There'd be nothing to see. You'd have been asleep. We followed you guys to work or to the store a few times.

Big fucking deal." She clicked her tongue against her teeth and shook her head at him. "Y'know, this third degree from my long-lost father, it's really sweet as hell. I come here and tell you that I'm your daughter, and this is how you treat me." She let out a little laugh. "Between the two of us, no one would ever guess that I'm the bastard here."

Dylan reached for Sheila's water and took a swig. "I'm sorry," he mumbled, touching his mouth again. "This whole thing took me by surprise."

"No shit."

He glanced toward the den. "What happened in there?"

"Beats me. It was that way when we came in."

He looked at the birth certificate again. "You mentioned your mom got married a couple of times. Do you have any brothers or sisters?"

She shook her head. "Nope."

"Did you get along okay with your stepfathers?"

"Nope. Neither marriage lasted long, and neither one of the assholes stayed in touch—which is just as well, because asshole husband number two seemed to take a more than fatherly interest in me, if you get my drift. I was twelve at the time."

Dylan sat up in the chair. "He didn't—"

"He came close, but nothing ever happened."

"Don't you have any grandparents?" he asked.

"Well, if your folks are alive, I do."

Dylan shook his head.

"Antonia's parents are dead, too. So I'm grandparentless. Are you trying to figure out who you're going to pawn me off on? Because there's nobody. I mean, for a while there, on and off, a friend of my mother's looked after me and helped raise me. But it was a long time ago, and that bridge is burned. She's totally out of the picture now. I don't have any aunts or uncles on my mother's side, either. In fact, I had to arrange my mom's memorial service. Some of her work friends chipped in for the funeral home. But mostly, it was up to me to put the whole thing together. I got a little help from this social worker at the hospital where they took my mother's body—or what was left of it. I got a crash course in what you're supposed to do with a corpse. It was really interesting."

"Your mother's work friends—"

"I'm not staying with any of them, and none of them want me."

"That's not what I was going to ask," Dylan said. "I was wondering if they knew about me."

"I guess," she said, her mouth twisting almost into a frown. "But it's not like anyone really gave a shit about you—except me. I mean, after all, it was seventeen years ago. It's not like my mom was still talking about you to her work friends."

Dylan nodded. He was thinking that perhaps one of Toni's work friends had texted Sheila the article about Toni's death. But what the girl said made sense. "So—you knew about me?"

"My mom never hid it. I grew up very aware that my father was married with this other family, and that he didn't know I was alive."

"I'm sorry," Dylan whispered. "That must have been really tough. Didn't you ever want to contact me?"

The girl gave him a sad smile. "Only about five hundred times," she murmured. "My mom had a couple of photos of you. And I have to admit, I googled you a lot and kept track of you over the years. A couple of weeks ago, after the funeral and all, I persuaded Brodie to take me up here from Portland, so I could check out you and your family. We're staying with some friends of his. I thought they were kind of cool at first, but I have to admit, they're pretty skanky. I can't stay with them much longer."

"Do they know about me?" Dylan asked. He was still thinking about the text—and whoever was lurking outside their house in the wee hours of Thursday morning.

She shrugged. "Maybe Brodie told them, I don't know. The point is, I have nowhere to go. I want to stay with you—at least until I figure out what I'm gonna do."

Dylan squirmed in the chair. It was the last thing he wanted. He couldn't even fathom how he'd tell the kids about her. He remembered what Sheila had said about Hannah possibly coming home at any minute. He started to shake his head. "I'm sorry, but I don't think that's an option right now."

She frowned at him. "Listen to yourself. *It's not an option*, like this is some sort of business deal or something. My mom never asked you for any help. She didn't ask you for a dime. But I'm asking you, my father, for a place to live for a little while after my mom just died. Is that too much?"

He didn't know how to answer her. "I—I want to help you, Eden. But you need to look at this from my perspective. We're strangers. Your mother never told me about you. I had no idea. For the past few days, you and your friend—and maybe his friends—have been bothering my wife. Now, you show me a birth certificate, and you think, suddenly, that makes us connected and everything's all right." He shook his head. "But it doesn't work that way. I'm sorry. Before I can let you stay in this house, before I can start being responsible for you, I need to verify that I'm really your father. We'll have to take a paternity test. I hope you understand."

She just stared at him.

"It's not that I don't believe you, Eden," he tried to explain. "But how do you know for sure your mom wasn't mistaken about who your father was? I mean, my name might be on the birth certificate. But how can you be absolutely sure?"

"I'm sure," she said. "And I really wish I didn't have to beg you to take me in, *Dad*. Because more than anything right now, I want to spit in your face."

CHAPTER TWELVE

Monday—5:27 P.M.

It was starting to get dark and chilly. Sheila realized she should have brought along a sweater or a jacket. Sitting on a swing, she clutched the cold chains on either side of the seat and gazed out at the gray water of Lake Washington. She was in a small playfield a few blocks down from Madison Park Beach. There was just the swing set, a few benches, and a neatly mowed strip of grass, where two boys had been tossing around a football. They'd left a few minutes ago. Sheila had come there to be alone and cry, but so far, she hadn't shed a tear.

She was wondering what her life would be like if she divorced Dylan.

She probably should have left him the first time she'd discovered he'd been unfaithful, but then she wouldn't have had Hannah, Steve, or Gabe. Still, that first time had nearly killed her. What a kick in the stomach to realize, during that horrible period—that *rough patch* seventeen years ago—while she'd been close to having a nervous breakdown, Dylan was screwing Toni, the party girl. And it wasn't a onetime thing, either. He'd admitted that he'd seen her for a whole month, the son of a bitch.

To so many of his other affairs since then, Sheila had managed to turn a blind eye. She convinced herself that he still loved her. He was a good provider and a devoted father. No matter what he did outside their marriage, he always stayed with her. And when each affair ended, there was usually a honeymoon period in which he was so devoted to her.

He compartmentalized when it came to his infidelities. These other women were something totally separate from his real life. His family mattered to him more than anything, she knew that. He was wonderful with the kids, and they adored him. Despite his faults, Sheila loved him—and the way he was with their children.

A few times, she'd threatened to divorce him, but they both knew she didn't mean it. She didn't want to nag him or be a watchdog. So she simply tried to ignore all the little red flags that came up when he was cheating. She didn't want to divorce him. She couldn't imagine trying to raise their children without him.

Besides, she'd known what she was getting into when she married him. All her friends thought he was an outstanding catch. Her parents adored him. He came from a well-to-do, respectable family. He was ambitious, charming, generous, and devastatingly handsome. Just walking down the street with him, Sheila would watch the passersby, their gazes locking onto Dylan. Sometimes, she felt like the invisible woman. At restaurants, they always got terrific service. Hostesses, waitresses, and even most waiters flirted shamelessly with him in front of her. Dylan lapped it up and chatted with them. In all the times they'd gone out to eat, his water glass had never been empty. She often felt compelled to tell him, "This isn't what it's like for normal people." In addition to being so good-looking, he was also naturally friendly. So everyone loved him—and remembered him. Sheila had lost track of how many times at parties someone would start to introduce them and have no difficulty remembering Dylan's name, but wouldn't remember hers.

About two years ago, Dylan had had a brief fling with a twentysomething barista. He was uncharacteristically sloppy about covering it up. Maybe, on some level, he'd wanted her to catch on and help terminate it. When she asked him why he felt compelled to see these other women, Dylan couldn't really answer her. He honestly didn't seem to know. "They're there," he'd said with a sorry shrug. Sheila didn't press the matter, maybe because she didn't want to hear if it was somehow her fault.

She remembered, during one of her bouts with insomnia around that time, she'd found an article online from *Psychology Today* listing ten reasons married men cheat. Dylan neatly fit into two of the categories:

Immaturity: He didn't think his actions had consequences. If he got away with cheating, it was like he'd never cheated. What the wife didn't know wouldn't hurt her, and all that. Sheila remembered seeing a clip on the national news during a hot spell and drought in New York City. Some kids had screwed open a fire hydrant to play in the spray of water. When a reporter asked one of the kids on the street why they were wasting water during a serious drought, the child replied "They shouldn't make it so easy for us."

That was Dylan with other women. It was so easy for him. And he was like a kid. No wonder he related so well to their children.

The other potential reason for his cheating was his *Uniqueness*. Dylan knew he was handsome and charming. He was special. He probably felt entitled when it came to sex. The rules simply didn't apply to him.

The *Psychology Today* article didn't address special circumstances—like the cheating husband being devastatingly handsome. Sheila had gotten used to Dylan's looks ages ago, but she still hadn't completely acclimated to the way other people reacted to him. Everyone thought she was so damn lucky to be married to him.

They didn't know what she had to put up with. In a way, she felt grateful that at least he was usually painstakingly discreet about his infidelities. He made it easy for her to ignore what went on behind her back. Privately and publicly, he was very hands-on and affectionate with her. So everyone thought she was quite lucky indeed.

But as of this afternoon, all bets were off. Sheila couldn't ignore the fact that he had an illegitimate daughter, conceived during the absolute darkest period of her life. And that girl was in their lives now—a walking, breathing, eating reminder of his infidelity and that horrible time.

Her cell phone rang.

Sheila reached inside her purse and checked the Caller ID. *Dylan again.*

She wasn't picking up. So far, there had been two texts, and this would be the second voicemail.

She thought about the public humiliation. It would soon get around that he'd had an extramarital affair and a child with another woman. Sheila realized people would stop thinking of her as lucky. Now they'd just think she was stupid, a complete nincompoop. That was a word no one used anymore, yet it seemed wildly appropriate for how she felt about herself at this moment.

Dylan was finished leaving voicemail number two.

Sheila gently swayed back and forth on the swing. She listened to the rusty chains squeak—and then she listened to Dylan's message:

"Hey, honey, it's me again," he whispered. "Please, call or text me so I know you're okay. I'm going out of my mind here. Like I started to tell you in the last message, I managed to get a walk-in at this clinic, and the girl and

I took a paternity test. They said I'll get the results tonight or tomorrow morning. After that, I dropped her off at the place she's staying while in town. God, it's a real dump, too. Anyway, she's there now. So she won't be coming back here to the house tonight. I called Matt Leonard and talked to him about all the legal angles—you know, custody, and what's going to happen to her mother's estate. I guess what I'm saying here is that we have to prepare ourselves for the possibility the test will be positive. I haven't said anything to the kids. I figure we should wait for the test results. Why tell them about it unless we absolutely have to? They're home. I convinced them you had a thing at the retirement home. Anyway . . . please, please, call and tell me you're okay. Or better yet, just come home. I can't stand this. I'm so sorry. I really—"

The voicemail cut him off.

Sheila shut off her phone. The kids were fine, that was all she needed to know. The rest of it was his problem.

And wasn't it just like him to be so practical about the whole thing? The poor girl came to them for help, and here he was, making her take a paternity test and phoning their lawyer. Of course, it was the smart thing to do. Sheila wondered what he planned on telling their children. That this girl was a long-lost cousin?

The wind off the lake seemed to whip through her, and she shuddered. She really should have brought along a jacket. Hell, she should have packed a bag. She didn't want to go back home tonight.

Sheila wasn't sure she wanted to go back at all.

9/24 Mon—5:30 P.M.

Glad I brought this journal with me. Gives me something to do while I watch her. I'm sitting in the car, across the street from a little park.

I didn't think she'd stick around the house in light of this afternoon's revelation. From the way she swills down the bourbon late at night, I was betting she'd go on a bender in some bar. Instead the stupid bitch came here to this playground, like a little kid running away from home. She's been here practically two hours now, just sitting on the swing. I can only guess what's going on inside that half a brain of hers.

I keep thinking about the gun I have tucked under the seat here. Wouldn't it be perfect if I could walk across the street, blow her brains out, put the gun in her hand, and then drive away? If only the gun were registered in her name, and there weren't people around. They'd find her there by the swing set. Troubled, mentally unbalanced wife shoots herself. Once investigators got an earful of what happened to her this afternoon, it would be an open-and-shut case of suicide. And if that wasn't good enough, they just needed to check into her history and what happened down in Portland.

Wouldn't it be funny if she just got up, walked down to the beach, right into the water, and then just kept walking until the lake swallowed her up? I'd sit right here and watch her drown herself. Maybe I'd even applaud.

Then all my work and planning would be in vain, of course. But I wouldn't mind. It would be a sweet sight to see.

Unfortunately, I know Sheila too well. She'll sit there and stew a while longer. Then she'll grab dinner someplace. After that, she'll slink home to the kiddies, and to him. That's how it's going to happen.

The poor, silly stupid bitch.
I'm going to make her sorry she didn't drown
herself when she had the chance.

It was nearly seven o'clock. Dylan was making the kids breakfast for dinner: pancakes, eggs, bacon, and sausage. The last time he'd cooked a big breakfast for everyone like this had been brunch on Mother's Day. Tonight, he was throwing the meal together out of desperation. The boys were excited, like it was a special occasion. But Hannah was being a pill, acting as if he was trying to poison her. She insisted on turkey bacon and egg whites only. Until last year, she'd eaten like a truck driver all the time and looked absolutely fine. Now she was skin and bones. What killed him was that later tonight, she'd probably eat half a bag of Cheetos with a Diet Coke. So really, why not have regular bacon and eggs for her meal?

The cooking was a welcome distraction. Sheila had been gone only three and a half hours, but he was terrified that she would do something rash. This wasn't the first time he'd been on suicide watch with her, but it was the first time in Seattle. Any minute now, he expected the phone to ring, and it would be some official-sounding voice on the other end of the line telling him that Mrs. O'Rourke had tied up rush-hour traffic while jumping off the Aurora Bridge, and they were still fishing her body out of Lake Union right now. Could he come down to the morgue in an hour to identify her?

He wished she would at least text him back: *I'm OK.* But then that would relieve some of his suffering, wouldn't it? As if he weren't paying enough for his sins with this girl showing up out of nowhere. Actually, he didn't blame Sheila for putting him through the wringer. But he knew how depressed she could get, and he was worried sick. He couldn't shake this sense of doom.

He knew it was too early for the paternity test results to be ready, but that didn't stop him from checking his email twice—just in case. Still nothing.

At one point, while he was flipping the pancakes, it occurred to him that if this were a regular Monday night, he'd have gone to the gym. And maybe he would have seen Brooke again. More than anything, he wished it were just a regular Monday night.

He'd told the kids they could eat in front of the TV downstairs or wherever they wanted. As he was serving up the plates, he kept thinking that, in all likelihood, there would be one more for dinner tomorrow night—and for many, many nights after that.

The Caller ID showed the time of his last voicemail: 9:23. That had been just a few minutes ago. Once again, Sheila hadn't picked up. Dylan had been pretty brief with this latest message.

Sheila sat at a window table in a pub called McGilvra's, across from Madison Park Beach. It had two walls of windows that looked out at Lake Washington. The waiter had cleared away her half-eaten French dip dinner over an hour ago. Nursing her second glass of merlot, Sheila feigned interest in the football game on the big-screen TV. She still didn't want to go home any more than she wanted to talk to Dylan.

Yet she checked his message: "Hey, Sheila," he whispered. She imagined him up in their bedroom, someplace out of earshot of the kids. "You've been gone over six hours now, and I'm going pretty crazy with worry here. I got the paternity test results back from the lab. They emailed me about ten minutes ago. I didn't know they worked this late, but I guess they do. So—I'll tell you about it when you come home. Then we can discuss it. Hurry home, okay? And please, be careful. And—just know, we'll work this out."

The son of a bitch, he figured he'd dangle that hook out there, and she'd bite. He must have assumed her curiosity would get the best of her. To find out the results of the paternity test, she'd either have to text him or go home. Either way, he could stop worrying about her—if he really was so terribly worried, like he said.

If not for the kids, she wouldn't be going back home tonight.

She already knew the test results. Sheila was almost certain the girl was his daughter. And they'd be responsible for her now.

Swell. She was stepmother to the pierced, peroxided, shoplifting street urchin who had been stalking and harassing her. And at one point earlier today, her darling new stepdaughter had called her a *fucking bitch*.

Sheila managed the household budget and accounts. As flighty as Dylan made her feel sometimes, she was actually the responsible, practical one. Financially, they were comfortable. They could afford college for both Hannah and Steve. But having three kids in college at the same time would plunge them into debt. Of course, Eden would probably be in jail in a couple of years. So they wouldn't have to worry about college tuition for Little Miss Sunshine.

Actually, Sheila felt sorry for her.

But at the same time, she hoped to God the girl didn't expect to stay with them. Sheila didn't think she could take it.

Someone was standing by her table.

Startled, Sheila looked up at the waiter. She realized she had tears in her eyes.

"Um, can I get you something else?" he asked, a bit bewildered.

She quickly wiped her eyes. "No, I guess I better head home," she said quietly. "May I have the check, please?"

CHAPTER THIRTEEN

Monday—9:52 P.M.

"I think something's up with Mom or Dad," Steve whispered. "Since when does Mom have a *sudden thing* at the retirement home? I get the feeling there's trouble. Dad's kind of on edge, like super serious tonight. Have you noticed?"

"Not really," Hannah sighed, her thumbs working on the keypad of her phone.

She sat on the other end of the sectional sofa from Steve. They were in the family room in the basement, watching some decent-to-horrible singing auditions on *The Voice*. But Steve had to back up and replay it every few minutes for things Hannah missed because she couldn't put her stupid phone down for two seconds. He used to love watching this type of TV show with her because they'd make fun of the contestants and crack each other up. But now, she was always so busy texting with her friends during every movie or show that it was a total drag to watch TV with her—and a painful reminder that he had no friends of his own.

Until last year, he and his older sister had been close. Hannah used to hang out with a very small group of sweet, funny, not-especially-cool girls she'd grown up with. They were like older sisters to Steve, and they seemed to like him, too. Then all of a sudden, Hannah got super status conscious and dumped those longtime friends. They never came over to the house anymore. She had this whole new set of friends, each one prettier, skinnier, and more stuck-up than the next. And Hannah and her new crowd wanted nothing to do with him.

She was pretty, too, now. Of course, she paid more attention to her looks than she ever had in her life. The only thing she stared at more than her phone was the mirror. She wore makeup now, and her long, light brown hair always looked beautiful. She'd become a total clothes-horse, too. Suddenly, she was popular. But as far as Steve was concerned, Hannah had been a lot more fun before she became cool.

Steve looked at her and then at the TV. She was so un-involved, she might as well not have been in the room. He would have had a better time watching TV with Gabe, who had already gone to bed.

"Did you see that mess on top of Dad's desk earlier?" Steve asked.

Eyes on her phone, Hannah shook her head.

"Well, he's put most of it away," Steve explained. "But when I came home, his desk was totally covered with heaps of paper and crap. And he's really distracted. He keeps checking his phone. I mean, usually he shuts it off when he comes home. Earlier, I heard him talking to someone. He mentioned a clinic and test results. Do you think one of them is sick, like seriously sick?" Steve glanced over at her. "Are you even listening to me?"

Tearing her eyes off the phone, Hannah looked up at him for a second and sighed. "Neither one of them is dying, you drama queen."

"*Drama queen*?" Steve repeated. "What's that supposed to mean?"

"Oh, it's just an expression, stupid. It's not a slur on your precious manhood."

"Okay, you explain to me what's going on. Mom supposedly has this unscheduled thing at the retirement home, and I hear Dad talking about some kind of medical tests . . ."

"If it's anything at all," Hannah said, "I'll bet one of those old farts at the home croaked, probably one of Mom's favorites. Either that or someone there just got the bad news that they're *going* to croak. Remember last year with Hildie, or whatever her name was? They told her she was terminal, and then Mom was over there all the time, and she was moping around here for like two weeks until the lady finally died. That's probably what it is."

"Maybe," Steve said. But why would his parents be so secretive about it? He was convinced that whatever was going on, it was something dire, something that would have an effect on all of them.

Steve didn't say anything for a few minutes. On TV, a young woman in a wheelchair was belting out Aretha Franklin's "Respect."

"Your girlfriend, Barbie Grimes, might be breaking up with her boyfriend," Hannah announced, consulting her phone. "Now's your chance to make your big move on her, hotshot."

She was being sarcastic, of course. Still, Steve wondered out loud: "Do you think she'd be interested to know there was a girl named Barbara Grimes, same age practically, and she and her sister were killed in a famous murder case in Chicago in the nineteen fifties? I wonder if she knows . . ."

"Oh, I'll bet if you told her that, she'd be fascinated. Completely charmed," Hannah replied, rolling her eyes.

"God, where do you get this murder stuff anyway? Could you possibly be any creepier? You're such a freak."

Frowning, Steve turned his attention back to the TV. The girl in the wheelchair was getting a standing ovation.

He heard the front door open and close upstairs, then footsteps and his parents murmuring.

"You can relax now," Hannah said, focused on her phone. "Mom's not dead."

Steve wondered if he should go up there and ask what was going on. But he heard the basement door yawn open. His mother came down the stairs.

"Is everything okay?" Steve asked.

From the bottom step, she gave them a tight smile. "Fine," she said. "Is your homework done, guys?"

"Like an hour ago," Hannah answered.

Steve just nodded. The way his mom had asked, it seemed kind of strained. "What's going on?" he asked.

"How much longer is this show on?" his mother asked.

"It's got like ten more minutes," Steve answered. "Why?"

"When it's over, your dad and I want to talk to you both up in the dining room. Okay?"

Both Steve and Hannah just nodded. Then their mother turned and headed back up the stairs. Steve heard more murmuring.

He glanced at Hannah, who had put down her phone. She stared back at him. For a moment, she looked so much like her old self—and she looked scared. "Shit, Stevie," she whispered. "Maybe she really is dying."

The test results showed a 99.6 percent probability that Dylan was Eden's father.

"She's your daughter, all right," Sheila hissed, pacing back and forth in the den. They had the door closed. "I trust her about as far as I could throw her, the little liar. If it wasn't her and her slimy boyfriend sending those texts and creeping around the house, then who was it?"

Dylan stood by his desk, sorting through papers and trying to tidy up what was left of the mess she'd made earlier. "I think someone in that dump where she's staying—one of the boyfriend's friends—they must have gotten wind of the situation, and they decided to screw around with us. Eden doesn't want to stay there anymore, and I don't blame her. I figure, tomorrow, we can put her in the guest room in the basement for a while, and then—"

"No, that's not going to work," Sheila interrupted. "For one, Hannah has called dibs on that bedroom. Do you want her resenting her new stepsister even more? Besides, I don't trust that little monster down there. I don't trust her upstairs near us, either, but at least with her sleeping upstairs we can keep closer tabs on her. I can just see her down in that basement room, sneaking her creepy boyfriend into the house through the laundry room door—or maybe sneaking out to meet him. By the way—and actually, this is very important. The boyfriend, that Brodie character, he's not setting foot in this house ever again. That's non-negotiable. You'll have to make that clear to her if she's staying with us. Our house, our rules."

"Honey, I'm not sure she'll agree to that."

"Well, she's your daughter. You make her agree. I'm not having that lowlife in our house or on our property. On top of everything else, I saw him shoplifting. In fact, you better check your precious CD collection, because he was going through it earlier today. He's probably on drugs. I wouldn't be surprised if she is, too. While you were getting that paternity test, you should have had the clinic do a drug screening on her."

Sheila could tell he was concerned now. She was
saying things he obviously hadn't even considered. She
was trying to be practical and realistic about this. If
she got emotional, she'd fall apart. "You know, we have
to be on our guard with her," she went on. "People on
drugs steal to support their habit. I'm telling you, when
they waltzed in here unannounced this afternoon, they
started looking around at everything, just like they were
shopping."

"Okay, okay," Dylan muttered, rubbing his forehead.
"She'll have to dump the boyfriend. And we'll look for
signs that she's on drugs."

"Doctor and dental appointments for her—this week,
if possible," Sheila said, pointing at him. "A lot of drug
addicts have terrible teeth. If we can't get a drug screening, we'll at least have some clues after Dr. Amato looks
at her teeth. She probably has a mess of cavities we'll
have to pay to fix, too, lucky us. And she's your daughter,
so you make the appointments. You explain to Dr. Chris-
topher and Dr. Amato just who she is."

Frowning, Dylan nodded.

"Tomorrow, we'll help Hannah move her things down
to the basement, and we'll put Eden in her room."

"Honey, the kids will be up here any minute. What are
we going to tell them?"

"What are *you* going to tell them?" she shot back.
"This is your goddamn mess, you can explain it to our
children." She nodded toward the dining room. "And just
so you know, I'm not going to sit in there and listen to
you *lie* to them, either. They deserve to know the truth."

"Oh, Jesus," he murmured. He actually had tears in
his eyes. He plopped down in his desk chair.

"Did you think you could get away with some other
story to save face?" she asked. "You should have known
the kids would find out about you eventually. Maybe you

can try to explain to them about our unspoken agreement, which has me calling you out on your shit every two or three years—just to remind you I'm not a complete idiot—and then you promising you'll never stray again. I wonder how that'll go over with our children." She sighed. "I did a pretty good job keeping them in the dark about your affairs. I suppose they'll end up blaming me, too. And maybe they should."

"I've told you that I wouldn't mind going to couples counseling," he murmured.

"Well, I'd mind," she replied. "I don't want to dredge up the past. I don't want to have to relive that pain. You're the one with the problem keeping our marriage vows, not me. You go see a therapist if you're so gung-ho on the idea."

He rubbed his forehead again and pinched the top of his nose between his eyes. "Hannah and Steve will be up here soon. I think it's best if we—we only tell them about the Eden situation . . ."

"Fine," she said. "Go ahead and make out like it was an isolated incident. Maybe the kids will believe you."

Looking hopeless, Dylan just stared at his messy desktop.

Sheila almost felt sorry for him, but not quite. She was still furious—and trying to be as calm, controlled, and practical as she could. She sat down on the edge of the desk. "By the way, we have to enroll her in school, too. You can send her to a private school to help avoid any embarrassment for Hannah and Steve, but that would cost us a small fortune. And the truth will come out sooner or later anyway. Plus, it would humiliate them even more if we were trying to hide it and their friends found out. So—we're probably better off sending her to school with them. You better brace them for that. On the plus side, this is a Seattle public school, so a lot of their classmates are from nontraditional families. It won't affect Steve or Gabe so much, but Hannah will not be pleased. I promise you that."

He wiped his eyes and looked at her. "Honey, I'm so sorry."

She sighed. "No one has slept down in that guest room for a couple of months. I'm sure the mattresses are fine. But you can test them out tonight, because you're certainly not sleeping in our bed."

He frowned. "Sheila, how's it going to look to the kids if I'm exiled down to the basement tonight?"

She heard Steve and Hannah coming up the basement stairs.

"It's going to look exactly like it is," she whispered. "Like their father is a lying, cheating bastard, and right now, I don't want anything to do with him."

"How could you do this to me?" Hannah asked their dad.

Everyone was at their usual spot around the dinner table. Steve hadn't said a thing so far. He didn't have to. Hannah was the one asking all the questions. And after every answer, she expressed utter horror, outrage, and disgust—enough for the two of them. She acted like this was something their parents had done specifically to humiliate her.

Steve was still processing the fact that he had an older sister he'd never known about—actually a half sister, specifically an illegitimate half sister. He still couldn't wrap his head around it.

Now he knew why his dad had been whispering earlier

about a clinic and test results. He'd been talking about a
paternity test.

Steve was so disillusioned with his father. He remembered how traumatized he'd been at age ten, after learning
where babies came from. He hadn't been able to look his
parents in the eyes for at least a week. They'd seemed so
alien to him. That was how he felt about his father now,
only worse. He knew his father wasn't perfect. But he
had no idea his dad was capable of anything so sleazy.

His father wasn't in public relations for nothing. He'd
delivered the news to them about their half sister in a
very smooth way, with a gradual buildup: *There's this
sixteen-year-old girl from Portland . . . her mother died
suddenly . . . she has no family, and she needs a place to
stay . . . I knew the mother . . . In fact, I knew her during
a period when your mom and I were having a lot of problems, and we were almost separated . . . I knew the
mother intimately . . .*

While his father had been talking—and Hannah had
been interrupting with an astonished "What?" and "Oh
my God, I can't believe this!"—Steve had glanced over
at his mom, staring at the soup tureen in the center of the
table. Her arms crossed in front of her, she hadn't said
a word.

And she was still quiet.

Steve kept telling himself that at least neither one of
his parents was dying. But still, it felt like something had
indeed died.

"So—let me get this straight," Hannah continued, turning to their mom. "That piece of street trash whose picture
you sent me—the same girl who was stalking you—she's
my half sister? And she's coming to stay with us?"

"Yes," their father said quietly. "And it would be a good
idea not to call her 'street trash.' I want you guys to be
nice to her. She's been through a very tough time."

"Well, just how long is she staying? A week, a couple of months, or what?"

"We're not sure yet," their father answered.

"Well, I'm not giving up my room for her," Hannah said, shaking her head. "Forget it."

"She can have my room," Steve finally spoke up. "I wouldn't mind giving it up if I can move down to the basement."

"No!" Hannah cried. "No, I'll move. I was promised the basement bedroom ages ago. She can have my room. I'll start cleaning it out as soon as I get back from school tomorrow. I prefer the basement anyway . . ." She abruptly got to her feet, almost tipping over her chair. "In fact, the farther away I can be from the rest of this family, the better. I just can't believe this has happened."

Tears in her eyes, she shook her head at their father. "Daddy, you were like my hero. How could you?"

Before he could answer, she swiveled around and ran out of the dining room. Steve heard her footsteps retreating up the stairs.

"She took that well, don't you think?" Steve's mother murmured, very deadpan.

His dad looked like he was in pain. Hunched forward, elbows on the table, he rubbed his face.

"What are you guys going to tell Gabe?" Steve asked quietly.

"We'll explain it to him tomorrow, your father and me," his mom answered.

"Does this mean you guys are going to break up?"

His mom sighed. "To be totally honest, Stevie, that's a good question."

"We're going to get through this," his father said, clearing his throat.

"How did her mother die, anyway?" Steve asked.

He saw a look pass between his parents. For a moment,

it seemed like the question caused even more tension than the one about divorcing. It was like he'd touched a nerve. His mother even shuddered a little.

"Um, they think it was an accident," his father finally answered. "She fell off the roof of her apartment building."

CHAPTER FOURTEEN

Tuesday, September 25—6:38 P.M.

Sheila was fixing her special lasagna for Eden's first dinner with the family and her first night in her new home. Sheila cringed inside at the thought of it. But she prepared the special dinner anyway. She even made one section meatless—in case the girl was a vegetarian.

She'd canceled two dance lessons so she could get ready for Eden today. Dylan had called in sick to work for the first time in four years so he could make doctor and dentist appointments for Eden, talk to their lawyer, call the high school about Eden's enrollment, and clean out the basement guest room, where he'd slept last night. The guest room was like the house's junk drawer; if someone didn't know what to do with something, then they threw it on one of the guest room's twin beds, set it on top of the desk, or stashed it in the closet. It was a major chore getting the room ready for Hannah.

Sheila had said about twenty words to Dylan all day. He would try to talk to her or give her an update on some task he had accomplished, and she'd utter the same icy response: *Fine.*

She must have said, "Fine," to him—and nothing else—about a dozen times today.

Once Hannah came home from school around four

o'clock, the three of them started stripping her bedroom walls of pictures and posters, clearing the shelves of books and trinkets, and emptying out the dresser and closet. They all worked together in angry silence—punctuated by an occasional question.

Dylan to Hannah: "Do you want this lamp?"

Hannah (sullenly): "Yes, and the bean bag chair, too. It's mine. I bought it with my babysitting money, remember?"

It was bizarre: a family working together in a room full of souvenirs, memories, and personal effects, and no one was talking. They were like a bunch of disgruntled, underpaid movers.

In a day full of packing and moving things, Sheila was tempted to pack her own bags and leave—if only for a few days. The notion of going to Vermont (she'd never been) to watch the leaves change and take a lot of contemplative walks suddenly seemed very appealing. But she felt a sense of responsibility to her kids to be here during this crisis. She felt sort of responsible for Eden, too. Even though Sheila intensely disliked her, she still thought the kid deserved a break. She would have kicked Dylan out of the house, but that would mean he wouldn't have to deal with any of this mess, and it was *his* mess. Besides, the last time she'd kicked him out of the house, he'd started up with "Toni." And look what had happened.

Sheila wasn't sure where he was sleeping tonight, but it certainly wouldn't be with her.

In keeping with her resolve to make Eden feel welcome, she changed the bedding and cleaned up Hannah's pillaged bedroom. On the walls, her daughter had left behind posters of the Eiffel Tower and *Breakfast at Tiffany's* that she was "sick of." But the walls were still marred with smudges and tape marks. Sheila partially covered the blemishes with a couple of cheaply framed posters they had in storage: Monet's *Water Lilies* and van Gogh's *Sunflowers*. She cut some flowers from her garden, put them in a vase, and set it in Eden's new room. She also got some notepads, paper, and pens and left them in the desk drawer. And on top of the desk, Sheila left travel-size soap, shampoo, conditioner, lotion, and a new toothbrush.

When Gabe came home from football practice at five, she and Dylan sat down with him in the dining room and tried to explain about the girl who was moving in with them tonight. Gabe didn't completely understand. "How did Dad have a daughter with this Portland lady if they weren't married and he's married to you?" he asked at one point.

That's an excellent question, honey, Sheila wanted to reply. But she let Dylan explain. Gabe didn't seem traumatized by the revelation, just confused.

Then Sheila had started putting dinner together.

At six, Dylan had left to pick up Eden. She'd arrived at the house with a backpack and two ratty-looking suitcases. Sheila had been hoping against hope that the girl might have cleaned herself up a little for them, maybe even gone a little easy on the Marilyn Manson eyeliner, but no such luck. She looked as punk-rock skanky as she had in all their previous encounters. And she smelled like cigarettes.

Hannah emerged from her new bedroom in the basement for exactly three minutes so Eden could meet her—along with the rest of the family. The introduction of the half sisters was strained: the princess and the Goth girl. They each nodded and uttered a cautious "hi," and then Hannah retreated to her new room. Steve, bless his heart, tried to be nice. He went to hug her and Eden flinched—like he was about to frisk her or something. Steve managed to get in a quick, painfully awkward embrace before backing away. Then he seemed totally embarrassed. Gabe just shook her hand and remained silent.

Sheila took Eden upstairs to show the girl her new bedroom. Dylan followed with the suitcases. In the bedroom doorway, Sheila told Eden that she could decorate the room however she wanted. "Do you have some furniture or things from your apartment in Portland?" she asked.

"We did, but the asshole landlord sold or donated it all because we were behind on the rent," Eden replied—with her dark-cherry lip curled. "I guess the janitor saved a couple of boxes of junk. It's in storage there."

Sheila said they'd try to get the boxes back for her soon. She assured her the art on the walls was just temporary. Dylan said he would repaint the room any color of her choice. Maybe they could pick up some paint samples tomorrow.

"Well, we'll let you get settled in," Dylan said, taking Sheila's arm.

Sheila gingerly wrestled away from him. "I'll be down in a minute," she said.

After Dylan started down the hall, she worked up a smile and turned to her new stepdaughter. "You can call me Sheila," she said. "I guess we got off to a rocky start yesterday. But I'd like you to think of me as a friend—and not your evil stepmother. I'm here if you need someone to talk to. And don't hesitate to ask for anything. I know all this must be pretty strange for you, but give us a try. You might end up liking us . . ."

She'd been thinking all day of what she'd say to this girl, something to break the ice.

Sheila had imagined the snarky punk girl's face softening, and then her saying, with a grateful smile, *I'm so glad you said that, Sheila. I have to admit, I've been a little scared that no one would like me. And I'm really sorry I called you a "fucking bitch" yesterday. I can tell you're a nice person. It was a terrible thing to say. Will you forgive me?*

Then Sheila would hug her, and the poor girl would start crying on her shoulder.

Unfortunately, that didn't happen.

After Sheila told her, "You might end up liking us," Eden just stared at her for a few moments, her eyes half closed.

"Is that all?" the girl asked. "Because I'd really like to be alone so I can unpack."

"Of course," Sheila said, with a pinched smile. "Dinner's in about fifteen minutes." She closed the bedroom door and retreated down the hall for the stairs.

Now, she was heating up the garlic bread and making the salad. Dylan was setting the dinner table. "How did it go upstairs with the two of you?" he asked, collecting the cloth napkins from the drawer.

"Fine," Sheila muttered, cutting tomatoes for the salad. "She's a real sweetie pie."

"That bad, huh?"

She turned her back to him and kept slicing.

Dylan sighed. "In the car, on the way here, I told her that—for now—her boyfriend wasn't welcome in our house. Maybe that's why she's a little hostile. I also told her about the doctor and dental appointments. I guess she hasn't been to either in quite a while."

Sheila just nodded. She could have bet on that.

"I used the doctors' appointments to segue to any previous or current medical issues—including alcohol or drug abuse, or allergies, or psychological problems . . ."

Smooth, thought Sheila. *The kid probably saw right through him.*

"She seemed to know what I was driving at," Dylan admitted. "She said she doesn't like the taste of alcohol, and she tried marijuana a couple of times and didn't like that, either. I don't think she'd tell us about trying pot if she wanted to hide something."

That's just where she's being clever, Sheila thought. "Well, she must smoke like a chimney," she said. "Did you get a whiff of her? Unless Donna Karan has a new scent called 'Ashtray,' that girl's a smoker. You better tell her she can't smoke in the house."

"I already asked her if she's a smoker, and she said no," Dylan explained. "She said everyone in that rathole where she was staying smokes. It's one reason she wanted out of there."

He touched her arm and smiled. "And that's the most you've talked to me all day. You even made a joke."

"It wasn't very funny," Sheila muttered. Turning away from him, she grabbed the potholders and took the lasagna out of the oven to rest. "Will you please finish setting the table? Then you can tell the kids—and her—that dinner's almost ready."

At the dinner table, Dylan desperately tried to get Eden talking, asking her if she was in any sports or groups at school, what her favorite subjects were, whether she'd traveled much outside Portland, and if she had any favorite TV shows. The girl kept her answers curt. Steve also tentatively tried drawing her out, but she wouldn't engage. And she wouldn't touch her food. Sheila had offered her meat or meatless, and Eden had picked a meatless portion of lasagna. But she just kept pushing the pasta around the plate with her fork.

"Honey, don't you like lasagna?" Sheila finally asked.

"My name's Eden," she said. She dropped the fork on her plate with a clank. "I can't eat this shit. I'm vegan. And this has cheese on it."

Sheila took a deep breath. "Well, why don't you have some bread and salad? And if you're still hungry after that, we can see if there's anything in the kitchen you might like."

"I can't eat the bread. It's got butter on it. That's dairy."

"God," Hannah muttered. "And you guys think I'm picky."

Dylan passed the salad bowl to Eden, and seemed to work up a smile for her. "After dinner, why don't you make a list of the foods you like? Tomorrow, we can go shopping."

"What?" Hannah said. "Is she getting a special menu? That's not fair."

Sheila said nothing, but for a change, she and Hannah actually agreed on something.

Dylan shot Hannah a look. "That's enough," he said under his breath. "Just chill."

"And I guess it's perfectly fine for her to say *shit* at the dinner table," Hannah continued. "If I did that, especially in front of Gabe, you'd bite my head off."

"I said *that's enough*," Dylan growled.

"I'm not really hungry anyway," Eden said. She got up from the table, pulled her phone out of the pocket of her hoodie, and looked at it as she left the dining room.

Sheila watched her head up the stairs. She got to her feet, grabbed her empty plate, and then marched around to Eden's place at the table. She swept up the full plate and set it on top of her own. Then she stomped into the kitchen and dumped both the plates in the sink with a loud clatter.

"Honey?" Dylan called tentatively.

Sheila ignored him. She grabbed a jacket from the hallway closet, threw it on, and then stepped outside. She figured she would walk around the block to cool off.

As she left the house, she slammed the front door shut behind her and spitefully hoped that the little bitch upstairs heard it.

* * *

Steve glanced at the fake-antique Union Pacific Railroad clock on his bedroom wall: a quarter to eleven. His new stepsister had been in the bathroom for sixty-five minutes so far. The shower had been on most of the time, too. Okay, so she *had* looked pretty grimy. But really, how the hell long did it take her to get clean? Hannah was always giving him grief about his long showers, but this girl was setting a new house record tonight.

Steve had heard the shower go off with a squeak about ten minutes ago. So what was she doing now?

He just needed to brush his teeth and wash his face. Plus, his acne cream was in there.

He finally headed down the hall and knocked on the bathroom door. "Hey, Eden?" he said timidly. He kept his voice down because he didn't want to wake Gabe, sleeping down the corridor. "I don't mean to rush you, but I need to get in there—for just a few minutes."

He heard an "Uh-huh," and wasn't sure if that meant she would be out soon, or, "screw you," or what.

Steve thought about going downstairs and telling his parents that his new stepsister was a bathroom hog, but he didn't want to be a jerk about it. He decided to give her a few more minutes. He retreated into his room, sat down on the edge of his bed, and waited.

When his dad had first told him about an unknown stepsister, Steve had felt sorry for her. It sounded like she'd had a lot of tough breaks. Even though she looked kind of skanky in the photo his mom took, Steve had made up his mind to give her a chance and be nice. But now that he'd met her, he found her very unfriendly, even kind of hostile. Plus, she stank. Sometime after the dinner from hell, he'd knocked on her door and asked if she wanted to watch TV in the basement with Gabe and him.

"You can pick whatever show or movie you want to watch," he called out so she could hear him past the door she refused to open. "Would you like to do that? Would you like to watch TV with us?"

"Not really," she called back, sounding annoyed.

"Okay," he said, giving up.

But before walking away, he thought he heard her whispering to someone. He figured she was on the phone with her skuzzy boyfriend.

His dad had told him to give her time to adjust. But Steve didn't like her, and he didn't feel so sorry for her anymore.

The person he felt sorry for was his mother, who—more than anyone else—seemed to be busting her butt to make this girl feel welcome. And more than anyone, she had every reason to loathe having her here. Steve couldn't quite forgive his dad for what he'd done. It was such a betrayal of his mom. Steve wondered if this was just the tip of the iceberg. Maybe his dad had cheated a lot more than just this one time, seventeen years ago. Steve figured that would kind of explain why his mom was sometimes emotionally fragile.

When his mom had first texted the photo of Eden and her boyfriend, she'd said they were shoplifters who were stalking her. They were potentially dangerous. But then, when his dad broke the news to them about Eden being his daughter, suddenly they took it back about how terrible she was. It was all just a misunderstanding, his father had said. But Steve wondered if his mom's original assessment of the girl and her boyfriend was correct. Steve still didn't trust her. He felt squeamish having her just down the hall from him while he slept. It was like having a member of the Manson family spending the night—only she'd be spending the next several nights, until God knew when. What was to keep her from sneaking her boyfriend in here in the middle of the night so the pair could kill the entire family? Of all the murder cases Steve had read about, some of the grisliest were when one family member killed another, or several others. No breaking and entering was necessary. The killer already knew the victim or victims—intimately.

Steve wished he had a lock on his bedroom door. Maybe he could set up some cans along his closed door before going to sleep tonight so if someone tried to sneak in, the cans would fall and the clatter would wake him up.

Down the hall, the sound of the bathroom door opening jarred him out of his thoughts. Steve stood up—just as Eden appeared in his doorway.

She had a towel around her waist and was drying her platinum and pink hair with another towel. Otherwise, she was naked. She had a tiny potbelly and plump, round breasts with large, pale rose nipples. Covering her left shoulder was a big swirly tattoo that looked like a thorn bush.

Stunned, Steve couldn't help gaping at her. "Jeez," he muttered.

"The bathroom's yours, bro," she said with a blasé smile.

Part of it was sexy, because she was practically naked. But it was repulsive, too. She was his half sister, for God's sake! Mostly, it was just jarring.

She sauntered down the hall, and then Steve heard her bedroom door close.

For a few moments, he couldn't move. He wasn't sure why Eden had done that. As far as Steve knew, it wasn't normal. He'd seen his mom and Hannah in their underwear, but they didn't walk around the house half naked with their boobs hanging out. And he—along with his dad and brother—didn't walk around bare-assed, either.

Maybe she was one of those free spirits who embraced nudity. But it didn't seem that way. It seemed deliberate, almost as if she was flirting with him or trying to shock him. He was a little turned on, but mostly he felt confused and uncomfortable. He wondered if he should tell somebody about this.

But at this point, who could he confide in?

His old friend, Adam, would have told him not to breathe a word about it to anybody. Steve could just hear him: "Are you nuts? Why mess up a good thing?"

But she was his sister, and this didn't seem good at all. It felt gross—and wrong.

Still a bit stupefied, he wandered across the hall to the bathroom. The door was open, and the light was still on. Steam wafted in the air, and it smelled like Dove soap. There was a puddle on the floor. Every towel had been used and tossed on the floor, on the counter, or into the tub. The place was a complete mess.

It was as if she'd done it on purpose—to screw with him.

Just like appearing in his doorway that way.

The divorcée who had moved in next door obviously owned a dog—a very unhappy dog. It barked erratically: long yowling spells, then a break, and then it would start barking again.

Sheila wondered what was wrong with the new neighbor that she'd let the dog go on like that so late. The clock on the nightstand read 12:38 A.M. Sheila had changed into her old pink pajamas. Her face was washed and her hair in a ponytail. She hadn't turned down the bed yet. She wondered how she'd be able to fall asleep with all the noise next door.

She'd delayed going to bed while Eden was still awake. She hated the idea of everyone asleep in the house other than that strange, insolent girl down the hall. Sheila simply didn't trust her. So while the kids went to bed, one by one, Sheila kept checking the strip of light under Eden's bedroom door. Dylan had been the last to turn in. Tonight, he was in Gabe's room, sleeping in the bottom bunk—probably very soundly, the son of a bitch.

She'd DVR'd a World War II spy movie on Turner Classic Movies: *36 Hours* with James Garner and Eva Marie Saint. It was good enough to keep Sheila from dozing on the sofa in the den. Still, she paused the movie a few times to tiptoe upstairs and check the light under Eden's door. The movie ended shortly after midnight, and she was happy to see that the light was finally off in Eden's room.

But now she had this stupid dog promising to keep her awake. It sounded like the dog was in a room directly across the way from her and Dylan's bedroom. Sheila guessed that the noise wasn't as bad in other parts of the house because everyone else seemed to be sleeping through it. She stood by the window, squinting at the Curtis house. It was dark. It didn't look like anyone was home—except the poor dog, who wouldn't shut up.

Maybe with an Ambien, and some cotton in her ears, and the radio on low for background noise . . . maybe then she could fall asleep. But she didn't want to get too dependent on the drug. And a part of her didn't want to be completely knocked out—not with that girl down the hall.

More than anything, she just wanted this awful day to end.

Dylan and Steve had washed the dinner dishes by the time she'd returned from her walk. She'd decided to take the high road and go up to Eden's room. "I'm not going to have you starve your first night here," she'd told her.

"Now, come down to the kitchen, and let's find you something to eat."

Once Sheila had gotten Eden in the kitchen, she opened up all the cupboards to show the variety of food on hand. She said she'd be happy to cook something, or Eden could just help herself.

"What stuff here is yours?" Eden asked warily.

"What do you mean?"

"I don't want to take anything that's yours and then, later, have you pissed off at me when you see it's gone."

Sheila figured this was something left over from the girl's relationship with her mother. She assured Eden that she could help herself to anything. But Eden insisted on having Sheila point out what was hers exclusively.

"Well, okay. I'm the only one who drinks the cranberry juice, but you're welcome to it. No one else eats the rice crackers, or the Special K, or the orange marmalade, or the Yoplait. But please, feel free to help yourself . . ."

Eden finally sat down in the dinette booth and ate a PowerBar, pretzels, and a Diet Coke. But that wasn't until after Sheila had pointed out practically every type of food that she exclusively liked. It was strange. She tried to imagine what kind of incident had triggered this idiosyncrasy. Maybe Antonia had once beaten the crap out of her daughter for finishing off a jar of olives or something.

Eden also asked if there was a Laundromat nearby where she could wash her clothes.

"I can do that for you," Sheila told her. "I do the wash for everyone else in the house."

"You mean, no one here washes their own clothes?"

Sheila laughed. "I don't think anyone else in the house even knows how to operate the washer or dryer. And sometimes, I feel like that's all I do around here. Just leave your clothes in a pile inside your door, and I'll take care of it."

Eden nodded.

Sheila wondered if a "thank you" or a smile would have killed the girl. But it felt like maybe they were connecting a little—finally. Then, without saying anything, Eden got to her feet and started out of the kitchen. She'd left a mess on the dinette table.

"Ah, honey, Eden?" Sheila said. "In this house, we clean up after ourselves."

The girl sighed and rolled her eyes. She stomped back to the table and grabbed the soda can and the PowerBar wrapper and dumped them in the garbage.

"We recycle, too," Sheila said, going over to pick the can and the paper out of the garbage. She tossed them in the recycling bin next to the garbage pail. "Here's where it goes. See? I mean, just for future reference."

Frowning, Eden watched her. "Yeah, I see. Is that all? Can I go now?"

Biting her lip, Sheila nodded.

She'd decided to spend the rest of the evening avoiding her, which had been easy. Eden had spent over an hour in the second-floor bathroom and the rest of the time barricaded in her new bedroom. Dylan had knocked on Eden's door to say good night, but Sheila had let him go solo on that venture. She'd had enough of Eden for one evening.

And she'd had enough of this shitty day.

She figured Ambien was the way to go tonight. Yes, it would probably knock her out, and she might not hear if Eden got up in the middle of the night. But the alternative was lying there wide awake, worrying, and listening to the barking dog. She just wished the kids' bedrooms had locks on the doors. The master bedroom and the guest room in the basement were the only ones with locks. Sheila convinced herself that Hannah was probably using the lock on her new bedroom tonight. It was clear that Hannah was pretty wary of Eden, too. Gabe had his dad in the bedroom to protect him, and Steve had the baseball bat.

Sheila went back into her bathroom and opened up the medicine chest to get her Ambien. Her hand automatically started reaching for it on the top shelf. But the prescription bottle wasn't there. It took her a moment to find the Ambien on the middle shelf, along with a prescribed medication for muscle spasms that she took whenever her back went haywire. Out of a habit developed when the kids were young, Sheila always kept prescription bottles on the top shelf where the kids couldn't reach them.

Someone had been through her medicine chest today.

"Goddamn it," she whispered.

Eden had been up here on the second floor by herself for most of the evening. Who else would have been in here? Had the little sneak been through all of her things?

Sheila hurried back to the bedroom and checked her dresser top. She had several perfume bottles there. The Estée Lauder, which she hardly ever used and kept behind the other vials, was now at the front of the collection. Sheila immediately checked her jewelry boxes to see if anything was gone. She kept her expensive baubles in one box and the cheap costume jewelry in another. She didn't see anything missing from either box. But maybe she just didn't realize it now. Maybe she wouldn't know a certain piece was gone until she went looking for that particular bracelet, necklace, brooch, or set of earrings.

God, she hated this. She felt so vulnerable—and violated.

And the damn dog next door was barking again.

Sheila glanced over at her purse on the chair beside her dresser. She'd kept her purse up here in the bedroom most of the night, thinking it would be safe up here. Talk about stupid. She reached inside and took out her wallet. The credit cards were all there, and she was pretty sure no money was missing. But her driver's license was upside down in the wallet's window.

Eden must have taken it out of the wallet and put it back wrong. The little street urchin wasn't even careful about covering her tracks. Sheila wondered what the girl had done with her driver's license. All she could think about was identity theft.

It was maddening. This girl was a stranger, and they were letting her into their house. Dylan had even given her the alarm code. What the hell was he thinking? What was to keep her from sharing it with her lowlife boyfriend?

Earlier, after hearing that Eden had been staying in a rundown dump, one of Sheila's main concerns had been the possibility of her bringing lice or bedbugs into the house. That seemed like small potatoes now. But it still seemed very possible, on top of everything else.

Sheila opened her door, crept down the hallway to Eden's room, and checked the threshold for the umpteenth time tonight. It looked like the lights were still off in there. A part of her wanted to double-check that Eden was really asleep—and in fact, in the room. There was always a chance the girl could have snuck out in the middle of the night. But if Eden was there in bed and awake, Sheila didn't want to get caught looking in on her. Then again, Sheila had every reason to barge in, wake up the little brat, and ask what the hell she'd been doing in her medicine cabinet and her purse. But she knew Eden would just deny it.

She slunk back to the master bedroom. Before accusing Eden of anything, she'd first check with her kids to make sure no one else had been in the bedroom. She would deal with it in the morning.

Sheila locked her bedroom door. She heard the dog next door let out a few more yelps. Yes, Ambien, and some cotton in her ears tonight. She just wanted to be unconscious. Half a tablet was her normal dosage, and she'd already cut a few pills in half. She checked that the pill half looked like all the others before she swallowed it with some water.

In the medicine chest, she found some foam earplugs Dylan had bought but never used. She worked them into her ears. The sound of her closing the medicine chest was muffled. She hoped it would block out the barking, too.

Switching off the bathroom light, she stepped back into the bedroom and glanced at her dresser top again. She wondered what Eden was doing in here anyway. Just snooping?

Sheila wasn't going to let it gnaw at her and keep her awake. She told herself again that it could all wait until morning. She was already feeling a bit drowsy.

The neighbor's dog barked again, but it sounded far off. With the blanket over her head, Sheila figured she'd hardly hear the barking at all.

She peeled back the bedspread, and that was when she saw a black thing crawling on her pillow.

Sheila reeled back.

The spider's body was the size of a quarter, with legs extending at least an inch. It almost looked like a tarantula.

Without thinking, Sheila grabbed the paperback off

her nightstand and swatted at the bug. But it crawled under her sheets. Sheila tore back the sheet and slammed it with the book again and again, killing it this time.

Trying to catch her breath, she took a few Kleenex from the box on her nightstand and cleaned up the mess. Then she checked under the pillows and shook out the bedding to make sure the bug didn't have a companion.

In a less panicked moment, she might have gotten a piece of paper and patiently waited for the spider to crawl on it so she could take it outside. But this bug caught her by surprise.

As Sheila flushed it down the toilet, her heart was still racing. At the same time, the Ambien was kicking in. She felt dizzy and weak. She shuddered at the thought of the bug guts on one little section of the sheets. But she was too damn tired to change the bedding right now.

Standing in the bathroom doorway, she looked at the rumpled bed with the coverlet on the floor. She felt queasy about sleeping in here tonight. She wasn't sure what to do.

But she knew one thing.

It was now quite clear what Eden had been doing in her room earlier tonight.

CHAPTER FIFTEEN

9/26—Notes

House alarm code: *08291940

WA state driver's license (also see photo):
#OROURSA267NP

O'Rourke
Sheila Ann (Driscoll)

DOB: 2/16/74

578 Roanoke Pl E
Seattle, WA 98102-0000

Sex: F—Hght: 5-6
Wgt: 120—Eyes: Blue
Class—End: None
Restrictions: None

Signature samples (see photo/scan—more to come)

Hair samples (from brush on dresser—enclosed)
Used Kleenex (from purse—enclosed)

American Express # (see photo/scan)
Visa # (see photo/scan)
Social: 328-35-4159

Wells Fargo Bank Account (checking):
#000073724995

Blank Checks (#2149—from end of current book)
*   (#2157—from new/unused book)*

DRUGS:
Zolpidem 10 mg (Ambien)
Robaxin 500 mg (for muscle spasms)
L-Theanine 200 mg (stress formula/nonprescrip)
Melatonin 10 mg (nonprescrip)
Aspirin
Women's Multivitamin Supplement
Vitamin D
Vitamin C

–No one else uses washer or dryer—possible
* short/electric shock*
–No one else does gardening—check fertilizer for
* arsenic or other toxins*

FOOD & DRINK ONLY SHE CONSUMES:
Cranberry Juice—poison? Eye drops?
Special K cereal—rat poison?
Orange marmalade—jar currently opened/fridge
Yoplait—one container now open/half
eaten/fridge
Rice Crackers
Pickles—jar opened/fridge
Tea—in bags
Half & Half—carton currently open/fridge
Bourbon—of course . . .

Not bad for one day!!!

–Handwriting samples are needed (check her desk).
–Kids' emails are needed

—Key to house needed (essential)!
—Password list needed!
*—Does she keep a journal? Only the best people
  do!* ☺

*—Going w/"Dad" to enroll in school & buy things
  for bedroom 1 P.M. ?*
—Stupid Sheila has dance classes starting at 2 P.M.
—House will be empty today from 1:30–3:30.

*I'm in now, and it feels pretty goddamn great.
More later.*

CHAPTER SIXTEEN

Wednesday, September 26—1:58 P.M.

"**H**ey, I was just going to leave a message," Dylan said on the other end of the line. "I thought you'd be too busy to pick up."

"My two o'clock lesson canceled on me at the last minute, so I'm here at the ballroom with an hour to kill until the next lesson," Sheila explained. She was sitting at a café table on the edge of the seating area in the large, empty ballroom. At this time of day, the second floor of the old building was pretty deserted, and even a bit spooky.

"So—what's going on?" Sheila asked. She kept a civil tone with Dylan. As of this morning, it had become necessary to talk to him in sentences with more than one word. After breakfast, she'd told him about her awful night and how it was obvious that Eden had gone through her things in their bedroom.

Despite the Ambien, she'd had a fitful sleep. She'd still heard the dog, though its barking had been slightly muffled by the earplugs. It had gone on all night long. Sheila had woken up around 4:30 and hadn't been able to go back to sleep.

Taking another day off from work, Dylan had an appointment to enroll Eden in the high school today, and the school administration wanted Eden there, too. After that, they were headed to True Value to pick out paint colors for her bedroom and then to Bed Bath & Beyond. The two of them would stop for lunch somewhere along the way. It was supposed to give them a chance for some father-daughter bonding. At least, that had been the plan.

At breakfast this morning, after the kids had left for school, she and Dylan had discussed it. He'd promised he would figure out a tactful way of asking Eden if she'd been in their room last night. "But, honey, I've got to admit, I think the spider in the bed was just a weird co-incidence. I mean, I see spiders in the house all the time. I just can't see her bringing it in her backpack—this pet spider in a jar with air holes in the lid—all so she could put it in our bed and terrorize you. It seems kind of dumb and childlike. It reminds me of the von Trapp kids slipping the frog in Julie Andrews's pocket in *The Sound of Music*. Do you really think she'd do something that silly?"

"Considering that we don't know her at all—and that she's been openly hostile to me—yes, damn it, I think it's quite possible she'd do something like that. And you should have seen the size of this damn thing. She did it to mess with me. And I want you to find out if she did."

She'd figured Eden would insist she wasn't anywhere near their bedroom last night. And Dylan would probably take the little brat's word.

Sheila had waited until the two of them had taken off for their appointment with the high school principal, and then she snuck into Eden's room. If the girl noticed anything was out of place, Sheila figured she could always use the excuse that she'd gone in there to see if Eden had left any dirty laundry for her. Eden hadn't. She also hadn't made her bed, and she'd left everything she'd worn yesterday—along with a couple of used bath towels—on the floor.

Sheila wasn't sure what she was looking for, but she

thought maybe she'd find a piece of her own jewelry that the girl had stolen last night. Or maybe Eden kept a journal. Maybe she was hiding some drugs in the room. Sheila searched the bedroom, even under the mattress. She also went through Eden's two suitcases. Eden had her backpack with her for the appointment at the high school. Sheila was careful not to get anything out of order—which was difficult, because everything was already a mess in both suitcases. The slob had crammed her dirty, smelly, rolled-up clothes (practically every item black) into the suitcases. Sheila didn't come across anything suspicious amid the toiletries and cosmetics. She found a sketchbook, full of some not-bad ballpoint pen renderings—dark, morbid cartoonish stuff. The girl had a fondness for these characters that were human, but with pig-faces—almost like the doctors and nurses at the end of that old episode of *The Twilight Zone* with Donna Douglas, "Eye of the Beholder." Many of the sketchbook pages were slightly puckered from the sheer quantity of ink used to scribble in the dark backgrounds.

In the back of the sketchbook, Sheila found a few photographs of a younger Eden and her mother. She was actually a cute little girl. She looked a bit awkward and chubby in one photo—obviously taken when she'd hit puberty. There was also a birthday card with a ballerina on a cake and *To My Daughter on Her 12th Birthday!* on the front. Inside, it was signed: "My grown-up girl, so proud of you . . . All the love in the world, Mom."

She'd saved a card from four years ago. So, at least, Eden had a little sentimental streak in her. And she was a mildly talented artist.

But Sheila left Eden's bedroom feeling she still didn't know the girl. She hadn't found anything new about the mother or her death. And she hadn't uncovered any evidence that Eden had been in her room last night, either.

She wondered if Dylan had found anything out yet.

"So I'm in the paint section of True Value," Dylan said on the phone. "Eden's in the bathroom."

Probably snorting cocaine, Sheila thought. "And?" she said.

"She starts school on Friday."

Holding the phone to her ear, Sheila drummed her fingers on the café tabletop with her other hand. "Okay," she said. "Well, that's good . . ."

"Even though she's a few months older than Hannah, because she missed a month of school, they're putting her in Steve's class for now. They said if she seems unhappy or unchallenged as a sophomore, they'll reassess in a few weeks."

"Did you explain to them just who she is—in relation to us?" Sheila asked.

He hesitated before answering. "Yeah, and you were right. No judgment. The principal, she didn't seem the least bit scandalized. Outside of Hannah having some issues about it being this great, big embarrassment, there really shouldn't be a problem."

"No, no problem at all," Sheila muttered.

"I meant with the school situation."

"Did you ask her what she was doing in our bedroom last night?"

He hesitated again.

"I'll bet she denied it and was outraged you even asked. Am I right?"

"Half-right," Dylan answered. "She said that, yes, she went into our bedroom for a couple of minutes last night. She was looking for aspirin and found some in the bathroom medicine chest. Then she saw your perfume on the dresser and tried some. She said she didn't think you'd mind, since you gave her this big speech earlier about how she could help herself to anything that was yours.

Then she got pretty mad, because she said—after you promised it wouldn't be a problem—you were obviously pissed off at her for helping herself to your stuff. She said you set her up. She thinks you hate her."

Sheila let out an exasperated sigh. "My God, I love how she's twisted this around. I told her she could help herself to anything *in the kitchen*. I didn't say she could go through our bedroom or look inside my purse. What about the spider? Did you ask her about the spider?"

"Yeah, I told her what happened, and asked if she knew anything about it."

"And?"

"Well, you're not going to like this, but she laughed. She said you can't blame her if we have spiders in our house. I've got to tell you, honey, I think she's right. Like I told you this morning, I've seen spiders in the house lately. It's fall. It happens. They're just spiders, and it's not a big deal. Can't you just drop it?"

Sheila said nothing. She knew Dylan would take the girl's side on this.

"Are you still there?" Dylan asked.

"Did you find out anything about what happened to the mother?" she asked. "I mean, was it a suicide, or an accident, or what?"

"The police think it was an accident. Apparently, she was up there on the roof working on her tan and drinking. Eden said she always made herself a thermos of Cosmopolitans and got a little sloshed while she soaked up the rays."

"Did you believe her?" Sheila asked. "Do you think that's what really happened? Antonia got drunk and fell?"

"Well, the police came to that conclusion, and Eden seems to agree with them."

"You don't think maybe it's a little too much of a co-incidence that it happened before—and in Portland?"

He didn't answer.

Sheila didn't say anything, either. She'd finally asked the question that had been on her mind since she received that anonymous text and the news story about Antonia's death. Neither she nor Dylan had acknowledged it out loud. For the past week, she'd been trying not to think about it.

"Yeah, okay, it's weird," he admitted. "But Sheila, do you really want to have this conversation now? On the phone? And she's out of the restroom, by the way, so I can't really talk."

"Is she right there?" Sheila asked.

"No, she's down the aisle, looking at paint samples."

"You said you were seeing Antonia during that bad time for us—or rather, right afterwards," Sheila said. She felt knots forming in her stomach. "The birth certificate confirms that. Did you tell Antonia about us, and what happened?"

"Sheila, do we have to talk about this *now*?" he whispered.

"I'm curious just how much Antonia could have told her daughter about us."

"I—I didn't discuss it with Antonia. But, honey, it was in the Portland newspapers. So I'm sure she knew."

Sheila winced. All she could think was that Antonia had probably told her daughter. And now, this girl had moved in with them. Hannah, Steve, and Gabe had no idea what had happened in Portland before they were born. Eden was probably just itching for the right moment to tell them, too.

"God, I hate this," Sheila whispered. Tears welled in her eyes.

"Sheila, no one blames you. No one's ever blamed you. And we aren't even sure how much Eden knows.

Listen. If you want, I can find out what her mom might have told her. Okay?"

Sheila felt sick to her stomach. "Okay," she muttered into the phone.

"I better hang up. She looks like she's getting bored over there in paints. She's already whipped out her phone."

"She's probably texting that creep. You've made it clear to her that we don't want him around, right?" Sheila wiped the tears from her eyes.

"Yes, I told you, I did that yesterday, and it went over like a pregnant pole vaulter. She wasn't pleased. Anyway, I better go."

"Okay. I'll see you in a couple of hours."

"Bye," he said. Then he hung up.

Sheila set the phone on the café table. Dylan usually finished their phone conversations with a "Love you," or "Bye, babe." But it was too soon to go back to that kind of sweet talk. And obviously, he damn well knew it.

Out of the corner of her eye, Sheila saw someone standing in the ballroom's doorway. She thought she recognized the army jacket and the shaggy blond hair. Startled, Sheila got up, almost tipping over her chair.

But this man was about forty. Except for the hair and the jacket, he didn't look a thing like that Brodie kid. "They told me downstairs that there's a restroom up here," he called to her across the room.

Catching her breath, Sheila pointed toward his left. "Just down the hall," she said.

"Thanks!"

Her phone rang again. Sheila snatched it off the café table. There was no name on the Caller ID, just a number she didn't recognize. She hesitated before answering: "Hello?"

"Hi, Mrs. O'Rourke, it's Artie from Hilltop Auto. How are you?"

"Fine," she said tentatively. She wondered why he was calling. "Ah, how are you?"

"I'm hanging in there, thanks. How's the car working for you?"

"Great, thank you. No trouble with the brakes at all."

"Are you missing a pair of driving gloves—brown, soft, and kind of fancy?"

She let out a little laugh. "Well, as a matter of fact, I did have a pair like that in the car, but I thought I'd mislaid them."

"They ended up in our lost and found. I told the boss, 'I'm pretty sure these are Mrs. O'Rourke's.' Anyway, I'm on my way to Northgate. I knew I'd be driving by your neighborhood, so I brought the gloves with me. Can I drop them off?"

"Oh, that's so nice of you," she said. "No one's home right now, but if it isn't any trouble, could you leave them in the mailbox?"

"Easy-breezy, I sure will," he said. "I'm only a couple of blocks away right now."

"Thanks so much, Artie. I really appreciate it."

"No worries," he said. "Take care, Mrs. O'Rourke." Then he clicked off.

Artie slowed the pickup as he approached the O'Rourkes' Craftsman-style house. Something wasn't right. A sketchy-looking guy in a camouflage jacket was headed up their driveway toward the garage. He was too old to be one of her kids and too young to be the husband. The guy didn't look like he belonged there at all. He kept glancing over his shoulder in a shifty way, like he was checking to make sure no one saw him. He ducked down a little walkway between the garage and some shrubs bordering the yard.

Artie pulled up in front of the house and parked. He shoved Mrs. O'Rourke's gloves in the pocket of his light-weight jacket. Climbing out of the pickup, he quietly closed the door and hurried up the driveway to the stone footpath beside the garage. He wasn't sure if the guy was cutting through the yard or what, exactly. But Mrs. O'Rourke was a nice lady, and Artie wanted to make sure this character wasn't up to something. He sure looked suspicious as hell.

The narrow walkway led to the backyard. Artie noticed the beautiful, tiered garden. He also noticed the sketchy-looking creep kneeling by the kitchen door, trying to pick the lock.

"Hey!" Artie shouted.

The guy froze.

In that moment, Artie realized he should have kept his mouth shut, stepped back to the stone path, and phoned the police. He'd just instinctively shouted. Now the guy was going to run, and Artie would have to chase him down.

But the guy didn't bolt. Defiantly glaring at him, the punk straightened up.

"What do you think you're doing?" Artie asked. He took his phone out of his pocket, and Mrs. O'Rourke's gloves fell to the ground.

Artie saw the guy had a gun in his hand—pointed at him. Artie's heart stopped. He didn't move a muscle.

"What am I doing?" the punk said, stepping away from the back door. He came toward him. "What did it look like I was doing, you stupid, cross-eyed fuck?"

"Hey, man, it's cool, okay?" Artie said, half-raising his hands in surrender.

Next door, a dog started barking.

"Shit," the guy muttered. He poked the gun at Artie's neck, nudging the barrel against his Adam's apple. Then he swiped the phone from Artie's hand. "Turn around. Move it."

Obedient, Artie started back down the stone path toward the driveway. He felt the gun tickling the back of his head. He couldn't quite get his breath. He couldn't believe this was happening.

The neighbor's dog stopped barking.

Artie grimaced. He'd hoped the dog barking would draw some attention his way.

"Okay, hold on," said the guy behind him. "Put your hands in your pockets, asshole."

Artie did what he was told. They stood by the side of the garage for a moment. He figured if he simply did what the guy said, he'd get through this and have a story to tell his friends later.

"Who the hell are you anyway?" the guy whispered.

"I'm an auto mechanic. The lady who lives here, I fixed her car last week. Listen, you've got my phone. Take it and go. That'll give you a good head start before I can find another phone to call the cops."

"So you fixed the car, huh? How did you like the job I did on the brakes?"

"You did that?" Artie started to turn around.

But the dirtbag jabbed him with the gun again, scraping the back of his neck just above his collar. It stung. Artie wondered if he was bleeding. "Keep looking forward," the guy growled. "Is that your pickup parked over there?"

Artie nodded. "Yes. You want the keys? Take it."

"No, I wouldn't do that to you. In fact, we're going on a little trip, you and me. Now, take out the keys and start walking. And no funny shit. Don't make me have to shoot you, asshole."

Artie pulled the keys from his pocket and walked

down the driveway toward the street and his pickup. He heard the distant laughter of children. He kept looking around, hoping to spot someone he could signal to. At the playground at the other end of the park across the street, he noticed the kids and a few adults. But they were too far away.

The punk was walking close behind him. Artie imagined the guy had the gun concealed in his pocket.

Approaching the pickup, Artie clicked the button on his key fob to unlock the truck. The parking lights flashed. "Listen, pal, take the pickup and get out of here," he said. "Nothing serious has happened. The cops will never catch you. You can ditch the truck, and I'll get it back eventually. Everybody wins."

"No, I can't have that," the blond creep replied. "You'd tell Mrs. O'Rourke about me. You saw me trying to break into the house. You know I screwed with her car brakes. Guess I shouldn't have told you that—me and my big mouth. Anyway, I can't have you hanging around here. Now, get in behind the wheel. You're driving."

Artie walked around to the driver's side. He watched the punk open the passenger door. One hand was still in his pocket. The guy waited until Artie started to climb into the car and got in at the same time. Then he took his gun out. "So start the car already, dumb shit."

Artie turned the key in the ignition.

"Looks like you've got practically a full tank," the blond guy announced. "I want to see some scenery— trees, mountains, rivers and shit. I'm thinking maybe North Bend or Snoqualmie. Let's take the interstate, south to 90."

Artie swallowed hard, shifted out of park, and pulled away from the curb.

"You got a lot of tools in back of this heap?" the guy asked.

"Some," Artie said.

"Got a shovel back there—and maybe a pick?"

Artie didn't dare ask why he needed a shovel and pick. He just kept his eyes on the road and shook his head.

CHAPTER SEVENTEEN

Wednesday—2:48 P.M.

Staring at her phone, Sheila studied the cover of the leaflet for Antonia Newcomb's memorial service, the one the anonymous caller had texted her on Monday. Sheila was still certain Eden or her boyfriend had sent it—along with the other text—but that didn't matter right now. At the moment, she was looking for the name of the funeral parlor where Antonia's service had been held. It was there on the bottom of the program cover: *March-Middleton Funeral Services—Portland, Oregon.*

She went on Google to find the funeral home's phone number.

For the last twenty minutes, she'd been sitting at the same café table in the empty ballroom, looking at Antonia's Facebook page. All those friends who wrote tributes, from "We'll miss you, Toni!" to "Gone too soon," to "I'll treasure the memories of my dear friend," how many of them really knew Antonia Newcomb that well? Hannah once told her that with Facebook, a lot of people haven't even met their "friends," or maybe the friends were former classmates or coworkers from years before. Sheila had spent the last twenty minutes checking, and the most touching tributes on Antonia's Facebook page were from Debbie Akin in Boulder, Sandy Kohring in Clearwater, Florida, and Katie Reynolds in Oklahoma City. Sheila wondered if any of them could tell her what Antonia's relationship with her daughter was really like. Did they have any special knowledge about Antonia's affair with Dylan? Did they know any details about Antonia's death that weren't in *The Oregonian* article?

Sheila seriously doubted it. If she wanted to talk with someone who really knew Antonia, she'd need a list of the people who attended her memorial service.

She glanced at her wristwatch. She had about ten minutes until her dance lesson.

She dialed the number for the funeral home in Portland. It rang three times before a man answered: "March-Middleton Funeral Services, this is David Middleton speaking. How may I help you?" He had a perfect voice for his profession; the tone was warm and reassuring.

Sheila figured her name was on their Caller ID, so she might as well be honest with the guy. "Hi, my name is Sheila O'Rourke. My husband and I are looking after Eden Newcomb—pardon me, I mean, Eden *O'Rourke*. Her mother, Antonia Newcomb, died about three weeks ago, and her memorial service was held at your funeral home. My husband is Eden's biological father."

It didn't seem too terribly humiliating as she explained it to a stranger over the phone—just a bit convoluted. This was the first time she'd said it out loud to anyone.

"Yes, how can I help you, Mrs. O'Rourke?"

"Well, Eden's very reluctant to talk about her mother's death. All my husband and I know about it is what we've read in a newspaper article published the day after Antonia's accident. We haven't been able to get any more details. I know it's a strange request, but I was wondering if you could tell me the official cause of death."

Mr. Middleton didn't say anything for a moment; then

he cleared his throat. "I believe the medical examiner concluded it was an accidental fall with multiple impact injuries. Is that any help to you, Mrs. O'Rourke?"

She wasn't sure. "Yes, thank you," she said with uncertainty. "There's another reason I'm calling. My husband and I weren't at the memorial for Antonia, but I was wondering if you kept one of those guest books— you know, with the signatures and the names and addresses of the people who attended the service."

"As a matter of fact, we still have it, along with some paperwork that your stepdaughter didn't pick up. Could we forward that to you?"

"Yes, please," Sheila said. "Would it be possible for you to overnight mail that to us? We can reimburse you, if that's a problem."

"It's no problem at all, Mrs. O'Rourke."

"Thank you so much. If you could send it to—"

"The address your stepdaughter gave us was: Eden O'Rourke, care of O'Rourke, Five-seven-eight Roanoke Place East, Seattle, nine-eight-one-oh-two. Is that still correct?"

"Yes," Sheila murmured. She was surprised to hear him read off the address. She was certainly glad she was getting the memorial service guest book. It was why she'd called. But it struck her as bizarre and unsettling that two weeks ago, Eden had already given their address as her residence.

It was like everything was falling into place for the girl—just as she'd planned.

The back seat and trunk of Dylan's BMW were full of junk for Eden's bedroom: a new bedspread, café curtains, a lamp, two big throw pillows, a clock radio, and other things from Bed Bath & Beyond. They had paint samples from True Value but no paint—which was just as well, since Eden had the worst taste. It was very Goth. Her first choice for a wall color was a dark purple that would have made the bedroom look like the inside of a tomb. Dylan imagined Sheila getting one look at it and throwing up. He'd talked Eden into considering some paler, more palatable colors. They'd taken samples of those, thank God.

Now they were on their way to Old Navy so she could buy some clothes. Dylan hoped he could talk her into purchasing at least a couple of items that weren't black. He figured this shopping spree should have been the ideal situation for a biological dad and his surprise daughter to bond. But so far, after he'd spent four hours and over $500 on this girl, she acted like the whole thing was a major drag. And just two nights ago, she'd seemed so needy and desperate for them to take her in.

Dylan tried to engage her in conversation, but for most of their time in the car, she kept her earbuds in and listened to music on her smartphone. She plucked out the buds to answer the occasional question, but otherwise, she kept her eyes on the phone screen and the buds in her ears. Dylan figured he shouldn't take it too personally. Hannah was just as bad.

He did manage to find out how much she knew about her mother and him. Toni must have been pretty candid with her because her information was fairly accurate. They'd met at the Hilton Portland, where Toni was working as a desk clerk at the time. She knew he was married. When he took her out, it was always to out-of-the-way places where they wouldn't run into someone who knew him or his wife. At no point did Toni ever ask him to leave his wife, and at no point did he ever say he would leave Sheila. But in fact, their marriage had been in trouble at the time.

Dylan and Eden hadn't talked about that part yet. And Sheila wanted him to find out just how much she knew.

It started to rain, and Dylan switched on the windshield wipers. He turned to Eden and spoke loudly so she could hear him over the music: "Are Hannah, Steve, and Gabe what you expected?"

She took out the earbuds. "What?" She looked slightly annoyed.

"I asked what it was like to meet Hannah, Steve, and Gabe. Were they anything like you'd expected? You said the other night that you'd googled me . . ."

"Yeah, but they didn't come up in any of the searches. It was just your work shit that came up, Starbucks and all that. It's where they had photos of you. My mother told me that you had a wife and three kids, but I didn't know much else about your family."

"How did she find out that I had three kids?" Dylan asked. "They weren't born until long after your mom and I went our separate ways."

Eden shrugged. "Beats me."

"Did your mom tell you anything about Sheila?" he asked carefully.

Through a Google search, she might not have come up with much about his personal life. But a search for "Sheila Driscoll O'Rourke, Portland" would have revealed some very distressing, personal details about Sheila. He wondered if Eden knew that.

Eden sat there, seemingly mesmerized by the motion of the windshield wipers. Dylan wondered if she was trying to think of just the right answer. She seemed pretty guarded. Sheila had said she didn't trust her. Dylan wanted to give his daughter the benefit of the doubt, but Sheila definitely had a point. He didn't even want to leave Eden alone in the house for now because it didn't seem too unlikely that the rest of the family would return to find her gone and the place ransacked.

"Did you know anything about Sheila before meeting her?" he asked again.

"You must not have told my mom much about her," Eden finally answered, "because she barely mentioned her—ever. All I know is that when you started seeing my mom, your marriage was on the skids. But then, things got better between you and Sheila, so it was *adios, Toni*. My mom said it wasn't a big surprise. She saw it coming, and your parting was friendly enough. The only surprise was me."

Dylan just nodded. It was a good answer. He wasn't sure if it was a hundred percent truthful, but it was a good answer. And it was what he'd tell Sheila she said.

Eden started to put her earbuds back in.

"Speaking of relationships," he said. "I hate to bring up a sore subject, but . . ."

She dropped the earbuds back in her lap and stared at him with her raccoon eyes.

"I was wondering about the boyfriend situation," he went on. "Are you still communicating with him?"

"I thought the deal was that your wife doesn't want Brodie coming over to the house. Now she doesn't even want me to talk to him or text him?"

"Eden, this whole boyfriend moratorium thing was my idea, not Sheila's," he lied. He didn't want her disliking Sheila any more than she already did. "And I wasn't laying down any more restrictions. I was simply asking if you plan to keep in touch with him."

She frowned at him and sighed. "Yeah, we've been texting. But if you're worried about him coming over or me seeing him again, you can relax. In fact, thanks to you and your wife making him feel so unwelcome, I think we're splitting up. He's headed back to Portland tonight. He might have even left already. So you and Sheila can have a high-five session about that. You happy now?"

Dylan squirmed in the driver's seat. He nodded at the Old Navy sign near the mall entrance. "Well, nothing like a new wardrobe to help you get over an old flame."

As soon as the words came out of his mouth, Dylan regretted it. But if he'd said he was sorry, she'd have known it was a lie.

She put her earbuds back in and glanced out the window.

"Words of wisdom from my 'love 'em and leave 'em' dad," he heard her mutter.

Dylan turned into the mall entrance and pretended not to hear her.

Artie listened to pebbles crunching and ricocheting under his pickup as he turned into the parking area for Rattlesnake Lake near North Bend. He noticed about twenty other cars in the lot, but several were already pulling out—probably because of the rain.

He'd been driving with this dirtbag for over an hour. He felt sick. Under his light jacket, he'd sweated through his shirt. Artie thought he might have a panic attack or pass out. Despite the rain, he kept his window cracked open because he couldn't get a normal breath. It didn't help that the scumbag in the passenger seat had smoked six cigarettes since they'd left Seattle.

For someone who looked like a dimwitted street punk, he was awfully sharp. All through the car ride—from I-90 to Cedar Falls Road—the guy hadn't taken his eyes off him or the road. The gun remained in his grasp, always pointed at Artie's gut.

Artie had only a vague idea what this was all about. It was obvious the creep was out to get Mrs. O'Rourke for one reason or another. Last week he'd sabotaged her car, and today he'd tried to break into her house. God only knew what else he was up to—and why.

Earlier, while driving past Mercer Island, Artie had asked the guy: "What do you have against Mrs. O'Rourke anyway? She's a nice enough lady. Is there some special reason you're picking on her?"

The punk had snickered. "If I told you, I'd have to kill you."

"Isn't that the plan anyway?" Artie had asked.

In response, the punk had chuckled again and said nothing more.

During the last hour, they'd passed only one cop car, parked along the side of I-90 in Issaquah. Artie had been tempted to speed up, maybe even swerve off the road—anything to attract the cop's attention. But the punk, almost as if reading his mind, had muttered, "Don't even think about it, asshole."

Artie had thought they might pass another police car somewhere along the way. But that one patrol car in Issaquah had been his only chance for help, and he'd blown it.

Now they were at a recreation area by Rattlesnake Lake. Sitting in the idling pickup, Artie listened to the rain on the truck's roof. He watched hikers and families hurrying toward their cars.

"C'mon, let's stretch our legs," the punk announced. "And if you try to talk to anybody or signal anybody, I'll shoot you in the head—and I'll shoot any other asshole who tries to get in my way. Got that?"

Artie nodded. He switched off the wipers and then turned off the engine.

"I'll take the keys," the guy said, holding his hand out.

Artie surrendered the keys to him. The guy climbed out of the car just as Artie did, never taking his eyes off him. They headed down a trail toward the rocky beach. The lake was beautiful. Even with the rain, it seemed placid and serene. On the other side of the water was Rattlesnake Mountain. It was covered with trees, the leaves changing to an array of fiery autumnal colors. It was a majestic and beautiful site. And Artie realized if he didn't do something, he would die there.

He remembered how, when they'd first gotten into the pickup, the creep had asked if he had a shovel or a pick. Obviously, the guy had intended to take him out to the woods somewhere, shoot him, and then bury him. But Artie didn't have a shovel. So what did the guy plan to do now?

He thought he saw a couple of people up on the mountaintop ridge, just specks in the distance. He'd read that the view from up there on the cliff was incredible. He'd also read that the place had the occasional suicide. Jumpers. Was that what this guy had in mind? Was he going to take him up there and force him to jump?

Artie zipped his jacket to the neck and turned up his collar. But he could feel the rain soaking through the nylon material, wetting his shoulders. He was cold, and he started to shiver. The creep walked alongside and slightly behind him. They seemed headed for the mountain's hiking trail, which led up to the ledge.

Along the pebbly shoreline, they passed fewer and fewer people. Artie imagined that during the summer the area would be swarming with tourists and hikers. But the place was clearing out, and now it was quiet. He listened to the rain on the lake—and the beating of his heart.

At the start of the hiking path, there was a sign:

RATTLESNAKE MOUNTAIN
TRAIL – 2 MILES

BICYCLES AND HORSEBACK RIDERS
PROHIBITED.

Artie abruptly stopped and turned toward the guy. "Listen, why are we doing this? Whatever your beef is with Mrs. O'Rourke, I don't care. Your secret's safe with me. It's not worth dying for. Is it really worth killing me for? You have the keys to my pickup. Just take it and go."

"Shut the fuck up and get moving, Lazy Eye," the punk growled at him. He took the gun out of his army jacket and aimed it at him.

Artie didn't know why he thought this creep would have an ounce of compassion. Artie hadn't had anyone mock him about his eyes since some d-bag bully back during his sophomore year in high school.

Artie started up the well-worn, snaky trail. The trees shielded them from the rain, but it became darker and darker the deeper they ventured into the woods. The trail was muddy in spots because of the precipitation. Artie could hear the raindrops hitting the leaves above them. It seemed to be coming down harder now. Mosquitoes and gnats swarmed around him. Artie kept swatting them away.

"Hey, buddy, can't you cut me a break here?" he said, treading along the path. He was still trying to reason with him. "You don't have to do this. I've got a wife and a three-month-old daughter at home. Please . . ."

He heard the guy cackle.

There was no way for the asshole to know he was totally lying about the wife and child. But Artie figured this guy wasn't about to feel any sympathy for him if he said he was gay. Artie had a boyfriend of eighteen months, Richie, and they'd recently moved in together. He'd finally found "the one." He and Richie were supposed to go to Crate & Barrel tonight to pick out a sofa. That was the plan. This coming Saturday, they had tickets to the Seahawks game. And now, none of that was going to happen, because he would be dead.

Stopping in his tracks, Artie leaned forward and braced his hand against a tree. He gagged, but managed to keep from throwing up.

"C'mon, move it." the creep grunted.

Though his legs felt wobbly, Artie pressed on, weaving around trees and shrubs, stepping over rocks and tangled roots. At times, one edge of the trail dropped off several feet. It was cold, but still muggy. After just a few minutes, Artie couldn't get his breath again and he was sweating even more than before. He hadn't realized the trail would be as steep as it was.

"Okay, hold up," the punk said, obviously winded, too.

Artie turned to look at him. He noticed the guy's old sneakers were covered with mud. Artie wore construction boots, so at least his feet were dry and warm. If it was two miles to the top, he wondered which one of them would give out first.

He heard people talking in the distance. Artie turned forward again and spotted a couple of hikers up the trail, headed down toward them. There couldn't have been many other people along the way because one of the guys just stopped where he was, unzipped his fly, and peed. Then they started moving again, coming closer. Artie saw their faces. The two guys looked like they were in their late twenties. They wore hiking gear and backpacks.

Artie figured this was his last chance to ask somebody for help.

"I know what you're thinking," the creep said, between gasps for air. He jabbed Artie with the gun. "Here's your big opportunity. Help is on the way, right? Well, it isn't, stupid. Those two aren't going to help you. Because if they try, then that's merely two more bullets I'll have to use. So you just nod and smile when they pass us, understand? Now, get going."

Artie reluctantly continued up the trail, stepping aside for the two other hikers to pass.

"You guys aren't letting the rain stop you, huh?" said the one who had been peeing.

Artie tried to give him a pleading look, but the hiker didn't seem to notice. Artie felt his last chance slipping past him.

"Are there still a lot of hikers on the trail?" the punk asked them in a friendly tone Artie hadn't heard from him until just now.

"You got the place practically all to yourselves," the second backpacker said over his shoulder. The two men continued down the path.

Artie turned around, hoping for one more opportunity to signal to them. But the blond creep shoved him and took out the gun. "I fucking warned you," he growled.

Catching his breath, Artie silently watched the two hikers as they trod down the hill through the thicket. They followed the trail around a huge tree and disappeared.

Tears in his eyes, Artie turned forward again and kept walking. He looked down at the pathway, desperately searching for a rock or something he could use to hit the guy. He figured he could stumble, grab a rock, spring up, and bash the asshole's brains in. He just had to catch the guy off guard.

Here he was, trying not to cry. But if he started bawling like a baby and then faked a fall, he could surprise the punk with a sudden attack.

They passed a sign posted to a tree with an illustration of a stick figure falling off a ledge and the warning:

CAUTION
STEEP CLIFFS AHEAD

Artie wondered if, once they got up there, the guy intended to put a bullet through his head or make him jump. He kept checking the muddy trail, looking for a rock, something about the size of a baseball. He couldn't believe this—a well-worn mountain trail, and not one single rock he could use.

He started crying, and the tears weren't phony. "Please, hear me out. I—I've got close to thirty thousand bucks in the bank. It's yours if you just—just—just give me a break." He took a labored breath. "Is whatever you're doing to Mrs. O'Rourke so important that you'd pass up a chance for thirty thousand bucks? We could go to the bank right now. It's still open. I'll get them to write a money order to cash. You can stand somewhere nearby and watch me the whole time."

He could hear the creep trailing behind him. There was no response. Was he actually considering the proposition?

To his right, Artie gave a wide berth to the low, crude log railing along a precipice on the trail's edge. It was about a thirty-foot drop into a gully below. He wondered if maybe he could just swing around and push the son of a bitch. With a little luck, the guy wouldn't have time to fire a shot before falling and breaking his neck.

"Jesus Christ, please," Artie whispered. "I don't want to die . . ."

He heard the punk cackling again. He imagined the smirk on his face.

That was it. Artie couldn't take any more. With his fist clenched, he swiveled around to coldcock him. But Artie's feet suddenly went out from under him as he slipped in the mud. He started to stumble—toward the cliff's edge.

"Goddamn it!" he heard the guy grunt.

Then Artie heard the shot.

Artie felt it in his upper chest, a hard punch that pushed him further toward the steep cliff. He tripped over the log railing and plunged toward the bottom of the gulch.

He blacked out before his body smashed through several tree branches and hit the ground.

Artie didn't see the shower of leaves and branches that followed and nearly buried him.

No shovel was needed after all.

CHAPTER EIGHTEEN

Sheila had completely forgotten about her driving gloves. She didn't think to check the mailbox when she returned home from work because she'd picked up the mail earlier.

Dylan and Eden had returned from their shopping excursion just after four. Their last stop had been Whole Foods, where Eden had purchased some vegan staples so she could prepare her own dinner tonight. Sheila told her she could cook whatever she wanted as long as she cleaned up afterward. The rest of the family would have chicken casserole—except for Hannah, who had called to say she was having dinner at a friend's house. Sheila figured it would be a while before Hannah willingly shared another dinner with their newly extended family. She was still furious at everyone. She acted like the existence of this new half sister was a travesty inflicted upon her and her alone.

While Eden was in her bedroom unloading the several shopping bags' worth of junk her guilt-ridden, absent father had bought for her, Sheila spoke with Dylan in the kitchen. He told her that Eden's slimy boyfriend was headed back to Portland today—for good. Dylan also assured her that Eden didn't seem to know much about her past at all. "Eden said she googled me," he whispered. "But if she googled you, hon, I don't think she would have found anything. I tried to google you when we were in Old Navy, and in order for anything to come up about Portland, I had to include your maiden name and 'Portland' in the keywords. So unless Antonia said something to her, I sincerely doubt Eden knows anything."

Sheila wasn't completely convinced. If the girl had any compromising information on her, she wasn't about to admit it now. No, she'd wait and come out with it when she felt it could do the most damage. She was probably lying about the boyfriend, too.

But Sheila didn't say anything to Dylan about her doubts. He already knew she didn't trust his daughter *or* her creepy boyfriend.

She started cutting up the cold leftover chicken for the casserole. She made a mental note that once she got the guest book from the funeral home and started questioning Antonia's friends, among other things, she'd find out what they knew about this Brodie character.

"Would you mind if I went to the gym tonight?" Dylan asked. "I haven't been since last Friday."

Standing over the cutting board, Sheila gave a shrug and inflicted another apathetic "fine" on him.

But instead of leaving for the Pro Club right away, he hung around, keeping busy at his desk in the den. Then he left at his usual time.

Gabe just missed him when he came home from football practice around five-fifteen. Then Steve walked in the door from gymnastics a few minutes later. Each departure and arrival was announced with a string of frenzied barking from the new neighbor's dog.

Sheila decided, if she didn't want another sleepless night, she had to nip this in the bud with the neighbor right now. But she'd do it diplomatically. She'd cut some flowers from the garden and take them over with a bottle of red wine. She'd welcome her to the neighborhood and, in as tactful a way possible, explain that she'd gotten about three hours of sleep last night—thanks mostly to the woman's stupid dog.

Slipping on her raincoat, Sheila stepped out to the backyard. While cutting an assortment of flowers, she was serenaded with more barking. She was on her way back inside the house when she spotted her driving gloves on the lawn, halfway between the kitchen door and the walkway on the far side of the garage.

That was when Sheila remembered Artie from Hilltop Auto, calling to say he'd drop off the gloves at her house. It sure was a strange place for him to leave them. It didn't make any sense. All she could think was that he'd left them in the mailbox as promised, and then later, someone must have taken them and tossed them back here. That didn't make much sense, either. It also meant someone had rifled through their mailbox and been in their backyard. Eden had been gone all day. Was this something her boyfriend had done—and if so, why?

Returning to the kitchen, Sheila set the gloves on the counter. For the flowers, she found a simple vase in the cupboard, one she wouldn't miss if the neighbor failed to return it. While she arranged the flowers, she kept wondering about the gloves. It was creepy and unsettling. She knew if she asked Eden whether or not her boyfriend had been around here today, she'd just deny it and say he was on his way to Portland.

Sheila told herself not to think about it now. She grabbed a decent bottle of red wine from their stash in the liquor cabinet, buttoned up her raincoat, and headed out the front door. On her way up the Curtises' driveway, she heard the dog yelping again.

As she rang the bell, the barking and yowling went

into overdrive. She stood on the front stoop for a minute. "Shut up!" she heard a woman scream inside the house. "Shut up!"

But the dog kept up its frantic barking.

Sheila stood there in the rain on the front stoop, holding onto the bottle of wine and the flower arrangement. She wondered if the woman had heard the bell. Even if she hadn't heard it, she would have known someone was at the front door from the way the dog carried on.

Sheila was about to ring again when the door finally opened.

The woman on the other side of the threshold was bent over holding a fully grown German shepherd by the back of its collar. She was in her late forties, thin with reddish hair pulled back into a ponytail. Sheila guessed she might have been beautiful at one time, but now she had a hard-edged, slightly burnt-out look—or maybe it seemed that way because she was scowling.

"Hi, I'm from next door," Sheila said, putting on a smile and talking loudly to be heard over the dog. "My name's Sheila. It looks like my timing isn't exactly ideal. I brought along something to welcome you to the neighborhood."

"Stop it!" the woman hissed, jerking the dog back by its collar. It let out a startled yelp and ducked back into the foyer.

Sheila winced.

With an exasperated sigh, the woman collected the vase of flowers and the wine bottle from her. She immediately set the vase on the floor, but she inspected the wine bottle for a moment as if she wasn't sure whether she'd drink it or use it to make spaghetti sauce. With a look that seemed to say "spaghetti sauce," she put the bottle on the floor, too. The German shepherd sniffed it.

"My name's Sheila," Sheila repeated.

The woman nodded. "Leah Engelhardt," she said, unsmiling. With a hand on the knob, she kept the door half closed. Sheila guessed it was meant to both keep the dog in and her out. "I'm really busy right now," the woman said. "Is there anything else you wanted?"

Sheila tried to smile. "Well, as long as I'm here, I was wondering if you were home last night. Your dog, I'm sure he's just not used to the new surroundings—"

"He's a she," the neighbor said impatiently. "Her name's Trudy."

"Well, I heard Trudy barking all night. And I'm sure I'm not the only one . . ."

"Yeah, well, dogs bark," she said shrugging.

As if on cue, Trudy started barking again.

"See?" the woman said. She turned and swatted the poor dog on the back of her head. "Quiet!"

Trudy let out another frightened yelp and backed away.

Sheila shook her head. "You really shouldn't do that."

"You want her to shut up, don't you?"

"Well, yes, but—"

"So I'll do my best to keep her quiet any way I see fit. Okay? Now, I really need to go. Thanks for stopping by."

Then she closed the door in Sheila's face.

Dressed in his street clothes, gym bag in hand, Dylan roamed around both floors of the Pro Club. He searched around the machines and free weights and in the classrooms where the gym hosted group yoga and Pilates sessions, but he didn't find Brooke anywhere.

She'd made it quite clear to him on Friday that they shouldn't see each other again. But since everything had gone to hell on Monday with Eden's unscheduled visit, he'd longed to be with Brooke. He wanted to be around someone who didn't look at him as if he were a criminal.

For the past two days, that was all he'd gotten from his family—including the daughter he never knew he had.

Brooke had made him feel important. He hadn't even kissed her. They hardly knew each other. Still, he'd missed her terribly these past few days. Just thinking about her was like a reprieve from the grim reality of his current situation. She was his salvation.

As he found himself back at the gym's front desk, Dylan felt so dejected.

He didn't want to work out. That wasn't why he'd come here. He thought about driving to Brooke's apartment building and parking outside—maybe he could catch her coming or going. He realized this was total stalker behavior, but he didn't care.

He was about to head out the door when he spotted her, coming from the hallway that led to the locker rooms. She had on her glasses, and her blond hair was swept back. She wore a dark blue rain slicker and carried a collapsible umbrella along with her gym bag.

When they locked eyes, Brooke stopped abruptly.

At first, she didn't look happy to see him, and Dylan's heart sank.

She shook her head at him, but then she smiled.

Dylan hastened toward her. "Thank God," he whispered. "I was so worried I'd missed you."

"I purposely came here early, so we wouldn't run into each other," she said under her breath. "I thought we agreed that we weren't going to get involved."

"I never agreed. You said something like that, but I never agreed."

Brooke just shook her head again and continued toward the exit.

The young man folding towels at the front desk called to them, "Have a nice night!"

"Thank you!" Brooke called back.

Dylan caught up with her. "I'm sorry," he whispered. "I had to see you tonight. I haven't been able to stop thinking about you. Listen, Brooke, if you really want me to leave you alone, I will. I mean it. Everything in my life is so screwed up right now. The last thing I want is for you to feel like I'm stalking you."

"Well, you kind of are," she said, heading down the stairs to the lobby. "And I'm sorry, too, Dylan. But I thought I made it clear the other night that I didn't want to see you."

Dylan stopped. He watched her continue down to the bottom step alone. Then she suddenly seemed to realize he was no longer beside her. From the lobby, she turned to gaze up at him, looking a bit lost. After a second or two, she turned back around and hurried out through the lobby doors. Once outside, she stopped and stood there in the rain, staring at the wet sidewalk.

With uncertainty, Dylan came down the stairs and stepped outside.

"It's so crazy," she whispered to him. "You drove me home and we talked for twenty minutes, and then we went to dinner together. We're practically strangers. There's still so much I don't know about you. But I can't stop thinking about you, either. It's not supposed to happen this quickly. It's not supposed to happen *period*. I love my husband. You love your wife."

Standing in the rain with her, Dylan took hold of her arms. "I know."

She let out a sad laugh. "After my big speech the other night, I was here on Monday, absolutely heartbroken when I didn't see you."

"Monday was a rough night for me," he said.

"Me, too," she replied. "I came here early tonight because I told myself I needed to avoid you. Yet I was still looking around for you, still hoping."

He leaned in to kiss her, but she pulled away. She glanced around—at the sidewalk, the street, and then toward the glass doors to the gym's lobby. "I know it sounds paranoid," she whispered. "But I can't get over the feeling that someone's watching us. Don't you feel it, too?"

Dylan shook his head. "No."

"When is your wife expecting you home?"

"In about an hour."

"I really don't want to go home yet," she said. "Can we just drive around?"

They hurried to his BMW. Once they were inside, he started up the car. Brooke shuddered, and Dylan switched on the heater. But he didn't shift out of park.

As they sat and listened to the rain, he realized he couldn't go anywhere until he told her the truth about everything that had happened this week. His hands on the steering wheel, he stared out the windshield. "Remember the other night, when you asked if I'd ever been unfaithful to my wife?"

"Yes . . ."

"When I told you that I'd never strayed, I was lying," he admitted quietly. "I don't exactly have a perfect record. It's happened a few times. And—well, one of those times from long ago has come back to haunt me." He turned to her. "I've disappointed everyone in my family. And now I'm going to disappoint you, too. But I can't lie to you. I care about you too much. I guess if this doesn't finish us, nothing will . . ."

"What is it?" she asked, a hand on his arm.

"On Monday, I found out I have a daughter I didn't know about. She's sixteen."

"Oh my God," she whispered. Then she let out a stunned little laugh. "I'm not judging you, but oh my God."

Dylan told her the whole story. They drove around the

Eastlake area for about twenty minutes. Except for asking a few questions, she didn't say much. One of the questions she asked was why he'd been unfaithful to his wife at certain times.

"It's not that I don't love her," he said. "I think, for both of us, our relationship just isn't very exciting or romantic anymore. I know it sounds selfish, but I get so frustrated with her at times. She's so—complicated. I've talked to her about couples counseling, but she doesn't want to go. Anyway, I'm sorry I lied to you the other night when I said I've never strayed. I wasn't ready to tell you the truth. I was afraid you wouldn't like me if I told you."

True to her word earlier, she didn't seem to pass any judgment. And it was the most honest explanation he'd ever given to anyone for why he cheated.

They ended up parking along a dark, narrow street by Lake Union. The rain let up, so they climbed out of the car and strolled down to an old wooden pier that jutted out beside a row of floating homes. The two of them were alone with a beautiful view of the water, the illuminated Space Needle, and all the lights in the buildings on the other side of Lake Union.

"Well, thank you for telling me," she said finally, after a few minutes of silence between them. Her shoulder pressed against his as they looked out at the dark water. "If you're asking for my advice, I think you really need to focus on being a father to your children—all four of them. I also think you and Sheila could use some couples counseling. What I don't think you need, Dylan, is to be meeting in secret with another woman."

"I know," he murmured. "I've screwed things up royally. I don't want to screw up your life while I'm at it."

She slipped her arm around his. "Still, I'm glad you told me. It makes me realize how miserable we'd make things for ourselves if we kept seeing each other, how miserable we'd make the lives of the people we love. Maybe—maybe we could just be friends."

He let out a sad little laugh. "God, I think that would make me even more miserable, being with you just as friends and nothing more."

"Me, too," she sighed. "I don't know why I said it."

He turned toward her and touched her cheek. "I need to get home, I guess."

She nodded.

He couldn't help it. He had to kiss her. When his lips met hers, Dylan forgot for a moment about everything else—including all the advice she'd just given him. She was kissing him back. He hadn't felt this way before about anyone. He couldn't let this be a good-bye kiss. He had to see her again.

Brooke pulled away for a moment. But then her arms moved around him and she pulled him closer. "We're going to end up paying for this. You know that, don't you?"

"I know, I know," he whispered. And then he hungrily pressed his mouth against hers once more.

CHAPTER NINETEEN

Thursday, September 27—7:16 A.M.

"Did anyone borrow my eye drops?" Sheila asked.

As usual, nobody paid any attention to her. Steve and Gabe sat in the kitchen's dinette booth with Dylan, eating their pancakes. The *Today* show was on the small TV. Hannah had just rushed in to grab a Diet Coke out of the fridge. She'd drink it while wolfing down a Special K bar on her way out the door. Her ride to school, Jennifer, would be honking the horn any minute now. In her bathrobe, Sheila ate standing up—nine-grain toast and coffee. Everyone else was dressed and would be gone within five minutes—including Dylan, who started back at work today.

Eden slept in, her last chance to do so for a while because she started school tomorrow. Sheila would be alone with her for part of the day. Later in the morning, Sheila had her dance classes at the retirement home, so, for a while, Eden would have the house to herself. Dylan had given her a key.

Sheila hated to even ponder the possibilities. She imagined the girl taking inventory of the silver and china in the dining room and maybe, once again, all her jewelry. Eden might even invite her boyfriend over, the one who was supposed to be in Portland. He could search the entire house with her and help himself to whatever he wanted.

Sheila told herself she was being paranoid. After all, she hadn't seen the boyfriend since Monday, so maybe he really was in Portland. Plus, Eden had actually been civil toward her last night. She'd cleaned up after making a special vegan dinner for herself—something with tofu that looked pretty disgusting. Dylan said she was settling in and making the bedroom hers. She'd hung some café curtains and put the new comforter on her bed, among other things. She'd mentioned that she wanted to shop for some posters in the Pike/Pine district. Sheila had offered to drop her off on the way to the retirement home this morning. So Eden really wouldn't be alone in the house for very long. What harm could she do?

Still, Sheila didn't want Eden home alone when the FedEx package arrived from March-Middleton Funeral Services. Though the package would be addressed to Eden, Sheila wanted to get her hands on it first so she could copy the names and addresses in the memorial service guest book. Afterwards, she'd give the package to Eden and pretend she'd opened it by mistake. It was sneaky and underhanded, but she needed to talk to Antonia's friends. She needed to find out the truth about Antonia's death and the daughter she'd left behind.

Besides, sometimes it was part of a mother's—or stepmother's—job to be sneaky and underhanded.

Dylan was in a positive mood this morning, despite having been exiled again last night to the old *Star Wars* sheets on Gabe's bottom bunk. Maybe his upbeat attitude had something to do with getting back to work and his normal routine today. Or perhaps last night's trip to the gym had helped.

At least one of them had gotten some sleep last night, Sheila thought. Thanks mostly to both of the bitches next door, Sheila had tossed and turned for hours. Trudy had had a bark-fest until about three in the morning. Sheila had figured her owner hadn't been home for most of it because no one could have slept through that.

She'd woken up this morning looking and feeling like hell. When she'd reached into her medicine chest for the Visine, she hadn't been able to find it. Yesterday morning, it had been in there—practically a new bottle, too. Of course, she'd immediately thought of Eden. But would the girl have gone into her medicine chest again, so soon after getting in trouble for doing it the night before?

Sheila had splashed some cold water on her tired, puffy eyes and figured she'd blend right in with the folks at the retirement home today.

She took her cranberry juice out of the refrigerator and poured the last of the sixty-ounce bottle into a glass. "I repeat," she announced. "Did anyone borrow my Visine last night?"

"Not me," Dylan answered. "You know I don't use that stuff. It's actually supposed to be bad for your eyes if you use it every day, hon."

"Oh, really?" she replied sarcastically. "I think you might have mentioned that to me—only about two hundred times since we've been married. I happen to like my eye drops in the morning."

"Visine cocktail!" Steve exclaimed.

Gabe laughed. "*Wedding Crashers*!"

"Do you have any idea what they're talking about?" Sheila asked Dylan.

He just slurped his coffee and shrugged.

She heard a car horn. It was Hannah's ride to school. Steve went to the same high school but took the bus.

"See ya!" Hannah said, heading out of the kitchen with her backpack, her Diet Coke, and her Special K bar.

"Think I can get a ride with you and your cool friends?" Steve called, razzing her.

"Yeah, right!" Sheila heard Hannah reply. Then the front door slammed.

"Steve, I don't believe hell has frozen over yet," Dylan said.

They ate in silence and watched the *Today* show.

Sheila took her vitamins and chased them down with the cranberry juice. The juice tasted a little funny. But she figured that was because it came from the bottom of the container.

She drank it all, finishing the glass.

By 10:15, Sheila felt the lack of sleep catching up with her. Or perhaps she just needed her Visine, because her eyes hurt and her vision was a bit blurry. She was okay to drive, but at practically every stoplight, she took off her sunglasses and rubbed her eyes.

Sitting in the passenger seat, Eden didn't seem to notice. She had her earbuds in and was staring at her phone for most of the car ride. She did, however, notice one thing as they approached the Pike/Pine area. "God, it's so hot in this car! I'm, like, suffocating, aren't you?"

Actually, Sheila was freezing. She'd been getting chills all morning. Still, she turned down the car heater for her stepdaughter. She figured she could endure it for another few minutes until she dropped Eden off. Then she'd crank the heat back up. She'd probably feel better once she got to the Summit Park Retirement Home. The thermostat there was always set at about eighty degrees, and despite the staggering heat, most residents wore sweaters. Yes, she was going to fit right in with her elderly friends today.

She pulled up to a loading zone in front of a grungy used-record store that Eden claimed had good posters.

Eden opened her door and then stopped to squint at her. "Y'know, you don't look so hot."

"Well, thanks," Sheila said with a jaded smile. "I didn't get much sleep last night. Anyway, I'll see you back home around three. Don't forget, the number 49 practically takes you right there."

Eden nodded. "Yeah, I know, thanks." She climbed out of the car and shut the door.

Sheila realized that Eden indeed knew about the bus. The number 49 was where Sheila had encountered her new stepdaughter's awful boyfriend.

Pulling back into traffic, she turned up the heat again.

To the beat of Bobby Darin's "Mack the Knife," Sheila led twenty-seven senior citizens in her Sit Down and Dance session in the lounge at the retirement home. The class occupied two rows of chairs in a semicircle. Sheila sat in front of them in an armless swivel chair. The class was geared for the more sedentary residents. For this session, Sheila was like a geriatric aerobics instructor: sitting there, raising her arms over her head, left, then right, and then a little jazz hands followed by some light kicks, left and right—all set to music and Sheila's vocal encouragement. No one ever had to leave their chairs. The residents had similar lessons three times a week from someone who called himself Mr. Lyle. But apparently, the group didn't enjoy the sessions with Mr. Lyle much. "Lyle plays this Lawrence Welk garbage," one of Sheila's favorite residents, "eighty-six years young" Estelle, had confided a while back. "I mean, please. My parents listened to that. I knew I liked you the minute you played Fats Domino."

The more lively class, held after lunch, involved actual dancing, usually the fox-trot or the waltz.

But Sheila didn't think she'd be able to hang in there for the second class. She was nauseated and still wracked with awful chills. All of her hand movements and kicking just made her sweat and feel worse. She wondered if she was getting the flu. She usually ate lunch with some of the folks from the classes. But right now, the very idea of eating anything made her stomach turn.

All she wanted to do was go home and lie under a heavy blanket. Instead, she had to keep a smile plastered on her face and wave and kick in time with Bobby Darin. She told herself the show must go on. Several of her students in this class had it a lot worse with their aches, pains, and frailties—and they had forty or fifty years on her. If they could keep waving and kicking, so could she.

She managed to get through another song: Dusty Springfield's "I Only Want to Be with You." But the room almost seemed to spin at times. And she couldn't keep anything in complete focus. Sometimes, everyone was just a blur. She felt clammy and light-headed. At one point, she thought she was going to pass out, but she worked through it and kept moving her arms from side to side.

Then, in the middle of The Beatles' "Ob-La-Di, Ob-La-Da," she felt her stomach churn violently. She jumped to her feet. "I'm sorry, excuse me," she managed to say. She bolted across the hall to the women's restroom off the lobby and ducked into a stall. The door slammed against the wall as she fell to her knees, the sound echoing off the tiled walls. She threw up into the toilet. It was one of those elevated toilet seats. Sheila practically had to stick her head into the opening not to splash vomit all over the place. Her hair kept touching the toilet seat, and the thought of it—along with the smell—made her puke again.

After rinsing out her mouth at the sink, she felt better but still a bit woozy. In the mirror, she saw her sallow, chalky reflection.

Sheila didn't even go back to her class. She asked Roseann, the pretty, thirtyish brunette at the reception desk, to tell her class and the next group that she was sick and had to go home. She told Roseann she'd pick up her music later in the week.

"God, Sheila, you look horrible," Roseann murmured. "Maybe you should see one of the doctors while you're here."

"No, thanks, I think I just need to get home," she replied, heading toward the exit.

The drive from the retirement home in Madison Valley to her house in North Capitol Hill was only about fifteen minutes. It was also very scenic, especially this time of year with all the colorful autumn trees along Lake Washington Boulevard in the Arboretum and snaky, wooded Interlaken Boulevard. It was usually a gorgeous, pleasant drive.

But now, halfway home, Sheila felt horrible. She should have listened to Roseann's suggestion about having one of the doctors examine her. Leaning forward and squeezing the steering wheel, Sheila wondered if she'd ever get home. She was certain she had a fever.

Whenever the kids had the stomach flu, she gave them 7UP and saltine crackers. That was what she craved right now. The combo had gotten her through some pretty bad bouts with morning sickness back in the day.

Whatever plagued her now reminded her of how sick she'd been during her first pregnancy, back in Portland. She didn't like to think about that period in her life. But lately, she'd been forced to reexamine it. That should have been a happy time, but every day was a struggle.

"I'm not having *our* baby," she remembered telling Dylan. "I'm having *Rosemary's Baby.*"

After two years of marriage, she and Dylan had been ready to start a family, and she'd imagined herself as one of those happy, glowing pregnant women. But she was sick, hormonally unhinged, and haggard all the time. It didn't help that, during all this, her mother was recovering from a bad stroke and had recently been diagnosed with advanced Parkinson's disease. So in addition to working full-time as an accountant, Sheila was also looking after her invalid mother—and throwing up two or three times a day.

Fortunately, Sheila's late father had left her mom well-provided for. She lived in an upscale high-rise in downtown Portland, one of those places with a doorman and a front desk clerk in the lobby. Sheila hired a series of visiting nurses to look after her mom in addition to the physical therapist. But just managing that—along with all her mother's bills and accounts—was a major headache. Her mother, a very gracious, sweet lady, couldn't stand half the nurses. She was always complaining about them. This lazy one was asleep on the sofa when she'd needed her in the middle of the night. That one let her marinate in her own pee for four hours after she'd wet the bed. This other one yelled at her, and even slapped her.

From the agency that provided the nurses, Sheila got reports that her dear mom was "difficult" and "abusive." Sheila didn't know who to believe.

Her mother was so miserable that she often got uncharacteristically snippy with Sheila. So it was quite likely she dished out the same bile to the nurses. But sometimes, it seemed justified—at least to Sheila. One nurse dressed her mother in some of her most beautiful dresses, outfits her mom had worn to parties and social events. Sheila would come to visit and see her in these expensive clothes, leaning against her walker or in her wheelchair. The clothes drooped over her emaciated frame, and they'd be on backwards because it was easier for the nurse to dress and undress her if the zipper was in front. It was such a small thing, but it broke Sheila's heart to see her mom like that. She knew it broke her mom's spirit, too. The apartment began to smell terrible all the time, which didn't help Sheila's all-day "morning" sickness. Once, while throwing up in her mother's bathroom, Sheila noticed several streaks of shit on the wall and floor that the nurse must have missed when cleaning up after one of her mom's accidents.

Through trial and error, Sheila managed to get a better crew in there. She regularly visited her mom after work and spent several hours over the weekend at her apartment. Every Wednesday night, Dylan would come over with takeout for everyone, including the Wednesday-night nurse, who had a crush on him. Sheila thought they were starting to get a handle on it.

But her mother didn't think so.

On the top floor of her mother's apartment building, seventeen stories up, there was a small gym, along with a bathroom and a dry sauna. At the physical therapist's recommendation, Sheila would take her mom to the gym to stretch or lift the one- or two-pound free weights. There was also a door to a rooftop track that wrapped around the building. Sixteen laps equaled a mile—or so said the sign by the door. The placard also warned:

NO UNSUPERVISED CHILDREN.

NO DRINKING.

NO SMOKING.

RESIDENTS & GUESTS
USE THE OUTSIDE ROOFTOP AREA
AT THEIR <u>OWN</u> RISK.

If the weather was nice, Sheila would push her mother in the wheelchair around the track, which was almost like a covered terrace. Beyond a waist-high railing was a spectacular view of the city, the river, and Mount Hood. They rarely encountered anyone else up there.

Sheila was close to six months pregnant that July evening when, during lap number seven, Sheila's mother begged her to kill her.

"I mean it, I just want to die," she cried. Her speech was a bit slurred. "I can't take this indignity. I'm such a burden on you, sweetie. I'm a burden on everyone. I hate this so much. And it's only going to get worse. I want this to be over with. I'm so sick. If you really loved me, you'd kill me. You'd find a gap in this railing and just push me off the roof."

Sheila moved around to face her mother, then bent forward so they were eye to eye. "Mom, for starters, there are no gaps in the railing," she said, trying to make light of the situation. This wasn't the first time since the stroke that her mother had mentioned wanting to die. "I know you're frustrated," Sheila continued. "The therapist said there'd be days like this. 'Mama said there'd be days like this . . .'"

The little joke and musical reference seemed totally lost on her mother, who gazed at her with that glassy, lifeless look that her face had recently taken on.

"It's really hard right now, but you'll get better, I promise," Sheila assured her. "It's part of the recovery process. Remember the Patricia Neal autobiography we listened to on tape? This period was really tough for her. But she got better. It's temporary, Mom. You have a lot to look forward to." She patted her own extended stomach and smiled. "Don't you want to be around to meet your granddaughter? I just know it's a girl. We both have a lot to look forward to—even though we both feel like crap right now. In fact . . ."

Sheila's smile faded. Bending over like that after those laps had suddenly made her nauseated. "Oh, God. Mom . . ."

Straightening up, she moved around behind the wheelchair and pushed her mother to the door. All the while, her mother kept waving her on. "Just go. I'm fine here, sweetie. Just go . . ."

As she struggled to prop open the door, Sheila felt the vomit coming up toward her throat. "Stay here," she managed to say. Then she rushed through the little gym to the restroom. She made it to the toilet just in time. She immediately flushed and waited a few moments to make sure there wouldn't be an encore. Unsteadily, she got to her feet, then wobbled to the sink to splash some water on her face and rinse out her mouth.

For a couple of minutes, she'd forgotten about her mother—and what her mother had been saying earlier. Her hand froze in the air as she reached for the paper towel dispenser. "Oh, Jesus," she whispered.

With her face still wet, she ran out of the bathroom and through the small gym. Then she stopped dead. She saw her mother just outside the door, slightly slumped over in her wheelchair, tapping her foot and waiting for her.

Still slightly dizzy, Sheila caught her breath. She wondered how she could be so careless and irresponsible. What kind of mother would she be to her own child?

Looking back on it now, Sheila remembered vowing never to leave her mom alone like that again.

As she passed the park and turned down her block, Sheila started crying. She shivered from the chills and tried not to think about throwing up. Now she had a headache, too. She just wanted to be home with a blanket over her. She just wanted her mom to take care of her.

Passing the Curtis house, she noticed that the new neighbor, Leah What's-Her-Name, had set out the garbage and recycling by the end of the driveway. There on the ground, right beside the two bins, was Sheila's vase full of flowers. Leah must have poured the water out, because it looked like the flowers were already dying.

Sheila was too sick to let it bother her right now.

She parked in the turnaround beside the garage. Climbing out of the car and walking for a bit helped. She collected the mail at the front door. Unfortunately, there was nothing from FedEx on the welcome mat.

Inside, she kicked off her shoes and headed for the refrigerator in the kitchen. She opened a 7UP and poured it into a glass with ice. She used it to help wash down an aspirin and a Dramamine from the stash Dylan kept for traveling. Since it fought nausea from motion sickness, she hoped it would help keep her from throwing up again. The 7UP's carbonation and lemon-lime flavor was like liquid heaven. She hadn't realized she was so thirsty.

She curled up on the sofa in the den. There, shuddering under a heavy throw blanket, she finally fell into a deep sleep.

When Sheila woke up nearly two hours later, she felt like a truck had hit her. But that was actually an improvement over her previous condition. She'd sweated through her clothes. So if she'd had a fever, it must have broken during the nap. She was more groggy than light-headed. Her stomach seemed to have calmed down, too.

She wondered if Eden had come home yet. If so, the girl was being awfully quiet. Sheila was too exhausted to get up and check. She remained there on the sofa for another half an hour. But then she decided a shower might help her feel better. Whatever bug she had, she seemed to be over the worst of it now.

Still, Sheila took her time walking up the stairs. Her legs felt rubbery. At the end of the second-floor hallway, she noticed Eden's open door. She padded down the hall and peeked inside the room. Eden wasn't there. But she'd left a neat pile of dirty laundry on the floor by her door with a Post-it on top:

Thank You! ☺

That was encouraging. Her street punk stepdaughter had actually shown a little consideration. Sheila's own kids had never bothered to thank her for washing their clothes. Sheila decided to put a load in the wash, then take her shower.

Down in the laundry room, with the heap of Eden's dirty clothes in her grasp, she noticed a small puddle of water on the floor, right by the washing machine. "Oh, God, now what?" she said out loud.

She dumped the clothes on top of the dryer, stuck Eden's Post-it on the side of the washing machine, and inspected the puddle. It didn't seem to be coming from under the machine. Maybe someone had spilled a glass of water there, although it seemed like a strange place for that. Sheila mopped up the water with a used towel from the laundry basket. As she stood up again, she got a dizzying head rush. Sheila braced herself against the dryer. It reminded her that she was still a little fragile.

She took her time loading the washing machine. Then she poured in the detergent, shut the lid, and turned the setting dial to "Rapid Wash." At the same time, with her left hand, she pressed the start button.

As soon as it clicked, a surge of current rushed from

her fingers up both arms and through her upper body. The shock felt like red-hot razors ricocheting inside her. For what seemed like an eternity, she was paralyzed. Both her hands were glued to the source of all that voltage. Sheila thought she was going to die.

She screamed and somehow managed to jerk her hands away. Recoiling, she staggered back from the shorted-out machine.

Breathless, she fell to her knees. Her head was spinning again. Everything was just a blur. Her arms felt so heavy. With the tingling, throbbing, fiery pain, her hands might as well have been in a vise.

As soon as her vision righted itself, Sheila glanced at both hands. On her left hand, the tip of her index finger was black. On the right, several fingers were blackened. She frantically rubbed her hands and arms, trying to massage the traumatized nerves.

Still dazed, Sheila looked down and noticed the Post-it that had fallen on the floor. It had landed faceup, with Eden's handwriting on it:

Thank You! ☺

Thursday—5:17 P.M.
Lynnwood, Washington

The wry-faced, sixty-something woman behind the counter at Quality Guns & Ammo on Highway 99 was all business. She walked with a limp as she moved to the register and set the box of bullets on the countertop.

It was a large store, with the weapons displayed on a rack behind the counter or in fingerprint-smudged glass cases. The place looked like it could use a good cleaning, and it smelled like garlic. Up near the ceiling, there was a closed-circuit camera in every corner.

The customer, a slim, attractive, fortyish woman with light-brown hair, had asked for bullets for a nine-millimeter Luger. The saleswoman had chosen an overpriced fifty-count box of 115-grain full metal jacketed ammunition. "That's twenty-six ninety-six, including tax," she said.

The woman pulled a pen and a single blank check out of her purse. "Do you take checks?" she asked.

Frowning, the saleswoman nodded. "I'll need to see a photo ID."

Leaning over the counter, the customer wrote out the check. Then she dug into her purse again, pulled out her wallet, and pried the driver's license from the sleeve. She handed it to the saleswoman.

The woman glanced at the license and then at the check. "Thank you, Mrs. O'Rourke," she said.

Then she started to jot down the license information at the bottom of the check.

Thursday—9:50 P.M.
Seattle

Some black-and-white movie with Humphrey Bogart was on Turner Classic Movies. Sheila had no idea which one it was. She was a bit disoriented. She'd just woken up from another nap on the sofa in the den.

She'd been too tired to cook—and she'd been too nervous about going near any electric appliances, at least for a while. So they'd had Chinese food delivered. Everyone had gotten whatever they wanted—including Eden, who ordered something with tofu. Sheila had managed to eat an egg roll and some wonton soup.

She still wasn't feeling a hundred percent but figured she was lucky to be alive after that electric shock. Her arms had stopped feeling strange after about an hour. And thank God, the blackness on her fingertips had washed off. But the fingers were still sore from a mild burn.

When Eden had come home in the afternoon, Sheila hadn't mentioned anything to her about the washing machine injuring her. She hadn't phoned Dylan about it, either. She'd gone upstairs to lie down again, then shower. She'd left a sign taped on the basement door:

Don't Go Near The Washing Machine!
It's shorted out — DANGER OF ELECTRIC SHOCK!
This is NO JOKE — KEEP AWAY.

When Dylan had gotten home, she'd told him what had happened and kept her suspicions to herself. Dylan had switched off the power down in the basement, then unplugged the washing machine and turned the power back on. Sheila had put in a call to an appliance repairman, who was supposed to drop by tomorrow morning.

Maybe once the repairman checked it out, he'd be able to tell her if someone had tampered with the machine.

She kept thinking about the load of dirty laundry Eden had left her—like she was setting her up for the kill. The boyfriend must have had something to do with it. Had Eden left her copy of the house key someplace outside for him? Sheila imagined her phoning him from that record store off Pine Street, giving him the key location, and telling him the alarm code. Brodie could have rigged the washer to short out. He'd probably even made that puddle of water by the machine. If Sheila hadn't wiped it up—if she'd been standing in that puddle of water when she'd pressed the power button—then she would be dead right now.

Sheila remembered telling Eden the other night that

no one else in the house even knew how to operate the washer or dryer.

In that same discussion, Eden had insisted she show her which food and drink items were consumed by her and her alone. Had the girl been making sure no one else in the family became ill—or perhaps died—from ingesting something she planned to taint with poison? Was that why no one else got sick today?

Eden could have snuck down to the kitchen at dawn and tampered with something that Sheila ate or drank. All sorts of packages, jars, and bottles were already open—and vulnerable.

Sheila sat up on the sofa. With the remote, she shut off the TV.

On her way to the kitchen, she stopped at the basement doorway and saw Steve coming up the stairs.

"I'm sorry, I'm sorry, I forgot to empty the garbage," he said. "I'm doing it right now."

"Thanks, Stevie," she said, patting his shoulder. "Is everyone else downstairs?"

"Just Dad and me. Hannah's in her *new room*," he added with a trace of bitterness. "Gabe went to bed. I think Eden's in her *lair*." Bending down, Steve reached inside the cabinet under the sink, where they kept the garbage and recycling.

Sheila watched Steve pull out the trash bag and the recycling bin. The empty Ocean Spray container was poking out of the top of the small recycling bin. Sheila numbly stared at it. Cranberry juice, coffee, cream, and toast. That was all she'd had this morning, a couple of hours before she'd started feeling ill.

"Hey, Mom?" Steve asked. He reached into the garbage, past some of the Chinese carryout containers. Then he pulled out the small bottle of Visine. "Weren't you looking for this earlier? It's still got some in it."

He handed it to her. The bottle was sticky—and still a quarter-full.

"Honey?" she said, staring at the bottle. "You said something this morning about a Visine cocktail. What were you talking about?"

Steve grinned and nodded. "In *Wedding Crashers*, they put Visine in this guy's drink and it gave him diarrhea. It was really funny."

"I'll bet," Sheila murmured.

Steve went out the door and headed toward the side of the yard where they kept the garbage and recycling bins.

Sheila looked at the dirty vial of Visine and wondered just how many drops Eden had put in her cranberry juice this morning.

Sheila sat alone at the breakfast table. She had the small TV on for background noise. There had just been a commercial for the local eleven o'clock news, which was supposed to come on at any minute.

The house was quiet. Not everyone was asleep yet, but they were in their respective bedrooms—including Dylan. She'd told him he could return to their bed tonight. She'd be bunking in with Hannah, whose room was about as far as Sheila could get from the sound of their new neighbor's barking dog. Dylan could put up with the canine crooning tonight.

The lights were on in the house across the way. So Ms. Congeniality must be home, which accounted for the blessed silence right now. Maybe Dylan would luck out and Trudy would remain silent tonight. That was fine. Her anger at him was starting to soften.

She would need him on her side when she talked to him tomorrow about his oldest daughter.

Sheila had gone online and googled "Visine Cocktail." It turned out that the *Wedding Crashers* scenario was a myth. Slipping Visine into someone's drink didn't cause the drinker to have diarrhea. No, the results of this prank were far more serious. Consuming several drops was known to cause, among other things, an alteration in body temperature, respiratory problems, blurred vision, nausea and vomiting, radical changes in blood pressure, seizures, and even death for the drinker.

The little bitch had almost killed her today—twice.

Of course, Sheila couldn't prove that Eden had slipped eye drops into her cranberry juice. And even if Sheila did prove it, Eden could always dismiss the whole thing— and so might Dylan—as a silly prank, like in *Wedding Crashers*. Eden could pretend she'd had no idea of the dire consequences. It was supposed to be a practical joke, nothing more. Right up there with planting a spider in her bed.

Now Sheila wondered if that spider was poisonous.

She thought about the brakes on her car, too.

How many times had she almost "accidentally" died since Eden's birth mother had fallen to her death? How many times since Eden had moved in? There might even have been a few failed attempts and close calls she didn't know about.

Sheila wanted to see what the appliance repairman said about the washer. If it looked to him as if someone had tampered with it, then that would be enough for her to make a case to Dylan—and to the police. By tomorrow afternoon, she'd also have that guest book from Antonia's memorial service. Maybe a few of Antonia's friends could tell her more about Antonia's daughter—

and perhaps a few "close calls" Antonia had encountered before her fatal "accident."

To go to Dylan with her suspicions at this point seemed futile. She would just come off as paranoid and maybe a little loopy from being so sick today. She'd wait until tomorrow, when she had more ammunition to back up what she felt in her gut.

For now, it looked like Eden was targeting her and her alone. Why, exactly, Sheila wasn't sure yet. But she believed Dylan and the kids weren't in any danger.

In the meantime, she was sleeping in Hannah's room—with the door locked.

Though her mind was racing, she'd decided to attempt sleeping tonight without the help of Ambien or bourbon. She'd try meditating.

The local news came on the TV. The blonde, fifty-something anchor began talking: "In our top story, a group of hikers at Rattlesnake Mountain this morning discovered what they thought was a dead body off one of the trails."

The picture switched to video of several squad cars and an ambulance in a recreation area by the pristine, picturesque lake at the base of Rattlesnake Mountain. The newscaster continued with a voiceover: "Thirty-three-year-old Arthur Merrens of Wallingford had been shot and left to die in the woods. Merrens was rushed to Swedish Hospital in Issaquah, where he's in critical condition . . ."

Sheila wasn't paying much attention. With a sigh, she reached over and switched off the TV. Then she went to get ready for bed.

CHAPTER TWENTY

Friday, September 28—11:51 A.M.

Sitting in the second-to-last row in his English Lit class, Steve watched Ms. Warren call on the new student.

He had a mild crush on Ms. Warren, who was about thirty-five and pretty with red hair and what appeared to be a great-looking body under those sweaters. Plus, she was nice. When she'd been late for class last week, Shane Camper had written on the blackboard: *Ms. Warren— Cougar or MILF?* But he'd erased it before she'd walked in. So Steve wasn't totally alone in thinking she was kind of sexy.

Eden, the new student, seemed to be doing her damnedest to make a lousy first impression on Ms. Warren. Throughout the class, she'd been fidgety to the point of distracting just about everyone—including Ms. Warren. She kept squirming in her desk chair, rolling her heavily made-up eyes, and yawning loudly. At one point, she even leaned over to the next seat and asked Eve Caletti, "When do we break for lunch in this shit hole, anyway?" The entire class heard her, too.

If Eden was acting like this to attract attention, it was totally unnecessary, because everyone couldn't help staring at her the minute she strolled into the classroom. She'd left the house this morning in a pair of jeans and a black cardigan over a sort of bruise-colored leotard top. Had his parents seen her without the sweater, they never would have let her leave the house, because the clingy top was practically transparent—especially around her breasts, which stretched the material to its fiber limit. Steve wasn't sure when she'd ditched the sweater. But now practically everyone in the school could see what he'd seen after her lengthy bathroom session on Tuesday night.

"Eden, since this is your first day here, you might not have read *The Scarlet Letter*, but if you've been listening to the discussion, I'm sure you've formed some sort of opinion of Hester Prynne. What do you think of her?"

Ms. Warren was obviously trying to put her on the spot and maybe get back at her a little for distracting the class.

"Actually, I read it last year," Eden muttered, slouched in her chair.

"Would you please sit up, Eden—and speak up?"

Asking Eden to sit up was a definite mistake, because when she did, she stuck out her chest, and it was hard to avoid looking at anything else.

"I said I've read it already," she announced. "And I thought it was crap."

A girl in the front row gasped.

Ms. Warren glared at Eden. "Would you care to elaborate?"

"The only pleasure I got from reading it was congratulating myself every time I finished one more boring page. Hester was a wimp. And it was so, like, convoluted. Plus, Hawthorne didn't know shit about women. And how many stupid coincidences could he have in there? The 'A' in the sky when there's a meteor—sure, yeah, like *that's* really realistic. What makes you stupid teachers think we're going to enjoy books when you force us to read something that's like a hundred and sixty years old? Maybe the book was a big hit back in eighteen-whatever, when people didn't have anything else to do. They didn't have radio, movies, TV, or the internet. Shit, they didn't even have electricity, right? So it was like, *The Scarlet Letter* or parlor games. If you want us to really *embrace* reading books, why don't you teachers put some good books, some semi-current best-sellers, on the reading list? *Game of Thrones*, and shit like that."

A couple of the more ballsy guys in the class laughed and applauded. Others were stunned into silence.

Ms. Warren was still glaring at her. She looked like she was trying to keep composed, but Steve thought he saw her nostrils flare. "First of all, Eden, foul language will not be tolerated in this classroom," she said evenly. "Secondly, I'd like to point out that if it weren't for classics like *The Scarlet Letter* paving the way, we wouldn't have the basic ingredients found in today's bestselling books. Perhaps if you read Hawthorne's novel a little more carefully—"

The bell rang, and everybody started to get out of their seats.

"Chapters twenty through twenty-four on Monday, people!" she announced over the din. "Eden, I'd like a word."

"I'll give you two: *fuck you*," Eden replied, not quite under her breath.

Steve heard it, and he was pretty sure Ms. Warren did, too. Ms. Warren was also Eden's homeroom advisor. So Eden was pretty dumb to tick her off.

Stepping out to the crowded hallway, Steve lingered near the door after Ms. Warren closed it. Through the glass, he could see her bawling out Eden for being such a smart-ass. Eden just stood there, defiantly pouting at her.

Steve was fascinated by his half sister, but he was

leery of her, too. He hadn't gotten another peep show since Tuesday night, though she was certainly making up for lost time with today's transparent top. Steve's dad had slept in Gabe's room for a couple of nights. So maybe that was why she hadn't walked around practically naked again. His dad had gotten a look at the mess Eden had left behind in the bathroom on Tuesday night, and he'd talked with her about it. So she wasn't being such a pig in the bathroom anymore, either. She spent most of her time in Hannah's old room with the door closed. Steve decided to give her some space and be friendly. He still wasn't sure if he liked her or not.

As for her behavior in school today, Steve tried to cut her some slack. Maybe she was just putting on a sexy, smart, tough-girl act so no one would mess with her. Steve imagined it was like one of those prison movies, when the new guy picked a fight on his first day in the slammer so all the other inmates would respect him. After all, she was in a new school, and maybe the word was starting to get around about her background. Steve wasn't sure how many people knew that she was his and Hannah's half sister and that she was living with them now.

He decided to hang around and make sure she wasn't in too much trouble. If she didn't get sent to the principal's office, he'd ask if she wanted to eat with him in the cafeteria. He didn't want her to have to eat alone on her first day.

Through the window in the classroom door, he watched her nod at Ms. Warren. Then, slinging her backpack over her shoulder, she turned and flounced toward the door. Steve approached her as she stepped out into the hallway. The crowd in the corridor was already thinning out. People were on their way to lunch. "What happened?" Steve asked.

She sighed. "I have to write a thousand-word report on the fucking *Scarlet Letter*," she groused. "And the bitch wants it on Monday. Well, that's not going to happen."

"You can borrow my copy of the book if you want," Steve offered. "It's already highlighted, with notes in the margins. Anyway, listen, I usually eat in the cafeteria with this guy, Sean Thomas. He's sort of new, too. He's from Boston, and he's a nice guy. You might like him. You want to eat lunch with us?"

Eden shook her head, "Not really."

Steve stopped, a bit taken aback by her abruptness.

He watched her saunter down the hallway without him.

Sean Thomas and Steve had a table by the window in the cafeteria. They picked at their gristly Salisbury steak and tater tots. Sean was skinny with green eyes and light brown skin. He was kind of a wise guy. Every time he said something funny in his Boston accent, he said it out of one side of his mouth. Steve was his only friend right now, and vice versa. They hadn't started hanging out together after school or anything, but since the beginning of the year, they'd had lunch together in the cafeteria practically every day.

Steve had told him about Eden being his half sister.

"Does she dress like that at home, too?" Sean asked. "You must be walking around with a boner all the time."

They weren't too far into lunch when Sean nodded toward the window. "Hey, isn't that her?"

Steve looked outside and saw Eden by the bike racks. She had her sweater on again, but it was open in front. She sat on a bench, eating and talking with this guy who looked just like her boyfriend, the one who was supposed to be in Portland. Steve was almost positive it was the same blond guy in the picture his mom had taken. The guy even wore the same camo jacket as the punk in the photo.

Steve watched the guy feed Eden a French fry. He could tell—even at this distance—that they were eating McDonald's. The guy offered her a bite of his cheese-burger, and she greedily took several bites. Steve could tell from the color of the wrapper that it was a cheese-burger, all right, and Ms. Vegan was gobbling it up and laughing.

Then the two of them stood up and walked away. The guy left the McDonald's bag on the bench. They were six feet from a trash can, and the lazy jerk left his garbage on the bench. Steve hadn't even met the guy, and already he didn't like him. He also didn't like the fact that Eden was lying to everyone about the jerky boyfriend being in Portland. And why the hell did she make up that crap about being vegan? Was it just to make things more difficult for his mom?

Steve watched them get into a car together and drive away.

He wondered if he should tell his parents about any of this. He didn't want to be a snitch, but he hated seeing her make chumps out of all of them.

"Hey, are you okay?" Sean asked. "Who was that burnout with your sister?"

Steve shrugged. "Beats me," he lied. He wished he knew Sean a bit better so he could confide in him. But he hadn't even told him about seeing Eden naked the other night.

"Why do these tater tots suck so much today?" Steve asked to change the subject. "Usually, they're okay, but these are like raw on the inside."

He'd taken a few unenthusiastic bites of the tough steak when his phone vibrated. Steve pulled it out of the side pocket of his cargo pants. It was a text. He didn't recognize the sender, but he clicked on the message. He wasn't sure if the text was really meant for him or not, because it didn't make any sense:

ASK YOUR MOM ABOUT YOUR AUNT MOLLY

"What's going on?" he heard Sean ask. "Who texted?"

Looking up from the phone, Steve quickly switched it off. "Um, nobody, some spam thing."

He didn't want to say anything, not until he found out what the text was about—and maybe not even then. Steve couldn't wrap his head around it. This week, he'd just found out about this sister he never knew existed. He'd also learned that his dad had cheated on his mom. And now, some stranger was telling him that he had an aunt out there somewhere.

As far as he knew, he had no aunts or uncles. So who was this Aunt Molly?

Despite what the text said, the last thing in the world Steve wanted to do was ask his mom about her.

CHAPTER TWENTY-ONE

Friday—2:57 P.M.

It wasn't there.

With two bags of groceries weighing her down, Sheila stopped at the front door. The FedEx package from March-Middleton Funeral Services still hadn't been delivered. She wondered if perhaps Eden's creepy boyfriend had found the package and made off with it yesterday when he'd come by to sabotage her washing machine.

She still didn't know whether or not the machine had been tampered with because the repairman had never showed up. Sheila had waited during his "arrival time window" of eight-thirty until eleven-thirty. At noon, she'd called the appliance repair place and was told that, yes, there had been a delay, and now he wouldn't be by until Monday. Sheila had figured telling them it was a matter of life and death wouldn't do any good, though it wouldn't have been far from the truth. She'd gritted her teeth and thanked the person on the other end of the phone when they'd told her to have a nice weekend.

She hadn't slept well in Hannah's room last night. Plus, she was still feeling a bit dicey today. She'd even gotten snippy with two of her favorite students during her one-thirty session. The soon-to-be-married Dante and Pattie were so sweet, and she'd gotten impatient with them over practically nothing. Or maybe it was simply because they were young and cute and in love, and she was bitter.

As she stepped inside the house and disarmed the code, Sheila wondered if it was too soon to call the funeral home and ask if they'd sent the memorial guest book yet. She hung up her coat, took the two bags of groceries into the kitchen, and unloaded them on the counter. She started putting things away—including some small, individual bottles of cranberry juice. From now on, everything she ate or drank would be in a smaller container. She wasn't touching anything that had already been opened.

She'd put away nearly all the groceries when she noticed something through the kitchen-door window. It looked like a large tree branch had fallen onto the lawn.

Sheila opened the door and stepped outside.

To her horror, she saw it wasn't a tree branch on the grass. It was one of the Japanese maple trees from her garden. It had been uprooted and tossed into the middle of the yard.

That was when she realized her entire garden had been demolished. The beautiful flowers and plants had been torn up from the roots and scattered on the grass. The birdbath was tipped over. The stones she'd painstakingly arranged were strewn all over the place. The garden was her pride and joy, and someone had completely destroyed it.

"Oh, no. Oh, no," she kept murmuring. Tears filled her eyes. It was all so utterly senseless.

For a few moments, she wandered amid the carnage as if it were a battlefield full of corpses. Devastated, Sheila started weeping.

"Who would do this?" she cried.

Then she heard a voice inside her head: *Do you really have to ask?*

* * *

Dressed in his suit and tie, Dylan stood in his back-yard with Sheila, Eden, and Steve. As he surveyed the damage to the garden, he listened to the high-pitched accusations and denials between his wife and this stranger who was his daughter.

It was close to four o'clock, and he should have been at the office. He wished he were still there.

Until all this happened, he'd been in a good mood today. Sheila had given the all-clear for him to work out tonight. He would hit the gym, all right. But he wouldn't be stepping inside. It was merely a rendezvous point for Brooke and him. They'd steal two wonderful, clandestine hours together.

On Wednesday night, all they'd done was kiss and neck on that old dock. Then they'd made out in the car like a couple of horny teenagers, but not for long, because he'd had to go home. Kissing, necking, and some fondling. Even if that was all they did tonight, he'd be happy.

But of course, he wanted more.

A mere thirty-five minutes ago, he'd been at his desk in his office, thinking about Brooke and tonight. That was when Sheila had called him. Hysterical, she'd demanded he come home immediately. "You need to see what your daughter has done," she'd said, enunciating each word with an angry tremor in her voice.

And now Dylan was looking at it.

His heart broke for Sheila. She loved this garden. She'd worked hard to make it beautiful. He completely understood why she'd become unhinged. Annihilating something so lovely just seemed cruel and pointless. He didn't want to think Eden had anything to do with it.

Apparently, Sheila had phoned Eden earlier. With no explanation, she'd asked her to come home immediately after school. Then she'd called Steve and asked him to skip gymnastics practice and make sure Eden came directly home.

At least, that was the way Dylan understood it from what Sheila had told him.

Now, the four of them stood at the edge of the demolished garden. And in Sheila's way of thinking, the perpetrator was returning to the scene of the crime. Dylan, feeling like a referee, stood between his wife and his daughter. Steve was at Sheila's side with his hand on her shoulder. Looking somber and uncomfortable, Steve said nothing.

"I didn't do this!" Eden cried, hugging herself. Dark eye makeup ran down her cheeks along with her tears. Despite the buttoned-up black cardigan she wore, she was shivering—maybe more with rage than from the autumn chill. "This is so unfair! How can you guys blame me for this? I was at school all day!"

Her loud protests prompted the new neighbor's dog to start barking.

"She's lying," Sheila insisted.

"I'm sorry this happened, okay?" Eden cried. "But you can't pin this on me! I wasn't even here! It's bad enough that I'm still getting over my mom dying. But I'm forced to live with somebody who hates me! This isn't my fault! How could I have done this? I told you, I was at school all day!"

"Please, Eden, you don't have to shout," Dylan murmured. "The neighbors . . ."

"Well, if you were at school the entire day," Sheila snapped, "then you must have gotten that scummy boyfriend of yours to do your dirty work."

"How could Brodie have done this?" Eden yelled, motioning toward the wrecked flower bed. "He's in Portland, you crazy bitch!"

"Hey!" Dylan warned, pointing his finger at her. "Now, that's enough."

All the while, the neighbor's dog kept barking.

Dylan took a deep breath, then edged closer to his son. "Stevie, can you take Eden for a walk or something?" he whispered. "Just get her out of here for a while until she calms down. I'll owe you." He turned to his daughter. "Eden, why don't you go with Steve, walk around the neighborhood, and cool down a little, okay? We'll figure this out."

Frowning at him, she wiped her eyes again. Then she swiveled around and headed toward the walkway beside the garage. Steve started after her. "Hey, hold up a minute!" he called. "I've got to talk to you!"

Once they were gone, Dylan waited for the stupid dog next door to stop barking. He took another deep breath, then put his arm around Sheila. He looked at the ruined patch of land in front of them. "Y'know, honey, it's not a total disaster," he said gently. "We'll buy some new plants tomorrow. We'll all work together to get this back into shape over the weekend. We'll make it a family project."

Sheila pulled away and glared at him. "Is that it?" she said. She shook her head at him. "Unbelievable. Are you really going to let your bastard daughter get away with this?"

His mouth open, Dylan gazed at her.

She didn't wait for an answer. Sheila turned away. Threading around the corpses of plants and flowers, she headed into the house.

"Hey, wait a minute, okay?" Steve called to his half sister. "Slow down!"

He was reluctant to chase after her. The way she

hurried down the steep street near his house, Steve knew she'd get to a point at which she couldn't stop herself. She'd end up falling and breaking her neck. The downhill incline toward Portage Bay was so sharp that Steve didn't dare take his bike or skateboard down the street. From this spot, near the top of the hill, he had a beautiful view of the bay, the floating homes, Montlake Bridge, and beyond that, part of the University of Washington campus. He also had a view of Eden's back as she continued to charge down the slope.

"I know you were lying!" Steve yelled.

That did the trick—almost. It looked like Eden tried to stop, but couldn't. She veered off the sidewalk and staggered toward a tree on the parkway. She grabbed its trunk to stop herself.

Steve took his time catching up with her. "I saw you having lunch with your boyfriend by the bike racks today," he said. "He's not in Portland. And you ditched history class after that."

Still bracing herself against the tree, she stared at him. She was panting. "I didn't wreck that garden," she insisted. "Jesus, so some flowers got trampled on. She's acting like somebody shot her dog or something."

"That garden's very important to my mother," Steve said.

"Well, I didn't touch it!"

"I don't believe you," he said. "And you still haven't explained why you lied about your boyfriend being out of town. I saw both of you eating a cheeseburger, too. I recognized the yellow McDonald's wrapper. What's this shit about you being a vegan? That's obviously a lie. What are you up to? What's your deal, anyway?"

Her eyes widened. Steve could tell he'd put her on the spot.

"Well?" Steve said.

"For starters," she said, a bit huffy. "That was an apple pie in Brodie's cheeseburger wrapper. I don't eat anything that once had a face. And I didn't eat any part of the pie that touched the wrapper. I had no idea that Brodie was in town. I was totally surprised when he showed up at school today. And yes, I ditched one stupid class so we could go for a drive . . ."

"And you guys drove here and demolished my mother's garden," Steve said.

Eden shook her head. "We went to Volunteer Park. Brodie just wanted to say good-bye to me. When he dropped me off at school later, he said he was leaving for Portland *right then*. His crap was in the back seat. He's probably halfway there now."

"I don't believe you."

"You really think I tore apart your mother's precious garden?" Eden asked. She waved a hand from her neck down toward her legs. "Look at what I'm wearing. It's what I've had on since this morning. You saw that garden. If I *had* destroyed it, I'd be covered with dirt from head to toe. Look at my hands." She shoved them in front of his face, palms up, then palms down. She obviously chewed her fingernails, which still had remnants of black polish on them. But her hands were reasonably clean.

Steve realized she had a point. The destruction of his mother's garden seemed like a crazy, impulsive act. He couldn't imagine Eden stopping to change clothes and find some gardening gloves before trashing the flower beds. Then she would've had to clean up and change back into her old clothes afterwards. It didn't make sense.

"Okay, maybe you didn't do it," Steve allowed. "But how can you be so sure your boyfriend didn't come back here and wreck my mother's garden?"

"'Cause he would have told me."

"He lied to you about going to Portland the other day. Why wouldn't he lie to you again?"

"Something came up at the last minute, and that's why he didn't go to Portland. He didn't deliberately lie to me. And if he trashed your old lady's garden, believe me, he'd have told me about it. It's something Brodie would brag to me about. He'd have called me from the road to let me know what to expect when I got home today."

Steve frowned at her. Again, her answer made sense, but he still wasn't satisfied. "Why didn't you just tell my parents—*our* parents—the truth?" he asked pointedly. "Why did you have to lie about your boyfriend being in Portland?"

"Because he's practically there now!" she said, exasperated. She rolled her eyes at him and then started to walk back up the hill. "What goddamn difference does it make? If I admitted that he was still in town, they'd have insisted—just like you did—that he did that number on the stupid garden. They wouldn't have listened to me. Your mother has it out for me. It's that simple. I can't say I blame her. But it's not my fault your dad screwed around with my mom. It's not my fault I was born."

Steve walked alongside her and didn't say anything for a few moments. There was still something else that bothered him. He gazed up at the steep hike in front of them. "Who's Molly?" he finally asked.

She squinted at him. "What?"

"Who's Aunt Molly?"

"I don't get it."

"Did you or your boyfriend text me this afternoon?" he asked, a bit winded by the uphill climb.

"No. Why would we? What are you talking about?"

"Nothing, forget it," he said. "You know, if you think my mom doesn't like you, it might help things a lot if you offered to help clean up that mess in the backyard."

His suggestion was met with silence. Steve figured she was either saving her breath for the uphill climb or she wanted him to mind his own goddamn business.

Ten minutes later, when they came in through the front door, they were met by Hannah. She'd stormed out of the kitchen and practically pounced on them in the hallway. "There you are!" she yelled at Eden, almost in her face, "Oh, sure, now you're covering yourself up with that hideous sweater."

Taken aback, Steve shut the door behind him.

His parents tentatively stepped out from the kitchen, where Hannah must have been venting at them.

"Go ahead, *Chesty*," Hannah said. "Show my mom and dad what you have on underneath that rag. Let them see what the whole school saw today. It's not humiliating enough that everyone in school knows we're related. But you have to make things even worse by putting your tits on display for the whole school! Go ahead, show them what I'm talking about. Let them see what you've got on under that ugly, homeless old-granny sweater. I dare you."

Sneering at her, Eden unzipped the threadbare sweater and shucked it off. To Steve, it almost seemed like an act of defiance.

"Oh, God," their father lamented. "Eden, what were you thinking? Please, cover yourself up."

"All day long at school, she was walking around like that," Hannah said. She shook her head at Eden. "As if you didn't already look like a train wreck, you have to go out of your way to dress like an alien prostitute from the wrong side of Mars."

Putting her sweater back on, Eden zipped it up. "Oh, bite me," she said.

"Okay. That's enough, you two," their dad said.

Steve noticed that his mother hadn't said anything.

She just stood there behind his dad with a disgusted look on her face, like someone who didn't particularly enjoy being right.

"Why in the world would you wear something like that to school?" his dad asked her. He rubbed the side of his neck.

Eden shrugged. "All my other clothes were dirty. I was going to keep my sweater on, but it was hot in those classrooms."

"Hey, y'know, there's this thing called a *bra*," Hannah interjected.

"Do me a favor," their father said to Eden. "Get rid of that thing, throw it out. I don't even think Goodwill would take it. Hannah, listen, could you do what sisters do and loan Eden something of yours to wear until we can get the washing machine fixed?"

"*Half sister*," Hannah corrected him.

"Fine, if you want to get technical." He let out an exasperated sigh. "I just figured, honey, since you seem to have your finger on the pulse of all the latest fashion trends, you might be willing to help her out a little."

Hannah rolled her eyes as if his request had put a huge burden on her. With her lip curled, Eden didn't seem too thrilled about the idea, either.

"Would it kill you guys to at least try to get along?" he asked.

His phone rang, and he pulled it out of the inside pocket of his suit coat. He stepped toward the dining room to look at the screen—almost like he wanted privacy, which struck Steve as weird. His father seemed puzzled as he glanced at the phone screen.

For a moment, Steve wondered if he was getting a message about Aunt Molly, too.

And I've missed you. I've been looking forward to this since Wednesday night."

"Dylan, your wife and family need you now—"

"And I need you."

"That's sweet. But it sounds to me like your family is going through a real crisis. You should be there for them. I'm just making things worse and more complicated for you."

"No, you're making things *bearable* for me," he said into the phone. His other hand tightened on the steering wheel. "If it weren't for you right now—if I didn't have these minutes talking with you—I'd completely lose it."

"Go see your daughter's teacher," she told him. "Be with your family tonight, Dylan."

"What about this weekend?" he asked desperately. He held the phone closer to his mouth. "Can you get away? I don't think I can wait until Monday. I want to see you before that. Please?"

"I don't know," she said. "Tell you what. Text me tomorrow, okay? Let me know if you can get away sometime. I'll see what I can do. I can't promise anything, Dylan."

"Okay, I'll see you tomorrow or Sunday."

"*Maybe*," she said. "I better let you go. You shouldn't be talking on the phone and driving at the same time."

"Thank you, Brooke."

"What for?" she asked.

"Anyone else would have been pissed off at me for screwing up our date tonight. And here you are, patiently listening to me go on about my wife and kids, and our troubles." He let out a little laugh. "You're pretty amazing. You should be the last person to remind me of my duty to my family."

"Yeah, well, I warned you I was going to be bad at this

'other woman' business," she said. "And I'm not pissed off at you about tonight. I just really want you right now."

Before he could respond, he heard the click on the other end.

Miranda Warren stayed late at the high school because she was in detention.

All the teachers got stuck pulling two separate weeks of after-school detention duty every year, and this was Miranda's first week. She felt like a prison guard—or that hotheaded teacher from *The Breakfast Club*—sitting from 3:30 until 5:15 in front of a classroom full of students being punished. Most of the kids were well behaved. She let them read, text, do their homework, or listen to music. They usually ended up in detention for minor offenses. Hard-core offenders got suspended or reprimanded some other way. So it was a passive group—no Judd Nelsons among them.

Miranda usually graded papers during the sessions, making the most of her detention time. But after five afternoons in a row, she felt as if she were being punished, too. Repeatedly leaving the school when the place was quiet and nearly empty had started to take its toll. There was something creepy about all those dark classrooms. She'd gone home exhausted every night this week. It would have put a real crimp in her social life—if she'd had one. Miranda was divorced with two sons, ages eleven and thirteen.

Right now, she was eager to go home, put her feet up, and order home delivery. The boys were spending the weekend with their father.

Unfortunately, Miranda had to stay in the empty classroom a little longer. She had to meet Eden O'Rourke's father, who was late for his 5:30 appointment. She knew the child's situation and wanted to sympathize. But after only one day with her, Miranda loathed the smart-ass, raccoon-eyed street punk. She probably should have sent Eden to the principal for her performance in English Lit this morning. Miranda always had at least one pain-in-the-ass, rebellious student every year who thought they were coming up with the revolutionary idea that the "stupid teachers" should be assigning popular fiction—everything from graphic novels to *Fifty Shades of Grey*—instead of the classics. Miranda had taken pity on Eden and merely given her a writing task as punishment. But then, after asking some of Eden's other teachers how they'd fared with Ms. Rebel-Without-a-Clue, Miranda had learned that the girl had ditched all of her classes after lunch. So Miranda had put in a call to the father.

She'd had Hannah O'Rourke in her English class last year and thought she was a bit of a princess, but pretty and nice enough. Her brother, Steve, reminded her of a lamb because he was so sweet and cute. Miranda hadn't met either of the parents. She hadn't had any of the O'Rourke kids in her advisory—until now.

She wasn't sure what to expect with Mr. O'Rourke, but she figured he must be pretty sleazy since he'd knocked up Eden's mother while married to someone else. Sleazy and stupid. He'd done all his dick-swinging about seventeen years ago, so Miranda imagined him as an ex-jock hunk, now fat and bald. Or perhaps he was the wormy, pompous professor type. Whatever. She would give him an earful about his delinquent daughter and get out of there so that she was home by six-fifteen.

The students in detention had filed out twenty minutes ago, leaving Miranda alone in a classroom that still smelled of teenage B.O. Kids didn't shower after gym anymore.

She finally stood up to open a few windows.

"Ms. Warren?"

"Yes?" She turned and saw him in the classroom doorway.

He was handsome, tall and lean in a blue suit with his striped tie loosened. He smiled. "I'm Eden's dad, Dylan O'Rourke."

She automatically touched her hair to make sure it was in place. "Oh, hi, I—I'm Miranda Warren." She turned and opened the window, furtively checking her reflection in the glass. Then she pointed at a desk in the center of the front row. "Won't you sit down, please?"

He sat in the desk chair. "Before we get started," he said. "I have to apologize for Eden's fashion choice today. When she left the house, she had a sweater on. My wife and I had no idea what she had on underneath until our daughter, Hannah, told us."

Miranda usually sat down at her desk during these parent-teacher meetings, but she took the seat next to his. She smiled and gave a little shrug. "Well, on the bright side, not one boy fell asleep during my English class with Eden today."

He laughed. "I'm glad you have a sense of humor about it."

Sitting just a foot away from him, Miranda felt like a high school girl again, sitting beside the class hunk. She found herself downplaying his daughter's every transgression today, even trying to make excuses for her. Nevertheless, he kept apologizing—and he seemed sincere, too. A couple of times, she reached over and touched his arm while she was talking. A part of her knew it was sort of inappropriate, but she couldn't help herself.

It wasn't just because he was handsome. He had an aura about him—a friendly, easygoing warmth. He seemed to pay attention to every word she said. He exuded a certain laid-back confidence without being cocky about it. Most of all, he was clearly attracted to her. She'd gotten that vibe from plenty of middle-aged fathers during these conferences, but it had never been a turn-on—until now.

"You know," she said, leaning in closer to him. "With everything Eden has been through lately, have you considered getting her into some kind of counseling or therapy? Maybe all she needs is someone she could talk to . . ."

"That's so funny you should say that, because I was driving around with her the other day to buy stuff for her new room, and that very thought hit me. But I wasn't sure how to bring it up with her. I mean, maybe she'd be offended if I said something. So I sort of dismissed the idea, and I shouldn't have. I'm really glad you made that suggestion, Miranda. Thanks."

"I'm sure you would have come back to the idea soon enough," she said, resting her hand on his arm again.

He put his hand over hers for a moment and then stood up. "I have to be honest with you," he said. "I was dreading this meeting. But you've been terrific. I've really enjoyed talking with you." He let out an awkward laugh. "By the way, are we done here? I don't want to rush you. At the same time, I don't want to keep you. I wasn't sure . . ."

Smiling, Miranda got to her feet. "It's okay, we're done."

"Well, I'll make sure Eden gets that paper turned in on Monday, and I promise, she'll be properly dressed when you see her."

Miranda moved to her desk to gather her bag and her

coat. "You have my number in your phone now. So feel free to call me—if I can be of any help, that is."

Miranda thought about the night alone at home ahead of her. She wasn't seeing anyone currently. She'd never gone after a married man before. It had been five weeks since her last date, and nine weeks since she'd had sex. Those numbers raced through her mind as Dylan O'Rourke came around behind her and helped her on with her coat.

"It's getting dark out," he said. "May I walk you to your car?"

Good manners—and good-looking, she thought. "Well, I'm not in the teachers' lot. Ever since one of the other teachers got her tires slashed three years ago, I've parked in a secluded spot about four blocks away."

"Well, then, all the more reason I should walk with you, Miranda," he said. "If you don't mind my company."

She smiled at him. "Oh, I don't mind a bit."

She wasn't kidding about the secluded parking spot for her older-model silver Toyota Camry. It was beside a huge pine tree on a poorly lit cul-de-sac. The walk had been more like five blocks, and several times along the way, she'd leaned into him and casually bumped her shoulder against his. For most of the walk, Dylan had to keep his hands in his pockets to camouflage a hard-on.

He couldn't help it. She was beautiful and giving him all the signals that she wanted him. That would have been tough to resist in almost any kind of situation. But he hadn't shared a bed with his wife in four nights. Everyone in his life was disappointed in him. And his plans for tonight—to be with the one woman he really wanted—

had been derailed. Brooke had said she wanted him, too. He could have been with her right now, inside her.

But now he had to wait.

Having Eden's teacher flirt with him was a nice consolation prize.

As they approached her car, Miranda pulled the key fob out of her purse and pressed the unlock button. The Camry's lights blinked. "Well, I'm not sure what I'm going to do with myself tonight," she said. "I'm all alone. Maybe I should just pamper myself, take a bubble bath or something, you know, do it up with candles around the tub and soft music playing . . ."

"Sounds pretty great," was all he said in reply.

She nodded and let a silent moment pass. "Listen, I've probably taken you blocks away from your car. Why don't you get in, and I'll drive you to wherever you're parked."

"You sure it's no trouble?"

"I wouldn't ask if it was."

"Well, thank you, Miranda." He moved around to open the driver's door for her.

"So polite," she murmured, climbing into the car.

Dylan got in the passenger seat and closed the door.

But she didn't start the car.

Her hand moved to his thigh. "Are you in a hurry to get home?" she whispered.

"I probably have about an hour," he replied.

"We could do a lot in an hour."

She leaned over and hungrily kissed him on the mouth.

He thought of kissing Brooke the other night. This wasn't quite the same, but it wasn't bad, either, this consolation prize.

Her tongue slipped past his lips. Dylan felt her hand

moving up his thigh, lingering on his erection. Then she pulled at his belt buckle.

Dylan reached inside her coat and started to unbutton her blouse.

He told himself that what Sheila and Brooke didn't know wouldn't hurt them.

CHAPTER TWENTY-TWO

Friday—6:38 P.M.

Sheila usually liked the slightly acrid, earthy smell of her garden. It meant new plants, recently shifted soil, and things growing. But now, as a chill rolled in with the night, her once beautiful flower beds stank of rot, destruction, and mud. She'd been working in the garden for two hours, collecting the broken flowers and uprooted plants, trying to determine if anything was salvageable. It was all mostly compost now. She raked the displaced topsoil from the lawn back into the garden, tossed the dead plants in a wheelbarrow, and collected some of the stones that had been scattered across the grass.

For a while, Steve and Gabe had been helping her. Gabe had gotten bored quickly and headed back inside. With just Steve and her there in the backyard, he'd started defending Eden, saying she couldn't have wrecked the garden because she would have been covered head to toe with dirt this afternoon. And according to Eden, even if her boyfriend were still in town, he wouldn't have sabotaged the garden without telling Eden about it. At least, this was the gospel according to Eden, as told to Steve during their brief walk together.

Sheila listened to Steve's defense and had to agree with his first point, at least. But, if neither Eden nor her obnoxious boyfriend had destroyed her garden, then who had?

For a great deal of the time while Sheila and Steve were talking quietly in the backyard, they'd had to contend with Trudy barking incessantly next door.

At one point, they'd gone inside so Sheila could prepare dinner. It was pasta night. She'd gotten the spaghetti sauce started with sausage, leftover meatloaf, and whatever else she could find and left it to simmer. Then she'd gone back out to the garden to work alone—though not completely alone. She'd still had Trudy's barking and yowling to keep her company. Hannah had briefly come out to the backyard, asking if she could borrow some of Sheila's makeup. "Eden's skin tones are closer to yours than mine," she'd pointed out, "which is kind of weird, since she isn't even your daughter."

Sheila had told her to take whatever she wanted.

Hannah was in heaven. Somehow, her agreeing to let Eden borrow a few items of clothing had escalated into Hannah performing a makeover. "I told her that the Goth, urban nightmare look is so yesterday," Hannah had explained. "Anyway, you won't believe how different she looks already."

That had been about forty minutes ago. It was obvious to Sheila that Eden had ingratiated herself with the kids now. She had Steve bamboozled into believing she was this wrongly accused innocent. And by letting Hannah play Pygmalion for a teen makeover, they were bonding. Gabe was in his own little world and, therefore, neutral. And Dylan was her father, so it was obvious whose side he was on.

That left Sheila as the only one in the family who didn't trust her.

It was getting too dark outside to keep working, and

Sheila figured Dylan would be home soon. So she started gathering up the yard tools.

The backyard lights went on, making the ravaged garden look even sadder. She noticed a girl coming out through the kitchen door. It took Sheila a moment to recognize Eden in Hannah's old jeans and a black turtleneck. Her face and hair actually looked clean. Hannah had obviously spent a lot of time and effort applying just the right amount of cosmetics to make the girl appear naturally pretty and unspoiled.

Eden approached her tentatively. She almost looked desperate for approval.

A rake in her hand, Sheila just stared at her. Dylan's daughter had been hiding a lovely face behind that awful Goth makeup.

But as far as Sheila was concerned, she was still a monster.

"I thought I'd start cooking my dinner—if that's okay with you," Eden murmured.

"Fine," Sheila said.

"Listen, I'm really sorry about what happened to your garden," she said, her voice quavering a little. "I know you don't believe me, but I had nothing to do with it. Anyway, I'd like to help tomorrow, getting it back to the way it was."

"It'll be a long, long time and a lot of work before it's back to the way it was," Sheila said coolly.

"I'd like to help out just the same."

Sheila figured this was her cue to toss aside the rake and hug her. But she couldn't. She kept thinking of Eden and that burnout creep stalking her, the texts, the spider in her bed, the tainted cranberry juice, almost dying of electric shock, and today, the garden.

"Go make your dinner," she said, tightening her grip on the rake. "And I'd like you to keep something in mind."

"What?"

"If one of my kids gets sick or hurt, if some sort of freak accident happens to any of them, I'm holding you accountable. I promise, I'll make you pay."

Tears came to Eden's pretty eyes. She looked like she was about to say something.

"Now, leave me alone," Sheila said, cutting her off. She went back to gathering up the yard tools and didn't even look at Eden.

A few moments later, she heard the kitchen door shut.

CHAPTER TWENTY-THREE

Brodie stood at the information desk at Swedish Hospital with a flower arrangement in his hand. The fiftyish, blond receptionist was talking to someone on her phone headset. She held up her index finger to let him know she'd be with him soon.

Brodie wore an ill-fitting white shirt, a secondhand tie, and dirty khakis. He didn't have on his army camo jacket. He figured people were on the lookout for a guy wearing one. From reading online accounts of the Rattlesnake Mountain shooting, he knew the police were asking potential witnesses for a description of anyone who might have been seen with the victim, Arthur Merrens, on Thursday afternoon. So in addition to ditching his trademark jacket, Brodie had also cut his shaggy, dark-blond hair and dyed it black. Unfortunately, he hadn't mixed the dye right, and his hair came out a dull charcoal color that didn't look natural.

According to the same online article, Arthur Merrens was in a coma, but his partner and family were optimistic about his chances for a full recovery.

"Well, you better hope he never wakes up," Brodie had been told. "Obviously, Sheila has no idea what happened to him. And I don't think the garage where he works knows he was headed to her place on Thursday afternoon. So for now, you're reasonably safe, except for all the people who saw you with him at the lake on Thursday."

She wasn't happy with him at all. And she could be a first-class, raving bitch when she wasn't happy.

"You must be brainless to have chosen such a crowded spot to get rid of him," she said. "And then you did a half-assed job of it. If he wakes up, he'll connect what happened to him with the O'Rourkes, and our whole plan will be shot to hell. I wanted to take my time with this whole thing, but now I'll have to wrap this up as soon as possible. You just better hope he dies."

So Brodie decided he had to nip this in the bud before it became a real problem. That was why he was at the hospital now. It was why he'd already walked around the place and checked out all the entrances and exits. It was why he'd parked on the street close by, instead of in the pay lot, to prepare for a quick getaway if he needed one.

He'd thought about smothering the guy with a pillow. It depended on how many monitors were hooked up to the guy—and how far the nurse's desk was from his room. Or maybe he'd just make it quick and sloppy. Brodie might not have been wearing his big army jacket, but there was still plenty of room in the pocket of his khakis for a switchblade. And it only took a few seconds to slit a sleeping man's throat.

The receptionist finished talking on her headset and finally got around to acknowledging him. "Thanks for waiting," she said, smiling. "How can I help you?"

"I have a delivery for Arthur Merrens." A bit of water spilled out of the cheap vase as he lifted it to show her the flower arrangement. "I need the room number."

"He's in intensive care," she said, not needing to look up the location of their newsworthy patient. She pointed to the elevators. "Just go up to the second floor, turn left, and follow the signs to the ICU. You can leave the flowers at the nurse's desk up there."

"Does he have a room number?" Brodie pressed.

"Just leave it with the nurse at the desk. One of them will sign for it." Then the women turned away like she was finished with him. "Good evening," she said into the headset. "Swedish Hospital, how can I help you?"

Frowning, Brodie headed into the elevator and rode up to the second floor. He followed the signs and found a pair of closed glass doors with "Intensive Care Unit" in black and silver lettering on one of them. Beyond the doors was an L-shaped counter. A heavyset, black, thirty-ish nurse with severely close-cropped hair sat at the desk. She was scribbling something down while talking on a corded phone. Brodie was pretty certain she hadn't yet noticed him.

He ducked into an alcove for a stairwell door. This would take more finessing than he'd thought. He'd have to sneak past the nurses' station to reach the rooms, then poke his head in each one until he found Merrens. It wasn't a big hospital, so maybe there were only a few rooms in this unit. If he timed it right and acted quickly, maybe he could be in, out, and down the stairs within two or three minutes.

Brodie peeked around the corner of the alcove. The nurse was still at her desk. She glanced up—toward him.

Brodie quickly shrank back. "Crap," he muttered under his breath.

He looked up toward the corridor's ceiling to see if they had any cameras recording activity in the hallways, but there were none. At least, he didn't see any from where he stood. Brodie waited a few more minutes, then cautiously peered around the corner again.

The nurse's station was deserted.

. Brodie smiled. He stepped out of the alcove and hurried through the glass doors. They were still swinging shut behind him when he slithered past the nurses' desk. He spotted the stocky nurse in the back room, checking something in a binder notebook. Brodie continued on down a short corridor. He accidentally spilled water from the vase onto the floor as he peeked into the first patient room, where an old woman lay in bed. The nurse tending to her had her back to the door. Brodie tried the room across the hall: empty.

Creeping down the corridor, he poked his head into the next room down. A man lay in bed shirtless, with a big bandage on his shoulder and upper chest. His face was bruised and scratched—from falling through the tree branches. It was Merrens, all right. He had a tube in his nose and a cuff around his arm, just above the ACE bandage around his wrist. It looked like he was sleeping. Behind the headboard was a barrage of wires, cables, and monitors. Flowers and cards covered a table on the other side of some kind of monitor on wheels. With their long ribbons tied to the table leg, two "Get Well" helium balloons floated above the little impromptu altar.

No one else was in there with him. It seemed perfect.

Glancing over his shoulder, Brodie skulked into the room. He approached the bed and carefully set down the vase of flowers on the already cluttered bedside table. An empty glass almost fell off, but he caught it just in time. He placed it back on the tabletop.

Brodie reached into his pocket for the switchblade.

"Hey, what are you doing in here?"

Brodie swiveled around to see a tall, wiry Latino guy with a goatee. He was in his late twenties and wore jeans and a sweater. He held a folded newspaper in one hand. He looked annoyed.

"I'm just delivering flowers, man," Brodie muttered. He pointed to the arrangement on the night-table. "Everything's cool."

"No one's supposed to be in here," the goateed man said, stepping inside the room. "How did you get past the nurses' station?"

The man's eyes narrowed, and Brodie sneered at him. "Why don't you just chill, dude?"

Heading for the door, he kept his hand around the switchblade inside his pocket. He was prepared to cut the son of a bitch if he had to. Brodie brushed past him.

It looked like the guy was about to grab his arm. "Hey, hold on a minute . . ."

Brodie didn't stop. He didn't even slow down. "I don't have time for this shit. I got deliveries to make." He ducked out the door and hurried down the hallway.

Brodie could hear the guy talking on the phone: "Hello? Yeah, this is Richie Cansino, Artie Merrens' partner, in the ICU. Can you get security up here right away?"

Rushing past the nurses' station, Brodie saw the nurse out of the corner of his eye.

"Sir?" she called to him. "Wait—"

He just kept moving through the double doors and to the stairway access.

His footsteps echoed in the cinderblock stairwell as he raced down to the first floor. Having studied the hospital layout, he knew there was a gift shop with both hallway and outside entrances. He'd cut through there and make a beeline to his car on the street. Brodie was pretty confident they wouldn't catch him.

But they'd be looking for him if he tried to make a return visit.

Minutes later, once he was inside his car, Brodie checked his rearview mirror. It didn't look like anyone was following him. He pulled into traffic and tried to catch his breath.

You damn well better hope he never wakes up.

He would have to break the news to her that things got screwed up again. She'd probably go ballistic. They'd just have to take a chance with the coma. Maybe the guy would wake up, maybe not.

She couldn't take her sweet time as she'd originally planned. Everything would have to be accelerated.

If the wife and the kid were going to die, it needed to happen soon.

CHAPTER TWENTY-FOUR

Friday—11:20 P.M.
Seattle

"**H**ey, honey, what have you got there?"

The house was quiet. Steve had snuck into the den while his mom sat at her computer desk in the kitchen. She'd had the radio on low—some oldies station. He figured she wouldn't be able to hear him or see him from there. But he must have timed it wrong, because she'd come around from her office nook to refill her water glass at the refrigerator.

Steve stopped in his tracks. He tucked the old photo album under his arm. "I was just going to look at some pictures before I went to bed."

The glass of water in her hand, she moved closer to him. He knew she could tell from a glance at the maroon cover that the photo album was the old one, the one with pictures from his parents' wedding and before they'd even met. Steve knew his dad had looked at this album just recently because he'd mentioned how much Eden had looked like his mom in an old photo.

Steve noticed his mom frowning slightly at the album he'd chosen. But then she worked up a smile. "I'm sorry," she sighed. "With everything that's gone on today, I can't remember if you have a game or gymnastics practice tomorrow . . ."

"Gabe's got a game. But I don't have anything going on."

She nodded and then kissed him on the forehead. "Well, thanks for skipping practice for me this afternoon. Hope I didn't get you into trouble with the coach."

He shrugged. "It's okay."

"And thanks for the help with the garden tonight." She reached up and touched the side of his head, by his ear. "Your hair's growing back. It looks good."

"Thanks." He faked a yawn. "Well, I'm going to get ready for bed."

She sighed again. "And I guess those bills online aren't going to pay themselves. I better get back to them." But she didn't move, and her eyes narrowed as she looked closely at him. "Stevie, I know, with everything that's been happening lately, it's been pretty strange. But are you okay?"

He nodded a few more times than necessary. "Sure, I'm all right. It's cool."

"Because if anything is bothering you, anything at all, you can talk to your dad or me."

"Nothing's bothering me," he lied. "I'm fine."

"Well, g'night," she said.

With the photo album still tucked under his arm, Steve turned and headed up the stairs to his bedroom. He really wished his mom hadn't seen him with it.

Before ducking inside his room, he glanced down the hall. From the crack under the closed door, he could see the light was on in Eden's bedroom. His dad had been in there earlier, talking to her about his conference with Ms. Warren.

Earlier tonight, Steve had tried to convince his mom that Eden hadn't wrecked the garden. But in pleading Eden's case, he hadn't been completely honest with his mother. He hadn't told her—or anyone else, for that matter—that he'd seen Eden's boyfriend outside school today. The guy hadn't been in Portland for the past two days, Eden had confided. To Steve, it felt like a secret between his half sister and him.

For all Steve knew, the guy could still be in town. He could have lied to Eden about leaving for Portland this afternoon. He could have lied to her about a whole bunch of things. Steve wondered what kind of power this scumbag held over her.

Minutes ago, he'd come close to telling his mom the truth about Eden's boyfriend. He'd also come close to asking her about Aunt Molly.

But it was obvious his mom was emotionally fragile right now. So Steve hoped to find something in the old photo album. Though he'd looked at these pictures dozens of times over the years, maybe he'd missed something.

He wanted to study the photos of his mom's side of the family. His mom was supposed to be an only child. At least, that was what his parents had led him to believe. But his faith in his parents' word had been shaken lately. He couldn't help thinking that his mom had a sister who had died, or maybe this Aunt Molly was in an institution someplace.

The album was a fat binder with photos arranged on each page under a transparent peel-back plastic sheet. The pictures were secured in place with some mild adhesive coating that had made the page edges turn brown. Searching through the book, Steve didn't see anyone who looked like a sibling in any of his mom's early childhood photos. In group shots, she was clearly with friends— like in the grade school graduation shot, with four young girls in their caps and gowns, and what must have been a high school prom picture, with a tall, dorky-looking, basketball-player type in a tux.

But Steve noticed something strange. His dad's childhood and young adult snapshots—on the opposite page from his mom's—were always a standard size: $3" \times 5"$ and $4" \times 6"$, with a rare $5" \times 7"$ in there. But many of his mother's early family photos were an irregular size—as if someone had cut them down, or maybe cut a certain person out of the shots. Even a few of his parents' wedding photos were like that.

Steve flipped back several pages to his mother's early childhood pictures. He carefully peeled back the plastic sheet and pried some of his mom's irregular-size photographs off the page. In Steve's own baby pictures, before photos went digital, his mom had written his name and the date on the back. He hoped to find some names and dates on the back of his mom's childhood pictures.

Some photos had notations on the back, but nothing that revealed someone had been eliminated from the shot.

But then Steve found a photograph of his mother as a preteen, standing on a beach, squinting in the sun. She looked very cute, and happy. But there were two shadows on the sand behind her. And it looked like another child's elbow was at the very edge of the cropped image.

Steve peeled the photo off the adhesive page and looked at the back. He read the faded script, which must have been his grandmother's handwriting, because it wasn't his mom's. Half the caption had been cut off:

June, 198
Door Count
Sheila & Mol

Suddenly it seemed possible that his mom had a sister. But why had they hidden *Aunt Molly* from him and Hannah and Gabe?

Last week, Steve might not have believed it.

But then, last week, he'd had no idea about his half sister.

Saturday, September 29—12:47 A.M.

Dressed in an old Sting concert T-shirt and sweat shorts, Sheila turned down her bedcover. No spiders, thank God.

She'd already flossed, brushed her teeth, and washed her face. The drapes were drawn, and the bedroom was dark except for her bedside lamp. She had the door locked. She'd fallen asleep last night without any bourbon or Ambien. At dinner tonight, she'd drunk a couple of glasses of red wine, but nothing else. She had a good book for bedtime. She would just read until she got tired—like a normal person.

The game of musical beds was still going on between her and Dylan.

Sheila had noticed when he'd come back from the teacher conference earlier tonight that he'd smelled of perfume.

"Do I?" he asked, taking off his suit coat and throwing it on the cushioned seat in their breakfast booth. He headed to the refrigerator for a beer. "It's probably Eden's teacher, Ms. Warren. She was one of those touchy-feely, close-talking, personal-space invaders. And I noticed she kind of overdid it on the perfume, too. I'll shower and change before I eat so you don't have to smell it all night."

He took a swig of his beer. "So—I heard the neighbor's dog bark a few times last night just as I was hitting the sheets, but that was it. Still, I didn't sleep well in our bed alone. So what are the sleeping arrangements tonight? Could you please just tell me now? I'd like to turn in early. I was actually getting used to Gabe's bottom bunk. I'll go back there tonight if that's how you want it."

Standing at the stove, Sheila wasn't sure how to answer him. She imagined a sexy English teacher hanging on Dylan the way she'd seen other women at social gatherings touch his arm or shoulder when they talked to him. She should have gotten used to it years ago, but still.

She finally shrugged. "I'm still not ready to go back to sleeping together like everything's fine, because it isn't."

He said he understood. He went to bed in Gabe's room at eleven o'clock.

Sheila thought he'd given in way too easily.

So now she had their bed to herself and a good book as a consolation prize. She got half a chapter read before the words started to blur. Switching off the light, Sheila slid down beneath the covers. She thought about Steve, taking the photo album up to his room tonight. She rarely looked at that particular album because none of her children were in it.

At least, that was her excuse.

But the truth was, even with so many of the photos cut down, she couldn't cut out the memories of when—and with whom—they were taken. She'd altered or completely destroyed so many of her family snapshots seventeen years ago. At the time, going through the collection had confirmed what she'd always thought. Her sister had gotten all the attention.

Molly was prettier—blond, blue-eyed, and dimpled, with perfect skin. No wonder their dad took so many photos of her. Sheila was six years older, the babysitter, the responsible one, the one who did everything her parents expected of her. In junior high and high school, she always made the honor roll. In her bedroom, she had a shelf full of sports and community service awards. And yet, it never seemed to be enough for her parents.

Molly called her a suck-up, Miss Goody-Two-Shoes, a total drag.

Their parents let Molly get away with everything. She went through school with Cs and Ds because she didn't apply herself. She wasn't even thirteen when she started drinking, breaking curfew, and going out with the wrong guys. Sheila remembered telling her: "I'm the suck-up, but you're the fuckup."

The remark had made Molly cry.

At the time, Sheila was in college, studying accounting and working part time to help pay for her room and board. Thirteen-year-old Molly had just been arrested. She'd been in a speeding car full of drunken high school kids when a cop had pulled them over. The other kids were two or three years older than her. Molly had drunk three Miller Lites, and one of the boys had talked her into taking off her bra under her T-shirt.

Sheila remembered how she held her weeping sister. She rocked Molly in her arms and kept apologizing for calling her a fuckup.

But it was the truth—just as it was true that Sheila really was kind of a suck-up.

It was only more of the same as they got older. Sheila used to study articles and essays about family birth order, sibling rivalries, and sibling roles. She thought she could figure out her relationship with Molly the way she could figure out a tough accounting problem. She often wondered if she and Molly kept each other in their assigned roles. Maybe if they were estranged, Molly would be more responsible and Sheila could cut loose and have some fun, stop doing everything she thought was expected of her.

Molly was away at the University of Oregon when their dad died and their mom got sick. Sheila handled everything, of course, even though she was married with a full-time job—and vomiting daily, thanks to the baby on the way. She handled all her mother's accounts, including bills from the University of Oregon. Sheila also wrote and signed the checks for Molly's "food money." Every month, she'd mail the check, along with a pathetic little note to Molly that their ailing mother would scrawl in her failing penmanship. Sheila got copies of her sister's grades, too, and they were abysmal. Molly, by her own admission, was partying all the time. She was just three hours away in Eugene, but she never had time over the weekends to visit their sick mother.

It drove Sheila crazy. Yet she wouldn't have trusted Molly to look after their mom anyway. Molly couldn't even look after herself.

That summer when Sheila was so sick and haggard, her sister remained in Eugene to lifeguard at a country club. She'd always been a good swimmer. So while Sheila worked herself toward a nervous breakdown, she imagined Molly working on her tan and partying nightly with her college friends. Meanwhile, Sheila kept signing those "food money" checks for her sister.

One night she got a call from Molly's roommate, Darcie. "Hi, Sheila, I just wanted to give you a heads-up that Molly's in the hospital tonight—and maybe tomorrow night, too," the girl explained.

"My God, what happened?"

"Uh, well, she took a bunch of sleeping pills this afternoon—like a whole bottle, prescription stuff. I don't know how she got them."

"Is she okay?" Sheila asked anxiously.

"Yeah, they pumped her stomach. They're keeping her overnight for observation. I guess, in cases like this, the doctors are always afraid the patient will try it again."

"So this wasn't an accident," Sheila said, hoping for some clarification. "She was trying to kill herself."

"Or maybe get some attention," Darcie said. "I'm not sure. I mean, Molly knows when I usually come home, and I'm the one who found her."

"Did she leave a note or anything?"

"No, but I'm pretty sure I know what the problem is. Molly's been really messed up lately . . ."

Lately? Sheila wanted to ask. She wiped a tear away. After the initial shock, she was starting to get frustrated. "What—what's Molly messed up about this time?"

"Well, she's been drinking even more than usual lately. There's this senior, Jesse, and they've been seeing each other off and on all year. He just graduated, and he's spending the summer here in Eugene. Molly's pretty hung up over him, but I think he's just using her. I don't know the whole story. I haven't even met Jesse yet. The other thing is that Molly's worried about whether or not the school will take her back next semester, because her grades were so bad."

This was the first Sheila had heard of Jesse, and the first time she'd heard of Molly actually caring about her grades.

"And she got fired," Darcie added. "I think it's because she kept showing up late for work—or not showing up at all. But Molly thinks it's political, because she was seeing a club member's son and his mother wanted to break them up."

"This is someone else—in addition to Jesse?"

"Yeah, this one's name is Brian."

Sheila sighed. "Has Molly asked for me? Does she want me to come down there?"

Because I can't, Sheila wanted to say. What with work, bouts of throwing up, and constant house calls to her sickly mother.

"Well, she could be out of the hospital tomorrow, so I wouldn't bother making the trip. But she definitely needs someone to pay the hospital and ambulance bills. And you'll have to send another check, too, because I need rent money. I've covered the last two months for her, and she owes me."

Sheila thought about how miserable and scared her kid sister must have been, having just tried to kill herself hours before, sitting in a hospital bed amid a bunch of strangers in another city, three hours away.

And yet Sheila couldn't help hating her.

Molly had a bedroom in their mother's apartment. It made no sense that they were sending her money so she could live in another city, where she no longer had a job, all so she could be near some guy who apparently didn't give a crap about her. If Molly was going to be irresponsible, she could do that a lot more cheaply at home.

There would still be a nurse on duty at her mom's place. So it wasn't like their mother would be left alone with Molly for any long stretch of time. In fact, Sheila even wondered if she could simply pay the nurse a little bit more to look after the two of them. Still, she thought about her mother in that wheelchair, up on the rooftop track, begging to be put out of her misery. Sheila wondered how her reckless, suicidal sister would have handled it.

But at the time, she couldn't think of any other options. So she asked Molly to move back home, at least until school started in the fall.

Lying in bed alone, once again unable to sleep, Sheila thought about how different things would have been if only her sister hadn't come home.

The dog next door started barking.

"Oh, God, spare me," Sheila groaned.

She glanced at the digital clock on her nightstand: 1:43 A.M. It had been a little over a half hour since she'd turned the light out.

Sheila wondered if she'd be better off sleeping in Hannah's room in the basement again. She wouldn't hear the dog down there. Obviously, she'd need some help falling asleep up here. Ambien or bourbon? Though she took it often enough, she still didn't completely trust Ambien. Dylan had told her that she'd once sleepwalked after taking Ambien, and another time, she'd had a whole conversation with him while asleep. Sheila didn't remember a thing about either incident. Some people claimed that while under the influence of the stuff, they had cooked and eaten a meal, even made love or driven a car—and then had no memory of any of it. For Sheila, hearing stories like that made a couple of shots of bourbon seem a lot safer.

Trudy was still going on at full volume. It was a distressed sort of yowling.

"What the hell's going on over there?" Sheila muttered, climbing out of bed.

Switching on the light, she made her way across the bedroom to the window. She moved the curtain to look outside.

Sheila let out a gasp.

The woman next door stood in her window, directly across the way. It was almost as if she was waiting for her. She wore a white, full-length nightgown, low-cut with straps. The lights were on behind her, making the gown practically transparent. She stared back at Sheila and remained perfectly still. She might as well have been a mannequin.

There was no sign of the dog, but Sheila could hear it yelping as if it were hurt.

Sheila quickly pulled the drape shut again.

"My God," she muttered. What was wrong with that woman? And what was she doing to her poor dog?

Sheila stepped out to the hallway to see if another bedroom light was on. Was everyone else sleeping through this?

It was completely dark in the corridor. Apparently, she was the only one awake.

Sheila decided to have a couple of shots of bourbon. It wouldn't make the barking go away, but at least she wouldn't care so much.

She headed downstairs to the darkened first floor. Sometimes, when she was the only one awake, all the deserted, shadowy rooms could be slightly eerie. But right now, she was too angry to be scared. She even considered throwing on her coat, going over to the neighbor's house, and banging on her door so she could have it out with her. It was almost as if this woman intended to make her life miserable. Maybe the neighbor was tormenting her dog in that room directly across the way just so it would bark when Sheila was trying to sleep. Why had the dog been relatively quiet the one and only night Dylan had slept in the master bedroom? Maybe last night the neighbor had seen Dylan in the bedroom before he'd turned off the lights. Maybe, since the drapes were shut tonight, the woman had gotten the dog to bark in hopes that Dylan would come to the window. Was that why she was wearing that skimpy nightgown—to give Dylan a show? Who wears a sexy nightgown like that when they're sleeping alone, anyway?

Sheila knew her mind was reeling. As paranoid as it seemed, she couldn't help feeling persecuted.

She wondered if that Leah woman was the one who had demolished her garden. After all, hadn't she thrown that flower arrangement away? She'd even left it out on the front curb with the garbage and recycling so Sheila would be sure to see it.

Switching on the light in the kitchen, Sheila padded over to the cupboard. Then she got out the Jim Beam and her favorite jelly glass.

The barking finally stopped—at least, for the moment.

Sheila turned to glance out the window at the house next door. None of the first-floor lights were on. Sheila couldn't shake the feeling that her awful new neighbor was standing there in the dark, studying her.

And she used to think the place was creepy back when it had been empty.

Sheila poured the Jim Beam. She started to reach for the glass but missed it and knocked it over. "Good one, Sheila," she muttered. "Swell . . ."

At least the glass hadn't broken. But she'd spilled bourbon across the boomerang-pattern counter. The pungent liquor smell filled the kitchen. Sheila grabbed a sponge, wiped up the mess, and then returned to the sink. As she wrung out the sponge, she felt something sharp bite into her hand in several places. It hurt like hell. "Shit!" she whispered.

Sheila quickly dropped the sponge and glanced at her hand. Her palm and two fingers were bleeding. The alcohol made the little cuts sting even more. She watched another spot on her hand start to bleed, and she noticed a tiny, embedded shard of glass. Wincing, Sheila picked it out.

She tore off some more sheets of paper towel and clutched them in her hand to soak up the blood.

She glanced over at the countertop again. The jelly glass wasn't even cracked or chipped. Where had the glass come from?

Then she picked up the bottle of bourbon. It was half full. What was she thinking? She'd broken her own, self-preserving statute. She'd told herself she wouldn't consume anything that had already been opened. And she'd opened this bottle sometime early last week.

Sheila set the wadded-up, blood-spotted paper towels by the sink. From the cupboard, she took out an old-fashioned glass. Then from the utensil drawer she dug out a small wire strainer. Setting the strainer on the glass, she poured at least three shots' worth of bourbon through the strainer.

She could see the ground glass in the strainer, glistening like diamonds.

She immediately thought of Eden. She thought of that sweet, innocent act she'd tried to pull over on her in the garden earlier tonight.

Sheila held the bourbon bottle up to the light, shook it a little, and watched the sparkling bits swirl in the amber liquid.

She wondered if the little bitch had put some eye drops in there, too, while she was at it.

Forty-five minutes later, Sheila took half of an Ambien and crawled into her bed again.

She'd left the light on in the kitchen, and another one on in the den. She wanted the woman next door to think she was still up. The whole time she'd been awake, Trudy hadn't barked at all. Whether or not that was just a co-incidence, Sheila wasn't taking any chances.

She'd hidden the bottle of bourbon on the top shelf of the kitchen cupboard behind some trays and chafing dishes she broke out only on special occasions. For the time being, it would be safe back there. Besides, no one in the house touched the bourbon except her.

Sheila had decided to keep the tainted bottle of Jim Beam because she wanted to try an experiment on Eden. At some point tomorrow night, she'd sit down with her stepdaughter. She'd apologize for all their misunder-standings. Then she'd propose they both have a very grownup toast to a new start with just a little bit of bour-bon. Certainly, Eden had tried bourbon before. All she had to do was take a few sips.

If the girl refused to drink it, then, as far as Sheila was concerned, that would be an admission of guilt. And con-sidering everything else that had happened in the last few days, it was just the tip of the iceberg.

Sheila still hoped to gather more information about her from some of Antonia's friends. She just needed to get her hands on that guest book from the memorial ser-vice. She counted on the FedEx package finally arriving tomorrow.

Of course, when she talked to Antonia's friends, she'd need to be tactful. But how could she tactfully ask them the question on her mind?

Do you think your friend, Antonia, was murdered by her daughter?

Right now, it seemed very, very possible.

Tossing back the bedcovers, Sheila climbed out of bed and started across the room toward the door. Her legs felt wobbly, and she realized the Ambien must have started kicking in.

Sheila checked the door to make sure it was locked. Then she made her way back to bed.

Her last thought before she lost consciousness wasn't about Eden or Antonia.

It was about someone she'd never even met. For some reason, Sheila thought of Ms. Warren. She imagined Eden's teacher earlier tonight, hanging on Dylan and getting her scent all over him.

CHAPTER TWENTY-FIVE

Saturday—3:28 A.M.
Shoreline

Miranda Warren was alone and half asleep in her queen-size bed.

Whenever she heard a strange noise in the house late at night, it was usually one of her sons snoring or thrashing around in his sleep. Their bedroom was next to hers. But Seth and Finn were at her ex-husband's this weekend.

Miranda was pretty sure the sound she'd heard—the one that had woken her minutes ago—had been a raccoon in her garbage. Her ranch house was on a wooded, dead-end street. The raccoons came out at night to scavenge, often in packs and sometimes with their babies. About a year ago, she'd heard a horrible racket in the tall evergreen right outside her window, and she'd realized it had been two raccoons mating. It seemed like a pretty crazy place to have sex, up in a tree.

But who was she to criticize? She'd just had sex in her car earlier tonight. It had been frantic, sweaty, and, at times, uncomfortable. But it had also been damn hot. She'd spent the rest of the evening with a smile on her face.

Yes, he was a married guy. And calling it unprofessional on her part was the understatement of the year.

Still, the whole wicked experience was exciting and sexy. Miranda told herself she deserved every pleasurable minute.

It was just too bad she'd had to go to bed alone tonight.

Miranda thought she heard another sound. *Just the raccoons looking for food*, she told herself again. If they made a mess outside, she'd clean it up in the morning.

She turned over on her left side and adjusted the pale blue quilt, tucking it under her chin.

Then Miranda remembered something. The garbage collectors had come Friday morning. There was no garbage, no food scents to attract the raccoons.

She lay there in the dark, suddenly afraid to move.

She'd have to roll over to reach for her bedside lamp or check the bedroom door. But she couldn't. She kept perfectly still and listened for the next sound. It was deathly quiet.

Miranda wasn't sure how much time passed, but she finally rolled over and blindly reached for the lamp. Her hand frantically fanned at the air for a moment before she touched the lamp base and worked her way up to the switch. She turned on the light.

Now he knows you're awake, she thought.

A floorboard creaked. It sounded like it came from the hallway.

She stared at the closed bedroom door. The lock on the doorknob didn't work. It was one of those things she'd been meaning to get fixed. But it only occurred to her on these weekends when she was alone in the house.

She thought she saw the knob twist to one side.

Stop it, she told herself. *Now you're imagining things.*

Except for her bedroom door, the house was all locked up. She'd checked everything before going to bed. She was fine. So she'd heard some noises outside. No one had broken in.

Wasn't it funny—that she'd think someone was coming to kill her on this particular night? Did it have anything to do with the fact that she'd finally had some great sex with a married guy? Could it be that she was feeling a little guilty? Maybe she thought she was going to be punished for actually having some fun. A shrink would have had a field day analyzing her right now.

Still, she was frightened.

Miranda figured she'd have to get out of bed and check every room in the house. It was ridiculous, but it was the only way she'd ever fall asleep again tonight.

She'd left her smartphone on the nightstand, right beside the old landline they still used on rare occasions. Grabbing her phone, Miranda switched it on so she could quickly call 9-1-1—if it became necessary. She climbed out of bed, shivering as the air hit her bare legs and the strip of midriff exposed between the top band of her pink panties and her small T-shirt.

In the corner of her bedroom, she had a basket of yarn and the beginnings of a sweater she'd been knitting for Finn, one of those projects she'd probably never finish. Miranda took one of the long knitting needles and tucked it under her arm. Tiptoeing toward the door, she put her ear to it and listened for a moment. Silence.

She opened the door and pulled the knitting needle out from under her arm. She told herself, if she saw an intruder, she'd aim for the eyes or the neck.

From the darkened hallway, she peeked into her sons' room. The door was open, and beyond it, blackness—except for a faint line of moonlight coming through a break between the window curtains. With trepidation, she reached in and switched on the light by the door. The bedroom was vacant. Messy, but vacant.

It was like that for each room in the house: a little messy, but empty, with no sign of a break-in. She didn't check the basement because it was unfinished, and too cluttered and creepy. The basement door off the kitchen had a lock on it, and Miranda double-checked to make sure it was secured. She also checked the locks to the kitchen and the front doors. She was fine.

Miranda went back to bed, but now she was too wired to sleep. She decided to read an article or two in *People* magazine until her eyes got tired. She left her phone and the knitting needle on her nightstand. She was halfway through a story about how a hunky TV star had kicked his drug addiction when she heard another noise. It seemed to come from right outside her closed bedroom door—another creak of the floorboards.

She hadn't checked the boys' bedroom closet. Someone could have climbed in through the window and hidden in their closet amid the clothes and toys.

Her cell phone rang, giving her a start.

She automatically thought something must have happened to one of the boys. It was almost four in the morning. Why else would anyone call at this hour? She figured it had to be her ex-husband. She snatched up the phone. "Yes? Gary?"

"Is this Ms. Warren?" It was a woman's voice. She was whispering.

"Who is this?" Miranda asked. Her heart was racing.

"It's Mrs. O'Rourke," the voice growled. "You look like a whore walking around in your underwear like that."

Horrified, Miranda stared at her phone—and at the Caller ID. It was her landline. The call was coming from the extension in the kitchen.

"What—what do you want?" Miranda said into the phone. She could barely talk. She could barely even breathe.

"I won't let you ruin my family," the woman said.

Miranda could hear the voice inside her house now.

She dropped the phone. Paralyzed with fear, she heard the footsteps coming closer, loud and quick. The light went on in the hallway. Miranda saw it under the crack in the door.

"Leave me alone!" she screamed, grabbing the knitting needle from the nightstand.

The bedroom door flew open. The light was behind the woman, leaving her face in the shadows. But Miranda could see she had dark hair. She wore a purple coat with the collar raised. She had a gun in one gloved hand. The other hand held something behind her back.

Miranda sprang up so she was kneeling on her bed. Tears in her eyes, she held the knitting needle in her shaking fist. But it seemed utterly useless. "No," she whispered. "Please, wait . . ."

From behind her, the woman pulled out Miranda's son's pillow, the one with the X-Men pillow case.

"Finn's pillow," Miranda whispered, dazed. "What—what are you doing with that?"

"They say it muffles the sound."

The woman held the pillow in front of the gun and fired twice. In the silence, the muffled shots still seemed loud.

Miranda screamed as those first two shots went off—and missed.

The third shot silenced her. She flopped back on the bed. The knitting needle flew out of her hand.

The woman dropped the tattered pillow and took a step toward the bed.

Miranda lay perfectly still, with her eyes open and a bullet in her throat. Beneath her neck and shoulders, a crimson stain began to bloom on the blue quilt.

And all the while, feathers whirled around the room like snow.

CHAPTER TWENTY-SIX

Saturday—9:22 A.M.
Seattle

Steve stopped raking leaves for a moment. He watched his dad, with a saw, cutting up the small Japanese maple tree that had been ripped out of the garden. Steve's mom had said the tree couldn't be saved. So his dad was dividing the battered-looking thing into sections so it could be bundled for the garbage collectors to haul away.

They wanted to get a head start on today's garden rebuilding project—and surprise Steve's mom, who was still asleep. She usually didn't stay in bed this late. Steve figured she must have had another bout with insomnia last night.

It was just he and his dad out there for now. Gabe had to conserve his energy for an "away" football game in Kent. Hannah would be there to cheer him on and represent the family, although her motives were actually self-serving. She had a crush on the older brother of one of Gabe's teammates. Apparently, he was going to the game as well, and she'd finagled a ride from him.

Eden had said something about helping with the garden today, but she'd slept in, too.

Between the leaves and the morning chill in the air, it really felt like fall. Steve could even see his breath. He and his father worked together without saying much.

He wanted to ask his dad what Ms. Warren had said about Eden last evening, but he figured it was none of his business. And his father wasn't volunteering any information. So they were quiet.

Besides, half the time, whenever they started talking, the dog next door would bark.

Steve was only mildly curious about the parent-teacher conference anyway. He'd been there for the whole showdown between Eden and Ms. Warren. So he didn't need to hear a recap.

What he really wanted to ask his father about was Aunt Molly.

Last night, after looking through the family album, Steve had gone online in search of anything about Molly Driscoll. It turned out there was a journalist with that name, so Steve kept coming up with articles she'd written. He'd been on Google for nearly an hour, but he couldn't find anyone he could connect to his mother. It dawned on him that maybe Molly was just a good friend of his mom's. Though he'd grown up without any actual aunts or uncles, as a kid he'd called a few of his parents' close friends Aunt This or Uncle That. His godparents, Aunt Judy and Uncle Bill, were actually his parents' next-door neighbors from when they'd first moved to Seattle. Maybe this Molly person had a totally different last name.

Whatever the case, it was obvious there was someone in his mother's life named Molly. And for one reason or another, she was a big secret. Steve kept wondering what had happened to her—or what she had done that was so horrible. It must have been pretty bad if they'd cut her out of all those family photos.

Had she murdered somebody? Steve's mind couldn't help going there, what with all the grisly true-crime stories he'd read. Among the many Google search variations he'd tried were "Molly Driscoll Murder" and "Molly Driscoll Killer." But he'd found nothing.

His mom hadn't been the only one unable to sleep last night. His mind racing, Steve had tossed and turned for at least an hour. At one point, he'd thought he heard someone come and go in the middle of the night. But maybe he'd dreamt it.

Abandoning his rake, Steve helped gather up the branches and sections of the small tree so his dad could tie them in a bundle. "Hey, Dad," he finally said. He spoke in a quiet voice so he wouldn't be heard inside the house—and so he wouldn't trigger another barking fit from the neighbor's dog. "Can I ask you something?"

Hunched over his work, his father stopped to look at him. "This sounds serious."

Steve shrugged. "I don't know, maybe it is."

His dad straightened up and took off his work gloves. "What is it, Stevie?"

He hesitated.

"You know, you can ask me anything," his father whispered. He smiled, reached over, and rubbed Steve's shoulder.

Steve couldn't quite look him in the eye. "Did—did Mom have a sister? Someone named Molly?"

The smile faded from his father's face. His hand dropped to his side. "What makes you ask that?"

Steve could tell he'd hit a nerve.

"I got this weird text yesterday," he explained. "Someone—I don't know who—sent me a message: *Ask your mom about your Aunt Molly*." He shrugged. "But Mom was so upset about the garden yesterday, I didn't want to upset her any more. I kept thinking the message must be about something awful."

His dad said nothing. Frowning, he wiped the sweat off his forehead with the back of his hand.

Steve told him about the cut-up photos in the family album—and the one with the writing on the back.

His father nodded soberly. "So this text you mentioned earlier," he said. "You don't have any idea who sent it?"

"I thought maybe it was Eden, but when I asked her, she didn't know a thing about it."

His father said nothing. He just twisted his mouth over to one side as if baffled and slightly ticked off.

"*Did* Mom have a sister named Molly?" Steve pressed. At the same time, he thought maybe he should stop asking. His dad obviously didn't want to answer him.

He glanced down at a chunk of the tree, then sighed. "Yes, Molly was her younger sister," he whispered. "But your mom doesn't like talking about her. It's still a very painful subject. I'm glad you came to me about this, Stevie."

Yet he didn't seem glad at all. He rubbed Steve's shoulder again. "Please, don't ask your mom about her, okay? Your instincts were right. You'd just upset her. For your mother, it's easier to pretend Molly never existed. I don't completely agree with that, but I have to respect it. Anyway, that's why we didn't say anything to you kids about her."

Steve thought of all those photos Molly had been cut out of. "Was she at your wedding?"

His father nodded. "She was the maid of honor. She and your mom were very close growing up."

"And now she's dead?"

"Yes, she died before you were born."

"How? What happened to her?"

His father sighed. "Molly had a lot of problems. Your mom did the best she could to help her. She's always blamed herself for what happened to Molly. They were never sure if it was an accident, or if she jumped . . ."

"Jumped?" Steve repeated. "What do you mean?"

"It was like what happened to Eden's mother," his father whispered, so quietly that Steve barely heard him. "She fell several stories off the roof of an apartment building."

Dazed, Steve stared at him. "When did this happen?"

"About seventeen—almost eighteen years ago," his father answered. He glanced toward the house. "You aren't going to say anything to your mother about this, are you?"

Steve quickly shook his head.

"Good. Let's just keep this between us, okay?"

"Sure," Steve murmured.

His father gave him a hug. "Thanks, Stevie."

For a moment, Steve's arms remained at his sides. He was so stunned that he forgot to return the hug. He smelled his dad's aftershave and felt his hand patting him on the back. Steve finally put his arms around him, but only briefly.

Breaking away, Steve squinted at him. "So that's weird Eden's mom died the same way as Molly."

His father put the work gloves back on. He knelt on the stack of cut branches as he tried to tie it up with a rope. The branches snapped under his weight. "Yeah, I know," he muttered. "What are the odds?"

Steve knew his father didn't expect an answer.

And he didn't expect any more questions, either.

The clock on the microwave read 9:58 A.M.

In her bathrobe, Sheila stood by the window in the kitchen door, a freshly poured cup of coffee in her hand. She'd put milk in it instead of cream because the cream had been opened earlier in the week, and it was one of those items she'd told Eden that she alone consumed.

In a sweatshirt that belonged to Hannah, Eden was raking leaves in the backyard with Steve. The two half-siblings were talking, but Sheila couldn't hear what they were saying because Dylan was mowing the lawn. With her face clean and her hair in a ponytail, Eden looked pretty. She seemed like one of the family out there.

Sheila wondered how many other items in the house had been tampered with. Was the girl impatiently waiting for her to drink, eat, or swallow something else? Maybe right now, Eden imagined her dead in her bedroom upstairs. Perhaps she was hoping a fatal dose of something or other had finally done the trick.

Sheila now realized she'd taken a big chance swallowing an Ambien last night. It could have been a tablet of arsenic, or some other kind of poison.

The doorbell rang.

No one in the backyard heard it because of the lawnmower. But obviously Trudy had, because she started barking next door.

Putting down her coffee cup, Sheila headed toward the front door. But when she realized it could be FedEx with that package from the funeral home, she started to run. Unlocking the door, she flung it open. She saw the FedEx delivery woman climbing back into her truck. On the front stoop was a package about the size of a gift box for a sweater. The package was addressed to Eden O'Rourke.

Sheila scooped up the box. It must have weighed about five or six pounds. As the delivery truck started to back out of the driveway, Sheila glanced at the return address on the package, just to make sure it was what she'd been waiting for: *March-Middleton Funeral Services*.

Ducking back inside the house, Sheila closed the door

and returned to the kitchen. She peeked out the window again. The three of them were still working in the yard. Sheila was pretty certain they hadn't heard the truck.

Grabbing a knife from the rack on the counter, she cut the tape along the sides of the parcel. Then, with her coffee and the package, she retreated upstairs to her room. She locked the bedroom door, sat down on the floor, and opened the box.

She felt a bit guilty when the first thing she saw was a note to Eden, signed by the man Sheila had spoken to on the phone the other day. But then she thought of the ground glass in her bourbon last night and quickly got over any qualms she had. The note thanked Eden for using the funeral home's services and explained that the enclosed materials were being provided to her free of charge. There was a sleek folder, full of paperwork, and a box with fifty thank-you cards for people who had attended the service, sent flowers, or made donations. There was also a stack of memorial prayer cards and leftover programs. And finally, there was the guest book. The cover was black, with GUESTS & TRIBUTES embossed in swirly silver script.

Sheila opened the book to the first page and read a note in very neat penmanship:

Dear —

Your mother was a lovely neighbor. Always a smile for everyone! She'll be missed.

I'm so sorry for your loss. My thoughts & prayers are with you at this difficult time.

Sincerely, Eileen Pollakoff
Bristol Apts.

The tribute on the next page was pretty terse:

Condolences,

Sid Parsons,
Caretaker, Bristol Apts.

Sheila imagined some neighbors from Antonia's apartment building must have carpooled over to the funeral home together because the first five signatures were all from people who had followed Eileen's lead and written "Bristol Apts." after their names. Like Eileen, none of them seemed to know Eden's name.

Some people merely signed their names. Most kept it brief, as Sid had.

In addition to Antonia's neighbors at Bristol Apartments, there was a set of mourners from a different camp. Close to ten coworkers from the Portland Hilton had signed the book. But only one of them seemed to know Eden's name. Another one had called her "Erin."

There were about thirty signatures in the book, and Eden's boyfriend, Brodie, wasn't among them.

Sheila figured, with a little research online, she could get the phone numbers for some of these people. The Hilton coworkers would be easy to contact. All she had to do was phone the hotel and ask for them.

But it wasn't as simple as all that. After looking up the number for the hotel, Sheila called and got the hotel operator. She asked to talk to Nancy Abbe but was told that Nancy didn't work weekends. Neither did Jay Simmons. She tried the next one on the list, Barbara Riddle, and found out she was no longer employed there. Sheila could tell the operator was getting impatient with her.

"I'm trying to track down some people who were

friends with Antonia Newcomb—Toni," Sheila told her. "Maybe you knew her?"

"No, actually, I didn't," the operator said, a bit snippy.

"Do you know someone there who was close with her?"

"No."

Flustered, Sheila glanced at the book again. "Is Debra Barnes working today?"

"I'll connect you."

Debra Barnes wasn't at her desk. But Sheila got her voicemail. She left a message: "Hi, Debra. My name's Sheila, and I was hoping you could give me some information about Antonia—*Toni*—Newcomb, specifically about Toni and her daughter, Eden. Could you call me? It's rather urgent. I promise not to take up much of your time." She left her number and clicked off.

Sheila didn't want to call the hotel and risk getting that same officious operator again. So she went online to look up the phone numbers for some of Antonia's neighbors. The site that was supposed to locate people seemed fairly accurate with the Pendleton Street Northwest address, but the phone numbers listed must have been old landlines. Sheila's first three attempts to call residents of the Bristol resulted in two wrong numbers and one number no longer in service.

She was about to try another neighbor's phone number when she heard the lawnmower stop. Getting to her feet, she padded over to the far window and glanced down at the backyard. Dylan was emptying the lawnmower's bag. Eden and Steve were still raking leaves.

As she sat down on the floor again, Sheila threw everything back into the box except for the guest book. She kept that, along with her phone, and then shoved the package under her bed. She heard Gabe in his room down the hall, playing the theme from *Captain America* on his computer, which he always did to psych himself up before heading to a football game.

Sheila tried the number listed online for Sid Parsons, the Bristol Apartments caretaker who didn't have much to say in the guest book. To her surprise, someone answered on the second ring. "Hello?"

"Hello, is Sid Parsons there, please?"

"Speaking."

"Hi, Mr. Parsons. My name's Sheila, and I understand you're the caretaker at the Bristol Apartments."

"Yeah . . ." he answered warily.

"I was hoping you might be able to tell me something about a resident there who recently passed away, Antonia Newcomb."

"Are you a reporter or with the police or something?"

"No. Actually, I'm sort of a distant relative—by marriage. Antonia's daughter, Eden, has become my responsibility. I'm looking after her now. But to be completely honest, I don't know much about the girl or her relationship with her mother—"

"Listen, I have one foot out the door here," he interrupted. "I can't talk now. But I have some of Antonia's personal effects. It's not much, just a couple of boxes of old photos I found when I was cleaning out the built-in hutch. They're just in the way here. Do you or the girl want them? I'll be back here after two-thirty, if you want to come by and pick them up."

Sheila hesitated. Was she willing to take an impromptu trip down to Portland?

"Ah . . . yes. Yes, I think I can get there later this afternoon," she said. "Listen, I was wondering if Antonia was close friends with anyone in the building. I'm hoping someone there could give me information about how she died. The newspapers were so vague about it—and so was Eden, for that matter."

"I'm the one you should talk to," Sid said with a hint of self-importance. "I saw her fall. I'll tell you about it when I see you this afternoon. I'll be around from two-thirty on. Now, I hate to cut you short, but I really need to get going."

"I'll see you this afternoon, Sid."

"Sounds like a plan," he replied. Then he hung up.

Sheila immediately went on the internet and checked Alaska Airlines for available flights to Portland.

Sheila booked herself on a flight to Portland that departed shortly after noon. She figured she could be at the Bristol Apartments by two-thirty. She might even have time to swing by the Hilton before catching her return flight. She'd be home by seven.

Getting dressed, Sheila felt as if she were losing her mind. She couldn't find her purple coat, and a pair of shoes was missing. They'd been in her closet just the other day. She immediately thought of Eden. But what would the girl want with a coat and a pair of shoes?

She could hear Gabe downstairs yelling to Dylan from the kitchen door: "Hey, Dad! I'm ready! I need to get to the game!"

"Give those scallywags a good thrashing!" Steve called in a fake British accent. He and Gabe had heard that once in a movie and thought it was hysterical. Now Steve said it to Gabe every time he left for a game.

"Let Hannah know we're leaving in three minutes!" Dylan called. "I'll be right there!"

Sheila heard the kitchen door slam, and this triggered Trudy next door to bark.

"Hey, Hannah, we're leaving!" Gabe screamed. "Shake a foot!" Gabe still didn't have all his sayings down.

Dressed and ready, with the memorial service guest book in her big purse, Sheila hurried downstairs to find Gabe pacing by the front door. He had two backpacks with him. "Sweetie, what's the second backpack for?" she asked, smoothing his unruly hair to one side.

"I'm spending the night at Jimmy Munchel's," Gabe explained. "Remember, I told you on Wednesday?"

She felt like a negligent mother for not remembering. "Of course," she said, crouching down to zip up his jacket. "Well, be careful." It was a stupid thing to tell him on his way to a football game, but she always said it anyway. "And if I'm not seeing you until tomorrow, I need an extra-strength hug and a kiss."

Gabe complied. "Can you tell Dad to hurry up?" he asked, breaking away.

Sheila headed through the kitchen and out the door. "Gabe is chafing at the bit," she announced to Dylan, who had put the lawnmower away. "He's doing his pacing routine."

The dog started barking again. "Hey, it sure looks great out here!" she said loudly so the three of them could hear her past Trudy's barking. "Thanks for cleaning up that mess. Can we delay getting to the garden until tomorrow? Hallie has an emergency and asked me to teach her lessons today. I'll be gone until seven. Do you guys mind ordering pizza again?"

Steve turned to Eden. "Do they even have vegan pizza?"

"No sweat," Dylan said, approaching her. "In fact, as long as you won't be around, I might hit the gym this afternoon." He turned to glance at the house next door. "God, I understand what you mean about that stupid dog."

"No kidding. It's not the poor dog, it's *her*," Sheila said. Then she yelled: "FOR GOD'S SAKE, WILL YOU GET THAT DOG TO SHUT UP! AND DON'T HIT IT! JUST TRY A LITTLE KINDNESS AND PATIENCE, YOU MORON!"

Steve seemed embarrassed and flabbergasted at her outburst. Then he and Dylan and Eden all exchanged looks, and they started laughing. Even Sheila realized how crazy she sounded, and she had to giggle. Dylan rubbed her arm. They were both smiling at each other—for a change.

"Don't forget to pick up the laundry," she said. "See you tonight."

Then she kissed him. It was just a quick good-bye kiss, but their first since Monday. Five days without a smile or a kiss or sleeping in the same bed. She'd broken her moratorium. She wasn't sure why. Maybe it was the way he looked in his sweatshirt and fall jacket, with just a little perspiration on his forehead. Or maybe it was because she was getting on a plane soon, though he didn't know it.

"Bye, babe," he whispered.

Sheila realized the dog had stopped barking. She glanced across the way to see the woman next door on the rooftop deck. Her hair ruffled in the slight breeze. But the sun was behind her, so Sheila couldn't quite see her face.

Still, Sheila felt the woman glaring at her—just as she had last night.

Dylan still had a hand on her shoulder when he looked up toward the neighbor. "Well, I think she got the message," he said under his breath.

Even with the woman's face swallowed up in shadow,

Sheila felt her contempt. It was all there in the stiff posture and tilt of her head.

"Bye, Mom!" Steve called.

She blew him a kiss and turned to Dylan. "See you to-night," she said. Then she started down the walkway on the other side of the garage toward where the Toyota was parked in the turnaround.

Somehow, she could still feel that woman's hateful stare.

CHAPTER TWENTY-SEVEN

Dylan dropped off Gabe and Hannah at the grade school. Gabe's teammates were already boarding the bus, parked across from the school's main entrance. Hannah's crush was parked three cars behind it. Dylan caught a glimpse of him from a distance. He was a slick-looking, dark-haired kid, driving an old red VW bug with the side mirror held up by duct tape. The guy scored some points with Dylan because he actually got out of the car and opened the passenger door for Hannah. But then Dylan wasn't quite sure if the kid was naturally well-mannered or if the gesture was just a fake-polite, Eddie Haskell thing he'd done because he knew her father was watching.

Dylan drove around the block until he found a parking spot. It was across the street from a playfield. Three teenage boys tossed a football back and forth on the leaf-covered grass. Dylan stayed in the car and took out his phone.

He would have the whole afternoon free. He'd given Steve $40 to take Eden out for lunch as a thank-you to both of them for helping with the yard work. After a rough start, Eden was now looking and acting more human. Dylan had also noticed his family seemed to be warming up to him again. He'd even gotten a kiss out of Sheila this morning. It felt like life might be returning to normal.

The only thing gnawing at him was this business about Sheila's sister.

He couldn't figure out who would have texted Steve about his Aunt Molly—or why. Eden had told him that she didn't know much about Sheila at all. Maybe some friend of Toni's was behind the text. It had to be the same person who had sent the text to Sheila last week along with the article about Toni's death. *Maybe you should ask your husband about this.* That was awfully similar to *Ask your mom about your Aunt Molly.*

Was it that Brodie character Eden had been hanging around with, or someone else? Dylan couldn't think what the person sending the texts looked to gain. What was the point in dredging up a lot of painful memories?

He'd always felt Sheila had gone about it wrong, dealing with her anger and grief by totally cutting Molly out of her life.

Dylan told himself that Steve was a good kid. He wouldn't say anything to his mother about Molly if he thought it would truly upset her. Still, Steve had to be curious as hell about this aunt whose existence they'd kept secret from him and his siblings. If he'd tried to look up Molly online, he probably hadn't had any luck. Dylan remembered how most of the newspaper accounts of her death referred to her as "Mary Michelle Driscoll." "Molly" was just her nickname.

Dylan remembered her wake. Sheila had been close to catatonic. He'd made all the arrangements for the wake and the burial. Since Sheila's family was Catholic and Molly's death was an apparent suicide, Dylan had gotten into a big hassle with some pigheaded old priest about Molly being buried beside her dad in a Catholic cemetery.

But they'd finally straightened it out. At the funeral parlor, Sheila was like a zombie, sitting in a chair near the closed coffin. People tried to talk to her and give their condolences, but she barely responded. They were lucky to get a nod out of her. A bunch of Molly's college and old high school friends had shown up. Dylan hadn't known anyone, and at one point, he desperately needed to get out of there. Outside, near the funeral home's side entrance, he saw two guys, old high school chums of Molly's—a couple of dirtbags, really. One of them hadn't even worn a tie or a jacket for the service. They were having a smoke.

"I can't remember," the one who was wearing a tie said to his friend. "Did you fuck her, too?"

The guy laughed. "Yeah. Shit, man. I was going out with her for like a month. But I'm sure half the guys in there right now banged her at one time or another. Man, she was crazy—I mean, fun, but really screwed up in the head."

"Yeah, but you know what they say—crazy in the head, crazy in the sack . . ."

This got a chuckle out of the one without the tie. "No shit."

Clenching his fists, Dylan had wanted to defend his sister-in-law's honor, go over there and punch their lights out. But it would have caused a terrible scene at an already awful occasion. Sheila was on the brink of a nervous breakdown. Another incident, even a small one, could have pushed her over the edge. Besides, the two dirtbags were right. Sheila's sister was promiscuous— and a bit crazy. Even Sheila knew that.

Sometimes, Dylan thought that craziness ran in the Driscoll family. He often wished he were with someone who wasn't so complicated, someone who was fun.

And sometimes, he just couldn't help who he was

attracted to. Right now, more than anything, Dylan wanted
to be with Brooke. He texted her:

> **I have the afternoon free. Can u break away and meet
> me? I'm alone right now if u want to talk. Would love to
> hear ur voice**

He pressed Send. Just a minute later, his phone rang.
Dylan saw it was her, and he answered. "Hi, are
you free?"

"No, Paul's in the shower right now, so I can't talk
long. How are you? I've missed you."

"I've missed you, too. Can you get away?"

He heard her sigh on the other end. "We're supposed
to go on some Puget Sound cruise this afternoon. It's a
work thing he's got to do. I could fake a headache and
try to get out of it. If he doesn't give me an argument,
then I'll be free. But—well, there's another problem. Remember how I've told you a couple of times I think that
someone's watching us?"

"Yeah?" Dylan replied warily.

"I'm pretty sure it's a woman," Brooke said. "Was
your wife asleep last night around four in the morning?"

"Why do you ask that?"

"Well, I got a strange phone call. It woke me up.
Thank God, Paul slept through it. A woman was on the
other end. She said, 'You're just a whore.' But she sort
of sang it, like it was part of a rhyme, or something. It
was so creepy. I couldn't go back to sleep. I checked my
Caller ID, and the call came from a public phone. I hate
to ask, but was Sheila home last night around four in
the morning?"

"I think so," Dylan said. "But I can't be a hundred
percent positive. We've been sleeping in separate quar-
ters lately."

It was strange, but Dylan found himself trying not to be furious with Sheila. The thought that she might be tormenting Brooke infuriated him. Brooke hadn't done anything to hurt her—except exist. It certainly seemed possible that Sheila had snuck out of the house in the middle of the night while everyone slept. After all, she hadn't gotten out of bed until ten this morning.

"Listen, I caught a glimpse of this woman who might have been following me yesterday afternoon," Brooke whispered. "I saw her outside my apartment building, and then later in the underground parking lot at the hospital. At least, I think it was the same woman. I didn't really get a close look at her. But do you have a photo of your wife on your phone that you can send me?"

Dylan hesitated. He didn't want to give Brooke a photo of Sheila. He wanted to keep the two of them as separate as possible.

"You know, I'm not exactly dying to see what she looks like," Brooke explained. "But I want to determine if she could be this woman."

"Let me put you on hold while I find a picture," Dylan sighed. He tapped into the photo gallery. Practically all of the pictures of Sheila showed her with one or more of the kids. He didn't want to send Brooke any of those. He didn't want to send her a shot of Sheila looking too pretty or sexy, either—and of course, those were the photos he'd saved on his phone. He finally found a remotely cute shot of her holding a pumpkin she'd carved last Halloween. He sent it.

He got back on the line with Brooke. "Are you there? Did you get it?"

There was silence.

"Brooke?"

"Yeah, I'm here. I'm looking at her right now. She's pretty. I didn't think she'd be this pretty. The woman I saw in the parking garage might have had lighter hair. I don't think this is her."

"You don't sound certain," Dylan said.

"Well, to be perfectly honest, I'm not certain. I guess there's still a chance it was her. Maybe I'm just being paranoid. Maybe I'm making too much out of a stupid phone call someone made while drunk. Anyway, I'm going to delete this photo right now."

"Good."

"Maybe I'll forget what she looks like," Brooke said. "I don't want to be thinking about her while I'm with you later this afternoon—that is, if I can get out of this cruise."

"You have to get out of it," Dylan insisted. They'd have at least three hours. Maybe he could get a hotel room downtown.

"Like I said, Paul might give me an argument . . ." Her voice dropped to a whisper. "I just heard the shower go off. I better go. If I can meet up with you, count on me calling in about forty-five minutes or less. Okay?"

"Terrific," he said.

"Bye, Dylan," she whispered. Then she hung up.

He clicked off and set the phone on the passenger seat. Dylan smiled.

But then he thought about that crazy phone call from a drunken woman at four in the morning.

"That was actually kind of fun this morning," Eden admitted.

Steve sat next to her on the number 49 bus. He'd offered her the window seat, but she'd told him to take it. His dad had given him forty bucks to treat Eden to lunch. The bus was headed toward the Broadway shopping district, where Steve remembered there was a vegan restaurant.

"I never had a backyard," Eden continued. "We always went from apartment to apartment. So it was cool to be out there with you and your dad—*our* dad. I'm still not used to that." She turned to smile at him. "I never had a brother growing up, either. It's kind of weird going to school and being in some of the same classes as you."

"Did you get into a lot of trouble for what happened in Ms. Warren's class?" Steve asked, wincing a bit.

She shrugged. "Your dad—*our* dad, I mean—he tried to pull this tough-guy act with me about it. I still don't really know him yet, so I half-expected him to beat the crap out of me. But then I realized he's not like that. He's kind of a softy. I can tell he feels like a real shit because he didn't even know I was alive these past sixteen years. Anyway, I think he wants me to like him. So he cut me some slack."

"Well, let me know if you need any help with your report on *The Scarlet Letter*," Steve offered.

She shook her head. "I'm not worried about that."

It was like she had no intention of even writing it. But Steve didn't say anything.

He thought about how she had to keep correcting herself not to say "your dad" when she was talking about their father. Steve understood completely.

If that wasn't enough, as of two hours ago, his dad—*their* dad—had just confirmed that Steve had an aunt he never knew existed. And she'd had *problems*. The type of problems that could lead to suicide.

He almost wanted to say something to Eden about how her mom and his aunt had died the same way. But then he remembered his promise to his dad not to talk about this mysterious, long-dead Aunt Molly. Besides that, he was pretty sure Eden wasn't exactly eager to talk about how her mother had taken a half gainer from the roof of their apartment building. So he just kept his mouth shut and looked out the bus window.

The bus came to a stop at Prospect Street, a couple of blocks before all the shops and restaurants on Broadway. The bus doors opened, and a few passengers started to get off at the stop.

"Y'know, I'm gonna spend the afternoon on my own," Eden said, quickly getting to her feet. "You go where you want for lunch. I'm not hungry. See you later." She rushed for the middle door, which had already closed. "Door!" she shouted. It opened with a hiss, and she jumped off the bus.

Steve was halfway out of his seat when the bus pulled away. Through the window, he glimpsed Eden heading east up a side street. He reached for the pull cord and yanked it to request the next stop.

He couldn't help thinking she was running off to meet someone.

Eden was headed in the direction of Volunteer Park, which was only a few blocks off Broadway. She'd mentioned going there with her boyfriend yesterday. She was new to Seattle, but she knew where the park was. So if she was meeting someone, the park would be a logical choice.

Steve moved to the bus door. It was still a block until the next stop, but he was impatient. He wanted to catch up with Eden. He'd follow his hunch and search for her in Volunteer Park.

Steve had another hunch. In fact, he was now almost certain her scumbag boyfriend had never left for Portland.

CHAPTER TWENTY-EIGHT

"That was where I was standing when I heard the scream."

Sid Parsons, the Bristol Apartments' caretaker, was in his early sixties and skinny, with a ruddy complexion and a gray crew cut. He had intense blue eyes that made him look a bit crazy. He reminded Sheila a bit of Dennis Hopper. He was dressed in a tie and a fall jacket, but his clothes had a slightly worn, thrift-shop look to them.

The seven-story building was from the twenties or thirties. Sheila admired what had to be the original outside light fixtures and the detail on the front door. Sid obviously did a fine job maintaining the building. There were rhododendron bushes and a small patch of neatly mowed grass on either side of the walkway to the front door. Sheila had found a parking spot across the street for her rental car.

She let Sid guide her by the arm to the mouth of a narrow alley. Two large dumpsters and four recycling bins were pushed against the side of the building. Sid pointed up to the rooftop. "That's where she fell from," he said. "She was naked—except for a pair of bikini bottoms. And like I said, she was screaming. A couple of the cops had a debate about that right here, while they were putting up the yellow police tape. By then, they'd covered her up, thank God. One of them said that if she'd screamed, it couldn't have been a suicide. And the other cop said no, that wasn't always the case. He knew of jumpers who screamed . . ."

Sheila had half-expected Sid to ask for an ID or some kind of proof that she was a relative of Antonia's. But when she'd buzzed him on the intercom and said they'd talked on the phone earlier, he'd come right out to meet her, no questions asked. And it didn't take any arm-twisting to get him to start in with his account of how Antonia had died. Sheila had a feeling it gave Sid a sense of importance.

With his finger in the air, he traced the trajectory of Antonia's fall. "She flew straight down toward that first dumpster. And there's no nice way of putting it. She hit the edge, so half of her went into the dumpster, and the other half hit the pavement there."

Grimacing, Sheila held a hand over her heart.

"Blood was everywhere," Sid went on, shaking his head. "I was covered in it. And the cops wouldn't let me change or wash up for the first hour. The clothes I had on were ruined. I had to throw them away."

Sheila imagined the scene in front of her. She turned toward Sid so she didn't have to look at the dumpsters. She figured it would be a while before she'd be able to look at a dumpster without thinking of Eden's mother. She cleared her throat. "The newspaper article I read didn't say if her death was a suicide, an accident, or foul play," she explained. "I asked Eden, and she seemed pretty certain her mother didn't commit suicide. What do you think?"

"I'd rule out suicide," he said. Then he stopped to squint at her. "You said you were a distant relative. How well did you know her?"

"I never even met her," Sheila admitted. "Antonia was a—a relative of my husband's. But he hadn't seen her in close to twenty years."

"Well, I don't mean to speak ill of the dead, but—well, let's just say that Antonia struck me as kind of a good-time girl. I mean, in my line of work, you end up getting to know people's garbage, and hers always had a lot of booze bottles. Plus, she had a string of boyfriends coming in and out of here. I could barely keep track of them. I can't see her getting down in the dumps and taking her own life."

Sheila thought of her sister, and she gave the man a sad little smile. "I don't know if her drinking a lot and having several boyfriends automatically rules out the possibility of suicide. Did any of the boyfriends strike you as dangerous? Did any of them give Antonia trouble?"

"I think a few of them gave her trouble," Sid said with a little snort. "I don't think she had the best taste in boy-friends. But I never heard about any of them coming back and threatening her, or anything like that. If you want to talk about the boyfriend who was trouble, then we should be talking about the daughter's boyfriend. He was bad news."

"You mean Brodie?" Sheila said.

"I never got the guy's name."

Sheila dug out her phone and pulled up the photo she'd taken of Brodie and Eden in the corridor outside the ballroom. She showed it to Sid. "Is this the guy you're talking about?"

"Yeah, that's him, a real lowlife," he grunted. "Is the daughter still seeing him?"

"She claims she isn't, but I suspect she's still talking and texting with him—unfortunately."

"You know, the minute that kid started hanging around

here, suddenly we had trouble. There were break-ins. People got their mail stolen. I was cleaning up his trash in the hallways and stairwells. This is a nonsmoking building, and I smelled cigarette smoke in the lobby and stairways all the time. I even smelled dope once. All that started when he began seeing the daughter. And he was hanging around the building the day Antonia went off the roof."

Sheila's eyes widened. "He was? Are you sure?"

Sid nodded. "I know because I was cleaning up a bunch of trash he'd left in the hallway and on the front walk."

"Did you tell this to the police?"

"Sure did. I guess they brought him in for questioning. Apparently, he had an alibi, because they let him go. They talked to the girl, too, of course."

"Was Eden around that day?" Sheila asked.

Sid shook his head. "I don't know where she was. I think she must have given her boyfriend a key because sometimes he came and went when neither one of them was even here." He took a handkerchief out of his pocket and wiped his nose. "Anyway, in answer to your question earlier, if the boyfriend didn't have anything to do with it, then I think Antonia's death was an accident. You know, she had a thermos of booze up there, so they think she was pretty sloshed."

"Yes, the newspaper article hinted at that," Sheila said.

Sid put his handkerchief back in his pocket. "So before I forget, do you want those boxes full of Antonia's stuff? I'd really like to get rid of them. They're just taking up room."

"Yes, please," Sheila said. "I—I think Eden would be happy to get them."

"Well, c'mon, follow me," he said, heading toward the front door.

"Do you know Eden very well?" Sheila asked.

"No, not really," Sid replied. He unlocked the door and held it open for her.

"Thank you." Sheila stepped inside the vestibule and onto an old tiled floor. "Wasn't Eden around much?" she asked.

Sid quietly closed the door behind him. "Well, I started working here about a year ago, and I didn't see the daughter until this summer. I don't think Antonia would have won any awards for 'Mother of the Year,' if you know what I mean. I think the girl was away at school or living with the boyfriend until mid-July or August. That's when I first noticed her—and the boyfriend not long after that."

Sheila remembered Eden saying that some friend of her mother's helped raise her for a while. Maybe one of Antonia's neighbors knew about the arrangement.

"Was Antonia close to anyone in the building?" Sheila asked.

Sid frowned and shook his head. "I'm pretty sure she didn't make any friends here. Some of us went to the memorial service together. Only a couple of others from the building bothered. We compared notes, and no one seemed to know Antonia very well." He nodded toward the lobby. "This way."

Sheila followed him up a few steps to the lobby. One wall contained rows of small brass mailboxes, each with a little window that had an apartment number on it. The carpet was worn, with a swirly, ornate pattern like something from an old movie theater lobby. The elevator with an accordion gate was original as well. By the stairs, Sheila noticed a slightly threadbare rose-colored sofa and a fake potted palm.

"Have a seat," Sid said. "The boxes are down in my apartment. Be right back." He headed down the stairs.

From her bag, Sheila pulled out the memorial service

guest book. She was wondering about the woman who had helped look after Eden. Could she be among the mourners who had signed the guest book? Sheila wondered if the surrogate mother was a friend or former friend of Antonia's from the Hilton. Maybe someone at the hotel could tell her more.

While waiting for her plane at Sea-Tac Airport, Sheila had tried to track down a few of the other names in the guest book. She'd managed to get ahold of four people: two former Hilton employees that hadn't seen Antonia in over a year and didn't know much about Eden at all; a former boyfriend who had never even met Eden; and an old high school friend who hadn't seen Antonia in over twenty years.

If what Sid had said was true, she could check off all the guest-book signers from the Bristol Apartments. None of them had been very close to Antonia. It was strange that no one really seemed to know this woman who appeared to be the life of the party wherever she went. At least, that was the impression Sheila had gotten from Antonia's Facebook page.

Sheila felt something brush up against her leg. She flinched, startling the gray tabby that had silently padded over to her feet. Staring at her, the cat arched its back.

"Oh, you scared me, you cutie!" she laughed. "I'm sorry." She set the guest book aside and held out her hand toward the skittish cat, trying to show she was friendly.

"That's my Jasper," Sid announced, a bit winded as he came from the stairway around the corner. He carried two medium-sized boxes. He plopped them down beside Sheila on the sofa. "The little son of a gun snuck out when I opened my door. He always does that." Sid scooped the cat up into his arms. "I'll help you take this stuff out to the car just as soon as I put this little guy back where he belongs." He took Jasper's paw and waved it at Sheila.

"Say good-bye to the nice lady, Jasper." Then he headed back toward the stairway with the cat.

He'd left the boxes stacked one on top of the other. The carton on top was a slightly beaten-up shirt box from JCPenney. Sheila opened it. She found a collection of snapshots, at least a hundred of them. It was a hodge-podge of current digital shots and old, slightly fuzzy photos that must have been taken with an Instamatic and flashcubes. Practically all of the photographs were of Antonia through the years, alone or with friends or boy-friends. There were several pictures of Antonia at the beach or pool, taut and tan in her various bikinis.

Sheila had to dig through a few layers of photos until she unearthed a picture of Eden. It was a school portrait from seventh or eighth grade. Eden looked awkward and cute, with badly cut bangs, a dimpled smile, and a striped turtleneck. Sheila turned the photograph over to look at the back. She found a note in loopy handwriting: *To Mom—XXX—Love, Eden.*

Sid returned, and Sheila put the school portrait back in the box and set the lid back on top. "Did you know anything about the woman who helped raise Eden?" she asked. "Maybe there was a woman who came by to visit Eden or Antonia."

Sid shook his head. "Like I said, Antonia had a lot of guys coming by, but no women. None that I know of, at least." He stooped down to pick up the boxes. "I need to watch my back here."

"Oh, let me take one," Sheila said, getting to her feet. She grabbed the top carton.

They carried the boxes out to her rental car and loaded them in the back seat.

Sheila opened the driver-side door to get in, then stopped, quickly scribbled down her number, and gave it to Sid. "If anything should come up or if you hear from any of Antonia's friends, please give me a call, okay?" She shook his hand. "Thanks so much for all your help. I really appreciate it."

"My pleasure," he said. "I wouldn't have felt right tossing out that stuff, but I didn't want to hold on to it, either. So you're doing me a big favor. And good luck with that—Eden." He gave her a lopsided grin. "I think you're going to have some trouble with that one."

Sheila watched him head back inside the building, then climbed behind the wheel of the rental. With the key still in her hand, she stared over at the alleyway by The Bristol and the first dumpster.

She couldn't help thinking about Molly. She never saw her sister's body after she'd plunged seventeen stories.

But she'd been the last one to see her alive.

At Sheila's insistence, Molly had moved back to Portland from Eugene for the summer and was living with their sick mother. After only two weeks, Sheila knew it was a huge mistake. Molly was still drinking and partying, looking up old high school boyfriends and going out with them. She called Sheila every day to complain about their mother's nurses. The nurses called every other day to complain about Molly. Her mother called twice a day—just to complain in general. It was more work than ever before. Molly would feel insulted if Sheila didn't trust her to handle a certain task; but when she tried to handle it, she'd screw it up, and then she'd phone Sheila or Dylan to come help her out. Dylan was working out of town a lot, so it was often left up to Sheila to handle everything.

Between her sick mother, her crazy sister, and the poor, battle-fatigued nurses, the whole situation was bizarre. Sheila and Dylan began calling her mother's apartment "Twin Peaks." Sheila would call and leave a message for Dylan on the answering machine: "I'm swinging by Twin

Peaks after work tonight. Do you want me to get takeout on the way home?"

During this time, Sheila was still nauseated and terrified something was wrong with the baby. She kept checking in with her doctor, who told her to avoid stress—which made her want to kill him.

One hot Thursday evening, after a bad day at work, Sheila figured she'd treat her mother, Molly, and the nurse on duty to Chinese food. She called Twin Peaks to ask them what they wanted her to pick up, but she got the answering machine. She left a message. When no one returned her call, she tried again an hour later, and the machine picked up again. That was unusual. Instead of swinging by Uptown China, their favorite Chinese restaurant, Sheila drove directly to her mother's.

The nurse wasn't there. Molly was gone. And her mother was in the bathroom, crying on the floor. Her mom had fallen while trying to get herself from the wheelchair to the toilet. There was shit all over the place. She was on some new medication that gave her diarrhea, and the smell was horrible. Sheila gagged as she undressed her mother and got her into the tub.

"Don't . . . the baby," her mother cried. "You shouldn't. Just leave me here, and let me die . . ."

While her mom was sitting on the shower stool, Sheila noticed a purple bruise forming on her hip. "What happened to Manuela?" Sheila asked. "Where's Molly? Why are you here by yourself, Mom?"

Her mother was too miserable and confused to answer.

Manuela was the Thursday middle-shift nurse: a stout, fiftyish woman with glasses and a streak of gray in her black, lacquered hair. She showed up in time to help Sheila dress her mom and finish cleaning up the bathroom. She'd gone out to get a prescription filled for her mom, and had told Molly as much.

Sheila did her best to swallow her anger. She had smeared poop on her clothes, so she went into Molly's bedroom to find something to wear while she threw her and her mom's soiled things in the wash. Molly's room was a mess. She'd brought almost everything back from Eugene. And that should have included some items that actually belonged to Sheila.

Ever since they were kids, Molly had had a habit of pilfering anything she wanted that was Sheila's—clothes, records, toys, stuffed animals. Sheila didn't care so much about losing the toys and stuffed animals since she'd out-grown them by the time her younger sister coveted them. But she hadn't wanted to give up one stuffed animal, a monkey she'd cherished and named Micky—after Micky Dolenz from *The Monkees* on TV reruns. Yet, somehow, Molly had made Micky the Monkey hers. She'd even taken him off to college with her—along with several other things she'd pinched from Sheila. It was a mystery to Sheila why her sister needed some of those childhood treasures while away at school. And it was a mystery what had happened to them, because they were all miss-ing now. It really irked Sheila, who would have liked to pass on to her own baby some of the things she'd cher-ished as a child—especially Micky the Monkey.

Molly was still a slob. Her bed wasn't made. Dirty clothes littered the floor. There were several half-filled glasses of soda or booze on her nightstand and desk, along with open bags of chips, an apple core, and other half-eaten snacks. In one of her calls to Sheila, Molly had complained that one of the nurses had refused to clean her room. "Molly, it's a medical service, not a maid service," Sheila had explained.

"Well, they're all just sitting around here, doing nothing most of the time," Molly had argued. "And this one nurse got all pissed off at me because I asked if she'd mind changing the sheets on my bed. She changes the sheets on Mom's bed. I really don't see what the big deal is."

Amid the debris on top of Molly's dresser, Sheila noticed several mini shampoo bottles and soaps from a Best Western hotel. She knew her sister was often out half the night with old boyfriends, but she didn't know Molly was bringing home souvenirs from her various sexcapades.

Again, Sheila tried hard to swallow her anger. In Molly's closet, she found a loose top and some jeans she could button halfway up over her ever-expanding baby bump. She phoned Dylan to say she'd be home late, and then she ordered dinner for her mother, Manuela, and herself. Molly showed up while they were eating. She'd been out shopping for clothes and had stopped by the store for a pint of their mom's favorite Ben & Jerry's flavor. There was something in the way she announced this—as if she expected kudos for bringing their sick mother some ice cream, like this was her big contribution to the caregiving arrangement.

Sheila was furious, but she patiently tried to explain to her sister what had happened. Molly claimed to have misunderstood Manuela about when she was picking up their mother's prescription. "I thought she was doing that tomorrow," Molly whispered. "Y'know, it would help if you hired some nurses who actually spoke English."

Sheila turned away from her sister and resolved not to say anything in the heat of anger. She avoided Molly for the next half an hour. She washed the dishes, took her clothes out of the dryer, and got dressed. When she was ready to leave, her mother and Manuela were on opposite ends of the sofa, watching *Friends*. She kissed her mother good-bye, then realized Molly was nowhere to be seen. "Do you know where my sister is?" she asked the nurse.

Putting down her knitting, Manuela pantomimed smoking a cigarette and then pointed upward. It was supposed to be a big secret that Molly often went up to the roof to smoke. "Well, say good night to her for me," Sheila sighed. "Thanks, Manuela."

In the corridor, as she pressed the button for the elevator, Sheila was so depressed, tired, and angry, she just wanted to cry. The elevator door opened, and one of the two people aboard stepped out. Sheila headed into the elevator and automatically pressed the lobby button.

"We're going up," announced the middle-aged man already in the elevator—just as the doors shut behind her.

"This is how my day's been going," Sheila tried to joke, but her voice was cracking.

As the man got off on twelve, Sheila impulsively pressed the button for the top floor. She needed to have it out with her sister. She was tired of venting to Dylan, who was damn tired of it, too.

There was no one in the exercise room or on the track. For a few minutes, Sheila wondered if there really was a communication gap between Manuela and Molly, because it didn't look like her sister was up here. Wandering around the track, Sheila called out her sister's name.

"What is it?" Molly yelled back.

Sheila spotted her with a cigarette between her fingers, coming toward her from the other side of the track's railing by some huge air-conditioning vents. The area didn't have any guardrail. The sun was just beginning to set, and the sky behind Molly was a blazing red. Sheila could hear a car horn from the street seventeen stories below.

"Molly, are you crazy?" Sheila cried. "What are you doing out there?"

"Oh, there's this narc in the building who gave me all sorts of shit for smoking up here, so I hide over there now." She nodded toward the vents and puffed on her cigarette. "What's with the look? Are you still pissed? I told you, it was all just a misunderstanding."

Shaking her head, Sheila clutched the top of the railing. "I can't do this anymore," she whispered. "I'm sick, literally nauseated all the time. What in the world made me think that you'd actually surprise me and help out a little bit here? You've only made things worse. You don't care about anybody but yourself. I have nurses threatening to quit because of you. I'm doing more work than ever. I'm so stressed out. I swear, if something happens to this baby, I'm going to hold you partially responsible."

"Now you're being melodramatic." Molly dropped her cigarette and stepped on it.

"Mom could have died tonight!" Sheila screamed. "She could have hit her head on the side of the toilet or the tub. *You* didn't see the bruise on her hip! *You* didn't see our mother crying and covered in shit because of *your* negligence. Outside of buying Mom ice cream once in a while—*with her money*—have you done anything to help? Have you spent any time with her exercising? Have you ever helped her to the toilet or bathed her?"

"That's what the nurses are for!" Molly cried.

"When are you going to grow up?" Sheila asked. "You're still this thoughtless, stupid, selfish, spoiled child. And I can't deal with you anymore. I can't take care of you anymore. I'm trying to look after our mother. I'm trying to take care of myself for my baby—and I'm doing a terrible job of it. I'm neglecting my husband. I thought you might rise to the occasion and chip in a little. But you're worse than useless, Molly."

Her pretty blond kid sister stood there on the side of the railing. She had tears in her eyes, and her lip quivered. "Well, I guess as far as you're concerned, I'm still just a fuckup."

Sheila nodded. "Yes, I guess you are."

She remembered all the times she'd yelled at Molly, made her cry, then hugged her and apologized. But she couldn't do that now. She backed away and shook her head. "You'll have to move out. Come up with some other kind of living arrangement," she said calmly. "I won't do this anymore."

She could hear her sister crying as she turned away. Molly called out to her in a broken voice, but Sheila kept walking.

She hardly ever allowed herself to look back on that night. She kept thinking about what the priest friend of her mother had told her about pretending it all never happened—"forget and forgive." Better to blot out all memories of her little sister and move on.

But Sheila was back in Portland for the first time in seventeen years. And she was sitting in a rental car, staring at a spot where another woman had plunged to her death. So she couldn't help thinking about Molly—and crying for her. That stupid priest's advice had never been any good. She'd never completely forgotten nor forgiven her sweet, stupid screw-up of a sister.

Sheila wasn't sure how long she'd been sitting in the car, weeping, when the ringing of her phone jarred her out of it. She checked the Caller ID: PORTLAND HILTON. She clicked to answer and cleared her throat. "Hello?"

"Hello, is this Sheila?"

"Speaking." She cleared her throat again and quickly wiped her eyes.

"This is Debra Barnes. You called me earlier about Toni Newcomb. I noticed on my phone your last name is O'Rourke. Is that right?"

"Yes."

"Are you Dylan's wife?"

"Yes," Sheila answered. "We have Eden staying with us now."

There was silence on the other end.

"Hello?" Sheila said.

"I was just thinking," Antonia's friend said. "I wasn't sure if I should give my congratulations or condolences. You mentioned in your message that you had some questions about Toni and Eden—and that it was *urgent*."

This woman sounded like she knew Antonia pretty well. At least, she seemed knowledgeable about the situation. She knew who Dylan was. "Well, it's urgent in the sense that I'm in Portland right now, and I was hoping we could talk," Sheila said into the phone. She glanced over her shoulder at the boxes on the back seat. "I have some old photographs of Antonia's. Maybe you could go over them with me, fill me in on some things. You might even want to keep some of the pictures."

"Well, that sounds too good to resist," she said drolly. "Plus, I'd be lying through my teeth if I said I had no interest in meeting you, Mrs. O'Rourke. I'm at work right now, and things are a little slow at the moment. How soon do you think you could get here?"

CHAPTER TWENTY-NINE

Saturday—2:51 P.M.
Seattle

Steve hid behind the hedges that circled one of the koi ponds in Volunteer Park. He knew he must have looked slightly suspicious, because he was the only one by the pond with his back to the fish. The pond had a twin to the north, just on the other side of the sculpture everyone called the "Doughnut." The name of the modern art piece was actually *Black Sun*, but the nine-foot-tall granite sculpture was undeniably doughnut-shaped. It sat on a long, rectangular pedestal with the park's reservoir to the west and the Asian Art Museum to the east.

From that spot, people had a breathtaking view of the Space Needle, Elliott Bay, and the Olympic Mountains. So the Doughnut was a popular meeting place. There were always people sitting on the stone pedestal and the park benches facing it. If Eden was meeting someone in Volunteer Park, Steve figured she'd rendezvous with them right there.

He'd gotten off the bus only two blocks after Eden had made her impulsive departure. On the hunch she was headed for the park, he'd practically run there to catch up with her. But the park was huge—over forty-eight acres, which included a conservatory, an old brick water tower with an observation deck, the art museum, several meadows and gardens, a playground, and a wading pool. Steve went over each area twice. He even checked out Lake View Cemetery, which neighbored the park, thinking it might appeal to Eden's Goth side. But the sprawling memorial park also had over forty acres, plus forty thousand graves. He couldn't hope to cover the whole area. He thought Eden might have gone to the graves of Bruce and Brandon Lee, which were a tourist attraction. He remembered where the headstones were and found a group of solemn admirers, but Eden wasn't among them. Still, the Lees' gravesite was near the top of a hill, and from there Steve had a sweeping view of the cemetery. He didn't see Eden anywhere.

He'd been searching for his elusive half sister for nearly two hours. He was hungry and tired, but he refused to give up. He walked back to Volunteer Park and paid for admission into the Asian Art Museum. It was a huge place, with several exhibit rooms full of paintings, sculptures, tapestries, pottery, and metalwork. But Steve zipped through the museum in about fifteen minutes. He wasn't looking at the art but at the people milling around the art. And Eden wasn't among them.

His feet dragging, Steve headed down the steps of the art museum. He was ready to give up. He wasn't sure what he'd hoped to find anyway. He'd just started to warm up to Eden, and he thought she had started to like him, too. And she'd seemed to be warming up to the family. But then she'd suddenly ditched him on the bus. So he couldn't help but think she must be up to something underhanded.

Gazing at the Doughnut across the way, Steve heard his stomach rumble. He was thinking that he'd kill for some fries and a Coke.

And that was when he spotted Eden, sitting on the sculpture's pedestal with some guy. At first, Steve thought it wasn't the boyfriend. Instead of the camo jacket, this guy wore a beat-up black leather jacket. Plus, his hair was short and a dull blackish color.

The couple seemed deep in conversation. Steve was pretty sure they weren't looking his way, but he took off his own jacket, which Eden had seen him wearing today. Tucking it under his arm, he tried to blend in with a couple walking south toward the big water tower. Once they passed the Doughnut's pedestal, Steve broke away from the couple and ducked behind the bushes encircling the koi pond.

Now Steve stood there, hiding behind the hedges for a closer look at their faces. The guy with Eden was the same creep in the photo his mom had taken. He had merely cut off most of his hair and dyed it black. It was weird how neither one of them looked like the punk kids in the photo anymore. But while Eden was prettier, the boyfriend only looked creepier.

They seemed to be arguing about something. Eden had this miserable, defeated expression on her face. The guy kept talking and stabbing his finger in the air at her. He put his hand on her arm, and she pulled away. Steve wished he knew what they were saying.

Eden got a phone call and took it. The boyfriend started tapping his foot impatiently, and then he glanced around. For a moment, he seemed to look directly toward the koi pond area—and at him.

Steve swiveled around and pretended to be interested in the carp swimming around the slightly murky water. After a few moments, he dared to glance over his shoulder and noticed Eden was off the phone.

Brodie was talking to her again, and she reluctantly nodded. He leaned in toward her like he was going to kiss her, but Eden suddenly got to her feet. Frowning, he stood up, too. The two of them headed south toward Steve. He ducked down behind the hedge and pretended to tie his shoe.

As they passed by the other side of the hedge, Steve could hear Eden: ". . . don't care what you say, I hate this. I don't want to be part of it anymore. You can . . ."

Her voice faded as the two passed Steve's hiding spot without stopping.

Steve slowly straightened up and peered over the hedge. Their backs were to him as they climbed inside a black Mini Cooper parked across from the water tower. Steve took a chance and sprinted across the street to the steps leading up to the old brick tower. From the tower's observatory, he might be able to see which way they were headed.

He ducked into the water tower's entrance and ran up the grated steel stairs. His footsteps echoed in the stairwell. He'd heard there were 107 steps to the top, and somehow that number had stuck in his head. By the time he reached the top of the stairs, Steve's lungs were burning. About a dozen or so people were up there, gazing out the tall windows. Past the bars and grating, the series of windows offered a 360-degree view of Seattle. A few of the sightseers gaped at Steve as he staggered out of the stairwell into the covered observatory and then to the closest window. His head was spinning, and he wasn't sure which window overlooked the area where the Mini Cooper had been parked.

The first window offered a view of the cemetery to the north and the University District beyond that. His house in Roanoke Park was in that direction. Through the treetops, he looked for the Mini Cooper on the main drive through the park. He didn't see it.

He moved from window to window in search of the

car. At the fifth window, he finally spotted the Mini Cooper, headed down a side street that led to the Broadway shopping district. Was the boyfriend taking her back to the bus stop where she'd gotten off earlier? It would make sense that they didn't want to be seen driving around together anywhere near his house, not when the creep was supposed to be in Portland. Even if he'd changed his looks, he was still recognizable.

Steve lost sight of them through the treetops after about three blocks. Still winded, he backed away from the window and plopped down on a bench. He was sweating and his heart beat furiously. As he caught his breath, Steve tried to figure out what he should do.

If he asked Eden for an explanation, she'd just lie to him again. His mother was still pretty upset about her garden getting trashed. Steve didn't want to make matters worse by telling her about this. He decided he'd talk to his dad. After all, Eden was his daughter, wasn't she?

His phone rang. He had his wadded-up jacket in his lap, and it took him a few moments to find which pocket his phone was in. He checked the Caller ID: SEAN THOMAS. Steve frowned at the screen before answering. His school friend rarely called.

"Hey," Steve said.

"Hey, have you heard the news?" Sean asked. "Ms. Warren was murdered last night. Somebody shot her in her house. A neighbor found her body early this morning. Can you believe it?"

The neighbor's dog wouldn't shut up.

All the barking certainly didn't help Dylan's bad mood any.

After talking with Brooke, he'd hurried home and showered. Then, thinking optimistically, he'd booked a room for them at the downtown W Seattle Hotel. He'd put the reservation on his business American Express and made a mental note to swing by the bank so he would have enough money to pay in cash when he checked out. It seemed kind of sleazy, but he didn't want any Seattle hotel charges showing up on his credit card bill.

He'd changed his clothes twice before settling on a relaxed, casual look: an Italian wool V-neck sweater, white T-shirt, and khakis. Then he'd waited for Brooke's call. And waited. She'd told him that if she could get away, she would call within forty-five minutes. Over an hour had passed, and he'd still waited and hoped. Then two hours had gone by.

Instead of room service at the W with the woman he worshipped, he'd had Campbell's chicken noodle soup for lunch with CNN on the TV in the kitchen. All the while, the neighbor's dog had serenaded him with its sporadic yowling.

He'd managed to cancel his reservation at the W without having any charges on his card. Now he was washing the dishes, trying to resist the urge to break something. It was obvious Brooke hadn't been able to get away, and now she was stuck on some cruise for the rest of the afternoon.

Dylan told himself that he should hit the gym—maybe work out some of his frustration and disappointment. It wasn't just thwarted expectations about the afternoon with Brooke that bothered him. For a while, he'd been able to put his worries aside while fantasizing about a few stolen hours with her at the W. But now he began to brood once again about the bizarre anonymous phone call to Brooke in the middle of the night. If Sheila hadn't gone out at four in the morning and made the call from a pay phone, then who had? Was it the same person who'd sent the text to Steve about Molly? The same person who had texted Sheila the article about Antonia's death?

The two texts seemed like they were related. Maybe they'd come from a friend of Antonia's who knew about Molly, someone trying to screw with him and his family. But that didn't explain the woman who was following Brooke or the disturbing phone call she'd received. How could some friend of Antonia's know about Brooke and him? Maybe Brooke was right about the call being a fluke. And it wasn't totally unthinkable that she'd feel some guilt and paranoia over getting involved with him. She wasn't the first woman he'd been with who thought she was being watched or followed. It kind of came with the territory when the sex was illicit. In a weird way, that was part of the thrill.

Still, Brooke was different from the others. Dylan felt very protective of her, and he couldn't just dismiss her fears.

From next door, the dog suddenly gave a distressed yelp. Then the barking started up again, louder and more insistent.

"What the hell?" Dylan muttered, turning off the water at the kitchen sink. Now he knew what Sheila had been complaining about. He couldn't remember the renter's name—Lee or Lena Something. Except for glimpsing her in silhouette on the Curtises' roof deck this morning, Dylan still hadn't actually met the neighbor. But he was already convinced she was a total idiot.

He could see out the window that it was just starting to rain. Grabbing an umbrella from the front closet, he headed outside and marched across the lawn to the house next door. He rang the front bell and listened to the dog go even crazier.

All at once, the door flew open. Dylan reeled back as the dog shot past him and sprinted toward the park.

Dylan gaped at the redhead standing in the doorway. She was barefoot, wearing jeans and a black blouse that was completely unbuttoned. She wasn't wearing a bra. She put one hand on her hip.

"Oh, my God," Dylan murmured. "Leah."

"The other day, your wife gave me a bottle of wine, Dylan," she said with a smirk. "Shall we open it up and drink to old times?"

CHAPTER THIRTY

"Toni and I were good friends for eight years—ever since I started working here. In fact, I was probably her best friend."

Debra Barnes stood over her desk, where she'd pushed aside some clutter so Sheila could set down the boxes containing Antonia's photographs. Debra kept taking sips from a tall Starbucks cup while looking over the pictures. The rim of the coffee cup was smudged with her crimson lipstick.

She was about fifty, and pretty at first glance, but she'd also made herself up very carefully. Sheila noticed dark foundation under her weak chin to make it stand out more. Her big eyes were accentuated with a lot of mascara. Her hair was the same color as Sheila's—light mocha brown—but Debra's hairstyle looked coiffured and stiff. She wore a casual lavender blouse and olive slacks, but Sheila guessed she planned to change into the black dress that hung in a dry-cleaner bag on the back of her closed office door.

Debra had explained that she was managing an event tonight and Sheila had caught her during the calm before the storm. She was the Hilton's banquet manager. Her cramped, messy office had a window looking out to the huge kitchen, where the staff was busily preparing food. An argument seemed to be going on between two of the chefs on duty. Debra ignored them.

Sheila glanced over Debra's shoulder as the woman inspected the snapshots. So far, there had been only a few pictures of Eden, all of them formal school portraits. However, Debra showed up in several of the photos in Antonia's collection. Sheila had told her it was okay with her if she wanted to keep those shots. She figured Eden wouldn't miss them.

"This is a blast from the past," Debra said, grinning as she examined a photograph of her and Antonia at a party. "Brandey and Bronson's wedding reception. Toni got plastered and made an ass of herself in front of Bronson's parents. Plus, there was a wardrobe malfunction I won't even go into. I think she ended up with the DJ that night. I was sorry I'd brought her as my plus one."

"I got the impression from Toni's Facebook page that she was kind of a party girl," Sheila said.

Debra laughed. "Yeah, *kind of.*" She set aside the photo in her keeper pile, sipped her coffee, and went back to the photos. The blotter on her desk already had a stack of photographs she'd looked at.

"Still," Sheila said, "Toni didn't have too many people at her memorial service, did she?"

"The thing about Toni was, she could be a lot of fun," Debra said, eyeing another picture. "Ha, look at this one. Anyway, Toni and I really got along here because she was good at her job, a real pro. But outside of work, she could be pretty selfish. She liked to drink and party. She had a wicked sense of humor. She was a regular laugh riot— until the fourth or fifth drink. Then she got mean and bitchy. She had a hard time keeping friends because of that. She never remembered hurting anyone's feelings or embarrassing herself. I really wanted to clobber her sometimes, until I finally figured out to avoid her after drink number four. Then we got along fine."

"How well do you know Eden?" Sheila asked.

"The first time I laid eyes on Eden was at the memorial service," Debra answered, glancing up from a photograph. "Toni wasn't mother material. Eden was raised mostly by this rich friend of Toni's, a woman named Cassandra—or Cassie. I forget her last name."

From her purse, Sheila pulled out the funeral parlor guest book. She wanted to hunt for the name. "Was this Cassandra person at the memorial?"

"Not that I know of. At least, she didn't walk up and introduce herself to me. She would have had to, because I've never met her."

Sheila flipped through the pages of the book. She would have remembered if a "Cassandra" or "Cassie" was in there. She shoved the book back into her purse and then nodded at the box of photos. "So if a picture of Cassandra was in there, you wouldn't be able to tell me."

"Nope, never laid eyes on her," Debra replied, staring at another picture. "God, look how tan Toni is in this one. The girl was certainly in good shape. Exercised every morning—if she wasn't too hungover."

"Can you tell me anything about the arrangement Toni had with Cassandra?" Sheila pressed.

The argument in the kitchen was getting louder, but Debra seemed impervious to it. She set another snapshot in her keeper pile. "Cassandra and Eden had a place in Clackamas, but it might as well have been Timbuktu, considering how rarely Toni saw them. She'd check in with Eden whenever she started feeling maternal—which was rare, believe me. I think she liked to remind the kid who her real mother was. By the time I got to know Toni, she and Cassandra were like 'frenemies.' There was a lot of jealousy between them—"

"Wait a minute," Sheila said, stepping around the desk to face her. "You said you've known Toni eight years. Was Cassandra taking care of Eden all that time?"

"Except for the occasional weekend or holiday or birthday when Toni wanted to play mother, that kid was with Cassandra in Clackamas practically since birth." Debra shrugged. "At least, that's the impression I got."

Sheila couldn't comprehend how Antonia could have given her baby to a friend to raise. No wonder Eden was kind of screwed up, knowing all her life that her mother had never really wanted her and that her father didn't even know she was alive.

Debra sipped her coffee. "Come last July, Cassandra dumped Eden on Toni's doorstep and moved to Florida—Tampa, I think. Toni thought she was chasing after some guy down there. Either that, or Eden had done something really awful to piss off Cassandra, which really doesn't seem too inconceivable. Anyway, can you imagine? Suddenly getting stuck in the role of full-time mom with this teenage daughter you barely know?"

Sheila nodded. "Yes, I can."

Debra laughed. "That's right. Sorry. Anyway, after only a couple of months, the girl—along with her boyfriend—really started to get on Toni's nerves."

"Brodie?"

Debra nodded. "Toni couldn't stand him. She kept telling me she wanted to ship Eden back to Cassandra in Florida. But she didn't have any way of getting in touch with her. I guess Cassie changed her email and phone number, and became totally incommunicado. Toni was going nuts with the kid living there in that small apartment. It was a two-bedroom, but still. The two of them simply didn't get along—and having that snaky boyfriend around didn't help matters at all. That's what Toni called him, 'The Snake.' Toni was ready to wash her

hands of both of them. She was even thinking of shipping
Eden up north to you and your husband."

Sheila folded her arms. "I was just about to ask how
much Toni told you about Dylan."

"His name came up a lot in the last month or two
while Toni knocked around the idea of pawning Eden off
on you guys." Debra set another photo in her keeper pile
and examined some more. She was almost shuffling
through them now, getting impatient. "But even Toni
thought that was kind of a rotten trick to pull on you
two—especially since she hadn't uttered a word to Dylan
about the girl. Plus, she liked him. Toni hooked up with
a lot of losers in her day, but she never had anything bad
to say about your husband. She had a soft spot for Dylan.
I think she always felt sort of connected to him because
of Eden."

Sheila tried to keep from frowning. "Did she have an
opinion about me?"

She figured Antonia must have thought she was a
complete fool.

Debra glanced up from the photograph in her hand.
"No, I don't think she'd really formed an opinion about
you—at least, nothing she shared with me. But I have
to admit, I was damn curious to meet you when you
called . . ." She tossed some photos in the box and sifted
through some others. "Well, lookee here," she said, pluck-
ing out one snapshot. "Speak of the devil."

She showed Sheila a slightly fuzzy photo, probably
taken before digital became popular. It was of a smiling,
youthful Antonia with her head on Dylan's shoulder. He
looked so young and handsome in his blazer and a tie
Sheila had bought for him. Antonia had on a red dress
with a low neckline. It looked like they were in a restaurant. Dylan had his arm around her.

"Oh, shit, good one, Debra," the woman muttered, reaching to take back the photo. "That was so dumb of me. I'm sorry. You don't want to see that."

Sheila held onto the picture. "It's okay. I would have found it eventually anyway." She tried to keep her voice steady. But she was angry, and her heart was breaking.

Debra picked up the stack of photos she'd collected. "Well, I'd like to hold on to these, if that's all right with you."

Sheila nodded. "I should go. I've taken up too much of your time already."

"I'll get one of the busboys to help you carry those boxes to your car," Debra said. "I'll make sure your parking's validated, too."

Biting her lip, Sheila studied the photo of Antonia and Dylan again. "How did you know this was my husband?"

Debra shrugged. "One afternoon about a month ago, when Toni was telling me about him, we looked him up on Google and found his picture. He's really good-looking. And he's aged well, too."

Sheila carefully slipped the photograph inside her purse. Then she started dumping the discarded photos into the boxes.

"Are you really sure you want to keep that one picture of them?" Debra asked. "I'm not sure I would."

Sheila nodded. "Eden might want a photo of her parents together," she answered quietly.

CHAPTER THIRTY-ONE

Saturday—4:11 P.M.
Seattle

"You're the one who rented from the Curtises?" Dylan whispered. "You're living here?"

He was so taken aback that he let her grab him by the hand and pull him into the house. She shut the door behind him.

Dylan had been in the Curtis house several times, so everything looked familiar in the living room except for all the unpacked boxes—and her. She didn't belong there.

She belonged in a sanitarium.

Crazy Leah Engelhardt.

He realized she was still holding his hand when she brought it up inside her open blouse and ran his fingertips over her breast.

Dylan yanked his hand away. He couldn't believe this was happening.

He'd only seen her in silhouette this morning. He had no idea Leah was his new neighbor. She'd moved into the Curtis house last weekend. All this time, she'd been right next door to his wife and kids—and yet somehow, she'd avoided being seen by him.

Dylan hadn't thought about Leah in years. He thought he'd put that nightmare behind him.

Leah had been his *Fatal Attraction* encounter seven

years ago. She'd sat next to him in business class on a flight to San Francisco. He remembered thinking she was a few years older than him, but still sexy and flirtatious. It seemed like a perfect no-strings situation. He'd told her up front he was married. She'd told him she was divorced—with such a lucrative alimony settlement that she had no desire to get seriously involved with any guy. That night, they went out to dinner at Marlowe and then had wild sex in her room at the Fairmont. Dylan had never been with anyone quite like her. She was uninhibited and even a bit perverse. She had sex toys, and the notion that she'd brought them along in her luggage for the TSA people to see simply baffled him. Some of the things she did to him were downright dirty—and hot. But he had his boundaries and needed to stop her a couple of times: "Hey, I'm sorry, but I'm not really comfortable with that . . ."

"I didn't take you for being such a square," he remembered her saying as they thrashed around on the floor. As she hovered over him, her red hair created a small tent around his face. "I thought you'd be more open-minded. But if vanilla sex is your thing, that's okay with me."

He remembered walking out of the Fairmont at one in the morning, feeling as if he'd survived the sexual equivalent of a fraternity's hell night. He felt a strange exhilaration for having gotten through such a weird, intense, exciting, sometimes scary, debasing experience.

He had no plans to see Leah again. He took a vigorous shower when he got back to his hotel that night and threw out the scrap of paper with her phone number and email on it.

She called him the following evening at his hotel. "Guess where I am," she said. "I'm downstairs in the lobby! I wanted to surprise you."

Stunned, Dylan lied and said his wife was there with

him. "She—um, she decided to surprise me, too," he whispered. "She's in the shower right now. I'm so sorry you came here for nothing. I hope you understand that last night was a one-time-only thing. I think it's better that way. Anyhow, it was really nice meeting you, Leah. Take care, okay?"

He thought he was being pretty clever—and tactful.

Four days later, she called him at work in Seattle. He figured she must have done some research to track him down at his office. "I have my sources," she explained. "I just had to make a few calls. That's all. How about if we got together for a long lunch—maybe at some hotel downtown? I'll bring my bag of tricks. Or maybe you can get away and spend the night at my place in Kent? We have to hook up. I bought you a very expensive present, and I want to give it to you in person."

Dylan tried to be honest this time. "I'm sorry, Leah, but no. I thought we had an understanding. What happened in San Francisco was a onetime thing. You shouldn't be throwing your money away on presents for me. I appreciate the thought. But it really isn't a good idea to get together again."

"I can't return a sterling silver ID bracelet," she hissed on the other end of the line. "It's engraved with your name on it. What am I supposed to do with it now? I don't plan on fucking anyone else named Dylan."

"I'm sorry, Leah, but—"

She hung up on him.

The next day, she showed up at his office. Fortunately, he was on another floor in a meeting all morning. But the receptionist, Dawn, said Leah had waited for him for three hours—and that she'd been pretty snotty to her. Dylan was on good platonic terms with Dawn, and confided in her that the woman was a stalker. So from then on, Leah was always told that he was unavailable, in a meeting, or out of town.

Leah called or emailed him at least twice a day. Several of the emails included nude photos she'd taken of herself. He deleted them and blocked her emails. He never picked up when she called, and she often hung up when it went to voicemail. But in one message, she told him, "I don't know why you're avoiding me. You're acting like that night we spent together meant nothing. But we bonded. You let yourself be vulnerable with me. I think I know you better than most people do—maybe even better than you know yourself. I just want to make you happy, Dylan. Are you afraid to be happy? Call me."

After she'd left that particular message, when she called again, Dylan finally picked up and bluntly told her, "Listen, I'm really sorry, but you're getting sort of Glenn Close on me—you know, like in that movie? Do you really want to be that crazy-stalker person? Your behavior is definitely coming across that way. I'm not interested in having a relationship with you, Leah. I don't want to be rude, but please stop calling me. And please stop coming by my office. I don't want to see you again. Okay?"

She hung up on him again.

She continued to call—sometimes several times a day—but she always hung up because he never answered.

Every day for a week, a black rose was delivered to their house for Sheila. The box was left on the front stoop when no one was home, and the card attached merely had *Mrs. Dylan O'Rourke* written in girlish handwriting. Dylan was convinced it was Leah. He was pretty sure she was watching the house, too. He thought he saw her a couple of times in the park across the street.

Dylan was terrified she was going to hurt Sheila or one of the kids. He came very close to telling Sheila the truth.

Then it just stopped—no more calls, no more black roses, no more visits to his office.

Dylan felt so lucky to have come out of it without any real damage done, other than the damage to his nerves. Leah hadn't boiled any bunnies, attempted suicide, or inflicted harm on anyone. Still, the crazy bitch had nearly given him an ulcer. It was a long time before he was able to stop worrying and forget about her. It was months before he could even look at another woman again.

Now, Leah was back—and living next door to him.

"Jesus, what are you doing here?" he asked, standing in the center of his neighbor's living room.

Leah leaned against the living room entryway, between him and the front door. Her shoulder-length red hair was mussed, and she licked her lips. With her blouse still open, she traced her finger from between her cleavage down to her flat stomach. The pose might have been seductive if it didn't seem so forced—and if she weren't so scary. "I just want to be near you, Dylan," she purred. "I know you had to push me away for the sake of your family. I understand that now. It's actually very admirable. But I want you to know that I've never completely given up on you."

"My God," he muttered, shaking his head. "How—how did you . . . ?"

"I knew where you lived, of course," she said, still doing that thing with her finger along her torso. "I've driven by your house hundreds of times over the years. Then I saw the 'For Rent' sign here. It was meant to be, don't you see? The rent isn't cheap, but I don't care. I've still got quite a lot of money."

Dylan kept shaking his head. He couldn't figure out why this was happening. She was still an attractive woman, and she probably still had her bag of sex toys.

He couldn't believe that, in seven years, Leah hadn't found some other guy to latch onto. It had never occurred to Dylan that she might still be stalking him. He hadn't even considered Leah when he'd been wondering about the texts to Sheila and Steve—or the woman who was following Brooke, phoning her at four in the morning. He realized it must have been Leah. Such scheming, bizarre actions seemed right up Leah's alley. And she'd just now reminded him that she had money. She could easily afford a private investigator to delve into Sheila's and his past. Dylan imagined some slimy detective giving Leah all the dope on Sheila's sister. The guy could have found out about Toni and Eden, too. Dylan imagined some private dick spying on Brooke and him. Didn't Brooke say she thought they were being watched?

"You look good, Dylan," Leah said. "It's been so long since I've been in the same room as you. Remember the last time? Being this close to you again . . ." Her voice dropped to a whisper. "I'm already wet."

"You stay away from my family!" he warned, stabbing his finger in the air at her.

"I'm just here to make you happy, Dylan," she said, unfastening the top of her jeans. "You don't have to worry about me saying or doing anything to hurt your precious family. I moved here for you—for us. I've made it easier for us to keep seeing each other. No one has to know. I make you happy, you make me happy. Don't you see? It's a win-win for you. Whenever you've had enough of that mousy frump you're married to, all you have to do is come next door to me. You two aren't even sleeping together. I can see that from my window."

"Wait a minute," he said. "You're the one who trashed the garden, aren't you?"

She let out a startled, fake laugh. "I don't know what you're talking about."

He didn't believe her for a minute. She was a terrible actress.

Leah peeled down her jeans, revealing a pair of champagne-colored panties.

"Those texts to my son and my wife, those were from you," he murmured. "And you've hired someone to follow me around, haven't you? Or maybe you're doing it yourself."

Leah shook her head and then stepped out of her jeans. "I really have no idea what you're talking about."

"The hell you don't."

"I just want to make you happy, Dylan." She tossed her jeans into the front hallway. "It's what I've wanted all along. Now, come on. Don't you like what you see?"

"I want you to pack up all your shit and move out of here," he growled. "I don't want you anywhere near my family. You're not going to intimidate me. I'll tell my wife about you. I don't care."

"Oh, big talker," she laughed. "Have I got you good and mad now, Dylan? Do you want to hit me? Am I making you hot? Go ahead, let me have it."

His fists clenched, Dylan stood there, frozen. He'd never struck a woman in his life. But right now, more than anything, he wanted to punch Leah in the face—especially if it meant he'd never have to see her again.

She came at him. "You want me, I know you do," she murmured. Her hands went for his belt buckle. Then she started to unfasten his khakis.

Dylan grabbed her by the arms, swiveled around, and pushed her toward the dining room. He just wanted her out of the way so he could get out of there. But Leah kept tugging at the front of his pants, groping him. Dylan got angrier and more frustrated. He slammed her into a side table. A fancy candle holder with a glass hurricane lamp tipped over, and the glass shattered with a loud pop.

Leah shucked down his pants and boxer shorts. Before Dylan could pull away, she had her arms wrapped around his neck. One leg locked around his. She thrust her torso against him. "Go ahead," she whispered. Her warm breath was swirling in his ear. "Tear off my panties, do it. I want you to."

Dylan pried himself from her arms. He almost tripped as he spun around to get away from her. He grabbed onto the back of a dining room chair to keep from falling. He regained his footing and started to pull up his boxers and pants. He realized he was standing in front of the window. He looked up.

Just across the way, Eden stood at his kitchen window, gaping back at him.

"Oh, shit!" he muttered, zipping up his pants. He was utterly humiliated. He staggered toward the living room to avoid being seen—though he knew it was too late.

All the while, he heard Leah cackling.

Dylan glanced back at her.

She hadn't bothered to move away from the window or even cover herself up. She seemed so smug and content, half-sprawled over the side table.

Her mocking, triumphant laugh seemed to follow him out the front door.

CHAPTER THIRTY-TWO

Steve kept wiping the raindrops off his phone screen so he could read the news article. It had taken him forever to find the story. He'd googled "Miranda Warren, Murder" and "Seattle Teacher Murdered," and come up with nothing both times. He'd begun to think that his friend Sean had punked him about their teacher having been killed. But after walking in the rain to the number 49 bus stop, he'd searched *Seattle News* and finally found a brief article. At first, he hadn't been sure it was about Ms. Warren. He'd thought maybe her photo from the teachers' section of last year's high school yearbook would be with the story, something to show what she looked like. But there was no picture. The headline read:

Shoreline Woman Shot To Death in Home

It was dated today and didn't go into a lot of details. Ms. Warren was forty-one years old. A neighbor woman and friend of Ms. Warren's had been jogging by her house early in the morning and noticed her door was open. She rang the bell. When no one answered, the neighbor stepped inside. She found Ms. Warren dead in the bedroom. She'd been shot once in the throat. The neighbor immediately called the police. There were no suspects in custody. The killer was still at large. Ms. Warren was divorced and had two sons, who had been spending the night with their father.

Steve shuddered as he read the article—and it wasn't just because he was damp and cold from the rain. As he put his phone away, he kept thinking about Eden.

Last night, he'd heard someone in the hallway outside his door. He'd first heard the footsteps at one in the morning, and then, again a little after four. Eden could have snuck out of the house and returned during that time. Maybe her boyfriend had picked her up and driven her to Ms. Warren's place. Maybe they'd killed her together.

Hiking up his jacket collar, Steve glanced down the street for the number 49. No sign of it yet. His stomach was in knots from a weird combination of hunger and dread.

Was his half sister a murderer? He knew for sure that she was a liar. He'd just seen her with her creepy boyfriend, who, according to Eden, was out of town.

All those true murder stories he'd read over the summer, and now somebody he knew had actually been murdered. It wasn't so fascinating when it happened to someone he knew and liked. He just felt sick and sad. He'd had a little crush on Ms. Warren. She'd always been nice to him.

Eden had been pretty bitchy to their teacher yesterday. And in her screwy way of looking at things, Eden seemed to think Ms. Warren was the one who had gotten her into trouble. Only a few hours ago, before he knew Ms. Warren was dead, he'd asked Eden about the thousand-word report on *The Scarlet Letter* that Ms. Warren expected from her on Monday.

Steve shuddered again when he recalled her answer: "I'm not worried about it."

Of course she wasn't.

With her arms crossed in front of her, Eden sat in a rocking chair. It had been in the basement guest room, but Hannah hadn't wanted it, so the chair had been moved into Eden's room.

Dylan stood in the doorway. His hair and the top of his sweater were still wet from the rain. He'd been in such a hurry to get away from Leah that he'd left his umbrella next door. Once inside the house, he'd anxiously called out for Eden, but she hadn't responded. He'd found her up here.

She was glaring at him. She seemed more annoyed than shocked.

"I'm sorry you saw that," Dylan explained, still trying to catch his breath. "But it's not how it looked. I know you'll have a hard time believing this, but she attacked me and started to pull down my pants."

Shaking her head, Eden gave him a dubious smirk. "Oh, I'm sure," she muttered.

"It's the truth!" Dylan insisted. "Her name is Leah, and she's crazy—certifiable. I met her on a trip to San Francisco years ago. We—we messed around one night, and that was supposed to be it. But, like I say, she's nuts. She started stalking me. She stopped after a while, and I thought I was rid of her. That was seven years ago. But now, she—she's moved in next door . . ."

Biting her thumbnail, Eden rocked in the chair and stared at him. She seemed slightly amused by the whole thing.

Dylan realized he sounded like a fool—a fool who had let his dick get him into trouble again and again. "I had no idea it was her next door until just fifteen minutes ago, when I went over there because her dog wouldn't shut up."

"It's quiet now," Eden murmured.

"The dog ran out the door when Leah opened it for me," Dylan explained, sagging against the doorway frame. "I wouldn't be surprised if she was torturing it just so the barking would unnerve us. The poor mutt seemed anxious as hell to get out of there. And that dog wasn't the only one, believe me. I wanted to bolt as soon as I realized our new neighbor was the same crazy woman I—"

"Screwed one night in San Francisco?" Eden concluded.

Frowning, Dylan nodded. "Okay, yeah," he muttered. "And it was a huge mistake. Maybe I deserved all the shit I got from her. I probably had it coming. But you need to believe me, because I'm being completely honest here. I wasn't having sex with her just now. She was all over me, but I was only trying to push her away."

Eden sighed. "If you're worried about me telling Sheila or the kids, don't sweat it. I won't rat you out."

"Thank you," Dylan said, breathing a tiny bit easier. "But that's not it completely. It's important to me that you believe me."

Dylan heard the front door open downstairs and flinched. He thought Leah might be barging into their house. He hurried down the hallway. "Who's down there?" he yelled from the top of the stairs.

"It's me!" Hannah answered. "Can I spend the night at Gwen's? It's okay with her mom and dad."

Dylan stopped halfway down the stairs to see Hannah in the front hall. Now that she'd come in from the rain, she pushed her sweater hood off her head. She glanced up at him with an expectant smile. "I just have a few things to pack. Gwen's waiting outside in the car."

"Well, wait a minute," Dylan said. "What happened to the guy you were at the game with?" He wanted to make sure she wasn't actually going off with him.

"Jared," she frowned. "He's a drip. I ditched him at halftime. So is it okay if I stay overnight at Gwen's? She's waiting, Dad."

"I guess it's okay. But you know your mother's going to check up on this."

"Thanks. Yeah, I know," she said, rolling her eyes. She headed toward the kitchen.

"Well, who won?" Dylan called.

"Gabe's team!" she shouted over the sound of her footsteps racing down the basement stairs.

Dylan headed back up to the second floor and then down the hallway to Eden's bedroom door. She was still gently rocking in the chair. "So did Gabe's team win?" she asked in a tone that said she didn't really care.

"Yes," Dylan said.

"Well, rah-rah for Gabe's team," she muttered.

"You didn't answer my question earlier," Dylan whispered. "Do you believe me about what just went on next door?"

"I guess so," she said. She got to her feet and sauntered toward him. She put a hand on the door. "Anyway, you don't have to worry about me saying anything."

"Thanks, Eden." He started to leave, but hesitated and turned toward her again. "Are you—disappointed in me?"

"You haven't officially been my father long enough for me to be disappointed in you," she replied. "Besides, my mother pretty much told me all about you. When it comes to sex, you're just like Toni."

She slowly closed the door in his face.

Dylan stood there for a moment. He was humiliated.

At the same time, he was confused. From the way she talked just now, it almost sounded as if Eden's mother and Toni were two different people.

Saturday—5:22 P.M.
Portland

Practically everyone in the terminal for the Horizon Air flight to Seattle looked miserable. Someone's baby was shrieking. There weren't enough seats in the waiting area, so people were sitting or lying on the floor. All the carry-on luggage and bodies made the small terminal into an obstacle course. And they'd just announced that the flight would be delayed twenty-five minutes.

Sheila was one of the many people standing. Antonia's friend, Debra, had helped her tape up the boxes of photos, and they now leaned against the wall behind Sheila. She'd already decided to cram them under the seat in front of her so she wouldn't have to battle for overhead space. Plus, she had visions of the boxes breaking open when she pulled them down, the photos spilling into the aisles. So she'd have no legroom, but it would only be for an hour.

Since arriving at the airport, Sheila had been thinking about Eden and her surrogate mother, Cassandra. While in the TSA line, she'd called Debra for some clarification about a specific matter they'd discussed, but she'd gotten her voicemail. Sheila had asked Debra to call her as soon as possible.

That had been only a half hour ago. At the risk of being pushy, Sheila phoned her again. Debra picked up this time: "Hi, Sheila?"

"Yes—"

"I was just about to call you back," Debra said. "Things are starting to get crazy here, so I don't have a lot of time. What's up?"

Sheila had a finger in one ear to help block out the baby's screams. "I wanted to ask you about when Cassandra suddenly left Eden with Antonia this summer."

"Yeah?"

"You mentioned that Cassandra has been incommunicado ever since," Sheila said loudly to be heard over the child's shrieks. "Do you know if Cassandra actually met with Antonia when she dropped off Eden? Or did Eden just show up at Antonia's on her own?"

"The way I understood it, Eden called Toni, giving her about an hour's notice. Then she showed up at Toni's place with all her earthly possessions."

"And Toni never talked to Cassandra about it—before or afterward?"

"Never heard a peep from her."

"Do you think it's possible that Cassandra's dead?" Sheila asked.

"What did you say? We don't have the best connection. It sounds like some kid is screaming over there."

"Do you think that Cassandra might be dead?" Sheila repeated. "I mean, it sounds like Toni just took Eden's word for it that her 'other mother' had moved to Florida."

There was silence.

"Hello?" Sheila asked.

"Yeah, I'm here. I was just thinking. Toni never said anything to me along those lines. But I guess it's possible Cassandra's dead. It would explain why Toni was never able to get ahold of her. Plus, I always thought it was strange that no one heard from her after Toni died."

"It seems awfully suspicious," Sheila said. "First, Eden's substitute mother disappears without a trace, and then a couple of months later, her real mother has a fatal accident . . ."

In the background on the other end of the line, Sheila could hear someone talking to Debra.

"Um, just a second, Sheila, I'm sorry." Sheila waited and listened to the muted conversation. "Okay, okay, I'll handle it," Debra said to whoever was there with her.

"Hey, Sheila, I'm sorry about that. Like I told you, it's crazy here. I need to go. So do you really think Eden might have bumped off Cassandra—and then killed Toni? I mean, I can't see her being clever enough to pull off something like that and get away with it, can you?"

Sheila sighed. "Well, I don't know. That's what I'm asking you. The caretaker in Toni's apartment building told me that both Eden and her boyfriend were able to account for their whereabouts when Toni was killed."

"Okay, then, there you have it," Debra said. "And Toni seemed pretty sure Cassandra was in Tampa—whether to chase after some guy or because she'd gotten fed up with Eden, Toni didn't know. Believe me, after a couple of months with that kid and her boyfriend, Toni was ready to dump her and disappear, too. I'll bet this Cassandra will turn up soon enough. Listen, I've got to go."

"Well, thank you," Sheila said, still not feeling satisfied.

"Uh-huh, bye," Debra said quickly. Then she hung up.

Sheila clicked off and slipped the phone back in her coat pocket.

Unlike Debra, she couldn't so easily write off the possibility that Cassandra was dead. She had no idea how airtight Brodie's and Eden's alibis were for the day Antonia had plunged to her death. Perhaps the police would have been tougher when questioning them had they known Eden's other "mother" had mysteriously disappeared. The pattern couldn't be ignored: First, the surrogate mother vanishes. Then Eden moves in with her own mother, and two months later, Antonia dies under very suspicious circumstances. And now, Eden was living with her—a new stepmother. Since Antonia's untimely demise, Sheila had narrowly avoided death several times.

She could have been on the highway when her car's brakes gave out. She'd survived poisoning and electric shock.

Then last night, she'd come very close to drinking a nightcap full of ground glass. It probably wouldn't have killed her, but it certainly would have put her out of commission for a while.

She remembered what the auto mechanic who repaired the Toyota's brakes had told her: "Somebody must be out to get you . . ."

An announcement came over the terminal speaker that pre-boarding for the flight to Seattle would begin in a few minutes.

Sheila glanced down at the boxes against the wall. She thought of the mere handful of photos of Eden inside amid hundreds of shots of her mother. She wondered once again if Cassandra was in any of the photographs. Maybe she'd simply ask Eden tonight. Then she could pour two glasses of that bourbon and ask Eden to drink a toast to her three mothers.

Sheila still wasn't certain what that girl was up to, or why.

But she planned to rip the lid off tonight and find out.

CHAPTER THIRTY-THREE

Walking through Roanoke Park, Steve passed the playground, empty because of the rain. He wasn't all that eager to get home. He imagined Eden was there, and he didn't want to see her. He knew his half sister was a liar. But now it seemed very possible that she was a murderer, too.

Steve was soaked. He'd waited for that stupid bus for twenty minutes, then finally given up and walked. A couple of blocks back, he'd stopped by a pizza place. He knew he was having pizza for dinner tonight, but he was starting to get a headache and needed something to eat. He devoured a big slice of cheese pizza and guzzled down a large Coke.

Now that he had some food in him, he was tired—and emotional. Cutting through the park, he started crying. He didn't care about that "boys don't cry" crap. He kept thinking of Ms. Warren. But that wasn't all. He was thinking of his family, and how much had changed in just a week. Steve didn't think he'd ever be able to look at his parents the way he used to.

He wiped his eyes as he approached a huge evergreen in the center of the park. There were three things he needed to do when he got back home. He wanted a hot shower. He needed to catch the local six o'clock news for an update on Ms. Warren's murder. Finally, he wanted to sneak into Eden's room and look for some evidence that she'd killed Ms. Warren. He didn't think he'd find a gun. Her boyfriend probably had it. But maybe Eden had a journal. Or she might have taken some souvenir from Ms. Warren's house after they'd shot her. Maybe she'd stolen Ms. Warren's personal copy of *The Scarlet Letter* or something weird like that. Steve was trying to think like her—to get inside the head of a murderer.

As he passed the towering evergreen, the house came into view. A cop car was parked in the driveway behind his dad's BMW.

Steve stopped in his tracks. Had the police come to arrest Eden already? Or maybe someone in the family had been hurt or killed.

Steve started to run toward the house. He told himself that if anybody had been injured, an ambulance would have been there. So many different scenarios raced through his head, all of them awful.

As Steve reached the street in front of his house, he saw two men step outside through the front door: a young, hulky uniformed cop and a tall, balding middle-aged guy in a tie and a windbreaker. They trotted toward the patrol car, obviously in a hurry to get out of the rain.

"Hey, excuse me!" Steve called, out of breath. He rushed up the driveway. "Is everything okay?"

The man in the windbreaker squinted at him. Steve figured he must be a plainclothes detective or something like that. "Who are you?" the man asked.

"My name's Steve O'Rourke. I live here. Is everyone okay?" Still panting for air, he anxiously glanced at the house. Several lights were on, but everything looked normal.

"We just needed to talk to your father about something," the man answered. "He can fill you in."

Steve watched the two cops jump into the patrol car and shut their doors. The vehicle's lights went on, but it didn't look like the two were going to leave just yet. Steve turned and headed for the door, but he hesitated on the front stoop. He noticed how quiet it was. All this activity, yet the neighbor's dog wasn't barking.

Letting himself in, he immediately called out, "Dad? Dad, what's going on?"

"Steve?"

From the front hallway, he saw his father and Eden seated at the dining room table, where his parents always had their serious talks with them. His dad stood up.

"What did the police want?" Steve asked, heading into the dining room. "Is Mom okay?"

"Mom's fine," his dad said.

"What about Gabe? Where's Hannah?"

"Gabe's fine. He's spending the night at Danny Lassiter's. Hannah's staying over at a friend's, too." He put his hand on Steve's wet jacket. "You really need to get out of these wet clothes—"

"I will. Just as soon as you tell me what's going on."

"It's your English teacher," his dad said soberly. He moved his hand up to Steve's shoulder. "I'm sorry. It's bad news, Stevie. She was killed last night."

Steve glanced over at Eden, sitting there staring down at the tabletop. She looked very solemn. He turned to his father. "I know," he said. "My friend Sean called and told me. What were the police doing here?"

"They got my number from Ms. Warren's phone, along with all the other people she spoke with last night," his dad explained. "So they wanted to talk to me. I guess they're trying to track down everything that happened in the last hours of her life. I had that conference with her last night, remember?"

Steve glared at Eden until she finally looked up and their eyes met.

She looked away. "I guess I wasn't very nice to her," she murmured. She got to her feet and started to clear off the table. She withdrew into the kitchen with a Coke can and a near-empty water bottle, which his dad must have served to the cop and the detective during their visit.

Steve turned to his dad again. "Were you the last one to see her alive?"

He squeezed his shoulder. "No, I asked the police the same question. After our conference, Ms. Warren drove home and ran into a neighbor who was walking his dog. Then she made a couple of calls."

Steve pulled away from his dad and walked toward the kitchen so he could look at Eden. She tossed the can and the water bottle into the recycling bin. He could tell she'd been listening to them.

He unzipped his jacket and then turned to his dad again. "Did the police say what time she was killed?"

"They said it was early this morning, some time before dawn. Are you okay, Stevie?"

He nodded. "So the cops wanted to talk to Eden, too?" Out of the corner of his eye, Steve noticed her in the kitchen, standing perfectly still.

"My conference with Ms. Warren concerned her, so they had a couple of questions, that's all." His voice dropped to a whisper. "Listen, take it easy on Eden. You heard her. She knows she was kind of a brat to Ms. Warren. And she doesn't feel very good about it."

His dad took his jacket from him. "I'll hang this up. You're dripping all over the place." He put his hand on the back of Steve's neck. "Are you sure you're okay?"

Steve just nodded.

"Well, why don't you go upstairs, take a hot shower, and put on some dry clothes? You'll feel better."

Steve nodded again and then broke away. He caught Eden giving him a wary sidelong glance from the kitchen. He could have cut through there to go up the stairs, but he took the front way.

Right now, Steve just wanted to avoid her.

With his head in his hands, Dylan sat at his desk in the den. He'd closed the door, which he rarely did.

It probably wasn't necessary. Both Eden and Steve were out of earshot: Eden in her room upstairs, and Steve in the shower. His cell phone was on the desk blotter in front of him, but Dylan hadn't yet made a call. He was just sitting there, trying to figure out what the hell to do.

Through the French doors in the den, he had a view of the backyard, not the house next door. For that, he was grateful. He didn't need any reminders that Leah Engel-hardt was back in his life. She'd driven off sometime between when Hannah had left with her friend and when the cop car had pulled into the driveway. The police's unannounced arrival had given Dylan his second big fright of the afternoon. He'd initially thought Leah had called them in some sort of bizarre plot to set him up and have him arrested for attempted rape. It would have ex-plained her weird sexual attack earlier, which had almost seemed premeditated.

But then, at the front door, the detective explained the reason for their visit. Dylan was shocked and saddened by the news about Miranda Warren. As soon as he sat down with the cops and started answering their ques-tions, he realized he had yet a whole new set of troubles.

He'd had sex with her just hours before she was killed.
But of course, he couldn't tell the police that.

Dylan told them that he and Ms. Warren had held their
discussion about Eden in the classroom. Afterwards, he'd
walked Ms. Warren to her car, parked several blocks away.
Then she'd driven him to where he'd parked, closer to the
high school. Dylan conveniently left out the extra time
he had spent with Miranda Warren in the front seat of her
Toyota Camry.

But how long would it be before the police figured
that out? The poor woman had been murdered, so they
would do an autopsy—if they hadn't performed one already. They would determine that she'd recently had sex.
Miranda had told him he didn't need to use a condom,
so his semen was still inside her when she'd been murdered. How long before the cops would be back with
more questions, including a request for a blood test?

Dylan realized what he needed to do. He'd have to tell
the police the truth, throw himself on their mercy, and
beg them to keep his indiscretion a secret.

He picked up the phone and started to dial his lawyer.

And while he had his lawyer on the line, he'd ask him
what he could do about that insane bitch next door.

One of Steve's classmates, Dana Roberts-Gold, was
being interviewed on TV. In many respects, she seemed
like a logical choice to represent Ms. Warren's students.
She was a pretty, photogenic brunette, a cheerleader, and
the vice president of their sophomore class. She always
sat through English Lit looking kind of bored or texting
on the sly, but still, for the TV cameras she'd worked up
some tears. Steve figured they must have pulled Dana
away from a football game for her brief segment, because

they had her standing in front of the school, and she wore an open jacket over her cheerleading uniform.

"Ms. Warren was one of the most popular teachers at the school," Dana said, her voice shaky. "Everybody liked her. She wasn't just a teacher. She was like a friend to so many of us. I'm going to miss her. It's hard to believe she's gone. I just don't understand how something like this can happen. It's so senseless . . ." Dana wiped away a tear.

On TV, they cut back to a silver-haired reporter, standing in front of Ms. Warren's ranch house. He wore a blue rain slicker and held a mic in his hand. Some rather subdued police activity was going on behind him—like the cops had been there a while and things were winding down. "As police continue their investigation into the brutal murder, there's no doubt that neighbors in this secluded area of Shoreline will be locking their doors and windows tonight."

Steve sat on the sectional sofa in the basement, staring at the TV. He'd showered, dried off, and was now dressed in jeans and a gray sweatshirt. He had his phone in his hand. He'd been searching online for more updates, but he hadn't really learned anything new there or from the local TV news report. Still, he couldn't help but think that if Eden really cared at all, she'd be down here, watching this with him.

He still wasn't sure whether Eden and her boyfriend had anything to do with Ms. Warren's murder. But they'd been acting awfully suspicious at Volunteer Park this afternoon.

He sat up when he heard someone hurrying down the stairs.

"Hey, Stevie." His father came into the family room with his jacket on. "I need to drive to the police station to answer some follow-up questions about Ms. Warren. I'm not really sure how long I'm going to be."

Steve's mouth dropped open. Had the cops figured out that Eden had killed Ms. Warren? Or maybe his dad was a suspect now. "What do you mean?" he asked, not hiding his concern. "What kind of questions?"

"Relax, it's no big deal. I'm guessing it shouldn't take more than a couple of hours, at the very most." His dad took out his wallet and gave Steve his American Express card. "I want you to order the pizzas, whatever you want, and gluten-free or vegan or whatever Eden wants, and a medium chicken and basil for Mom and me—and a salad. Mom will probably be home before me."

Steve stood up. He shoved the credit card into the pocket of his jeans. "You mean you're leaving me here alone with Eden?"

"Yeah, you two keep the home fires burning."

"Can I go to the police station with you?" he asked.

"No, you'll be more comfortable here. Besides, I want you to keep Eden company. I think she's kind of shaken up about Ms. Warren."

His father turned and started back up the stairs. Steve anxiously followed him. He wanted to tell his dad that he wouldn't be comfortable at all—and he was pretty shaken up about Ms. Warren, too. Helplessly, he watched his father head for the front door.

"I've told Eden I'm heading out," his dad said, stopping by the front closet. He took out a small, collapsible umbrella and opened the front door. "Do me a favor and check in on her in a little while. I texted Mom, so she knows where I'll be. Make sure to lock up after me, and don't answer the door for anyone except the pizza delivery person." He stepped outside, then turned back. He pointed to the Curtis house. "Don't answer if that woman next door comes by. I was over there today, and she's crazy. I'll explain later. I doubt she will, but if she does come over, call me."

"Why? What happened?"

"Like I said, I'll explain later." His dad gave him a quick kiss on the cheek. "Love you."

His father ran to the car with the umbrella tucked under his arm. Steve waited by the front door, watching his dad back out of the driveway and drive off. He wondered what had happened with the lady next door. Maybe she and his dad had gotten into an argument about her dog barking all the time.

Steve closed the door, double-locked it, and fixed the chain in place.

But that wouldn't keep Eden's boyfriend out if he was on his way over. Eden would simply let him in.

Steve had an awful feeling in his gut. He thought about inviting over his friend, Sean, so he wouldn't have to be alone with Eden. But why put his friend at risk, too? As soon as Eden figured out that he was on to her, she'd kill him and anyone else in the house.

He wanted to run away, just grab his coat and get out of there. But then Eden would be alone with his mom. And Eden seemed to resent her as much as she had Ms. Warren.

Steve glanced up the stairs toward the second floor. He didn't hear her up there.

He headed down to the basement, figuring he'd feel safer two floors away. The TV was still on, and he sat down on the sofa again.

But then an unsettling image came to his mind. It wasn't of Ms. Warren, shot in the throat in her bedroom. The image was from one of the many true murder stories he'd read. It was a fuzzy, black-and-white photo of Kenyon Clutter, murdered along with his sister and parents in Kansas in 1959. Dressed in a T-shirt and jeans, the boy was hog-tied to the arm of a sofa in the basement of his house. He'd been shot in the head. He was the same age as Steve.

Steve didn't want to be found down here in the basement, just like the Clutter boy.

Grabbing the remote, he turned off the TV, jumped off the sofa, and headed upstairs. At the top of the steps, he switched off the basement lights.

He took a butcher knife from the knife block on the kitchen counter. Sitting down in the dinette booth, he switched on the kitchen TV. He set the knife on the cushion beside him.

Then he prayed his mom or dad would be home soon.

CHAPTER THIRTY-FOUR

The flight had boasted free Wi-Fi, but it was worthless. Sheila had to wait until they touched down at Sea-Tac to access her texts or voicemail. When the plane finally landed, there was a long voicemail from Dylan at 6:15.

"Hey, hon," he said. "I might not be home when you get back. So just a reminder, Gabe's spending the night at Danny Lassiter's. Hannah wanted to stay over at Gwen's house, and I said it was okay. Steve is home with Eden. Now, here's the thing. Don't panic. But I'm headed to the police station. I have some disturbing news. Eden and Steve's teacher, Ms. Warren, the one I met with last night . . . she was killed early this morning in her house, sometime before dawn. Anyway, I'm going to talk to the police. I think, because I walked her to her car after our conference, they figure I might have seen something. I don't know. Anyway, I hope to be home by eight or nine at the latest. If I'm stuck there any later, I'll call or text. Okay? Sorry to drop this bombshell on you in a voice-mail, but you're not picking up. Anyway, love you."

Sheila replayed the message, just to make sure she'd heard him right. She was having a hard time compre-hending the news that Steve and Eden's teacher had been "killed." It sounded like she'd been murdered, but how? She wondered if it had been some kind of drive-by shooting, or a break-in, or what.

Sheila had never met Ms. Warren. She was sorry to hear about her death. But she remembered the woman's perfume had been on Dylan last night.

What really troubled her, though, was that, right now, Steve was alone in the house with Eden. There was every indication Eden had targeted her mother figures: Cassandra and her real mother. And now she was targeting her stepmother. So far, she hadn't tried to hurt Dylan or any of the children. But Sheila still didn't trust her alone with Steve.

Sheila looked out at the tarmac from her window seat as the plane taxied toward the gate. Her legs were cramped because of the space taken up by the boxes under the seat in front of her. Over the PA system, the flight attendant welcomed them to Seattle.

Sheila waited for the announcement to finish before she tried to phone Dylan back. She didn't want him to know she was on a plane. She'd told him she was subbing for Hallie today.

The call went directly to Dylan's voicemail. Sheila didn't leave a message. She figured he was still talking to the police.

She hung up and tried Steve's number. He answered after one ring: "Mom?"

"Hi, I just got a message from your dad," she said. "Are you okay?"

"Yeah, I—I'm fine," he said. But he sounded anxious. "Are you coming home soon?"

"I should be there in about an hour. It's just you and Eden at home right now?"

"Yeah, she's up in her room, and I'm in the kitchen."

"Dad said your teacher was killed early this morning.

What happened?" Sheila noticed the woman in the neighboring seat turned to stare at her. She must have overheard.

"Yeah," Steve said. "Somebody broke in and shot her in her house."

"Does she—did she live anywhere near us?"

"No, she lived in Shoreline. It was on the news tonight. You won't be home for another hour?" He still sounded worried.

"That's right. This must be such a shock for you, honey. Are you sure you're okay?"

"Yeah, I'm fine, I guess."

The plane stopped at the gate, and the seatbelt sign went off with a *ding*. All at once, nearly everyone was standing and reaching for the overhead bins.

"What was that?" Steve asked.

"The elevator," Sheila lied. "I'm in the hallway outside the ballroom. There's some event going on next door, and it's kind of crowded."

The woman sitting next to Sheila shot her another inquisitive look. Sheila tried to ignore her.

"Well, I'll wait half an hour before ordering the pizzas and salads," Steve said. "That way, you'll be here when they arrive. Okay?"

"That's great. Thank you, sweetie. I'll see you soon."

"Okay, bye." He hung up.

Sheila clicked off. The rows in front of her were starting to clear out. She bent over to retrieve the boxes, which were hard to balance with the photographs sliding around inside. As she waited for the row ahead of hers to empty out, she told herself not to worry. Steve couldn't have been too upset if he was talking about ordering pizzas.

Still, she didn't like that he was alone there with that girl.

Sheila knew she'd be driving over the speed limit all the way home.

The kitchen TV's On Demand wasn't working. Steve had to settle for a *Seinfeld* rerun to distract him as he sat in the breakfast booth. He'd already seen practically every episode of the show. This was the one with "shrink-age." For a few minutes, he'd almost been able to forget about his worries—and the kitchen knife at his side. But he'd muted the TV to talk to his mom.

He was about to turn the volume back up when his phone chimed.

It was a text. He thought maybe his mom had forgotten to tell him something, or maybe it was his dad texting from the police station.

But when he checked the Caller ID, it showed UNKNOWN. The last time he'd received a text from an anonymous sender, it had been about his Aunt Molly. He read the cryptic message:

Thought you should see this. Your mother's a dangerous woman

There was an attachment.

"Shit," Steve muttered. Once again, he hesitated, knowing that by clicking on the link he might be downloading a virus or spyware. But he couldn't help wondering what made his mother "dangerous." He took a deep breath and clicked on the link. An article from *The Oregonian* popped up. It was from seventeen years ago, dated July 17. Steve stared at the headline:

Portland Woman, 20,
Dies in Fall

POLICE INVESTIGATE CIRCUMSTANCES OF
UNIVERSITY OF OREGON STUDENT'S DEATH

Steve adjusted the phone screen to zoom in on the photo in the article. It was of a very pretty blonde with a dimpled smile. The caption read: "Mary Michelle Driscoll, 20, plunged 17 stories to her death from the top floor of her mother's Portland apartment building. She had planned to start her junior year at the University of Oregon in September."

Steve perused the article, which explained that Mary Michelle—apparently Molly's legal name—had gone up to the roof to smoke. Steve's mom was the last one to see her alive. It seemed they'd argued, and his mother had left her kid sister alone up there. Steve couldn't help wondering if his mom had said something horrible enough to compel Molly to leap to her death. The article didn't indicate that his mother was to blame or that she might have pushed her sister off the roof or anything like that, but it seemed possible. Whoever had forwarded the article to him apparently believed so.

Steve thought about those irregular sized photos in the family album, from his mom's childhood snapshots to the wedding pictures. He remembered that photo of her as a young girl on the beach and the shadow in the sand alongside her.

Now that shadow had a face.

He glanced at his Aunt Molly again. She was incredibly pretty and sweet looking.

Who had sent this to him? The most obvious candidate was upstairs in Hannah's old room.

Steve figured that since Eden's mother had been messing around with his dad in Portland seventeen years ago, she must have known about Molly. She could have read this article back then. Hell, she could have clipped it out of the newspaper and saved it. Maybe she'd told Eden about the death of Mary Michelle Driscoll.

Switching off the TV, he got up from the booth, taking his phone and the knife with him. He checked the entire first floor. He looked out through the windows for any sign of someone lurking outside in the rainy night. He also double-checked the locks on the doors. Once back in the kitchen, he returned the knife to its slot in the knife block on the counter. He hated giving it up, but he figured he'd look like an idiot knocking on Eden's door with a knife in his hand. At the moment, he was more afraid of her boyfriend showing up than he was of her.

Steve headed upstairs. Passing his own room, he remembered the bat at his bedside and made a mental note to grab it if the boyfriend tried to get in.

As he approached Eden's closed door, he thought he heard her crying. Steve listened for a moment, then knocked.

"Yeah, come in," she answered, her voice cracking.

Steve opened the door to find Eden sitting on her bed in jeans and a red sweater. She wiped the tears from her face and sniffled. "What's going on? What do you want?" she asked.

"Are you okay?" Steve asked.

"Do I look okay?" she shot back. She wiped her eyes again. "Sorry. I didn't mean to jump on your case. I feel awful. I was such a shit to that lady in class yesterday. I was trying to act so cool, trying to impress everyone on my first day. Instead, I just came off as an asshole. I was so mean to that poor woman, and now she's dead."

Steve noticed the phone beside her on the bed. "Did you just text me?" he asked.

She cleared her throat. "What?" Before he could answer, she shook her head. "No, I was following the tweets about Ms. Warren. Did you know she had two kids?"

Steve nodded.

"You should read some of the things they're saying. Everybody from that class thinks I'm a supreme bitch. I guess some of the things they're saying about me are true. But a couple of girls even suggested that I killed Ms. Warren. Can you believe that?"

Steve didn't answer her.

She wiped her face with the sleeve of her sweater. "Did you say somebody texted you? Was it about Ms. Warren?"

He shook his head. "It was about something that happened to my mom around the time my dad hooked up with your mother. Or maybe before, I'm not sure."

"Well, what was it? What happened?"

"I thought you might be able to tell me," Steve said.

Frowning at him, Eden leaned back on the bed. "I have no idea what you're talking about. Why would I know stuff about your mother from like seventeen years ago? That makes no sense. Dylan—*our dad*—grilled me about that the other afternoon, acting like I might *know* something. What I knew was my father had a wife and family in Seattle, and no clue I even existed. Except for a few other details, that was the extent of my knowledge about you guys until I moved in here. Not that I really care, but what supposedly happened? What's this big mystery?"

Steve leaned against the doorway frame. He shook his head. "It doesn't matter."

If she really had no idea about it, he didn't want to tell her. It was a family secret, and Eden still didn't quite feel like family to him. Besides, she'd piqued his curiosity once again about her possible role in Ms. Warren's murder. It was interesting to hear that he wasn't the only one who suspected her.

"Was that you I heard getting up in the middle of the night?" he asked.

"Last night?" She sighed. "Yeah, I woke up and couldn't fall back asleep. So around three in the morning, I tiptoed downstairs and looked at some of your photo albums in the den."

Steve figured he had the album she probably wanted to see—the one with photos of their dad around the time when he knew her mother.

"It was weird looking at those pictures of your family." She reclined on the bed, propping herself up on one elbow. "Like I said, when I was growing up, I knew about you guys, but not really. I realized I had a half sister around my age and two younger half brothers. It was kind of interesting to see all of you back when you were little—this whole family he had that I wasn't part of."

"I'm sorry," Steve murmured.

"What do you have to be sorry for? You didn't do anything." She swept some hair away from her face and gave a wistful smile. "Y'know, you were a pretty cute little kid. I think I would have really liked growing up with you, being your big sister. I used to imagine you were this really cool little brother . . ." She let out a long sigh and then sat up. "Anyway, not to sound sappy or corny or anything, but I just want to say that you're actually even cooler than I imagined. It was fun hanging out with you and our dad this morning. I had a really good time."

Steve was flattered, but still a bit wary of her. "You said the same thing on the bus—right before you ditched me."

Eden shrugged. "Yeah, I know, sorry. All that togetherness, all that family—it gets a little scary when you're used to being alone. I just needed to be off by myself for a while."

"But you weren't by yourself," Steve said, studying her. "Maybe you won't think I'm so cool when I tell you I went looking for you after you got off the bus. And I finally found you in Volunteer Park—with that guy . . ."

He expected her to get angry or deny it. But Eden just nodded glumly. "So you saw us, huh?"

"You told me he was going back to Portland yesterday."

"That was the plan." She stood up. "I really did go off to be by myself, but then he called me and said he was still in town. He wanted to get together and talk. So I met with him."

"What did you guys talk about?"

She leaned her backside against her desktop. "Well, for one thing, I asked Brodie, face-to-face, if he trashed your mom's garden. And he said no, but he wished he'd thought of it. Anyway, he didn't tear apart your mother's flower beds, and neither did I. Somebody else did. Your dad figured out who did it. Ask him."

Steve narrowed his eyes at her. "Okay, I will," he murmured. It was weird, but he believed she was telling the truth. He was curious about who might have destroyed the garden—and why his dad would know. Maybe it was the crazy lady next door, the one his dad had warned him about.

Steve forced himself to put that aside for a moment. He didn't want to lose track of what Eden and Brodie were doing in the park.

"What else did you and your boyfriend talk about?" he asked.

"Well, you can stop calling him my boyfriend, because he isn't anymore. We had a very long discussion about that. We're history."

"Really?"

Sauntering toward him, Eden patted him on the arm. "Really," she said. "I don't think you have to worry about seeing him again."

Then she headed out the door and started down the hall for the stairs.

Saturday—7:20 P.M.
Snoqualmie, Washington

Brodie leaned on the shovel to rest for a minute. "What was that line from *Young Frankenstein*?" He grinned up at the shadowy figure standing over him. "What did that guy with the weird eyes say? *'At least it's not raining'*?"

Actually, the light precipitation worked to his advantage, softening the ground as he dug the grave. Brodie stood in the hole, now about five feet deep. He thought that was enough. No one was about to stumble upon this site. They were in a tiny clearing in the middle of the woods with no nearby trails. To get here, they'd hiked for nearly ten minutes from where they'd parked the car.

But his boss wanted him to keep digging for a while longer. She stood over the grave with a flashlight in one hand and an umbrella in the other. The light was trained steadily on him.

Brodie had been in her employ for five months. It was an interesting client-worker relationship that included sexual favors in addition to weekly cash payments. She'd promised to pay him extra for this grave-digging detail. She was very obliging when he demanded more money for any particular chore—and that included the bonus he'd insisted upon for being an accessory to murder.

She'd already explained to him that the grave was for the son, Steve O'Rourke, who would go "missing" tonight. Brodie had been curious about his role in making the kid disappear. But his employer had told him that Eden had it covered. She was alone with him right now.

This took Brodie by surprise, because they'd been keeping Eden pretty much in the dark about everything. For one, the stupid girl actually thought he was in love with her. The truth was he'd been stringing her along all this time. In fact, it had been tough for him to keep a straight face while she broke up with him in the park this afternoon—like he could give a shit. And like she wouldn't just cave and take him right back if he told her how much he needed her. Some of these girls who grew up without fathers were such easy marks.

He wondered why all this responsibility was being heaped on Eden all of a sudden. But the answer was pretty clear when he stopped to think about it. He'd screwed up and was being punished because that cross-eyed cretin who'd caught him trying to break into the O'Rourke house was still alive. The local news reported the guy was no longer in a coma. He was actually responding to people now. So how long would it be until ol' Lazy Eye was sitting up, eating his Jell-O, and describing to the cops in detail everything that had happened to him on Wednesday?

Brodie had already promised his employer that he'd return to the hospital tonight to take care of the guy—for good this time.

He went back to digging. "Y'know, I just don't get it. These plans to whack the O'Rourke kid tonight are really coming out of the blue here. Eden didn't mention it this afternoon. You usually tell me what's going on at least a few days ahead of time."

"Yes, well, there was a sudden change of plans," she replied, standing over him with the flashlight.

"How the hell do you expect me to do my job when you keep changing things on me at the last minute?" he complained, scooping out another shovelful of earth. "The whole idea was that we'd take our sweet-ass time with this, deliberately driving that bitch toward another nervous breakdown—and then suicide or a fatal accident. I thought the job was supposed to take about a month. And here it's hardly been a week."

"Yes, I know," his employer agreed. "But I've had to hurry things up a bit. I didn't count on your blunder the other day."

"I told you I'd fix it tonight."

"There are other things I didn't count on."

He chuckled. "You mean, like Dylan O'Rourke not being able to keep his dick in his pants?" Brodie kept digging. "It's only a matter of time before the police realize he was banging that teacher instead of erasers after school. And when they do, they'll be watching him and that house pretty damn close."

"Exactly," she said. "That's another reason I'm speeding things up."

"So when do you think you'll have this wrapped up?" Brodie asked, hoisting more dirt with the shovel. "I'd like to know how much longer you'll need me."

Out of the corner of his eye, he saw the beam from the flashlight go askew. Brodie glanced up to see the light aimed at the trees above them. He realized she was reaching for something in her bag.

"Actually, after this little chore here, I won't need you at all," she said.

She tossed aside the open umbrella. It fell to the ground slowly, the fabric catching on the air.

The flashlight blinded Brodie for a moment. Then he saw the gun in her hand.

"Christ, no," he whispered. He let go of the shovel and backed into a wall of dirt. "Wait—"

She fired.

He let out a gasp as the first bullet ripped through his chest.

A second shot hit him in the forehead.

Brodie fell over dead in the fresh grave.

CHAPTER THIRTY-FIVE

Saturday—7:33 P.M.
Seattle

"They've got four bottles of red wine in here," Eden said, standing in front of the open liquor cupboard in the kitchen. "Do you think they'll notice if one is missing?"

"Yes," Steve said, standing behind her.

She took one of the bottles and handed it to him. "C'mon, let's put on our jackets, go out, and get drunk someplace—like down the hill from here, where all those boats are."

"Now?" Steve asked, incredulous. "What are you, nuts? It's raining out. And we just ordered pizza like twenty minutes ago. I thought we were going to watch *Blade Runner 2049*."

They had decided to eat their pizza and watch the movie On Demand on the TV in the den. Steve sometimes preferred being in the den to the basement when no one else was home. It felt safer there. He was hoping the movie would take his mind off Ms. Warren's murder and that text about Aunt Molly. Plus, he still didn't know what to think about Eden. He was touched that she'd cried for Ms. Warren. But part of that was for herself, too, because everyone in English Lit class thought she was a tremendous jerk. On the other hand, he did feel sorry for her, and he was flattered that she'd said he was cool.

Still, he couldn't be sure that her slimy boyfriend—or ex-boyfriend, or whatever he was—wouldn't suddenly show up. Maybe Eden was trying to lure him down to Portage Bay so the guy could jump him and beat him up, or worse. It could be part of a kidnapping plot, for all he knew. Even if he trusted her completely, the notion of going out in the rain to get hammered with his half sister didn't really appeal to Steve.

His parents had made it clear that if he wanted to drink, he could do it in the house with their booze while they were home. If that was some kind of ploy to take the fun out of drinking for him, Hannah, and Gabe, then the buzzkill had worked pretty well so far.

"I really have no desire to go out and get drunk, I'm sorry," he told her.

"Remember when I said earlier that I thought you were cool?" Eden asked. "Well, I take it back."

She grabbed the bottle out of his hand, then found the corkscrew in the drawer—pretty easily for someone who had just moved in five days ago, Steve thought. He wondered if she'd secretly made a study of where everything was in the house.

Eden opened the bottle almost like a pro. Then she poured herself a glass and chugged down a few swallows. "Don't you just want to be bad sometimes?" she asked.

He backed away from her and sat down on the edge of the dinette booth. "Not really."

"You should really learn to loosen up."

"The other night, you came by my bedroom door, and you were, like, naked," Steve said. "Was that you just being bad?"

Leaning against the kitchen counter, she took a sip from the glass and rolled her eyes. "I guess that was me being pretty stupid. I was trying to mess with you, intimidate you, whatever . . ." She looked down into the glass. "Almost the same stupid way I was trying to mess with Ms. Warren yesterday. That backfired, too." She took another hit of wine. "Maybe that's why I'd like to go some-place and get drunk right now, so I don't have to think about any of it. And I want my brother to come with me."

"My mom will be here pretty soon," Steve said. "She's going to freak out if she comes home to an empty house. I don't want to do that to her. She's going through a lot right now."

Eden frowned. "You mean like having to put up with me?"

"Okay, sort of," he admitted. "But there's other stuff, too." He was thinking about his Aunt Molly. After read-ing that old newspaper article and the comment from the person who'd sent it, Steve wasn't sure he could ever look at his mom the same way again. She must have said or done something to cause her sister's death. Why else wouldn't she have ever told her children about their aunt and erased all evidence that she'd ever existed?

He realized Eden was staring at him. She had her head tilted to one side. "You really care about them, don't you?"

"You mean my parents?" Steve shrugged. "Sure. Didn't you care about your mom?"

Eden took another swig of wine. "I wasn't as lucky as you've been. I wasn't part of a *real family* growing up. I was caught between two bitches who were both shitty at being mothers."

"You had two moms?" Steve asked. "But that's a real family, too. You mean, like lesbians? That's cool . . ."

"No," Eden frowned. "Antonia was my birth mother, but I was raised by her onetime best friend, Cassandra. By the time I was like ten, they could barely stand each other. Cassandra never let me forget that Antonia almost had me aborted."

"Wow," Steve murmured.

"Yeah, but Cassandra talked her out of it, paid all the hospital bills, and then took me off her hands. At the same time, Antonia was constantly reminding me that she was my *real* mother. Honestly, Antonia was like the worst mother ever, but Cassandra was no prize, either. I don't think she ever really liked me much. I think she just liked the idea of being a mother to *Dylan's daughter* . . ."

"She knew my dad? What, did she have an affair with him, too?"

"No, but when her best friend screwed him and gave birth to his daughter, that practically made Cassandra's head explode." Eden slugged back some more wine, draining the glass. She quickly refilled it. "She was so in love with your dad. And you want to hear the funny part? She met him only a few times. He hardly knew her. The first time they met, it was at some department store—and it was like love at first sight for Cassandra, even though they talked for only five minutes.

"It was through Antonia that they met again. Cassandra figured that fate had brought them together once more, or some sort of bullshit like that. But Dylan had barely remembered her. And by then, Antonia was already hooking up with him. I'm pretty sure he still doesn't remember her. In fact, I'm certain of it. Anyway, raising his daughter was Cassandra's consolation prize. Maybe if she'd slept with him, she would have gotten him out of her system. Instead, Cassandra became obsessed with him and his whole family."

"What do you mean?" Steve asked anxiously. "Obsessed—like how?"

"Nothing, forget it." Eden took another swallow of

wine. Steve could tell she was pretty sloshed. "I've said too much," she muttered, shaking her head. "You're not supposed to know any of this. It's my fault, everything that's happened. And thanks to me, they consider you a liability. I'm sorry. You're a nice guy. You deserve a break."

"*Liability*?" he repeated. "What's that supposed to mean? Who's *they*?"

Eden started crying. "Why didn't you want to run away and get drunk with me?"

Steve didn't understand what she was trying to tell him. He figured she wasn't making any sense because she was drunk from the two glasses of wine she'd practically chugged down.

Still, he was suddenly afraid again.

He heard a car coming up the driveway. It was probably his mom or the pizza guy. Or it could be someone else entirely.

Steve stood up, but then he couldn't move for a moment.

He was too scared of what he might see when he looked out the front window.

At the front door, Sheila gave Steve a fierce hug. She was so relieved to see he was all right. She didn't want to let him go. "Are you okay?" she asked, just to be sure.

Steve broke away first. "Yeah, I'm fine," he said.

But he wasn't quite making eye contact with her. And that was one of his little quirks when something was wrong. Sheila couldn't figure out if he felt guilty about something or if he was upset with her. She reached up and smoothed the new growth of short brown hair back from his forehead. "I was so sorry to hear about Ms. Warren."

Looking down at the floor, he nodded. "Yeah, it's really weird."

Sheila glanced back at the driveway and her car. She'd left the boxes of Antonia's photographs on the passenger seat. She'd retrieve them later. She closed the door and took off her coat. "How's Eden taking it? Where is she, by the way?"

"She feels pretty lousy about it," Steve answered, hanging on the newel post. He faced the stairs. "She just went up to her room. The pizza should be here soon."

Sheila hung up her coat. "Have you heard from Dad? Is he still at the police station?"

"I guess so. We haven't heard from him since he left."

She gently patted his back and headed into the kitchen. In the sink, she noticed a glass that hadn't been rinsed out and the remnants of red wine around the drain. She smelled the glass. "Steve?" she called.

With his hands in his pockets, he wandered into the kitchen. "What?"

An eyebrow raised, she showed him the glass. "Did one of you decide to have a glass of wine before dinner?"

He shrugged. "You've always said it was okay to help ourselves."

"Yes, as long as one of us—your father or I—is home. You know the rule. Is that why you haven't been able to look me in the eye since I came through the door?"

He checked the floor again. "No."

Sheila let out an exasperated sigh. "What am I thinking? It wasn't you. It was *her*, wasn't it? She's the one who was helping herself to the red wine. Probably one of the thirty-dollar bottles, too." She marched over to the liquor cabinet and saw the corked, half-empty bottle of cabernet in front. She picked it up and noticed a fresh red ring on the shelf. She wiped it and the bottom of the bottle with a paper towel, then set the bottle back in the cupboard.

She turned to Steve again and put a hand on his cheek. "I'm sorry to go accusing you," she whispered. "I should have known. And you—you didn't say a word. So listen, you can pat yourself on the back for not ratting on her. It's okay."

But he didn't say anything, and he still wouldn't look at her.

"Steve, what is it? What's wrong?"

He finally looked up. "Mom, did you have a . . ." He stopped himself.

"What?" she asked. "Did I have what?"

"Nothing," he muttered, pulling away from her. "It's just been a really weird day, that's all."

Sheila wondered if he'd somehow figured out that she'd lied to everyone about where she'd been today. Or maybe he was just really troubled about what had happened to his teacher. News like that would upset any kid, and Steve was pretty sensitive.

He started to wander toward the front hall.

"Honey, if you're going upstairs," Sheila said, "could you ask Eden to come down here? I need to talk to her."

He turned to gaze at her. A look of dread passed over his face.

"Don't worry. She's not in trouble—at least, not for drinking."

He sighed and then headed toward the front hall again. "Eden!" he yelled from the bottom of the stairs. "Eden, can you come down here? My mom wants to talk to you!"

Sheila went to the cupboard where she'd hidden the bottle of Jim Beam with the ground glass in it. She figured if Eden wanted to drink, she'd have a tough time turning down a couple of shots of bourbon—unless, of course, she'd tampered with that particular bottle.

"This ends here," Sheila said under her breath. She set the bottle of Jim Beam on the kitchen table and then pulled two fancy, old-fashioned glasses from the cupboard. Sheila was determined to confront Eden to-night about the attempts the girl had made on her life, and about what had really happened to the two "mothers" before her.

Sheila heard the footsteps plodding down the stairs, then whispers.

"I didn't say anything!" Steve muttered. "She found your glass in the sink."

A moment later, Eden stepped into the kitchen. She was barefoot. Sheila still wasn't used to how pretty she looked without the Goth makeup. Eden leaned against the counter. "So are you going to jump all over my ass because I had a couple of glasses of wine?" she asked.

"No," Sheila smiled and shook her head. "Just next time you feel like drinking any alcohol, we have a rule in this house that your father or I need to be home when you indulge. That way, if you get sick, or anything happens, someone's here to help. Is that understood?"

Eden gave a snarky little salute. "Yes, ma'am."

Sheila sat down in the dinette booth and then motioned to the spot across from her. "If you want to get a good quick buzz, you're better off with bourbon," she said. She opened the tainted bottle of Jim Beam. "Now, maybe you've already figured this out, but sometimes, late at night when I can't sleep, I take a shot or two to help me relax. C'mon, sit."

With a trace of apprehension, Eden slid into the booth and sat across from her.

Steve came through the kitchen doorway. He leaned back against the counter, folded his arms, and watched them.

Sheila poured about two shots' worth into each glass.

"I was going to help myself to some of this last night, but I took an Ambien instead. Anyway, there's enough left in this bottle to help take the edge off for both of us."

"Mom," Steve said. "Why are you acting so weird?"

She ignored him and raised her glass. "Listen, Eden, I'm so sorry we got off to such a rocky start. Let's put all these misunderstandings and all this nonsense behind us. I'd like to drink to a whole new beginning."

The girl eyed the glass suspiciously. She didn't pick it up.

"What's wrong?" Sheila asked innocently.

"Steve's right," she murmured. "This is kind of weird."

Sheila kept her poker face. Of course, Eden wasn't going to drink it. She recognized the bottle she'd tainted with ground glass and God only knew what else.

"Why won't you drink with me?" Sheila pressed. She put her glass down on the table. "I'd like us to be friends. You don't want to drink to a fresh start?"

Eden squirmed and let out a little laugh. "I'm, like, not even legal."

"When I wasn't home, you went through half a bottle of wine," Sheila pointed out. "And now you won't even have a little drink with me. I made a toast, Eden."

With a sigh, Eden picked up her glass. "Fine," she muttered. "Here's to fresh starts and adult supervision."

Sheila raised her glass and clicked it against Eden's. She waited and watched as Eden brought the glass to her lips.

She realized the girl really was about to drink it. All at once, Sheila lunged forward and swatted the glass out of Eden's hand. The bourbon spilled down the front of the girl's sweater. With a loud crash, the glass shattered on the kitchen floor.

"God, Mom!" Steve cried, recoiling. "What the hell?"

With a hand over her mouth, Eden looked horrified—

and hurt. She obviously had no idea why her stepmother had suddenly knocked the glass away.

"I'm sorry!" Sheila whispered. She reached over to pry Eden's hand from her mouth. Sheila was worried she might have cut the girl's lip.

Eden shrank back and slapped her hand away. Her lip wasn't bleeding. But she was crying. "Get away from me, you crazy . . ." She banged into the table as she stood up.

Sheila noticed she was barefoot. "Honey, be careful of the glass!"

Tears in her eyes, Eden stared at her in astonishment. Then she looked down at the stain on her pullover. She shook her head and ran out of the kitchen.

Wincing, Sheila listened to the rumble of her footsteps as she ran up the stairs.

"God, Mom, what was that all about?" Steve whispered.

"An experiment gone wrong," she muttered.

Sheila couldn't explain to him what she was trying to do. With a wad of paper towels to protect her from the shards of glass, she started to clean up the mess on the floor.

Steve grabbed some paper towels, too. He crouched down and started wiping up the bourbon. "Shit!" he grumbled. He dropped the wet paper towel and stared at his bleeding finger.

"Let me see," Sheila said, concerned. She reached out to him.

He jerked away. "It's okay. I can take care of it." With his wounded finger raised, he ducked into the bathroom.

"Let me know if you need the tweezers or a magnifying glass!" Sheila called, feeling useless.

He didn't answer.

He probably thought she was crazy, what with the way she'd acted toward Eden. But he'd been acting strange toward her even before that. Something was wrong. Tending to finger cuts was basic mom stuff, and he wouldn't even let her see it.

Dejected, Sheila finished wiping up the mess on the kitchen floor. She poured the bourbon down the drain and tossed away the bottle. Then, bending over the garbage, she shook the ground glass out of the sink strainer. Finally, she fetched the Dustbuster out of the broom closet to make sure she'd gotten all the bits of glass off the floor. While the mini vacuum roared, she kept glancing up to see if Steve was out of the bathroom yet.

At least she'd proven something with that stupid little experiment. It was obvious Eden had no idea the bourbon was tainted. Sheila was almost positive she'd been about to drink it. And after she'd gotten the glass smacked out of her hand, the girl's hurt and confused reaction had seemed genuine.

If Eden wasn't responsible for the ground glass in the bourbon, could she be innocent of all the other acts of sabotage—all those near-fatal misses? Maybe it had been her boyfriend breaking into the house and setting up those booby traps without Eden knowing about it. Or was somebody else behind it all?

Sheila hadn't gotten a chance to ask Eden about her "other mother," Cassandra. Now she'd have to wait for the girl to cool off before broaching the subject with her—and that might take another hour or another couple of days, depending on how long Eden held a grudge.

Steve emerged from the bathroom with some tissues wrapped around his index finger.

"Did you get all the glass out?" she asked, switching off the Dustbuster.

He nodded. "It was a big piece."

"Don't you need a Band-Aid?"

"It's fine," he muttered, still not looking at her.

She approached him. "Honey, I know you think what you just witnessed was pretty crazy, but there was a reason for what I was doing—"

The doorbell rang.

Sheila sighed. "That's probably the pizza. I'll get it." She set the Dustbuster on the counter. "Why don't you go upstairs and try to convince Eden to come down and eat? She probably won't talk to me. But over dinner, I'll do my best to explain to both of you what all that nonsense with the bourbon was about." Sheila worked up a smile and patted his shoulder. Then she started for the door.

A few steps behind her in the front hallway, Steve turned and silently treaded up the stairs.

Sheila collected the pizzas and salads at the door and made sure the delivery girl had been tipped. Carrying everything into the kitchen, she started to wonder about Dylan, and how much longer he'd be at the police station.

As she set down the pizza boxes, she listened to the familiar rumble of Steve running down the stairs. "Eden!" he yelled. "Eden, where are you?"

He staggered into the kitchen. "Did Eden come down here?"

Wide-eyed, Sheila shook her head.

"She's not in her room," Steve said, out of breath. "Her stuff's gone, too. She must have slipped out, Mom. She's not here."

CHAPTER THIRTY-SIX

Saturday—8:01 P.M.

Dylan wondered if he'd ever get out of there.

At least the cops hadn't put him in one of those stark interrogation rooms with the one-way mirrors. Dylan was in a slightly cramped office, sitting in a hard-backed chair across from the same lanky, forty-something detective with the square jaw and receding hairline who had interviewed him earlier. His last name was Laskin. A cluttered old metal desk was between them, and somewhere, amid all that clutter, a small, digital voice recorder caught everything Dylan said. Detective Laskin had asked his permission to record the session. He'd also reminded Dylan that he could have his lawyer present. An hour and a half ago, Dylan hadn't thought it was necessary. But now he was beginning to rethink that decision.

He'd already gone over his revised, uncensored story twice while the detective listened, jotted down a few things, and made a chain out of paper clips. The other cop—the stocky young blond guy who'd come to the house with Laskin—had quietly stood in the office throughout Dylan's first retelling of what had happened with Ms. Warren. He'd left about forty minutes ago. But Dylan could still see him through the window that looked out onto a busy, open office. There were more cops milling around, six desks with ancient computers, a water cooler, and a Mr. Coffee machine—which explained the burnt coffee smell. Dylan noticed the stocky cop casually migrating from desk to desk, talking to his peers.

Detective Laskin had already assured Dylan that they wouldn't go public with the more intimate details of his story as long as the information had no bearing on the outcome of their investigation. Still, it seemed a safe bet that the blond cop was telling his pals out there about the witness in Laskin's office, now recanting an earlier story to admit he'd banged a homicide victim just hours before her murder. Every once in a while, Dylan caught one of the cops looking at him—and maybe it was just his imagination, but they seemed either smugly amused or disgusted by his presence there.

He'd already given Laskin every juicy detail of his encounter with Miranda Warren, using all of his public relations expertise to finesse things with the detective. He explained how he'd been caught by surprise earlier when they'd shown up at his door with the news about Ms. Warren. And they'd questioned him in his home with his daughter present, so naturally he had been reluctant to tell them how he'd been intimate with her teacher. But he was trying to set the record straight.

Now the detective wanted to hear it a third time. It was embarrassing. Dylan was tired, and sweating. His Italian-wool sweater was too warm for the stuffy, humid little office. He just wanted to go home.

"You indicated earlier that I wasn't a suspect," Dylan pointed out, shifting around on the hard chair. "Is that still true? Because I can't believe you want me to tell this story again. I swear to you, I didn't leave anything out of the last two versions I just told you. You've gotten the whole, unabridged story here."

Laskin nodded. He was still playing with his paper clips. "Just one more time, from when the two of you left the school."

Dylan rubbed his forehead. "Oh, God."

"The thing is, Mr. O'Rourke, for all we know, Miranda Warren might have had a stalker—or a student who was in love with her, or a student who had a grudge. There's a chance someone might have seen you with Ms. Warren, maybe even when you two were in the car together. And maybe that set them off. Your story here might provide us with a motive for her murder. Whoever broke into that house and shot her didn't steal a thing. Now, please, when you left the school, it was getting dark out."

The phone rang, and the detective answered it. Dylan guessed the call must have had nothing to do with Ms. Warren or him, because Laskin put down his paper-clip chain and started hunting through a stack of papers on his desk. Then he got back on the line and said something about an incident report dated September third.

During this lull, Dylan remembered what Brooke had mentioned about someone following her around. Had the same person been watching him and Miranda Warren? He thought about crazy Leah next door. God only knew what she was capable of.

He'd left the kids alone in the house, and now he wondered if they were safe.

Or maybe Leah was targeting Brooke. She didn't seem to regard Sheila or the kids as any kind of competition or threat—or at least, she'd indicated that today. But if Leah had been following him and seen him with Miranda Warren, that could have sent her over the edge. And if she'd murdered Miranda Warren, she might go after Brooke, too.

Or was he just tired and paranoid and jumping to conclusions? Maybe he was simply overreacting to the horrifying revelation that Leah was back in his life. She was crazy, but was she really capable of murder?

He wondered if he should say something to Laskin. But then he'd have to explain about Leah. He didn't mind that so much—especially if it got her off his back and out of his life. But he'd also have to expose Brooke. The police would want to question her about the woman who had been tailing her and that phone call in the middle of the night.

And if he said anything, he'd be stuck there for at least another two or three hours.

As soon as the cops let him go, he would phone home to make sure everyone was okay.

Then he would call Brooke.

Detective Laskin finally hung up the phone. He leaned back in his chair and picked up his paper-clip chain again. "Okay, Mr. O'Rourke, so—you two left the school together, and it was getting dark out . . ."

Both Sheila and Steve had tried to call Eden, but there had been no answer.

Though they had a ton of food, neither of them were able to eat more than a slice of pizza. Sheila hadn't eaten all day, but she had absolutely no appetite.

At Sheila's suggestion, the two of them sat at the dining room table with their pizzas and Cokes. Part of her just needed to get out of the kitchen, where Steve had witnessed that bizarre scene between her and Eden. Besides, the dining room table seemed an appropriate choice because she wanted to have a serious discussion with Steve.

She told him about her trip to Portland, along with everything she'd learned about Eden's mother and Cassandra. Steve was mildly surprised to learn about her secret trip. But the revelation about Eden's other mother was no shock. He said Eden had told him earlier tonight about Cassandra raising her. He said Eden hadn't given any indication that this Cassandra person might be dead—just that she and Antonia had been crummy mothers.

Sheila also told him about the attempts on her life— the brakes on her car, the shorted-out washing machine, the Visine in her cranberry juice, and the ground glass in the bourbon.

He was astonished. "Why didn't you say anything, Mom?" he asked, leaning forward, elbows on the table.

"It was all happening in plain sight, in front of everybody," she said. "I knew each little incident was connected and premeditated. But I didn't have any proof. I figured Eden was responsible for everything—until about a half hour ago, when I saw her ready to swallow that bourbon with the ground glass in it. That's why I knocked the drink out of her hand." Sheila picked up her half-eaten slice of pizza. "You must have thought I was crazy. Clearly, Eden thought so."

"Mom, I saw her today in Volunteer Park. She was meeting that Brodie guy. He's not in Portland. He keeps telling her he's leaving, but he hasn't yet."

"Why am I not surprised?" she replied, nibbling on the pizza. "I was blaming her for everything, including the garden. But I'll bet it was that sleazy creep all along."

"Eden said she's certain he didn't trash the garden."

"Well, obviously the guy's been lying to her about a lot of things."

"She said Dad figured out who wrecked the garden."

Sheila put down the slice of pizza and stared at him.

"I have a feeling it's the lady next door. Before leaving for the police station, Dad told me not to open the door if she came over to the house. He said she's crazy. I guess he went over there this afternoon and talked to her about the dog barking or something."

Sheila had been wondering last night whether Leah might be responsible for destroying the garden. But what could the woman next door have against her?

Steve took a swig of Coke and glanced at his watch. "Do you think one of us should try phoning Eden again? Or maybe we should call Dad."

There was a hard thump on the front door.

Sheila got up from the table and hurried to the door, with Steve right behind her. She looked through the peephole. No one was outside. She thought about the noise they'd just heard. It hadn't really sounded like someone knocking, but more like something had hit the door.

"Who's out there?" Steve whispered, hovering behind her.

"I don't think it's anybody." She opened the door and peered outside. She still didn't see anyone.

"Look," Steve said, pointing to the front stoop.

Sheila glanced down at the spattering of dirt, gravel, and mud. She turned and noticed the grimy dirt mark on the door. Somebody had hurled a dirtball at the house— and just missed the stained-glass window in the front door. Sheila stared out toward the lawn, searching for someone hiding in the shadows behind a tree or bush. She couldn't help thinking that, at any minute, the perpetrator would throw another dirtball—this time, at one of them. She dared to take a step outside. "Eden?" she called. "Eden, are you out there? Please, I want to apologize."

There was no answer. It was quiet, except for the sound of the wind and the light rain. A few leaves scattered across the wet lawn.

"Mom, there's something in the front seat of the car," Steve whispered.

He'd scared her for a moment, but then Sheila looked over toward the Toyota and remembered. "Oh, those are just a couple of boxes full of pictures that belonged to Antonia."

"Do you want me to get them?" he asked.

"It can wait, honey," she said nervously. "They're okay out there."

But Steve went into the kitchen and returned a few moments later with her car keys. Sheila figured that at least there was an alarm on the fob, in case they needed it.

She kept thinking that Eden was probably out there in the dark, watching them. Or maybe it was her boyfriend, Brodie. Someone had thrown that dirtball. Was it to draw them out of the house for some reason?

"Hey, Eden?" Steve called, brushing past Sheila and handing her the keys as he stepped outside. "Hey, Eden, are you out here? We've got pizza inside!"

Sheila reached out to stop him, but she was too late. He started toward the car.

Reluctantly, she followed Steve to the Toyota. The rain was more like a light mist, but it was still damp and cold out. With the device on the fob, she unlocked the car, and the parking lights blinked. Sheila expected to feel a gravel-packed dirtball smack into her face at any second. Or maybe it would be something worse.

Usually, Steve was pretty timid about things that went bump in the night, but here he was, grabbing the boxes out of the car. Maybe his curiosity about Eden's mother had overridden his wariness of the situation. Or maybe he was just being brave for her.

Sheila shut the car door and pressed the locking device on the fob. The car lights blinked again. "Here, let me take one of those," she said, catching up with him.

"I'm fine," Steve said. As he carried the boxes toward the house, he kept stopping to glance around.

Sheila followed him to the front door. She figured if Steve went over the photographs with her, maybe he'd recognize someone he'd seen hanging around outside the house or at school.

She was about to shut the door, but someone came charging up the driveway, seemingly out of nowhere. Sheila froze. It took her a moment to recognize Leah from next door.

"You took my dog, didn't you?" she screamed. "What did you do with her?"

It dawned on Sheila that she hadn't heard any barking since she'd returned home.

Steve set the boxes on the foyer floor and came up behind her. "Is that the crazy lady from next door?" he whispered.

"Yes," Sheila said under her breath. She made sure to place herself between Steve and Leah, who flounced up the walkway to the front stoop.

She shook her head at the woman. "No, we haven't seen your dog."

"I don't believe you," Leah hissed. Her tawny hair was a tangled wet mess. Sheila wondered if she was drunk. "You're lying."

"Why would one of us take your dog?" she asked calmly. "And if we had it here in the house, you'd certainly hear it barking. Anyway, I have no idea where your dog is."

"Are you sure your husband didn't see her?" Leah pressed.

"I'm positive." Sheila glanced down at the dirt on the front stoop, which was quickly turning into mud from the rain. Then she glanced at Leah's hands. They were dirty. "And if you throw anything else at our house again, I'll call the police. Is that understood?" She backed up and started to close the door.

"I thought your husband would know where Trudy was because he was the last one to see her," Leah said.

Her hand on the door, Sheila stopped to stare at her.

Leah's eyes narrowed. "You see, the dog slipped out and ran away when Dylan came over to fuck me this afternoon."

Sheila was stunned speechless.

"Jesus," Steve whispered.

"You mean, Dylan didn't tell you?" Leah's face lit up with a superior smile. "Oh, yes, the two of us go way back. We had a very serious, very passionate affair years ago. It was wonderful. You remember the black roses, Sheila? I sent those because I felt sorry for you."

Sheila remembered the roses all right. She felt sick to her stomach.

And all this was being broadcast in front of her son.

"Dylan used to say you weren't bad-looking," Leah went on. "I saw you from a distance often enough when I was watching your house. But I didn't realize until the other day, when you came by, that up close, you're rather plain and frumpy . . ."

Sheila felt Steve pulling at her.

"Get the hell out of here!" he yelled, stepping between her and Leah. "You can't talk to my mother like that. My father said you're crazy. He would never touch you—"

"Stevie, don't even bother." Sheila tried to pull him inside. She could feel him shaking.

"Really, he wouldn't touch me?" Leah laughed. "Well, just ask your sister, the pale blond one. She saw us from your kitchen window this afternoon." Hands on hips, she grinned at Sheila. "Dylan and I did it in my dining room. He had me on the table. The girl was watching."

"Get out of here!" Steve screamed. He swiveled around.

Before Sheila knew what was happening, he pushed her inside the house. Then he slammed the door shut.

"Mom, don't listen to that crazy skank," he said. He held onto her arms so tightly that her circulation was nearly cut off. "Dad said she was nuts. He would never . . ."

But then he trailed off, and his grip on her arms loosened. "You don't actually believe her, do you?"

"Of course not," Sheila lied.

She remembered those black roses, and she knew her husband.

But their son didn't need to know.

Sheila worked up a smile and wrapped her arms around him. He was still trembling. "Thanks for coming to my rescue, Stevie," she said, patting his back.

She pulled away and double-locked the door. She realized she was shaking, too. Any minute now, she expected a rock to smash through one of the front windows.

Bending down, she took one of the boxes and carried it into the kitchen. She set it on the dinette table, then reached over and pulled down the window shade so that they wouldn't have to see the house next door.

Steve followed her with the other box, setting it on the seat cushion. "How about that wacko anyway?" he said with a skittish laugh. "I can't believe her, throwing dirtballs at the house and coming up to you and saying that crazy stuff."

Sheila went to the other windows with a view of the house next door and lowered the shades. She knew Steve was trying to convince himself that what the woman had said wasn't true.

"I know," she said, drawing the curtains in the dining room. "She's definitely off her rocker, as my dear mother used to say. I guess we don't have to wonder anymore who wrecked our garden." She picked up the pizza boxes and the plates and took them into the kitchen. "Listen, Stevie, my head is suddenly splitting. I think I'll go upstairs and lie down for a little while—just a few minutes. Will you be all right by yourself down here?"

He nodded. "Is it okay if I look at Eden's pictures?"

"I'm sure she wouldn't mind," Sheila said. "There aren't too many of Eden. But let me know if you recognize anyone." She glanced toward the window. "And come get me if you hear anything more from the dirtball lady."

Up in her bedroom, Sheila closed the drapes, kicked off her shoes and stretched out on the bed.

She believed every word that crazy woman had just said.

Poor Eden. Between seeing her father copulating with a neighbor and then having her stepmother slap a drink out of her hand—after proposing a toast—small wonder the girl had run away tonight.

Sheila kept thinking, *How could he?*

Less than a week after learning that he'd fathered an illegitimate child who was now grown and turning their lives upside down, Dylan was screwing the next-door neighbor, some basket case he'd already been with years back. She wasn't even pretty. *How could he?*

He hadn't changed at all in seventeen years.

Sheila remembered the "rough patch" she'd tried so hard to forget.

Forget and forgive, forgive and forget. That was what the priest friend of her mother's had told her.

She recalled that hot July night, after finding her frail, sickly mother abandoned and lying in her own feces in the bathroom. Sheila was still feeling nauseated from perpetual morning sickness. And she'd finally had it out with her useless, self-centered sister. She remembered Molly with tears streaming down her pretty face and her blond hair blowing in the wind. She stood on the other side of the security railing on the rooftop deck of their mother's apartment building, the blazing red sunset behind her. Sheila had turned her back to her.

She started to walk away. Then, past the noise from the roof's air-conditioning vents and the distant traffic below, she heard her sister call to her a second time. "Sheila, please, wait."

If only she'd kept walking back into the building and that rooftop gym, how different things might have been. But Sheila stopped and turned around.

"You're right," Molly cried, her hands gripping the railing in front of her. "I'm a terrible sister. I don't blame you for hating me. I hate myself. But it's not my fault. You can't choose who you fall in love with."

Sheila tried to remember the name of the guy who had graduated that year, the one her roommate had said Molly was crazy for—so crazy that she'd swallowed all those sleeping pills and ended up in the hospital. Sheila shook her head. "Are you talking about—what's his name—Jesse?"

Molly wiped her eyes. "There's no Jesse. There was never a Jesse. I made him up. I didn't want anyone at school to know I was seeing a married guy."

Sheila remembered holding onto her swollen, extended belly, and somehow knowing what Molly was going to say.

"This whole year, during almost all of his trips out of town, Dylan's been seeing me," Molly admitted. "We're in love, Sheila. I'm sorry. We didn't plan on this happening. It's nobody's fault. Neither one of us wanted to hurt you."

Staring at her, Sheila just shook her head over and over. She remembered wanting to kill her.

But she didn't remember anything else after that.

There was a two-hour gap between that moment and when she returned to her and Dylan's apartment. It was lost time. The drive home should have taken twenty-five minutes. But Sheila didn't remember leaving her mother's building or getting into her car.

According to Dylan, after getting the call from the police, he'd waited and watched from their apartment window until he finally saw her car.

Sheila didn't even remember parking the car. But when she saw Dylan come out the front door of their apartment building, it was like she was waking up from an awful dream. His arms out, he slowly approached her. "Honey, I'm so sorry," he whispered.

She didn't hug him back. She realized Molly must have been telling the truth. She figured her sister must have called and told him about their discussion on the rooftop deck. That explained why he was apologizing. Sheila stood, stiff in his arms, thinking, *Does he think he can just hug me and say he's sorry? Does he really think that's going to make everything all right again?*

She was about to pull away, but he was holding her tightly.

"The police just called an hour ago," he whispered in her ear. "Where have you been? Your mom, the nurse, we've all been trying to get ahold of you. There's been a terrible accident. It's Molly . . ."

No one ever actually blamed her. She told the police that she'd had a brief argument with Molly on the rooftop deck. No one actually said anything about her possibly pushing her sister off the edge of that roof, though a couple of newspaper articles may have hinted between the lines. One look at Sheila in her advanced state of pregnancy and the police knew she would have had a hard time climbing over that railing. Besides, she and her sister had argued all their lives. No one had ever ended up dead before.

Sheila had a vague recollection of wandering along the

riverwalk downtown during that lost time. So she told the police that was where she'd been for the unaccounted-for ninety minutes. She said her doctor had prescribed a lot of exercise and walking.

There was every indication that Molly had leapt to her death. A few of Molly's college friends had come forward with accounts of other suicide attempts in addition to the incident with the sleeping pills. Apparently, the attempts to kill herself were always over this "Jesse" no one could ever track down.

Sheila didn't think she'd ever forgive Dylan. She kept asking him: *How could you?*

"I didn't mean for it to happen," he confessed to her in the early morning hours after Molly's death. The police had left and they were finally alone in their apartment. They were both devastated and exhausted. "I've never been unfaithful to you, Sheila," he explained. "I've never loved anyone but you. Then about a year and half ago, after your dad died and Molly went away to college, I had that trip to Eugene. Remember? You wanted Molly and me to get together while I was there. But I already knew how she felt about me. She'd been dropping all these hints. Anyway, we got together, got drunk, and—well, it happened. Remember how we didn't see much of her at all for about a year? I told her that we had to stay away from each other. To Molly's credit, she agreed. She understood. But then after you got pregnant, she suddenly became clingy and demanding. She kept calling me at work, telling me I had to drive down to see her. She threatened to tell you about us. I couldn't let that happen. You've been going through such an awful time. Hell, it's been tough on both of us. I thought I could smooth things over with Molly and we could somehow be friends. So I kept seeing her. She threatened to kill herself if I stopped. She tried a couple of times. I didn't know what to do. I was trying to get out of it gracefully without anyone getting hurt. I'm so sorry, Sheila . . ."

She didn't tell the police about Dylan's affair with Molly. The only person she told was the old priest friend of her mother's. Of course, he advised her to stay with Dylan and work things out: *forget and forgive, forgive and forget*. He'd come to her mother's apartment that week—not only to console her mom about Molly, but also to give her last rites. In the days following Molly's death, their mother starved herself. She was too frail to attend Molly's funeral.

Sheila remembered how Dylan did everything he could to make it up to her. He cried and begged for her forgiveness. He handled Molly's funeral arrangements and took over the around-the-clock nursing care for her mother. He devoted himself to helping Sheila heal. Everyone thought he was the best husband in the world.

Her mother died just a week after Molly was buried. Dylan made all the funeral arrangements again.

It was at her mom's funeral that Sheila realized something was wrong with the baby. She started bleeding in the cemetery.

She lost the child. It was a girl.

No one understood how she could want to leave her dear, sweet husband, who had been at her side practically the entire time during her hospital stay. Their separation lasted six weeks.

Looking back on it now, Sheila figured it must have been about two weeks after he'd moved out that he met Antonia. He might have even fooled around with some other women during that brief interim.

Sheila took him back because she didn't have anyone else. In a month's time, she'd lost her sister, her mother, and her baby daughter. She'd also lost her husband, but at least he was still alive. And he was calling every day to tell her how sorry he was, how much he missed her, and how much he still loved her. So Sheila decided to *forget and forgive, forgive and forget*. To help make that strategy easier, Sheila insisted they move away from Portland.

By the time they'd settled in Seattle, she was pregnant again.

She cut Molly out of all the photographs in the family albums, and they never talked about her. But it didn't really work. It just left a gap. Besides that, she'd forgiven Molly years and years ago.

It was Dylan she had a hard time completely forgiving.

That was the first time she found out that he'd been unfaithful. And it had practically killed her.

But since then, it had happened again and again. She told herself that it was his one flaw. He was a good father, a good lover, a good provider. And despite all the other women, he always came back to her. Yet, even though she turned a blind eye to every affair, it still killed her a little bit each time.

From the bed, Sheila looked over toward the window. She thought about the house on the other side of those closed curtains. She thought about what Dylan's long-lost daughter had seen going on in that house today.

Instead of asking, *How could he?* she finally had to ask herself, *How could you keep taking him back?*

Sheila turned away from the window and cried.

CHAPTER THIRTY-SEVEN

Saturday—9:19 P.M.

Dodgeball was on the kitchen TV with about a hundred commercials and all the best gross-out gags cut out. But it really didn't matter. Steve had the TV on mostly for background noise while he sorted through the pile of photos Eden's mother had saved.

He was still feeling kind of weird for yelling at that crazy woman next door. Maybe he had a minor case of post-traumatic stress disorder or something. He didn't like confrontations, especially with adults. Plus, he'd never encountered anyone who had so openly attacked his parents, screaming insults at his mother and bad-mouthing his dad. He kept thinking of all these clever, cutting things he should have said to her. It was extra disturbing that this nutcase lived right next door. Steve had to resist the urge to peek past the curtains and check on what she was up to in the house across the hedges.

All that drama had somehow made him hungry, and he'd put away three more slices of pizza while half-watching the movie and looking at the photographs. He was careful not to get any grease on the pictures.

It was actually pretty boring, going through the photos of some stranger. His mom was right about there being only a few snapshots of Eden, mostly school portraits in which she looked pretty dorky. It was easy to identify Eden's mother. She was the thin, tan brunette in about ninety-nine percent of the shots. In some of the older photos, Antonia was with a woman who looked like her wannabe twin. They both had on a lot of eye makeup, and their shoulder-length dark hair was kinky-curly. Steve wondered if the lookalike gal-pal in those pictures was Eden's "other mother," Cassandra. She wasn't quite as pretty or flashy-looking as Antonia. Steve looked for names on the backs of the photos, but all he found was an occasional notation with the month and year. The photos ranged from 1997 through 2002. Antonia looked pregnant in a couple of the pictures. There were about a dozen shots of this other woman with Antonia, and Steve set them aside. He couldn't find any current pictures of her.

Steve wished that the photo collection was more interesting. He really wanted to take his mind off what that crazy woman had said about his dad. If he'd heard those awful accusations before last week, he'd have quickly dismissed them. But since Eden had come into their lives, Steve had a whole different, slightly dismaying view of his dad. He couldn't help wondering if there was some truth in the ridiculous things that lady had said.

And what the hell was happening at the police station? His dad had said he'd be home by nine at the latest.

Steve's phone rang, and he dug it out from under a pile of photos he'd viewed. He saw on the Caller ID that it was Eden. He clicked on the phone. "Hey, where are you?" he asked.

"Well, I've pretty much run away, so answering that question would kind of defeat the purpose of the whole thing, y'know?"

She could be just as sarcastic as Hannah at times.

"Listen, my mom's really sorry about that thing

with the bourbon," Steve explained. "Somebody put ground-up glass in the bottle, and she thought it was you. She figured you'd refuse to drink it. But when you almost did, that's when she slapped the glass out of your hand. See?"

There was silence on the other end.

"Eden? Are you there?"

"Somebody put ground glass in her bourbon?"

"Yeah. They also put Visine in her juice to poison her and short-circuited the washing machine."

More silence.

"Are you there?"

"Did our father come home yet?" she asked.

"Not yet."

"Well, have you or your mom let him know that I've run away?"

"I haven't. I don't know about my mom. She's upstairs. We were kind of hoping you'd come back."

"Well, I'm not. Could you call our dad and let him know I'm sorry?"

"Listen, just come home, okay?" Steve let out a nervous sigh. "Did you see our dad with the woman next door this afternoon?"

"Yeah, I saw them. Why are you asking?"

"She came by here a little while ago. She said the two of them were getting it on in her dining room, and you saw them. Is that true?"

"Yeah," she muttered. "Dylan tried to convince me that she, like, tried to rape him or something. He said she attacked him and pulled down his pants. I guess it's possible. But to me, it sure looked like he was screwing her."

Steve slumped a bit in the breakfast booth. "Well, thanks for being honest," he mumbled. He wondered if there was any truth to his father's explanation. Steve wouldn't have put it past the woman to sexually attack his father. At the same time, he wouldn't have put it past his father to mess around with that woman, even if she was kind of a skank.

"Will you give that message to our dad for me?" Eden asked.

"That you're sorry you ran away?" Steve said. "Won't you please just come back? We have your special vegan pizza here—and *pictures*. My mom went down to Portland today and got all these photographs that your mom had saved."

"Well, she had no business taking my mother's stuff," Eden said. "What's she planning to do with the pictures?"

"I think she was going to surprise you or something. I don't know. Why are you wigging out about it?"

"I'm not wigging out. It's nothing. Forget it."

"You know that Cassandra woman you told me about? Is she alive or dead?"

"She moved to Florida. Why are you asking about her?"

"Did she kind of look like your mom at one time— I mean, like around a year or so before you were born?"

Again, there was silence on the other end of the line.

"Eden?"

"I really wish you'd run away with me when I asked you earlier tonight. This isn't how I wanted it to turn out. I'm sorry about everything. Anyway, be sure to call Dad and tell him I'm sorry."

"I don't get this," Steve said. "Why don't you just call him yourself?"

"Because I'd rather he hear it from you," she answered. "Listen, earlier tonight in the kitchen, your mom was worried about me walking on the glass, and she called me 'honey.' Is that what she calls you sometimes?"

"Yeah, sometimes," Steve replied. "She calls all of us that sometimes—Hannah, Gabe, and me."

"Neither one of those bitches who raised me ever called me that—at least, never in a nice way," Eden muttered. "I do feel bad about your mom. I feel bad about this whole thing. Listen, I'm sorry, okay? It—it would have been nice having you for a brother."

She hung up.

Leah Engelhardt realized she'd left her back door ajar.

She'd been up and down the block in the rain, looking for her German shepherd, calling for her. She even brought along a box of Milk-Bones and shook it as she walked down the street. She'd discovered that the sound of the rattling dog biscuits quickly brought Trudy out of hiding. It was one of the cute little things she'd learned about the dog in the short time she'd owned her. But the rattling box of Milk-Bones hadn't worked this time. Trudy was still missing.

Stepping inside the house, Leah shut and locked the door behind her. She set the box of dog biscuits and the leash on the kitchen counter. Peeling off her damp jacket, she threw it over the back of the chair at her breakfast table.

It had been nearly an hour since she'd confronted Dylan's pathetic wife and their snot-nosed son. Part of Leah was still riding on that high. She'd felt exhilarated telling Sheila O'Rourke about the affair with Dylan, finally getting it out in the open like that. She could tell Sheila remembered the black roses, too. Leah wished she'd had a camera to capture the look on Sheila's face when she told her about Dylan having sex with her this afternoon. Hell, it was even more satisfying than destroying the bitch's garden had been.

Leah knew the only obstacles standing between her and Dylan were his stupid wife and those three kids.

She'd never really gotten over being dumped by him years ago. And over the past several months, all that passion, rage, and yearning had been stirred up again by a series of phone conversations with Leah's new "friend."

The anonymous woman had one of those blocked numbers, so Leah had no way of calling her back. She'd started out just leaving messages. Leah still remembered the first one: "That Dylan O'Rourke was a fool to let you go."

That had been all. Then she'd hung up.

But it had gotten Leah's attention. It was like hearing the voice inside her head, the one reassuring her that she was right and everyone else could go to hell. But now it was somebody else's voice, almost as if she had her own personal cheerleader: "That wife of his is such a frump. Stupid Sheila, I call her. Dylan would be so much happier with you . . ."

It got so that Leah looked forward to the calls. The woman wanted to remain anonymous, referring to herself as a "concerned friend," which was frustrating. Leah would have loved to sit down with her, mix a batch of martinis, and talk about Dylan. Her "concerned friend" admitted that she'd been with Dylan, and he'd unceremoniously dumped her, too. A private investigator who owed her a favor had been able to track down the names of several other women Dylan had been with. The detective had even gained access to some of Dylan's old emails. "That's how I got your name," her friend told her. "And oh my God, those emails you wrote him were hot. So sexy! How could Dylan just ignore you like that? After reading what you wrote and seeing what you look like, well, I guess I don't feel so bad anymore that Dylan dumped me. What a fool he is! You're gorgeous, Leah."

Her friend texted her shots that looked like surveillance

photos of Dylan and his family. One batch showed them in a restaurant, and another bunch was from a Fourth of July celebration. In some of the shots, her anonymous friend had defaced Sheila's image. Some of the embellishments were lewd and pretty funny.

Leah's new friend also sent her a notice that the house next door to Dylan's was on the market to rent. The accompanying text message simply read:

U have to move in!

Leah was no fool. A part of her knew the woman was setting her up for something. But she wasn't ready to push away someone who told her everything she wanted to hear. It was like having a fan, someone completely devoted to her. Plus, Leah believed that a couple of women working in secret together could really make a man suffer and repent. Her friend assured her that they'd meet someday.

Meanwhile, the notion of living next door to Dylan was just too good to pass up. Before moving in, Leah couldn't quite decide if she wanted to make his life miserable or if she wanted him back.

"Make Sheila's life miserable," her friend suggested. "Have fun. And you'll get him back eventually, Leah. He won't be able to resist you."

Her friend always knew what she wanted to hear.

Leah got a look at the layout of the place. What really appealed to her was how, from one of the bedrooms, she could look through the window into Dylan and Sheila's bedroom. After securing the rental, one of the first things Leah did was go to the pound and adopt the noisiest dog there. In confidence, one of the employees at the shelter had even tried to talk her out of it.

After moving in, Leah was delighted to see that Dylan

wasn't even sleeping with Sheila. Leah was dying for her friend to call so she could share this little tidbit with her. But the woman hadn't called or texted since Leah had made the move.

That first night, when she'd seen Sheila alone in the bedroom, Leah locked Trudy in the bedroom across from hers. On the other side of the door, she'd shaken the Milk-Bone box to get the dog all stirred up, thinking she had a treat. And just to make sure Trudy kept barking, Leah opened a can of dog food and left it outside the closed door. She knew the animal would go crazy from the smell. All night, Trudy kept howling and scratching at the door. Leah knew it was a mean thing to do to the dog, but she couldn't stop giggling when she thought about Sheila just across the way.

Leah didn't stick around very long, though. The constant barking was unbearable. She slept at the Four Seasons that night, and the next.

On Thursday night, she'd been about to go through the routine of torturing Trudy again when she noticed Dylan alone in the bedroom across the way. He was in his boxer shorts and passed by the window only twice before the light went out. There had been no sign of frumpy Sheila.

The dog got a break that night. And the following evening, Leah dressed in a sexy nightgown and kept a vigil at the window, waiting for Dylan to return. She imagined Dylan's surprise when he spotted her across the way. She even indulged in a little fantasy in which the two of them drove each other crazy masturbating for each other.

Unfortunately, Sheila was back in the bedroom that night, spoiling all of Leah's plans. Leah went back to torturing the dog instead, but Trudy was growing tired of the routine and didn't create quite as much of a racket as she had the previous nights.

Leah hadn't expected to grow so attached to the damn mutt. But now that the German shepherd had been gone six hours, Leah was worried about her. Leah didn't think she'd be able to sleep tonight unless the dog was in the house. She glanced out the kitchen window. All the shades were drawn next door, and there was no sign of Trudy in the backyard.

Suddenly, she heard a scraping noise upstairs. Leah froze. It sounded like something had been dragged across the floor.

Leah told herself she simply wasn't used to this house. Without the dog scurrying around, the strange quiet was unsettling. Every little noise was exaggerated.

She glanced at the kitchen door. How long had it been open—ten or fifteen minutes? That was certainly long enough for someone to sneak into the house and creep upstairs.

The floorboards creaked above her.

Leah looked up at the ceiling. That wasn't the sound of the house settling. It was the sound of footsteps. She backed up and bumped into a stack of moving boxes by the breakfast table. A box cutter fell from the top of the stack and hit the floor with a clank.

The footsteps above suddenly stopped.

Leah swiped the box cutter off the floor and padded into the front hallway. She stopped at the bottom of the stairs. The sounds had seemed to come from the room in which she'd locked the dog those nights she'd been trying to drive Sheila crazy. But Leah couldn't be certain.

She pushed the little lever on the side of the box cutter, and the blade slid out. As she crept up the steps,

Leah could hear the footsteps again—coming from that same bedroom.

A part of her felt a strange thrill at the notion of a burglar. Her heart was racing. She'd never killed anyone before. The prowler might not even know she had the box cutter in her hand until it was too late and she'd slit his throat. But maybe it wasn't a burglar. Perhaps Sheila O'Rourke or the son had snuck into the house. Or maybe Dylan was waiting for her upstairs—naked and back for more after today's interrupted session. By the time she reached the dark second-floor landing, Leah was still scared. But she also felt like this was part of some exciting, dangerous game.

The footsteps stopped again. Her intruder must have heard her skulking up the stairs.

Leah glanced inside the bathroom: empty. The shower curtain was open, so she didn't even need to switch on the light or step inside the bathroom to double-check.

She heard a light thud and shuffle of papers, like someone had dropped a small book on the floor in the master bedroom. Leah hurried to the bedroom and switched on the light. An open *Architectural Digest* was on the carpeted floor directly in her path. Some of the mail-in subscription cards had fallen out. Scanning the room, she noticed that the closet door was open. On the bed, someone had laid out some of her sex toys.

She was trembling now. Yet she couldn't help hoping it was Dylan, playing with her, taunting her. She hurried across the room to the master bathroom, where the door was ajar. She opened it and quickly switched on the light. The shower curtain fluttered. As she ripped the curtain open, the hooks made a scraping noise on the curtain rod. No one was hiding in the tub.

She heard two knocks. They seemed to come from the hallway.

She padded across the bedroom, noticing the magazine again. Her intruder must have thrown it into the bedroom from the hall. By the time Leah reached the door and peered down the shadowy corridor, she could hear water running. It came from the bathroom she'd checked earlier.

Unnerved, she raced down the hallway to the darkened bathroom. Water flowed from the sink faucet. With a shaky hand, Leah turned it off. She emerged from the bathroom, angry now. At one end of the hallway was the second bedroom, where she'd kept the dog those nights she wanted to torment Sheila.

At the other end of the hall to the right was a wrought iron spiral staircase that led up to the rooftop deck. She'd been up there earlier today, enjoying the spectacular view of Portage Bay—and Dylan in the ravaged garden next door.

Leah thought she saw something move by the staircase.

"Who's there?" she yelled. She tightened her grip on the box cutter. Her nerves were frayed. "I'm sick of this! Who's there? Quit fucking with me!"

"I will," she heard a woman murmur behind her, "as soon as you quit fucking with my husband."

Leah swiveled around. A woman in a purple coat stood just outside the second bedroom's door. She looked like Sheila at first glimpse. Yet the voice, though familiar, wasn't Sheila's. It was too dark to make out the woman's face.

But Leah could clearly see the gun in her hand.

Shaking her head, she backed toward the spiral staircase. "Who are you?"

"Drop the box cutter, Leah," the woman said quietly. Her face was still in the shadows.

Leah backed into the staircase. Obediently, she set the knife on one of the lower steps. It clanked, metal against metal. "Who the hell are you?" Leah said, raising her voice.

"I'm Mrs. O'Rourke," the woman whispered. "And I won't let you ruin my family."

CHAPTER THIRTY-EIGHT

Saturday—9:41 P.M.

> They gave me a bathroom break. I'm still at the police station.
> I should b home in an hour or so. Is everyone ok? XXX

While Dylan waited for Sheila to respond, he checked the last text he'd sent—along with the time he'd sent it: 9:19 P.M.

> R u still on the cruise? I need to talk with u and hear ur voice.
> Please call asap. It's urgent. Concerns that woman following
> u. I may come by ur place to check on u. Please call.

There was still no response from Brooke.

Sitting at the wheel of his BMW, Dylan anxiously glanced at his wristwatch.

His phone chimed. It was a text from Sheila:

> We r fine. Hurry home.

It seemed a bit curt, like Sheila was pissed off at him about something. Then again, what else was new? Dylan texted back:

> C u soon!

He'd lied to Sheila in the earlier text. Detective Laskin had finally let him go about twenty-five minutes ago. Laskin had told Dylan they probably wouldn't go public with the intimate details of his story, but there was no guarantee of that. And they might want to talk with him again.

Dylan hadn't said anything to the detective about Leah or Brooke. But he couldn't stop thinking about the woman who had called Brooke in the middle of the night and might have been following her. Could it have been Leah? Could she have been following and watching him when he'd been with Miranda Warren, too?

He'd parked down the street, a block from the precinct station. The minute Dylan had climbed inside his car, he'd texted Brooke.

That had been twenty minutes ago.

Now, he was about a mile away from the police station, and he'd just bought himself another hour before Sheila expected him home. He needed this time so he could talk to Brooke and make sure she was all right.

Dylan couldn't help thinking something bad had happened to her. He hadn't heard from her since this morning, when she'd said she would try to get out of going on the Puget Sound cruise with her husband. Dylan figured she'd been unable to wiggle out of the trip or find a moment alone to text him. But it had been ten hours, for God's sake, and now he was worried. He needed Brooke to tell him that she was all right, and then he'd be able to breathe easy again.

The BMW had been idling for a few minutes. Dylan finally switched off the ignition. He was in a guest parking space in the half-circle driveway in front of Brooke's ten-story building. He knew he was taking a chance of fouling things up with her husband if the guy was home, but Dylan had to make sure she was okay.

Climbing out of the car, he figured if the husband answered the intercom or the door, he'd say that he knew Brooke from Children's Hospital. He'd say that his daughter had been a patient there—no, his and his *husband's* daughter had been recently released from the hospital, and Brooke had been so nice, and he was sorry to drop by unannounced, and blah-blah-blah. He'd be fine, he'd finesse this. He just hoped Brooke would answer the intercom and the husband would be out, or asleep, or in the shower.

By the glass double doors to the lobby, Dylan checked the resident call box, but he couldn't find the name *Crowley* anywhere. Was that her maiden name? There must have been about a hundred people living in the building. Her husband's name was Paul. Dylan started going through the listing, pressing the pound sign for the next name and then the next, hunting for someone with the initials *P* or *B,* or a couple with the initials *P & B*. He'd gotten through about twenty names when a white-haired, fifty-something man wearing a brown leather bomber jacket stepped out of the building. "Excuse me," Dylan said. "I'm sorry to bother you. But do you live here?"

The guy gave him a wary look. "Yes."

"I'm trying to get ahold of Brooke Crowley, but I don't see her name in the directory."

The man squinted at him. "Is she a guest of someone who lives here?"

"No, she lives here. She's lived here for a couple of years."

The man shook his head. "No, there's nobody here by that name."

Dylan laughed. "But I just dropped her off here last week. *Brooke Crowley.* Her husband's name is Paul. Paul and Brooke . . ."

"No, you've got the wrong building," the man said, looking like he was ready to move on. "Maybe it's the next building down—or the next one. People get the three buildings mixed up. They kind of look alike."

"No, I'm sure it's this one," Dylan said.

The man started to walk away.

"Y'know, there must be a hundred residents in there," Dylan yelled at the man. "I'm sorry, but how can you be so sure my friend doesn't live here? You can't know everybody in the building, buddy."

Hands in his jacket pockets, the man turned. "A hundred and sixteen residents," he called. "And I'm president of the condo board, *buddy*. It's my job to know everybody who lives in this building. Try the next building over."

He turned and continued walking. But he kept looking over his shoulder.

Dylan finally retreated to his car. He stopped and rattled off a quick text to Brooke:

Where r u? I'm at ur place. Please call!

He sent the text and set down the phone. He looked up at the ten-story structure. Brooke didn't live in the next building over or the next one. It was this building.

"What the hell?" he murmured to himself.

Trembling, Leah stood by the wrought iron spiral staircase. She stared down the darkened corridor at the woman in the purple raincoat—and at the gun in her hand. Leah realized the intruder was wearing thin, nearly transparent surgical gloves.

"You're not Mrs. O'Rourke," Leah said.

"Not yet," she replied. She took a step forward into the light from the master bedroom.

Leah didn't recognize the woman. There was a passing resemblance to Sheila. The light brown hair was almost exactly the same cut and style, only this woman's hair looked like a wig. Leah knew enough about makeup and hairstyles to discern a wig from real hair. And this was a wig—a decent one, but still a wig. The woman was in her forties, and pretty—the kind of prettiness money could buy. She'd had work done, at least some Botox around the eyes and forehead. Leah knew because she'd had the same kind of work done.

"Say something else," Leah whispered. "I know your voice . . ."

"We've talked on the phone enough, Leah. I'd think you should."

"It's *you*," Leah laughed. "My *concerned friend*."

The woman stepped forward, past the shaft of light pouring from the bedroom, and then stopped. She was in the shadows again. But Leah could still see the gun in her steady hand. "I told you we'd meet eventually," the woman said.

Leah let out another nervous laugh. "Aren't we on the same side?"

"We were. In fact, my compliments on the job you did on Sheila's garden. That was really inspired."

"Well, thanks," Leah said with a baffled smile. She wondered when her friend was going to put down the gun.

"Me, I was working on Sheila from inside. I had a brilliant plan to drive Sheila insane, to the point of an apparent suicide or some fatal accident that could have been avoided. Did you ever see that old movie *Gaslight*?"

Leah shook her head.

"It doesn't matter. The objective was to clear the way for me. I had someone in the house providing me with lots of valuable information. I also had someone else sneaking in there when no one was home, creating little booby traps and tampering with certain food and beverage items only Sheila consumes. I was able to do some serious damage. In fact, I nearly killed the bitch a couple of times. I certainly messed her up some. But what you did to her garden . . . well, that really left her devastated. Bravo, Leah."

"It was my pleasure." She still had a brittle smile plastered on her face. "Now, I thought we were friends. Why don't you put down the gun? I'll make us a couple of drinks."

"No, I need to keep a clear head for all the work I still have to do tonight."

Leah wished the woman would step out of the darkness again so she could see her face. She still wasn't sure if the gun was just a precaution or if the woman actually intended to use it.

"That business with the dog was pretty brilliant, too," the woman said. "I had those two people working for me—kids really—but you . . . well, you didn't even know you were working for me. Still, I think you were the most effective one. Remember that detective I told you about—the one who dug up the names of so many of Dylan's girlfriends?"

"Yes," Leah answered, wide-eyed.

"The detective drew up profiles of each one, and without a doubt, you took the prize. For a while there, you were so relentless, like a little honey badger. I read some of those emails you wrote to Dylan, and I said to myself: 'If she moves in next door, that insane bitch is going to push Sheila over the edge.' And honey, you haven't disappointed me."

Leah moved back and almost tripped over the bottom step of the spiral staircase. She grabbed on to the railing.

"Can't we talk without the gun?" she pleaded. "We're supposed to be friends."

"First, do me a favor. Gently toss that box cutter on the floor—in front of me."

Leah tried to swallow, but her mouth had gone dry. She picked up the box cutter and lobbed it over toward the woman. It landed near her feet.

"Good girl," she whispered. Then she nodded toward the staircase. "Sit down."

Leah was obedient. But the metal step had a grating that dug uncomfortably into her buttocks. "I thought you were going to get rid of the gun. Like I said earlier, you and I are on the same side."

"You were—until you screwed Dylan this afternoon."

Leah was stunned the woman knew. She shrugged helplessly. "Well, why come after me? You and I both know he's slept with dozens of women."

"Yes, I expected him to be unfaithful to Sheila. But I'll be damned if he cheats on me."

"You're seeing him?"

The woman nodded. "He's very much in love with me. He's been leaning on me a great deal while his wife becomes more and more unhinged. And I'm in love with him. I knew him way before you did, Leah. I lost him to my best friend. But she's dead now."

"What—are you killing all the women Dylan has slept with?"

"No. I threw my friend off a rooftop because she stood in the way of my plan. If I was intent on killing every woman Dylan has slept with since he married Sheila, I'd need an army." She snickered. "But that was the old Dylan. He loves me now, and no woman is going to spoil that. I happened to see him slip up yesterday with a schoolteacher—in her car, no less. So she had to die. I killed her last night."

Leah squirmed on the grated step. She'd heard something on the radio this afternoon about a high school teacher shot to death in her home in Shoreline. She wondered if that was what her "friend" was talking about.

"And you, Leah," the woman said. "You fucked him this afternoon, so now you're the one who's fucked."

She quickly shook her head. "But I didn't. Nothing really happened."

"That's not what my girl told me. She saw the two of you screwing on the dining room table."

"It just looked that way!" Leah insisted. "I—I admit, I tried to seduce him, but nothing actually happened. So—so it must be that he really is in love with you, because he didn't want me. I swear, that's the truth . . ."

Leah wondered if this ploy would help save her life. "So—you win," she said with a scared, pathetic little laugh. "Hell, you can't blame a girl for trying. Besides, I didn't know he was yours. And anyway, you don't have to worry about me. I'll move out tomorrow and clear the field for you. Nothing happened with him this afternoon. The girl got the wrong idea about us. Okay? I mean, you don't have to kill me . . ."

"Oh, I'm not going to kill you," the woman said quietly. "Sheila O'Rourke will. Sheila killed that schoolteacher last night, too. She shot her in the throat."

Leah didn't understand. The woman wasn't making any sense.

"This is Sheila's coat I'm wearing," she explained. With the gun muzzle, she pointed down to her feet. "And these are Sheila's shoes. I have hair samples from Sheila's hairbrush. And it's only a matter of time before investigators find the strands I left behind in that teacher's bedroom. They won't be able to trace the gun, but the bullets will lead them straight to Sheila. She bought them on Wednesday and paid for them with a personal check."

"So you're framing her for this teacher's murder?" Leah asked.

"Not just *her* murder." The woman slid a gloved hand into her coat pocket and carefully took out a scrunched-up tissue. She let it drop on the floor. "Sheila's DNA will be found here, too. I'm afraid they'll think she was an awful sloppy murderess. But then, when someone goes on a killing spree and then shoots herself, she can't be expected to cover her tracks."

"Killing spree?" Leah repeated.

"Those plans of mine to eventually drive Sheila to an apparent suicide," the woman explained, "they had to be accelerated, thanks to certain things beyond my control. I really didn't count on the teacher—or you. And there's someone in a hospital in Issaquah that I still need to take care of. This 'killing spree' is part of my plan B. And actually, I think it works out even better than the original plan."

Leah inched backward off the bottom step of the spiral staircase and up three steps. She gazed at the woman through the railing bars. She couldn't think of any possible way to escape other than maybe running up the steps to the rooftop deck. Once she got the door open, she'd scream and scream—if she was able to get that far without being shot. There were some potted plants and garden tools up there. She might be able to use one of the tools as a weapon. Leah couldn't think of anything else—except to keep this woman talking and stall her. "Who else is going to die in this killing spree?" she asked. "I mean, we're friends, right? I'd like to help."

"You've already done your part, Leah. Dylan knows my girl saw you two screwing this afternoon. By the time

I'm done, he'll assume his wife found out about the two of you and went berserk—just like she did last night with that schoolteacher he screwed. You've provided Sheila with the perfect motivation to go on a rampage. The evidence will show she shot two of her husband's most recent illicit lovers before killing her son and herself tonight. That ought to help Dylan keep his zipper shut from now on."

Leah stared at her. "Then you'll move in on him, and he'll be faithful to you? Is that it?"

She nodded. "Plan B. Dylan is already turning to me for comfort. After a suitable grieving period, we'll move away and raise our daughter together, along with his two other children."

Leah shifted around and scooted up two more steps on the spiral staircase. "But you said he knew you from before," she pointed out. "Are you going to keep pretending you're someone else for the rest of the time you're with him?"

"I've already changed my life around to raise his daughter. And I've killed for him. I don't mind changing my identity, as long as I can keep him."

"Your daughter, is she the pale blonde?" Leah asked. "I didn't think she was part of the family seven years ago . . ."

"Yes, she's mine—and Dylan's."

Leah moved up another step. "Where is she now?"

"She's run away, right on cue—as instructed. She's made sure that the son tells Dylan she's gone. That way, when the killing starts, she won't be a suspect or even a potential witness."

Leah stole a glance up at the landing to the rooftop deck access. She was halfway there. "But—well, aren't you worried she's going to give you away eventually?"

"She isn't in on everything. I think she has a pretty

good idea about what's going to happen tonight to her stepmother and half brother. And I suspect she has some misgivings. But I'm the only real parent she has, and she'll do what I tell her. Still, I should get going."

Leah got to her feet and watched the woman raise the gun.

"*Sheila* needs to start killing," the woman said.

"No, wait, please!" Leah begged. She stood up and desperately raced up the narrow metal steps, but lost her footing a few steps from the top. She slammed her knee against the edge of a step and tumbled back down the spiral stairs with a clatter. She heard bones snap as her arm banged against the wrought iron steps and railing. She landed at the bottom of the staircase, helpless. Her body wracked with pain, she gasped for breath.

Gazing up, Leah tried to focus on the woman standing over her with the gun. The woman's face was expression-less. Past the ringing in her ears, Leah almost didn't hear the woman whisper: "I'll give Dylan a kiss for you . . ."

But she clearly heard the gunshot.

CHAPTER THIRTY-NINE

Saturday—9:59 P.M.

Steve listened to the water pipes humming. It sounded like his mother was in the shower upstairs.

Dodgeball was wrapping up on the kitchen TV. Steve had set aside a small stack of photos of the woman he suspected was Eden's "other mother." He was now dumping all the other photographs back into the two boxes. If they were supposed to be in any special order he was screwed, because he hadn't been paying attention.

Steve kept thinking about his phone conversation with Eden nearly twenty minutes ago. He wondered why she kept telling him to call their dad about her running away. She knew their father was at the police station and probably couldn't take the call. And why didn't she just call him herself? It didn't make any sense.

She kept saying she was sorry, too. It almost sounded as if she were planning to kill herself.

Or was she sorry about something else? Something that was about to happen here in this house tonight? Steve remembered another thing she'd said: "I really wish you'd run away with me when I asked you . . ."

A loud bang from outside made him jump.

It sounded like a gunshot. It came from the Curtis house, where that crazy lady was staying. All he could think was that, earlier tonight, she'd thrown a dirtball at the house. Did that nutcase own a gun?

Steve was almost afraid to look, but he moved the curtain aside and tried to see if anything was happening across the way. Except for a light in one second-floor window, the house was dark.

Moving away from the kitchen window, Steve ran to the foot of the stairs. "Mom?" he yelled. "Mom, are you okay? Can you hear me up there?"

There was no answer—just the hum of pipes.

He turned and looked at the front door. Instead of just hurling dirtballs at it, maybe the crazy lady now intended to shoot her way in.

Running back into the kitchen, he swiped his phone off the table and dialed his dad's number. It went directly to voicemail. "Shit," Steve murmured, anxiously awaiting the prompt. *Beep*.

"Hey, Dad, when are you coming home?" he asked. "I—I just heard a gunshot outside. At least, I think that's what it was. The crazy lady next door was over here earlier tonight, ranting at Mom and saying all sorts of creepy stuff about you. And Eden's run away. I'm really worried. I keep thinking Eden might kill herself or something. What's taking you so long? Mom's upstairs in the shower. She wasn't feeling well earlier. I'm worried about her, too. Could you—could you just come home? I feel like something bad is about to happen."

"Thank God," Dylan said.

With the phone to his ear, he hurried through the light rain toward his car. He'd left the BMW parked in front of Brooke's building while he'd gone next door to check the resident listing on the call box. There hadn't been any

Brooke Crowley or Paul Crowley listed as living in that building, either.

"Where are you?" Brooke asked.

"I'm out in front of your apartment building. Didn't you get my text?"

"No. What are you doing there?"

"I was worried about you."

There was a beep from his phone—his call waiting. Dylan ignored it.

"Listen, I couldn't find you anywhere on the call box," he said. "And I ran into some guy who said he was president of the condo board or something. He said he'd never heard of you."

"Oh, that guy. He did that to another friend of ours just last week. I've only introduced myself to the guy like twenty times. The condo belongs to Paul's sister. We're subletting. It's her married name on the call box."

"Well, could you come down and meet me?"

"I'm not there. But I do need to see you, Dylan. In fact it—it's kind of an emergency."

He stopped in front of his car. "What's going on? Are you okay?"

"Not really. Can you meet me at Ray's Boathouse? Do you know where that is?"

"Yeah, it's in Ballard," he said. The restaurant-bar was also about half an hour away.

"I should be there in about five minutes," she said, her voice shaky. "I wouldn't ask you to come if it wasn't important. I really need you right now. I'll explain everything when you get here. Okay?"

Dylan ducked into the BMW and shut the door. "Can't you at least tell me what this is about?"

"When you get here," she said. "And please, please, hurry. I love you."

She clicked off.

Frazzled, Dylan started up the car and peeled out of the condo's driveway. He tried to think of the most direct way to Ballard. Every route that came to mind from Capitol Hill to Ray's Boathouse seemed convoluted—full of stops through neighborhood centers. He switched on his wipers again and turned down Belmont Avenue, like he was headed to his gym.

Brooke had sounded upset, maybe even scared. Had Leah tracked her down and threatened her? Brooke had said it was an emergency. She wouldn't have asked him to drop everything and drive to the other side of town just because she was feeling blue or had argued with her husband.

Dylan sped down the high, curved overpass. The road was slick with rain. The car started to skid, so he eased off the accelerator. At the bottom of the overpass, he hit a red light. "Shit," he muttered.

Impatiently tapping his fingers on the steering wheel, he realized something. With the trip to Ballard, there was no way he'd make it back home in an hour, like he'd told Sheila in his voicemail.

He also remembered that someone had tried to call while he'd been talking to Brooke. Dylan checked his phone. Steve had left a voicemail.

A car horn blared—right behind him. Startled, Dylan saw the light had turned green.

He tossed the phone on the passenger seat and stepped on the gas.

He told himself he'd listen to Steve's message at the next red light.

Steve knocked on his parents' bedroom door. He had his phone in his other hand. He could hear the shower roaring in the master bathroom, where his mother had been for at least twenty minutes now. With everything that was happening, he couldn't help worrying about her, too. She'd gotten an earful from that crazy lady tonight, and he kept thinking about how his dad had once called his mom "emotionally fragile."

Steve had heard stories about people killing themselves in bathtubs. They slit their wrists open and bled to death. The tub full of warm water was supposed to dull the pain, or something.

"Mom?" he yelled. "Mom, can you hear me?"

The shower kept going.

Steve opened the bedroom door. It was dark, but there was enough light from the hallway behind him that he could see the bedroom was empty. The bathroom door was closed, and he noticed the thin strip of light at the threshold. Steve was about to knock and call to his mother again, but then, past the sound of the shower, he heard a noise downstairs.

He rushed out to the hallway. It sounded like someone was trying to get in the front door. He heard the key in the lock.

He hoped it was his dad. Or maybe Eden had changed her mind and come back.

Steve hurried to the stairs, then stopped halfway down—just as the front door opened. He was baffled by what he saw. He couldn't make out the woman's face. But if he didn't know any better, he'd have thought it was his mother letting herself inside. The woman had the same kind of hair as his mom, along with a purple coat his mother sometimes wore.

The phone rang in Steve's hand.

The strange woman in the foyer glanced up at him. It wasn't his mother, of course. And it wasn't the crazy lady from next door. But there was a passing resemblance to the woman he'd seen in those photos with Eden's mom.

She had a gun in her hand—pointed at him. "Don't answer it!" she commanded. "Let it ring."

Steve started to tremble. He stole a glance at the Caller ID. It was his dad calling.

"Put the phone down, Steve."

How did she know his name? He half-turned and set the phone over to the side on a step behind him. It kept ringing. Steve turned to face her again. He kept thinking of all the true-crime murder stories he'd read. And now it was happening to him.

"Good boy," she whispered, like he was an obedient dog. "Now, where's your mother?"

The water pipes squeaked as Sheila turned off the shower. She'd had a long, hard cry while sitting in the tub with the water washing over her. She hadn't wanted Steve to hear her sobs.

She could no longer turn a blind eye to Dylan's infidelities—not now, not when her children knew about them. She used to reassure herself that Dylan always came back to her after fooling around with other women. But Sheila now realized maybe that wasn't such a good thing.

As she dried off, she tried to come to grips with the fact that she had to leave him. She'd already known that, on some level, when he'd texted her from the police station about a half hour ago. He'd asked if everything was okay. And she hadn't bothered to tell him anything about the woman next door or his daughter running away. She'd just answered with an apathetic "fine" and "hurry home," or something along those lines. She didn't care anymore. If she did, she might have called him back and screamed at him or cried.

Sheila heard her cell phone ringing in the bedroom.

Throwing on her bathrobe, she wondered if it was Dylan, or maybe his daughter.

Sheila opened the bathroom door and froze.

Steve sat on the bed. A woman, wearing Sheila's missing purple coat, was beside him. Gazing at Sheila, she held a gun to Steve's head. She flicked his earlobe with the barrel.

Wincing, Steve tapped his foot, the way he always did when he got nervous. He had tears in his eyes.

All Sheila could do was shake her head. "Please . . ." she whispered. She couldn't say anything else. She could barely breathe.

"Fetch the Ambien out of the medicine chest for me, Sheila," the woman said quietly.

On the nightstand, Sheila's phone stopped ringing.

She remained paralyzed in the bathroom doorway. Behind her, steam wafted into the bedroom. She didn't know the woman. But with the coat and the hair, it seemed the stranger was trying to look like her.

"Top shelf, Sheila," the woman said. "Get the Ambien."

Sheila realized Eden must have told her where it was. She wondered if maybe Eden's surrogate mother was alive after all. "Cassandra?"

"Get the goddamn Ambien!" she barked. She jabbed Steve with the gun. "Now!"

Steve let out a startled cry.

Sheila retreated into bathroom. Her hand shook so much that a couple of bottles fell from the top shelf and clanked into the sink as she grabbed the prescription bottle.

"A glass of water, too," Cassandra called from the bedroom.

Sheila filled a glass with cold water and then hurried back to the doorway. In the bedroom, both Cassandra and Steve were on their feet. Sheila noticed the woman was wearing surgical gloves. She still had the gun pressed against Steve's temple. "Get in there with your mother," she said to him. "I want you to take three of those pills."

"No," Sheila said. She quickly drew her hands in toward her stomach, spilling some water down the front of her robe. The bottle of pills rattled in her unsteady hand. "What for? Why are you making him take sleeping pills?"

"Three won't kill him," Cassandra said. "It'll just put him in a deep, deep sleep. Or would you rather have him awake to see what's going to happen to you?"

Sheila backed up to make room for them in the bathroom. She handed the water glass to Steve. Then she struggled with the bottle of Ambien. She finally got it open and shook out three pills.

On the nightstand, her phone rang again.

"Let it ring," Cassandra said. "In fact, bring the phone to me."

Biting her lip, Sheila handed Steve the three pills, then hurried to the nightstand. She set down the prescription bottle and retrieved the phone. She kept thinking that, so far, none of the kids had been hurt. All of Eden's and Cassandra's malignant labors had targeted her, not the kids. There was a chance she was still their sole target, and Steve might survive this.

At the bathroom doorway, Sheila handed the woman the phone, still ringing.

With a little smirk, Cassandra slipped it into her coat pocket. "That's probably your husband, saying it'll be another hour or so before he comes home. Right now, he's got something—*someone*—more important to tend to."

The phone stopped ringing.

Steve stood trembling in the bright light of the bathroom. He held the pills in one hand and the glass of water in the other. For a moment, he furtively looked at Cassandra as if he might have a chance to catch her off-guard. Sheila almost hoped he'd make a move now. He could smash that glass into her face—or into her neck.

But Cassandra turned toward him and tickled his ear with the gun barrel again. "Swallow the pills, Steve," she whispered.

From just across the threshold in the bedroom, Sheila watched and winced.

Steve locked eyes with her, and she nodded. He swallowed the three pills with a couple of loud gulps of water.

"Look at me," Cassandra told him, pulling the gun away. When Steve turned toward her, she stuck the barrel under his chin. "Open up."

Steve opened his mouth. She quickly glanced inside to make sure the pills were gone. "All right, hand the glass to your mother."

He did what he was told. Sheila looked down at the glass, still about half full.

Cassandra poked Steve's shoulder with the gun. "Let's get you to your bedroom and have you lie down," she said, almost sounding benign. "Those pills work fast for beginners. C'mon, Sheila, you lead the way."

In her darkened bedroom, Sheila stopped to glance at the closed curtains.

"What—are you wishing the curtains were open so Leah could see us?" Cassandra asked, practically reading her mind. "If she was watching right now, do you think she'd call the police? She wouldn't lift a finger to help you. Anyway, it doesn't matter. Leah is dead."

"The gunshot," Steve murmured.

"That's right, Steve. Now, let's get you ready for a nice, long nap." She glanced at Sheila, then over at the nightstand. "Grab those pills and hold on to that glass of water. We're not done with them yet."

Sheila hesitated before hurrying over to the nightstand and snatching up the prescription bottle. She slipped it into the pocket of her robe.

She led the way as the three of them moved down the hall, past the stairs to Steve's room. Cassandra was behind him with the gun at the back of his neck. As she stepped into her son's room, Sheila reached for the light switch beside his door.

"Leave it off," Cassandra said.

Sheila stepped aside and watched as Steve and Cassandra came through the doorway. Steve was teetering. "My legs feel funny," he muttered. "Is this happening already?" His speech was slurred.

Sheila started to reach out to him.

"Leave him be," Cassandra warned.

Sheila helplessly watched her son weave toward the bed. She remembered the first time she'd taken an Ambien. She'd felt it in her legs first, too. That had been only one pill. She couldn't imagine what three pills felt like.

Steve looked dazed as he sank down on the edge of the bed. He didn't seem aware that anyone else was in the room. He went into a coughing fit. He covered his mouth. Sheila thought he was choking. She started to offer him the water. "Here, honey—"

"Stay where you are," Cassandra said, the gun still trained on Steve.

Sheila backed away. After a few moments, Steve stopped coughing. He shook his head over and over, as if struggling to stay awake. "Mom . . . I'm . . . I'm sorry . . ." he murmured, his eyes closed.

"Go ahead, lie down, Steve," Cassandra whispered.

"Just . . . for . . . a second." He fell back onto the

mattress and curled up in a fetal position. "Mom . . . don't let her . . ." But his voice faded, and then he sighed.

"Let's just watch him for a minute or two," Cassandra whispered.

Bewildered, Sheila glanced over at her. Cassandra had a smile on her face.

"They look so sweet when they're sleeping. It didn't matter how much of a little shit Eden could be, she always looked like an angel when she was asleep."

She turned the gun on Sheila, and the smile was gone from her face. "Where are the pills?"

With a nervous sigh, Sheila pulled them out of the pocket of her bathrobe.

"Your turn," Cassandra said. "Just one pill for you."

"Why? What for?"

"Something to take the edge off," Cassandra said. "If you're drowsy, you won't be able to resist much."

"What are you going to make me do?"

"You won't have to do anything, Sheila. I'll do all the work—all the staging."

"Staging?"

"I want it to look like you were a kind, thoughtful mother, and you drugged your son before putting a bullet through that little angel's head."

Horrified, Sheila stared at her.

"Then you'll shoot yourself in the head, too, Sheila," she whispered.

"Why are you doing this?" Sheila asked, tears in her eyes.

"It's nothing personal. You're merely in the way—just like Antonia was. Now, c'mon, take the pill."

Sheila suddenly hurled the glass at her. Water doused the bed. The glass completely missed Cassandra and smashed against Steve's desk. Steve barely stirred. Shards of glass covered the floor.

Glaring at her, Cassandra aimed the gun at Steve's head. "All right, fine," she breathed. "We'll do it without the pill. It was just a whim. I wanted it to look like you had to drug yourself to pull off this murder-suicide thing. But the truth is you wouldn't need a pill to take the edge off, would you, Sheila? You've already had some practice in killing. After all, didn't you murder your own sister?"

Sheila automatically glanced over at Steve, still not moving. It was like a kick in the stomach to hear her refer to Molly. "I—I didn't kill my sister," she whispered.

"I hired a private detective to dig up everything he could on Molly," Cassandra said. "Your sister might have fooled some of her school friends about who she was seeing, but she wasn't very skilled at covering her tracks. When did you discover Dylan was screwing her? Was it the night she died? The newspapers said you two argued on the roof about caring for your mother. Your mother's nurses said that was an ongoing problem—not exactly a strong motive for killing your own sister. I'm guessing that's one reason why the police never went after you. But you and I know what the argument was about. After tonight, people will reexamine what happened in Portland seventeen or eighteen years ago. Some will say you've killed before for the same reason you killed tonight: an unfaithful husband. Others will just say that suicide ran in the Driscoll family."

"How much was Eden in on all this?" Sheila asked.

"She's always been good at following orders and not asking questions. She suspects certain things, but I've kept her in the dark about a lot of it. She tries to act tough, but she lacks the killer instincts you and I have, Sheila." She raised the gun. "Now, c'mon, I want them to find you in the bedroom. Let's move."

Sheila took a last look at Steve on the bed and reached to touch his face.

"I said *move it*," Cassandra growled.

Tears in her eyes, Sheila headed to the hallway. She desperately tried to think of a way out of this. Maybe she could talk her into letting Steve live. She glanced over her shoulder at the woman. "Listen," she said, "If you really—"

"No, *you listen* to something," Cassandra interrupted. With a forceful shove, she pushed Sheila across the threshold into the master bedroom. "In all his time married to you, Dylan hasn't changed one bit. You just weren't woman enough for him, Sheila. You failed. Do you know how easy it was for me to hook him? I got that dimwit Brodie to nearly run him down in his car at a crosswalk one afternoon, and I was right there to save Dylan's life. And he needed saving—*from you*. Dylan and I talked for only few minutes. But three weeks later, when I arranged our next 'accidental meeting,' this time at the gym, he still remembered me. Dylan asked me out right there. He wanted me. And it wasn't just sex, Sheila. He cared about me. I told him some bullshit story about a son I had who died, and Dylan lapped it up. I knew I had him that night. You want to hear something funny? We haven't even fucked yet, and he's already mine. He should have been mine seventeen years ago. Toni had no right . . ."

"*You* killed her," Sheila said.

Cassandra laughed and nodded. "You're not as stupid as you look. But then, I guess that's not fair. You're actually very pretty, Sheila. I guess in my mind, I had to make you out to be a frump, unworthy of Dylan's love. But you're not so bad. Neither was Toni. But you're just like her in the sense that you're in my way—you and the boy sleeping down the hall. Once the two of you are gone, I'll be on my way to becoming Mrs. Dylan O'Rourke. Dylan and I will move away with our three children. He'll want to move—too many bad memories here. Don't worry. I'll be a good stepmother to Hannah and Gabe. And if it turns out your children don't like me, I can always arrange for an accident . . ."

Sheila shook her head. "Your grand scheme isn't going to work, Cassandra. Dylan's not going to fall for—"

"Dylan's already *fallen*," Cassandra interrupted, "He's in love with me! You should have heard him just a couple of nights ago, explaining to me how much I matter to him, how you're no longer any fun. Do you know where he is right now, Sheila? I can tell you one thing. He's not coming to your rescue."

She reached into the pocket of Sheila's purple coat, pulled out the phone, and tossed it to her. Startled, Sheila almost dropped it. She backed up until she bumped into the foot of the bed.

"Play back that last message you missed," Cassandra said. "I know who it is—and what he's going to say. It's your husband. Dylan's going to be late tonight because he's supposed to meet me. He doesn't care about you, Sheila. You poor, pathetic thing. I'm the one he really loves. He's waiting for me right now. Go ahead and turn it up so I can hear, too."

Her hands still shaking, Sheila clicked on the Messages icon and turned up the volume. Cassandra was right. It was Dylan's voice:

"Honey, it's me. I'm on my way home." It sounded like he was crying. "I'm so worried about you and the kids. Steve called a little while ago, something about a gunshot. And now, neither of you is picking up . . ."

Sheila saw the stunned, horrified look in Cassandra's eyes. Then her expression twisted in anger as the message continued.

"Please, call me back as soon as you can. I'm in the

car, speeding home. I should be there in ten minutes. I love you."

"That bastard!" Cassandra slapped the phone out of Sheila's hand. She had tears in her eyes and she shook violently. She looked like a madwoman. "This isn't right! He's supposed to be in love with me! Goddamn it, he can't be coming here . . . he can't . . ." She kept shaking her head over and over. "This can't be happening! That motherfucker hasn't even bothered to call me to say he'll be late . . . or . . . or . . ."

Grimacing, she let out a furious scream. She raised the gun over her head.

Before Sheila realized what was happening, the gun butt came down and bashed her across the temple.

With a startled cry, Sheila crumpled to the floor. The pain was excruciating, but she was still half conscious. Blood trickled down her cheek from just above her ear. She couldn't lift her head from the carpet.

Sheila opened her eyes. Everything was a blur.

But she could hear the woman stomping down the stairs—and the sound of a car in the distance speeding up the street.

That son of a bitch had said he was in love with her.

But when push came to shove, the wife and kiddies always came first.

She'd loved Dylan for seventeen years. She'd raised his bastard daughter. She'd sacrificed for him and killed for him.

One distress call from his kid, and he forgot all about "Brooke" and all the feelings he claimed to have for her. If he truly loved Brooke—if he truly loved *her*—he wouldn't be rushing home to his wife and child right now.

At the very least, he could have called her and asked her to wait for him. She'd made it very clear that Brooke desperately needed him. She'd even hinted that Brooke might be in danger. But he'd just blown her off.

How could he?

Cassandra marched out of the house with Sheila's purple coat flapping open and what looked like Sheila's hair tousled by the wind and rain. She clutched the gun in her gloved hand.

She heard the squeal of tires as Dylan's car turned the corner at the end of the block.

He just couldn't wait to get to the wife and kids.

Enraged, Cassandra bolted down the walkway toward the wet, shiny street. Past the tears in her eyes, she saw the BMW speeding toward her. She thought she saw Dylan behind the wheel. But then the headlights blinded her for a moment.

"Son of a bitch!" Cassandra screamed.

She raised the gun and fired four times. The shots rang out over the sound of screeching brakes.

Dylan's BMW swerved, jumping over the curb and smashing into an elm tree. There was a deafening din of glass shattering and metal twisting. The car horn blared. The tree rained branches and leaves onto the mangled, smoking wreck.

Dazed, breathless, Cassandra stared at her handiwork. She couldn't see past the smashed windshield. But she noticed blood on the splintered glass.

All she could think was, *Serves him right.*

Cassandra realized the sound of the crash and the incessantly blaring horn would get the attention of everyone on the block. But if anybody saw her, they'd glimpse a woman looking like Sheila, in Sheila's coat. Later, they'd think they saw Mrs. O'Rourke—just moments before she ducked into the house to kill her son and herself.

But they wouldn't see her slipping out the back door and cutting through the side alley before the police arrived.

Cassandra couldn't make out anything inside Dylan's demolished BMW. She couldn't even see if the airbag had deployed. But nothing seemed to be moving in there. Smoke continued to spew from under the smashed hood. Beneath the chassis, a puddle of greenish fluid bloomed on the wet pavement.

For a moment, she was overwhelmed with regret. Seventeen years of loving a man, of feeding her obsession for him, and now he was completely lost to her. But she refused to dwell on that. She had her own survival to think about.

Cassandra glanced at the gun in her hand.

She turned and marched back to the house to finish what she'd started.

Before he heard the shots and the crash, Steve had been struggling to stay awake.

While his mom and that Cassandra woman had been in his bedroom, hovering over him, Steve had pretended to be unconscious. He'd heard what the woman had said about his dad screwing around—even screwing his sister-in-law. And he'd heard her give a painfully credible argument for why his mom might have murdered her sister, Molly.

He wished he could easily dismiss all of it as bullshit. But he couldn't. At the same time, he couldn't waste time thinking about it, either—not at that moment.

He had a bitter taste in his mouth from the Ambien. He'd used his tongue to push the tiny pills up between his cheek and his upper back molars. He'd faked a coughing fit and spit the pills into his hand less than a minute after pretending to swallow them. But they'd already started to dissolve and, as much as he'd tried not to, he'd still swallowed some of the sediment.

By the time Cassandra led his mother at gunpoint out of his bedroom, Steve felt a strange, chemically induced battle raging inside his body. Because of the drug, he was overwhelmed with fatigue. Yet his heart beat furiously. Along with his panic came a rush of adrenaline. The combination made him uncontrollably jittery and weak as he reached for the baseball bat at his bedside.

The mattress springs squeaked as he struggled to his feet. He worried that Cassandra might hear him, but he could barely hear them talking. He was able to make out his dad's voice. It sounded like one of them was playing back a voicemail message.

As Steve tried to cross the room, his legs were wobbly. The pills seemed to be shutting down his motor skills. With a shaky hand, he braced himself against his desk, then his dresser, and then the doorway. The baseball bat wavered in his other hand. He felt so rickety. He kept thinking he might collapse at any minute.

"*That bastard!*" he heard Cassandra scream. She started ranting, but Steve couldn't make out the words. He heard his mother suddenly cry out, followed by a thud. It sounded like she'd fallen on the floor. Seconds later, Steve heard someone running down the stairs. He wasn't sure what was happening. His brain seemed to be shutting down along with his limbs. Was his mother escaping down the stairs? Or would he find her on the bedroom floor, dead?

With his hand against the wall to keep his balance,

he teetered down the hallway toward his parents' room. He heard his mother's phone ringing. From the hall, he could see it lighting up on the carpet of the darkened bedroom. Then, once he made his way to the door, Steve saw his mother lying there—her arm outstretched, trying in vain to reach for the phone. His mom had lifted her bleeding head from the carpet, and she was now trying to drag herself across the floor.

"Mom!" Steve gasped, rushing to her. He crumpled to his knees, nearly falling down beside her.

"The phone," she muttered, nodding toward it. Her eyes were half closed. The trail of blood from above her ear dripped off her chin onto the carpet.

Steve crawled over to the ringing phone and snatched it up. "Dad?"

It was Eden. "Steve, you and your mom need to get out of there," she said in a rush. "My mother—Cassandra—I think she's going to kill you guys. I'm sorry. I—"

"Call the police!" Steve gasped, cutting her off.

"I just did," she said. "Are you okay?"

Steve heard tires screeching outside, then gunshots. It sounded like they came from directly in front of the house. Within seconds there was a deafening crash. Then a car horn wailed.

Steve immediately thought of his dad. Was he the one in the car?

"Oh, God, call the police," he cried into the phone.

"I told you, I called them," Eden said. "They're on their way—"

"Hang up, so I can call them, too."

"I'm sorry!" Eden clicked off.

Steve let go of the bat so he could call 9-1-1. A part of him still couldn't trust Eden. He had to call the police himself. But his hands shook so much that he couldn't work the three numbers on the phone's keypad. Frustrated, he dropped the phone and crawled to his mother. She was even more helpless than he was. Steve dragged her over to the bed and propped her up against the side of it. He tugged the coverlet off the bed and pressed the material to the bloody gash above her ear. "Hang in there, Mom," he urged her. "Please . . ." He grabbed her hand and made her hold up the makeshift swathe herself.

That was when he heard footsteps on the stairs.

He tried not to think about the crash or the shots fired. There was no time. Steve grabbed the baseball bat and got to his feet. The room spun around him as he staggered to the doorway.

From there, he managed to focus on Cassandra, hurrying up the stairs with the gun in her hand. She wasn't looking up.

But then, near the top step, her eyes met his.

She only saw him for a second before Steve, with all the strength he could muster, hauled back and slammed her in the face with the bat.

Cassandra let out a howl. She flopped back and plunged down the stairs. Her body smashed against the banister railing with a loud *crack* and continued to hurtle down the steps. A shot reverberated in the hallway just seconds before she hit the floor.

Steve realized the gun must have gone off in her hand.

Sprawled on the hallway floor, her head tilted to one side, Cassandra was perfectly still. One leg was turned at an impossible angle. Beneath her head, a crimson pool slowly spread across the tile floor.

The front door stood wide open. The wail of a car horn reverberated in the hallway.

Dazed, Steve couldn't be sure she was really dead. Making his way down a few steps, he clutched the banister and squinted down at Cassandra. The wig she'd been wearing was askew and matted with blood. Her eyes were open in a dead stare. It looked like she'd shot herself under the jaw on her right side.

He heard his mother calling to him in a frail, panicked voice. "Stevie? Honey, are . . . you . . . okay?"

"Yeah, Mom!" he answered her. Still leaning on the banister, he turned and struggled up the stairs.

Past the incessant wail of the car horn, he heard sirens. The blessed sound seemed to be getting louder and closer.

Eden had told him the truth about calling the police.

It may have been a little late, but his half sister had finally come through for them.

EPILOGUE

"Y ou're up!" Gabe declared.

Steve was just stepping out of the second-floor bathroom in his pajama bottoms and T-shirt when his little brother startled him with a big hug. He had a terrible headache, but he still thought it was kind of sweet of Gabe.

"And you're home," Steve said to Gabe.

"Yeah, so is Hannah. She's downstairs with Mom. We can't go outside. Did you see the TV news trucks out there?"

"Seriously?" Steve asked, retreating toward his room. A part of him wanted to go look out Gabe's window, but he was too tired and sick to care that much.

Gabe headed down the hall to the top of the stairs. "Hey, Mom!" he yelled. "Steve's awake!"

He heard a dog bark downstairs. He stopped in his bedroom doorway. "What was that?"

"We've got a dog now," Gabe explained. "It's the neighbor's. She got shot, she's dead—the neighbor, not the dog. I guess it showed up when all the cops were here last night. Mom says the dog can't stay, but I think we can talk her into letting us keep her. Her name's Trudy, but I'm calling her True."

Nodding, Steve made his way back to his bed and sat down. He rubbed his aching forehead. He loved his little brother, but Gabe was just a little too hyper for him right now. He stood in Steve's doorway and tapped the toe of his sneaker at the doorframe. "Guess what? The hallway downstairs was a 'crime scene' until just like a couple of hours ago. How cool is that?" Then he suddenly got serious. "They towed Dad's car away this morning. It's totaled. You should see the dent in the tree."

"What's the latest on Dad?" Steve asked, his eyes closed.

Before his brother could answer, their mom appeared in the hallway behind Gabe. She had a bandage on the side of her face, along the hairline by her ear. "Okay, give Steve a break," she said, her hands on Gabe's shoulders. She turned him around and gave him a gentle push in the direction of the stairs. "Go play with True. And stay inside."

She disappeared for a moment, then stepped back into the room with a glass of water and two pills. "Don't worry," she said. "It's just aspirin. The doctor said you'd have a headache, and you'll probably sleep on and off until midafternoon. So why don't you take these and go back to bed?"

Steve chased the pills down with practically the whole glass of water. He hadn't realized how thirsty he was until just now. His mom took the glass from him, then bent over and kissed his forehead. He crawled under the covers, but instead of lying down, he propped his pillow up against the headboard and sat up. "How are you?" he asked.

His mom pulled out his desk chair and sat down. "I'll live."

He could hardly remember anything that had happened

last night after the police arrived. "I forget. How many stitches did they give you?"

"Seven. I'm tired mostly. The police had me up late answering questions, and I was up again early this morning to answer some more."

"How's Dad doing?" Steve asked.

"He's having another surgery right now, as we speak," his mom sighed, "on his left leg, which is shattered . . ."

"I thought they said the airbag worked."

"It did, but he still has a lot of injuries—especially on his left side. He's got whiplash, and all sorts of lacerations. There are broken facial bones, too. They'll probably have to rewire his jaw."

Steve thought about how handsome his dad was. "He won't look the same, will he?"

His mom shrugged. "I don't know. We'll see. He's going to need plastic surgery. They said the bullet went through his right shoulder. But it's all the other injuries that'll keep him in the hospital and rehab for a while."

"Where's Eden?"

"She's in police custody, but our lawyer says we should have her back tonight—or tomorrow at the latest."

Steve remembered what that Cassandra woman had said about Eden just obeying orders and knowing very little about what was really going on. But now his mom filled him in on the rest. His head was still throbbing, so Steve didn't catch every detail. But his mother said that the police had searched the Capitol Hill apartment Cassandra had subleased under another name. They'd found a journal with a step-by-step account of what Cassandra had done and what she still planned to do. That included framing his mom for the murders of Ms. Warren and the crazy lady next door. The journal also exonerated Eden— to a point. But it was obvious Eden was complicit in some of her "other mother's" schemes. She'd furnished

Cassandra with a lot of personal information about his mom, and she'd secretly passed their house key to her boyfriend so he could let himself in while no one was home. This was early on—during the first day or two she'd stayed with them—but it was still pretty serious. His mom was in the middle of throwing out every package of food and every beverage container that was open. And an electrician was supposed to come by later this morning to check all the appliances, plugs, and switches to make sure nothing had been tampered with. His mom was pretty sure they were safe, but she wasn't taking any chances.

As for Brodie, Cassandra's journal indicated he wasn't in Portland. As of yesterday afternoon, he was dead and buried in some woods in Issaquah. The police had little to go on as to the exact location of his gravesite, and it might be a while before they found him. According to the journal, Eden had been kept in the dark about it.

But obviously, Eden had put together that something was about to happen to Steve and his mom last night. The fact that she'd tried to warn them—and ultimately called the police—was a good sign.

Apparently, Eden was being very cooperative with the police. She'd told them that Cassandra had a whole stack of journals at one time. "So I guess they're turning the apartment upside down looking for a key to a locker or safe deposit box," his mom said. "Because the only journal they found was the current one. But I guess it's pretty thorough. One of the detectives told me this morning that it was practically like a signed confession."

Steve shifted restlessly against his pillow. "Was there anything about Molly in her journal?"

His mom let out a wary sigh. "The police checked with me about a lot of things in Cassandra's journal to confirm whether they really happened. They didn't ask me anything about my sister."

"Or the private detective Cassandra hired?"

His mom shook her head. "There was no mention of him, either, as far as I know." Her eyes wrestled with his for a moment. "Was last night the first time you heard about Molly?"

"No, on Friday at school, somebody—I guess it was that Cassandra woman—she texted me about her. Then last night, I got another text with a newspaper article about how Molly had died."

His mother's face twisted into a frown. "That wasn't in the journal, either—not as far as I know. The police asked me about the two texts she sent me. She mentioned those in her writings. But the police didn't say anything about her texting you. That's strange."

"Who else could it have been?" Steve asked numbly.

"Well, maybe the police will ask about it later." His mother sighed. "I have a feeling they're not finished with us yet—just like those reporters outside."

"What are they doing out there, anyway?"

She shrugged. "You slept through everything while the police were here last night and early this morning. Right now, I think they're waiting for one of us to step outside—like the groundhog on Groundhog's Day."

"Are we going to the hospital to see Dad today?" Steve asked.

"He probably won't be in any shape to see anyone after he gets out of surgery. They have him on all sorts of medication." She let out a sad laugh. "But yeah, we're going—if you're up for it. You heard some pretty upsetting things about your dad, and I know they must have hurt. But he came through for us last night. If he hadn't shown up when he did, you and I wouldn't be here right now."

"I'd like to go see him," Steve said quietly.

"Good." But she winced a bit. "I guess it's not just your dad you've heard upsetting things about. Did you want to ask me about Molly, honey?"

Steve couldn't bring himself to say anything. He just shrugged.

"What that woman said last night about your father and Molly is true," his mom whispered. "But I didn't kill my sister. I was six months pregnant at the time—"

"With Hannah?"

"No, it was a baby I lost. I didn't think you kids needed to know about that, either." His mom went to touch the bandage on the side of her face, but then moved her hand to her mouth instead. "There was a guardrail on that apartment building roof—and Molly was on the other side of it, a restricted area where all the building equipment was. I couldn't have gotten over or around that railing. And your aunt was in a lot better shape than me at the time. She was a swimmer. The police took one look at me, and they knew I couldn't have pushed her off that roof."

"The woman said the police didn't know about Dad and your sister," Steve pointed out quietly.

"No, they didn't. I think the only people who knew about it are your dad and me—and some priest I talked to. I'm pretty sure he died a while back."

"And Cassandra—and the private detective guy," he added.

She nodded. "And now you."

"I won't tell anybody," Steve promised.

"I'd just as soon you didn't," his mom said, her voice a little shaky. "I'm hoping this private detective doesn't show up with all these revelations for the press. Your dad will have enough scandal to live down as it is."

"Are you going to tell Hannah and Gabe about Molly?"

Steve asked. "Or will you just keep pretending she never existed?"

His mother glanced down at the floor. "I've been thinking about that all morning. I'm telling them this afternoon. I don't want to take a chance of them hearing it on the news or reading it online, if it should come out."

"Sounds like a talk for the dining room table," Steve said with a tiny smile. He readjusted the bedcovers. Then his smile faded. "Didn't you keep any pictures of her at all?"

His mother let out a long sigh and shook her head. "I got rid of all of them. I really wish I hadn't now. It was so stupid of me."

Steve reached over to his desktop and grabbed his phone. He pulled up *The Oregonian* article that had been sent to him last night. He adjusted it to zoom in on the photo of his pretty blond aunt with the dimpled smile. "Here's one," he said, holding out the phone to his mom. "In case you want to show Hannah and Gabe."

She hesitated. "I—I haven't looked at a picture of her in seventeen years," she whispered. But she finally took the phone from his hand. Her eyes filled with tears as she studied the photograph. "Look how pretty she was. And this isn't even a very good picture of her."

Steve pulled back the sheets and scooted down the bed so he was sitting across from her. His mom couldn't stop looking at the photo of her kid sister.

He held her hand while she cried.

And he realized that there were worse things in this world than being a bit emotionally fragile.

Friday, October 5—2:01 P.M.

Dylan had been moved from intensive care to a private room at Swedish Hospital on Wednesday. But he still looked pretty awful. He was propped up in the bed with his left arm in a cast. His left leg was also in a cast, suspended by a contraption above the bed. The facial swelling had gone down, but his once handsome features were bruised, puffy, and half-covered with bandages. He wore one of those plastic cervical collars for his whiplash. It had sort of a brownish yellow tint to it, a sickly color. His jaw was wired, so he couldn't speak very clearly beyond the braces clamping his teeth together.

Most of the nurses understood what he was saying. The staff was friendly and attentive. But as she sat at his bedside, Sheila thought of how the nurses and orderlies might have been fawning over him right now if he'd merely hurt his leg or something. The gorgeous face that had always gotten him so much attention and admiration was unrecognizable now. His specialness was gone.

The private room was jammed with flowers, get-well cards, and balloons. He had a steady stream of friends coming to visit, a lot of them from work. But for Hannah, Steve, and Gabe, the visits were sort of an obligation. Their father had become a source of embarrassment. His infidelities were the focus of so many news stories. After all, two of Cassandra's murder victims had had sex with Dylan within a day of each other. And Cassandra had killed the mother of his illegitimate child. Online, he was being compared to Anthony Weiner and John Wayne Bobbitt. He'd become a punch line.

"How are the kids?" he asked through the wiring for his jaw.

Sheila started. "Oh, I thought you were sleeping."

"Yeah, I was sort of dozing," he muttered. "Yours right ah our eyes."

Sheila squinted at him. "I'm sorry . . . what?"

"Yours right ah our eyes!" he said louder, a bit impatient.

"Oh, I'm *a sight for sore eyes*," she said, nodding.

"Thanks, honey. Um, the kids are fine. I think things are calming down a little at school. They're no longer feeling like the center of attention. But then, Eden started back today. So maybe we're back to square one. I'll get all the scoop when they get home."

She'd taken Eden back into the house on Sunday night, although the lawyer was still sorting everything out. The kids did their best not to treat her like Lizzie Borden. Steve was the most forgiving of all of them, of course.

Cassandra had been cremated yesterday. Eden had asked Sheila to drive her down to a little wooden dock by some floating homes on Lake Union, near Eastlake. The girl had scattered the ashes of her "other mother" there. Eden had told Sheila that, when the police let her read Cassandra's journal, she'd learned that her substitute mother had a special affection for that spot. Sheila wondered what had happened there, but she didn't ask. She'd stayed in the car while Eden scattered the ashes. She was a bit surprised that Eden, on the way back to the car, unceremoniously deposited the funeral urn in a dumpster. It was as if she didn't want a thing to do with her other mother anymore.

But the girl wasn't completely rid of her. Sheila had been surprised to learn that Cassandra's estate was worth close to eight hundred thousand dollars, and Eden was the sole beneficiary. The lawyer would be settling all of it in a month or two.

The police still hadn't found Brodie's body. Arthur Merrens had given them a full account of how Brodie had tried to murder him. He was out of the hospital now, and Sheila had gotten his number from Hilltop Auto Repair. She talked with him on the phone for twenty minutes. She thanked him for returning her gloves—and apologized for all the trouble he'd gone through returning them. She planned to make a lasagna dinner and bring it over to his and his partner's place tomorrow.

The police hadn't been able to find any more of Cassandra's journals.

Sheila had asked one of the detectives if there had been anything in Cassandra's journal about sending one of her children a text or a newspaper article. They told her no. So she still didn't know for certain who had contacted Steve about Molly. Maybe it had been Brodie. Maybe they'd never know.

Nobody asked Sheila about the private detective Cassandra had once hired to dig up dirt about Molly. It looked as if Dylan's affair with her sister would remain a secret.

Some in-depth online articles had mentioned Molly's suicide, but they didn't go into it much. Sheila was glad she'd told Hannah and Gabe about her. Considering everything they'd been forced to process that Sunday, the revelation wasn't too traumatic. Earlier this week, Steve had printed up the newspaper photo of Molly and given it to her. Sheila thought about framing it and putting it on display with the other family photos in the den.

It also reminded her of another photograph.

Last night, around bedtime, Sheila had knocked on Eden's bedroom door. She presented her with the photo of Dylan and Antonia. "This is from that collection of pictures your mother had," she explained. "I'm sorry I didn't give it to you earlier. I set it aside and totally forgot about it. Anyway, I thought you might want to frame it, or something . . ."

Sitting on her bed, Eden studied the photo and shook her head. "I'm not framing this," she said. "It's a good picture of them. But I'm not putting it on display."

"Why not?" Sheila asked.

"Because it might hurt you," Eden replied. "And I've already done enough to hurt you."

Sheila leaned down and kissed her stepdaughter on the forehead.

Of the kids, Eden seemed the most wounded, but also the most forgiving toward their father. Gabe had said a couple of days ago that he didn't want his dad coming to any of his football games, although Sheila thought he would change his mind by the time Dylan got out of the hospital. Hannah considered her father a total embarrassment and seemed one step away from applying for witness protection relocation or something along those lines. But she was still as popular as ever at school. Things hadn't changed much for Steve. But yesterday, a girl he had a longtime crush on—Barbie Something—approached him in the cafeteria and asked to interview him for the school newspaper. So he was pretty pumped about that.

Sheila told Dylan about it at his hospital bedside. She talked about how she'd have to put off restoring the garden until next spring. And she told him that the kids adored their new German shepherd, True, but the dog's obvious favorite was her. She rarely left her side, especially when no one else was around.

It took Dylan two tries before Sheila finally understood the meaning of his response: "*Maybe she senses that you're a little lonely.*"

"But I'm really not that lonely, Dylan," she told him. "You don't have to worry about me or the kids. I think we're all going to be okay."

He didn't say anything. He just closed his eyes.

Sheila got to her feet. "I'll be by tomorrow afternoon."

He nodded painfully. "Thanks for coming."

As she walked down the hospital corridor, Sheila wondered if he'd ever get his handsome looks back. Either way, he'd be out of circulation for a while. But then, even with a face full of scars, he'd probably go back to his roving ways.

She would divorce him, but not until after the kids had gone off to college.

If she left him any sooner than that, Eden would probably end up with him, and the girl needed a good mother for a while.

In the meantime, she was no longer so averse to couples counseling. In the past, she'd been afraid a therapist might somehow make her realize that she'd killed her sister. But in her heart, Sheila knew she couldn't have. She'd also been worried a therapist might provide the kind of clarity that made leaving Dylan something she'd have to do.

But she wasn't afraid anymore.

Of the two of them, Dylan was the one who should be worried what he'd learn about himself in therapy.

Sheila stopped by the hospital gift shop, where she found a pretty frame for Molly's picture. Yes, she would put it in the family room, so she would never forget her sister.

And neither would Dylan.

"Did your wife leave?"

Dylan opened his eyes to see the nurse—a friendly, plump, fifty-something black woman named Loretta. She carried a slightly ratty-looking stuffed-animal monkey. Tied to its hand were a small card and a ribbon attached to a pink helium balloon with GET WELL in silver and blue letters. Loretta set the monkey on his bedside table.

"You just missed her." Dylan strained to be understood through the metal braces. "What's that?"

"Your daughter dropped this off a couple of minutes ago," Loretta explained.

"My daughters are both in school right now."

"Well, this girl was a very pretty blonde, about eighteen—a sweet thing," the nurse said. "She looked like you—like your pictures on the news. Anyway, she said she was your daughter." The nurse untied the small card and handed it to him. "This monkey's awfully cute, but he looks like he's been around for a long, long while."

With his good hand, Dylan brought the card close to his face and squinted at it. The message was in a girlish script:

Get well soon.

Love,
Micky the Monkey
& Me

"I don't know what this is about," Dylan said.

The nurse took the card from him and set it on the table. "Well, maybe it's one of those private jokes, something you shared with her a long time ago."

She headed out of the room. "Sleep on it," she called. "Maybe you'll figure it out. It'll come back to you . . ."